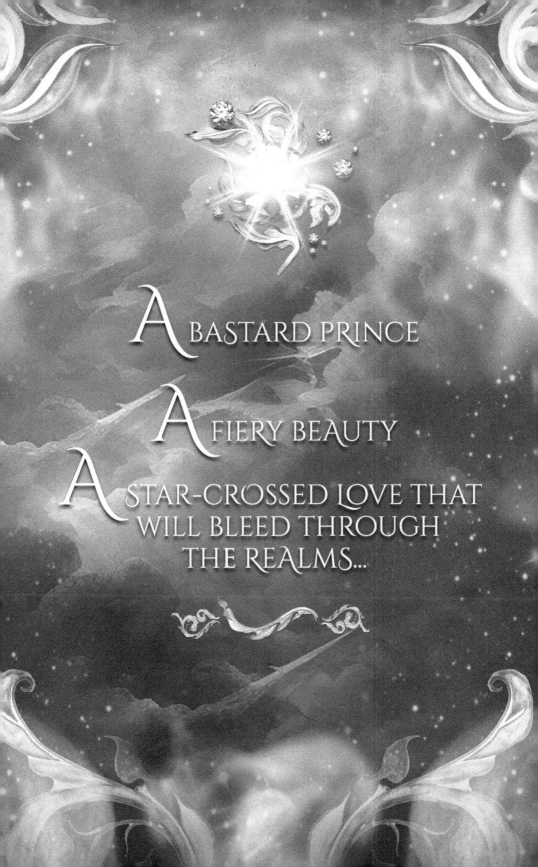

A bastard prince

A fiery beauty

A star-crossed love that will bleed through the realms...

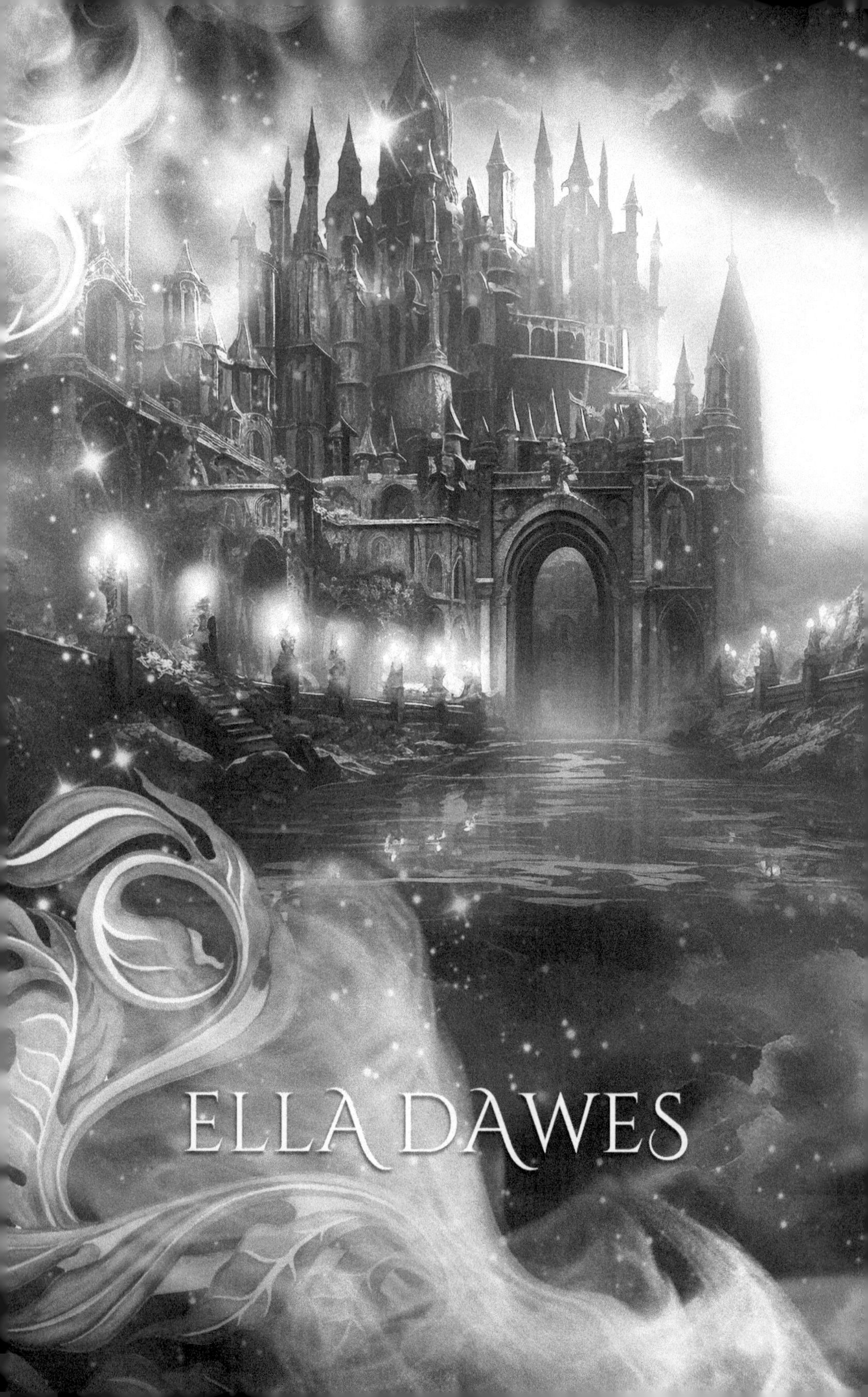
ELLA DAWES

THE BLEEDING REALMS

CONTENTS

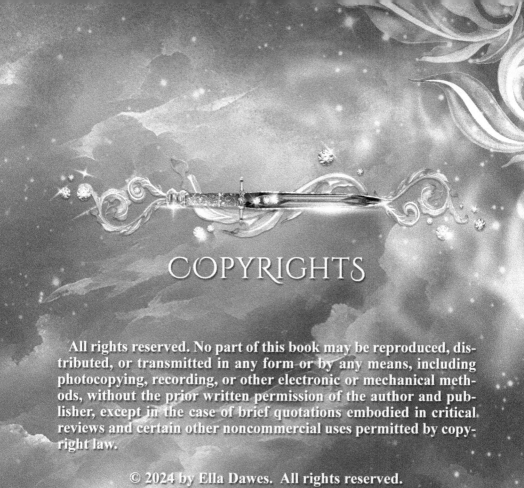

COPYRIGHTS

ISBN: 979-8-9892-6992-1

Edited By The Girl with the Red Pen
Sensitivity Reader: Ashley Birkenhauer
Cover Design By K.D. Ritchie at Story Wrappers
Special Edition Interior Design & Formatting By Stephany Wallace @ S.W. Creative Publishing. All Rights Reserved.

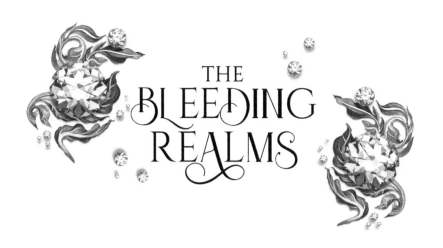

THE BLEEDING REALMS

COPYRIGHTS

A Gilded Roots Publication:
March 26, 2024

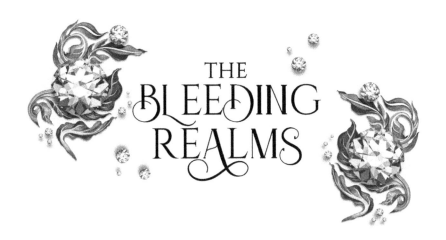

THE BLEEDING REALMS

CONTENT WARNING

Although *To Bleed A Kingdom* is humorous, fun, and a bit quirky, it also contains dark and violent elements that may be difficult for some. Triggers contained, but are not limited to, fantasy gore and violence, vulgar language, nonconsensual sex, graphic sex, and PTSD.

TO BLEED A KINGDOM

BOOK 1

DEDICATION

To all the broken souls who have felt themselves shatter one too many times, never forget that once you find the strength to piece yourself back together and choose to embrace all your jagged flaws and imperfections, you'll discover the stronger, more beautiful version of yourself that you were always destined to be.

PROLOGUE

QUEEN ADELPHIA

All I see is blood. On the walls, the floors, the tables, and the ceiling, splattered and pooling on every available surface. Gagging as that distinctive metallic scent overpowers me, I cup a hand to my mouth and sweep my gaze through all the gore decorating the once grand, crystal room. Limbs severed. Throats slashed. Heads decapitated. Intestines dangling from gutted torsos. Splashes of orange, green, blue, and teal magic streaks across the room as fae and immortals alike defend against humans with…

I don't understand what I'm seeing. It almost appears as if the humans are deflecting their powers with just a thought, but that can't possibly be right. Humans don't have magic. Never once throughout Vanyimar history have the gods blessed their race as they have immortals and fae.

A splash of bright orange hair catches my eye and I flit my gaze to a female, a Water fae, judging by her sharpened ears and the single aquamarine jewel near the outer corner of each eye, backed against a wall. She raises a teal glittering hand and a blast of water shoots from her palm, spearing the throat of an attacking human.

But with throat intact and no signs of drowning, the man doesn't miss a step as he raises his sword and slices clean through her neck. Her head tumbles to the floor along with her disconnected body, and the man turns his back on her, advancing on another.

Frozen within the doorway, my heart thunders against my chest as the sounds of the dying blast into me. Their screams, cries, grunts, and moans fuse one with the other to become a single roar reverberating into my ears. My eyes dart from one horrifying sight to the next until I spot the lone dead man sprawled at my feet. Inappropriately, I wonder how I was able to open the door, considering his location before I glance at his face and notice something strange.

At first I assume he is human, for no immortal has ever been killed by a human, but when I look near his open-eyed gaze, I notice he doesn't lack the jewels of a human, but neither does he have the sharpened ears or the jeweled markings of a fae. He has a sapphire and starlight jewel near the outer corner of each eye. Sucking in a gasp, I realize he's not a man, but a male. More precisely, an immortal!

Breaths punching from my chest, my horror intensifies as I scrutinize all the dead littering the throne room floor. They're all immortal and fae, not a single human amongst them. How can this be? It's not possible!

As much as I don't want to say it aloud, even to myself, we immortals and fae are superior. We're stronger, faster. We heal within moments and wield immense powers. To humans, we're indestructible. Even their most highly trained men can't compete with our males.

Attempting to grasp the magnitude of this situation, my eyes pass over all the fae and immortals defending themselves with swords, daggers, and their Gifts, desperately fighting for their lives, but felled within moments. My gaze eventually lands on the Captain of our Guards, Atlas, our most skilled and feared warrior, locked in battle with a human. Their swords are crossed, and I hear the hiss of steel on steel as each one attempts to gain ground against the other.

Both gritting their teeth and holding their stance, their twining swords appear to be held at an impasse until the human's sword begins to slowly inch in Atlas's direction. The time seems endless, but no more than a moment passes until the human suddenly thrusts forward, his blade vanishing into Atlas' chest, only to reappear in a spray of crimson through his back. Atlas cries out and falls to one knee. Faster than I can blink, but before his dying body drops to the floor, the human cuts off that cry with a gurgle, slashing Atlas' throat from ear to ear.

Tears streaming down my cheeks, body trembling, my shock fades as I desperately search for my male. Eyes darting from one end of the room to the next, my shaking becomes more violent the longer I search with no sign of his presence… until I spy a shock of platinum blonde hair in a sea of scarlet. I brace myself against the doorframe, my knees nearly giving out in relief at the sight of him alive. But then I look at him. Really *see* him as I ignore all the death and misery surrounding me to focus all my attention on him.

My heart stutters to a halt.

My husband, King Valor of Cascadonia is kneeling before his throne – a place where no king is ever intended to kneel – with one human on each side restraining his arms behind his back. His platinum blonde hair is disheveled and soaked, blood flowing through his immortal markings to drip down into his piercing green eyes. With a start, I realize the human he kneels before is none other than the human King of Brecca, King Rainier himself. Rainer says something to him that I'm unable to make out at this distance. Then he tosses his head back, roaring in laughter, before he raises his sword above Valor's head.

This isn't real. This isn't happening.

Valor can't die. He just can't! It's not meant to be this way. We're supposed to rule this kingdom together. To have long, fulfilling lives with a home full of children. Loving them and watching them grow until they marry and have their own babes. We're meant to fight, to play, to love, to cherish one another for hundreds of years at least, but we've barely had a decade together and I can already feel Fate's cruel fingers ripping it all from my grasp. All my hopes, my dreams, my future, disintegrating as if they are no more consequential than sand scattered in the wind.

No!

I shake my head, denying the truth. This is not the end; this is not my fate. Any moment now, Valor will disarm his human attackers and burn the traitorous bastards to ash. But as I watch him struggle to dislodge his captors and see the frustrated snarl on his face, I know that my dreams won't be coming true.

That uncanny sense Valor has whenever I enter a room has his head turning in my direction. Meeting his gaze, my mind flips from one scenario to the next as I imagine all the ways I can save him, but my sobs strengthen and a black hole of despair consumes me when I realize I can't save him. That I won't.

He smiles that smile that always manages to melt my heart, and nods his head in understanding. If our situations were reversed, he'd do no differently. Not because we don't love each other, and not because we aren't willing to die for the other, but because of the two beings we love more.

The battle falls to the wayside as I drown in his beautiful green eyes. So full of life and love. Until blood bubbles between his lips from the sword speared through his throat. His eyes widen momentarily, then just as quickly, glaze over in lifelessness.

I bolt, racing out the door and into the hall.

Don't think. Don't feel. Don't think. Don't feel. Don't think. Don't feel.

Rounding a corner, my heeled shoes wobble beneath my feet and I slam into a wall. Slowing, but not stopping, I remove one unstable shoe along with the other before pushing harder, using all my immortal strength to pump my legs as fast as possible.

A scream suddenly pierces the air, echoing throughout the palace, and my terror reignites at the realization that the battle is no longer contained to the throne room.

Don't think. Don't feel. Don't think. Don't feel. Don't think. Don't feel.

My chest heaves, my heartbeat is erratic, and I just watched the love of my life slayed in front of me, but all my focus is on moving my feet faster. To get to them. Before someone else does.

I pass rooms burning with fire and filled with smoke. Another completely flooded. A screaming human attached to a wall, held captive by a carnivorous plant eating him alive. A fae shapeshifted into a wolf is staked to the floor, partially skinned and burned. Too many dead. Some human, but mostly immortal and fae. Immortals, human, fae. All screaming, crying, fighting, and dying, but I don't pause for any of them. No matter what I see, no matter what I hear, I don't stop. Not even when I round the last corner to my destination and see a human man fucking a fae female's bloody corpse.

Door within sight, my feet skid across the wooden floor and I ram my shoulder into the frame, pushing the door open and shut all in a single motion.

The snick of the lock is deafening. My gasping breaths are abrasive to the ears in a room that should be filled with squeals and giggles yet is completely silent. No longer able to keep my terror at bay, I squeeze my eyes shut and press my forehead to the back of the door, praying that the gods haven't completely forsaken me.

Please be safe. Please be safe. Please be safe.

"Mama?"

A choked cry rips from my lungs. Slapping my palms to my face, I hurriedly swipe away the tears streaming down my cheeks and turn to face my sweet baby boy.

Green eyes stare questioningly back into mine from where he sits on the floor playing with wooden blocks. I see my mother in him with his soft heart, as well as how his power manifested identically to hers with his sapphire and starlight jewels. But when I look at his platinum blonde hair and bright green eyes, my heart constricts painfully with how much he looks like his father.

Attempting to control my breathing, I look to the crib where my two-month-old daughter, Aurora, is sound asleep.

They haven't made it here. Not yet.

"Mama?"

With a watery smile, I kneel down next to him. "Theon, where's Cinna?"

He points to the door. "Left."

"She left?"

He nods.

I sit back on my heels, my mind roaming back to the corpse I saw being defiled in the hallway. With the panic lessening now that I've reached them, I can place a name to the ravaged face. Cinna. The children's wet nurse. She must have gone to see what all the noise was about.

Get to the Palace Keep.

Knowing we have only a few minutes at best, I compartmentalize my grief of another senseless death and stand. Retrieving a dagger from my thigh holster, the very same dagger Valor forbade me from leaving our chambers without, regardless of how much I argued against it, I stab my skirt above the knees, slashing all the way around until I have a large piece of fabric. Slipping the knife back into its holster, I wrap my chest several times with the cloth and place the still sleeping Aurora into the makeshift sling.

Patting Aurora's bum, I force a smile and grab Theon's hand, tugging him to his feet. "We're going to play a little game today."

His green eyes light up. "Game?"

"Yes." I nod, pulling him behind me. "We're going to play hide and seek."

"Daddy play?" he asks, his expression brightening.

My smile falters. "No, sweetie. Just you, me, and Aurora."

"Where's Daddy?"

He's dead.

"He'll be along shortly," I lie, careful to keep my smile in place.

We stop before the door connected to mine and Valor's chambers and I place my ear against the wood, listening for any sounds. Hearing nothing, I unlock the door and peer down at Theon.

"We're going to play it a bit differently today. We have to move very fast and very quietly." I swallow nervously before continuing. "You may see some frightening things out there, but you can't make a sound. No matter what."

His excitement dims and he nods in confusion, but says nothing more.

Tightening my grip on his hand, I inhale a fortifying breath and swing the door open.

Not a soul in sight.

Releasing that pent-up breath, I give Theon a reassuring squeeze and walk through the door, moving as quickly as his little legs can manage. Staring straight ahead, I ignore everything, shoving away each memory called forth as I pass through the adjoining rooms.

The dining area where Valor blew raspberries on Aurora's belly while we had breakfast this very morning. Valor's office, where he would pretend not to notice the giggling Theon hiding beneath his desk. The receiving room where we snuggled up every night as a family while Valor recounted tales of gods, dragons, and legendary immortals' mighty quests.

Ignoring it all, my eyes remain fixed on the door to my

bedchambers, the door that will lead us to the secret passageway that leads to the Palace Keep. The door that will be our salvation. Hope rekindles as I step before that solid slab of oak. As I reach for the bronze handle, my fingers barely graze the cool metal before it swings open from the inside, revealing a man on the other side.

We both freeze, staring wide eyed at one another. Me in terror, him in shock that quickly shifts to excitement.

A slow smile spreads across his face and he cups his hands around his mouth, calling out, "I found them!" Gleeful eyes then drop to Theon and the man unsheathes his sword.

Horror like I've never known consumes me and I lurch towards Theon, curling my body over his and Aurora's as the man thrusts his blade. A sharp, fiery pain suddenly pierces my side and I scream, Theon and Aurora's cries an echo of my own.

"Shit." He rips the blade free, and I scream again as he snatches me up by the wrist, snapping the bone with a crack as he tears me away from Theon.

"Fuck!" he barks, his wide eyes staring at my limp hand. "We weren't supposed to hurt you. Only the heirs."

At the mention of my children, my cries cut off and I bury my pain and panic as I summon my most dominant Gift. Palms shimmering a glittering teal, a stream of water streaks towards the man and invades his open mouth.

Considering how many times I witnessed the humans deflect magic tonight, one would assume it'd be no surprise when nothing happens. But I'm stunned that when I expect him to drown, he laughs instead, thoroughly unaffected.

"That won't work on me," he sneers.

Rage and desperation fuel my determination to live and save my children at all costs. My power burns brighter, near blinding as I release a wave of water that swiftly surrounds him. Cycling faster and faster, the water cocoons his entire body in a speeding cyclone.

He laughs and stares at the cyclone in awe, mesmerized at the sight of the water recoiling from his skin when he slices a hand through it. “That won't work, either.”

“But *this* will.” Quickly unsheathing my dagger, I lunge forward and stab him in the eye.

“Aaaah!” He tugs the dagger free with a wet slurp, the blade tumbling from his grasp and clattering to the floor. He then slaps his hand to his now knifeless eye, blood gushing between his fingers as he drops to his knees and falls face first to the floor, dead before his face even touches the wood.

Knowing that our location has been compromised, I grab a sobbing Theon and carry him under my arm, running towards the door. Kicking the dead human aside, I rush into mine and Valor’s bedchamber, slam the door shut, lock it, and bolt across the room to the wall beside my bed. Placing Theon on his feet, I flatten my uninjured hand on the wall, searching for the groove that unlatches the hidden door. The sound of excited shouts and multiple sets of boots begin pounding in our direction. Theon sobs harder, Aurora joining him.

Panic crawls up the back of my throat as I swipe my hand back and forth with no sign of the latch.

Where is it?!

Theon screams and I jolt at the first strike against the door, a cold sweat beading across my brow as I move my hands faster and faster until … *finally*! Fingertips curving beneath the groove, I unlatch the door to the hidden passageway and shove Theon through.

As I take my first step to enter the passageway, the door to my bedchamber begins to splinter. I pause, my foot hovering above the threshold as I peer down at my son.

They know I'm here, but they don't know they *are. Even if they heard their cries, I could say they were my own. If they come in here and can't find me, they'll search and find the hidden door.*

A fierceness only a mother can feel engulfs me as I look down at my terrified son. Staring into the exact replica of his father's dark green eyes overflowing with tears, I realize I can't go with him. They might not discover the passageway. They may even give up their search eventually. But I'm not willing to take the risk.

Removing Aurora, I quickly unwrap the sling and wrap it around Theon's body, placing a trembling and sobbing Aurora inside it.

"Mama?" Confused eyes dart between me and Aurora.

"Take your sister and follow the passageway until it ends," I say, praying that he'll be able to bear her weight. "There's a room at the end of the corridor with beds and food. There's lots of toys, too! I'll come and find you when I can."

His sobs worsen and he gasps. "No!"

"I can't go with you, baby," I say with an apologetic smile.

Crouching before them, I press my lips to Aurora's forehead and hug them both tightly to my chest, feeling the wetness of tears as I place a soft kiss on Theon's chubby cheek.

"I'll find you," I whisper. "I promise." Heart shattering, I stand to my feet and peer down at him. "Run, Theon."

Then I shut the door on Aurora's cries and Theon's anguished face, just as a worn boot punches through the broken door.

Adrenaline wavering, I cradle my broken wrist to my chest and place my opposite hand against the wound on my side, feeling my life force slither between the webbing of my fingers as I stumble before my bed and collapse to my knees. Suffering from grief, pain, heartbreak, and exhaustion, I bow my head and watch my blood slowly pool onto the oak wood floors, lacking the strength to acknowledge the methodical footsteps slowly approaching.

"Lift her," a deep voice demands.

Rough hands drag me to my feet and I release a strangled cry. Slowly lifting my head, I meet the glacial-eyed stare of the Savage King himself, King Rainier.

His face betrays no emotion as he scrutinizes me from head to toe. "She's wounded," he coldly states. "Were my orders not clear when I said no harm is to come to her?" His jaw hardens. "Find who did this."

The greasy man standing beside him shuffles his feet. "I think it was Ptorik."

Rainier glances over his shoulder, seeing the dead body beside the doorway. "I'm assuming that's Ptorik?" Rainier asks, returning his cruel gaze to mine.

The greasy man nods his head.

"And whose responsibility was it to ensure my orders were executed properly?"

Silence.

"Who?" Rainier growls.

"M-m-mine," the greasy man stutters.

The air thickens menacingly as everyone holds their breath for Rainier's response.

"You disobeyed me."

Without breaking my gaze, Rainer darts his hand out and crushes the man's throat with a speed and strength unnatural for a human. Mouth gaping like a fish, the man stumbles to his knees while clutching his throat and collapses to the floor, squirming desperately for breath.

"Disobedience is an act of betrayal," Rainier tosses over his shoulder to the gangly man at his back. “There's no place for disloyalty in my court.” Stepping forward, Rainier’s lips tug up into a savage grin as he leers at me. “Hello, Your Majesty.”

Scanning his handsome face, staring into those cruel glacial blue eyes so full of triumph, I wonder how I was ever able to endure his presence. Sweeping my gaze over his black hair that almost appears blue, I suck in a pained breath when I see the gold crown atop his head, studded with orange topaz and starlight jewels and speckled with blood. My stomach roils into itself when I realize whose blood it's speckled with. Valor's blood. Valor’s crown.

“How?” I don't need to ask why. Cascadonia is a prosperous kingdom. Mild weather, a fruitful growing season, rich in coin and beauty. As for Rainier’s kingdom, Brecca is an arctic wasteland. An inhospitable landscape made even harsher for the human dominated kingdom where they have no fae or immortal citizens to alleviate the strain. Rainier may be a king, but he’s a king of a barren land and destitute people. A king of nothing.

Rainier smiles. “The Goddess of Death gifted us absolute protection against your power.”

I scoff, a flash of fire searing through my wound with the act. “We are Uriella’s favored. Her crown jewels. Desdemona would never defy her so openly.” None of the gods would.

“Oh, yes!” He laughs, a rumbling, arrogant sound. “The Goddess of Life's golden pets. But it would seem you are no longer her crown jewels. For you are not from her loins, and she has born a son. With Azazel, no less.”

“Impossible,” I breathe. “The Stars forbid it.”

Always one for showmanship, he waves a finger, tsking. “The Stars are fickle entities and will do as they please. And what they wish for is for the Mother of Life and the Creator of All to bear a babe.”

If this is true, it will upset the balance even more than it already is. Any child born from that union would have limitless power. Power that could rival all the gods, maybe even the Stars themselves. Too much power for one being. An abomination. One that the gods would not allow to live.

Stars save us.

"Ah." Rainier chuckles in glee. "You see it now, don't you? Uriella's favor means little to the gods when they're already condemned by hunting her only natural born child."

"What does Desdemona get out of this agreement?" I ask, swallowing thickly, seeing now this is so much more than a battle between kingdoms, but a war against gods. "I doubt she needs a human for anything."

His face shudders. "Her plans are not your concern. What should be, is that Desdemona granted me a taste of her power, giving me the means to conquer Cascadonia. And when I prove my loyalty to her, she'll bestow her full blessing on Brecca and *we* will be the ones favored by the gods."

I laugh bitterly, blood spurting from my wound as the vibrations tear it open even more. "You mean you'll be her slaves."

Glacial blue orbs narrow. "A faithful servant. And with her guiding hand, I'll rule over all of Vanyimar."

Walking toward me, he stops a few paces away, speaking in an alarmingly quiet tone. "Where are your children?"

Lifting my chin, I say nothing, my hard gaze boring into his cruel one.

"If you tell me, I'll spare your life." Silence. "I know you've hidden them somewhere." His lips tighten. "I'll find them one way or another. At least this way you can live."

Rainier's eyes suddenly brighten, smiling in triumph when I lean forward. My shoulder and wrists screaming, I curse the man shackling my wrists between his impossibly strong grip as I overextend my arms and arch toward Rainier. “Fuck. You.”

That arrogant smile falls, his gaze hardening as he takes two large strides towards me, stopping when the tips of his shoes rest against my bare toes. Leaving only a breadth of space between us, he shapes his hand as if it's a spear, and an agonized scream tears from my throat when he stabs his hand into the seam of my wound, twisting his fingers.

Screaming and sobbing, my vision wavers and I begin to lose consciousness. Left hand still torturing me, his other strokes my hair with mock affection. “Shh shh… It's alright,” he soothes. “Tell me where the children are and the pain will stop.”

“I don't know!”

“You don't know?”

“No!” I scream on a sob, desperate for the pain to end, but not desperate enough to betray my children.

He pulls his fingers from my wound and gently places his blood-slicked hand upon my cheek along with the other, delicately cradling my face.

“You're lying.” Blue eyes roam my face. “Gorgeous,” he murmurs. “You're even a legend amongst immortals, did you know that? They say your beauty could rival Uriella herself.” He traces his finger softly down my cheek as his eyes glaze over in lust, his voice hoarsening. “You truly are stunning.”

Revolted by his touch, I jerk my head from his grip and spit on his face.

Rainier stills, and a foreboding silence fills the room as he slowly wipes the glob off his cheek. Then his face contorts into a snarl and he grips my chin hard enough to break bones. Eyes maddened from rage he snarls, “*Where are they*?”

Tremors racking my body, I shake my head as much as I’m capable within his bruising grip.

A vicious light suddenly flashes within his eyes. Still gripping my chin, he slowly slides his opposite hand along my neck, his fingers trailing down my collarbone. Once he reaches the top of my dress, my chest clenches in fear as I struggle to free my arms with no success.

He rips the top of my gown, my breasts bouncing free as he slips his hand beneath one, cupping it. As affectionate as a lover, he slowly traces my areola and I swallow back bile as he tweaks my nipple to a pebbled state. Spreading his hand to encompass my entire breast, I cry out once he begins kneading it. But that cry quickly turns to a torturous scream when he viciously clenches my breast, then twists.

Shutting his eyes, he rests his forehead against mine and I feel the heat of his breath caress my face when he releases a hunger-fueled groan.

"Tell me where they are," he demands, his voice thickened with lust. "I cannot rule Cascadonia uncontested while your children still live."

All my pain, all my grief, all my fear and disgust swirls together, coalescing into an unmanageable whirl of chaos that swiftly morphs into a volatile mixture of rage and hate.

Pale green eyes expressing every ounce of loathing for him and his despicable race, I scream, "Never! I'll never tell you!" With heaving breaths, I promise, "You'll never find my children and you'll never rule Cascadonia. Even with a goddess's favor." I laugh, a crazed, bitter sound. "No immortal or fae will ever bow to a filthy human."

Rainier's features contort into a blistering rage and he backhands me, throwing me from my captor's grip to land face first on top of the bed. Head swimming and vision full of stars, I'm unable to regain my senses before I feel the weight of Rainier's body lying atop my back, pushing me into the bed.

"You always were a sanctimonious little bitch, weren't you?" he says scornfully. "Never knew when to keep your mouth shut. Valor thought you to be spirited." He laughs. "What a fool he was. Never realized that bitches must be trained to obey."

He grinds his growing erection against my ass, prodding me. I squirm, crying out when he fists his hand into my hair and jerks my head back, licking up the column of my arched throat.

Pressing his lips to the lobe of my ear, he growls, "A bitch must be broken before she learns to heel."

Placing his hand across the back of my head, he crushes my face into the mattress before shoving off.

"Hold her."

The lifting of his weight is quickly replaced by hands pressed upon my upper back. Accompanied by the sounds of a belt unbuckling and clothes rustling, Rainier sneers, "I bet you've never been fucked by a human cock before. Never *demeaned* yourself that way, have you?"

When I hear a ripping sound and a cool breeze brush my lower region, a feeling of dread slithers within me as I fight to remove the hands holding me down to no avail. Feeling his weight return along my back, I lock my ankles to prevent the inevitable, but his thighs easily spread my own.

"Don't worry, Your Highness. I'll solve that issue for you," he promises, right before I feel a ripping, burning pain as he forcefully invades my body.

Savagely tearing apart my lower half, my breath whooshes from my lungs and I suck in another, releasing a bloodcurdling scream as he ruts on me like a feral animal. Screaming and sobbing, I try to buck, scratch, kick and punch, but all I manage to do is squirm minutely and claw at the bedding.

My disgust and devastation at being violated, along with the feeling of filth, of Rainier's defilement of my body and his perversion of such a sacred act, creates a fissure in my soul. I begin to weep.

Head bobbing, I stare unseeing at the wall violently wavering back and forth due to his manic thrusts, and I stop fighting. Tears drying, body limpening, I choose to see nothing, to hear nothing, to feel nothing. Instead, I float outside my body and imagine a world where my husband isn't dead, my children are safe, my home isn't overrun by enemies, and I can't feel a human usurper swelling inside me now, grunting his release. He softens inside me before I feel the slippery withdrawal of him, but all I do is stare, seeing nothing.

At the sound of him buckling his belt, I feel his seed slither down my thighs and feel the heat of his breath between my thighs as he says to the other man, “Look at that pretty cunt dripping with my cum.”

He laughs manically, his words and actions intended to demean, but they no longer have the ability to wound me. Even when I hear an earsplitting roar and his laughter abruptly cuts off, his weight slamming on top of me and crushing me into the bed, obscuring my vision.

With the sounds of shouts and the clashing of swords that quickly cease, I do nothing. I see nothing. I feel nothing. Not even when the weight is removed and a wide eyed Cascadonia guard fills my vision.

“Your Highness!” He turns his head to speak to another. “It's her! It's the Queen!”

Another roar, followed by a wet squelching sound, and the guard’s gaze snaps above my head. “Get him out of here!”

“Are you injured?” the guard asks, returning his gaze to me.

I say nothing.

At my silence, timid hands begin to roam my body, only for

him to quickly jerk them back, horror lining his face as he stares at the blood slickening his fingers.

"She needs a healer!"

A dark-skinned arm suddenly snaps out, fisting the back of the guard's tunic and throwing him across the room. Those very same arms lift me off the bed, careful not to jostle my wounds, and cradle me to his chest.

With the swaying motion of the guard carrying me towards the door, my eyelids begin to descend and my body starts to shut down. But I quickly snap them open when I notice a lone male standing in the corner near the door.

At first, I assume him to be one of the guards, but then I notice his clothing. His *human* clothing. Battling consciousness, I force my eyes to remain open once I realize I recognize him. He's one of the humans who restrained Valor when he was killed, but… he's not a human at all.

With his sun kissed skin, pillowy lips, and blonde, wavy hair, he's the most attractive male I've ever seen. His luminous, bluish silver eyes are stunning, yet his markings are strange and he lacks the two or four jewels that would signify his power as immortal or fae. He's not human, but he's not fae or immortal, either. He's something *other*. But what he is doesn't concern me. All that does is he's just as responsible as Rainier for my husband's death.

I attempt to signal the guards to the traitor in our midst; call out, whisper, even issue a small grunt, but with the remainder of my blood seeping from my wounds, my lips refuse to shape the words. Powerless and unmoving, I can only watch as the male weeps silently. Struggling to contain the consciousness trickling between my fingers, only a sliver of my vision remains as the guard carrying me nears him. That's when an impossible realization dawns on me. The guards aren't even aware of this creature.

It's as if he's concealed himself from everyone's sight but my own, and he's as much of a specter as my dear Valor.

Tearing his gaze from mine, the weeping male ambles toward the door. And it's as he vanishes over the threshold, but before my eyes slide shut, I'm finally able to sense the spark of new life bloom within my womb.

CHAPTER 1

DARIUS

34 Years Later

With a swipe of my sword, I slice through the Soulless' neck, severing bone and sinew along with the creature's connection to its master. Tugging a cloth from my pocket, I wipe away the Soulless' black blood from my blade, watching its cloak of ruby flecked, black shadows disperse on the wind, returning to its patron's goddess as the undead's body returns to its natural state.

Dead. Unanimated. Decomposing. No more glowing red eyes, no more death magic, and no more insatiable need for blood. Just as it should be. Just as it should have always been.

Hearing a screech, I turn toward the sound and find a Soulless snapping at Kace's neck. The Nature fae's blue eyes are widened comically as he extends his arm to keep the mindless creature at bay. When his emerald jewels illuminate, I watch and wait, expecting him to use his Nature magic to defend himself. But I'm proven wrong when the battle hardened fae begins slapping at the demon's face, screeching like a female. Sighing, I press my boot to the mud-slicked ground, ready to assist, when a sword suddenly spears through its skull.

Griffin, a large male with cropped brown hair and the markings of an Air immortal with a sapphire and starlight jewel near the outer corner of each eye, appears calm and collected as he tugs the sword free from the creature's skull. Even when the Soulless' body slides down Kace's, leaving a trail of putrid body fluids in its wake.

“Oh, gods!” Kace snaps forward on a gag, retching over the crumbled dead.

“You probably shouldn't be hanging your head directly over its rotting corpse,” Griffin says, his lumbering footsteps rising in volume until he reaches my side. “I imagine the scent of decay is much more potent when you’re all but rubbing your nose in it.” He shrugs, seeming indifferent. “Just a suggestion.”

Intelligent enough to accept his advice, Kace kicks the Soulless away, then resumes his heaving.

Giving Kace a moment to himself, I look over all the lifeless creatures scattered across the forest floor. Several appear just as they always do. Emaciated, hairless, with leathery, sunken skin. Of course, one could never forget their clawed hands and dagger-like fangs, made even deadlier when their jaw widens enough to swallow an adult male's head whole.

Better to suck your blood and your soul along with it, I suppose.

Most of them obviously passed some time ago, but for some, the lack of decomposition is concerning. They still have patches of hair and their skin oozes as if transitioning to their companions' leathery state. They’re fresh, which means they haven't been dead long. It's rare to find freshly deceased Soulless, and there's four in this party alone.

Where did you come from?

They must have come from somewhere, and these Soulless have been dead no more than a month. Eyeing the dead's clothing, I notice their leather vest and trousers. A material not made available to Brecca – home to the Soulless’ masters – but guaranteed to be in any male Cascadonian's wardrobe.

Already knowing there aren’t any missing persons or deaths unaccounted for in Cascadonia, I wonder if there have been any missives from our neighboring kingdoms reporting differently. I would hope they would relay this or any other information regarding Soulless activity within their borders, but kings and queens never carry much thought for anyone but themselves. No matter how noble they present themselves.

No answers forthcoming, I search through the trees for the several hundred spans-tall stone wall surrounding the capital city of Cascadonia, thinking of all the inhabitants residing within. All the souls I'm oathbound to protect.

Too close.

The Gods Cursed are getting bolder. Increasing in frequency and in larger numbers, the masters to the Soulless are commanding them practically to our gates. This month alone we've had three attacks, not including this one. And with the newly dead adding to their ranks, it's vital we learn where these new creatures originally came from.

Unsettled, I return my gaze to Kace, who's wiping his mouth with the back of his hand.

"I got it in my mouth," Kace says, his eyes rounded in horror.

I cringe. "What?"

"I got it in my mouth!" He jabs a finger at the dead creature. "The Soulless. I got its body juices in my mouth. Ach!" He hunches over and gags for a moment more, then straightens, attempting to compose himself, but still appearing a bit green.

"Then maybe you should have summoned your Gift instead of slapping at it like a hysterical female," I chastise. "Or fought it off like the trained warrior you are."

"I panicked! I've never had one get close enough to bite me." He pauses, his brow furrowing. "There was what? Eight of them? We've never fought that many at once."

"No, we haven't." Blowing out a weary breath, I turn away

from Kace and begin making my way back toward the city gates, Kace and Griffin following behind.

"Their numbers are increasing," Griffin echoes my thoughts.

I nod in agreement, but say nothing more, listening to the crunch of Fall leaves beneath our boots.

"They had several new Soulless in this group," Kace notes.

"Four," Griffin adds.

"Their clothing… it isn't Breccan," Kace says, his body popping in and out of view as he slips between trees. "Where did they come from? What kingdom?"

"I don't know," I reply through gritted teeth, hating that I can't give him a definitive answer. Hating even more what I suspect that answer may be.

"The Kings Council is today," Griffin reminds me.

Rubbing my eyes, I groan internally at the thought of enduring another Kings Council meeting, wishing there was some way I could avoid another session of listening to the petty squabbles and drunken snide comments of the ruling monarchs of Vanyimar. But as acting Captain of the Guard, my presence is, unfortunately, mandatory.

Griffin places a large hand on my shoulder, pivoting me to face him. "This affects every kingdom, Darius. You must bring it to their attention." He pauses, conveying the severity of his thoughts with an arch of a brow. "Despite what orders you may receive."

Often others look at the quiet, muscular immortal who prefers his own company and assume him to be dim-witted. Yet, Griffin is anything but. He may not speak much, but when he does, his words are carefully selected and delivered with a keen intelligence that I've not found in another. I wouldn't dare to refuse his advice.

Mentally preparing myself for the punishment I'm sure to receive, I jerk my head in assent.

"At least this will give the rulers something else to argue over," Kace says, chuckling darkly as he rushes past. "Besides which one of them has the biggest cock."

A fae born in the lower class, Kace has always held an aversion towards royals and the members of nobility. Son of a courtesan and his father's identity unknown, his upbringing was darker than most.

Hungry and poor, Kace was no more than a child when he began slinging pots, shining boots, and occasionally pick pocketing. He has a first-hand account to the cruelty and selfishness of the nobility towards those less fortunate.

"You *do* know males aren't the only ones on the Council, right?" I ask Kace, watching him swing from tree to tree. "It also contains Queen Celene and Queen Adelphia."

"Oh, yes. I know *all* about Queen Celene," he drawls her name, bowing beneath a rather thin looking branch before swinging to another.

"You don't know a godsdamn thing about her." I chuckle, tossing a stick at him that he dodges easily enough. "That female would eat you alive."

Dropping to the ground, he bounces on the balls of his feet, his eyes glimmering. "I would love for her to eat me. Do you think she can shapeshift just her throat? She *is* the Shapeshifter Queen. Oh, gods!" He groans, biting his fist. "She could literally gobble my entire dick. Swallow it whole!"

Griffin chuckles. "Her being a queen, and you being…" He pauses, gesturing towards Kace with a wave of his hand, "*you,* I doubt you'll be able to get near enough to ask." Inhaling a deep breath, he cringes. "And with the scent currently wafting off you, she'd mistake you for a Soulless and kill you on the spot."

Griffin and I laugh, but Kace appears genuinely shocked at his words.

"I'll have you know I'm a fantastic lover. *A-ma-zing*," he says with a proud lilt to his chin. "Queen Celene should feel honored to have a male such as myself in her bed." He scrunches his nose in disgust, glancing down at his guards vest slickened with black blood. "Even if I am smothered in Soulless juices."

Griffin smirks. "No matter how amazing you are, her guards won't allow you anywhere near her."

"No, no. You're right." He rubs his chin, mumbling as he walks past. "I need to study the rotation of her guards. Find their weakness. Lie in wait for my chance to sweep her off her feet. Then, we'll get married and make a bunch of panther babies."

Cocking his head to the side, he scrunches his face in thought.

"Or would they be cubs? I'm not exactly sure how that works. In the meantime, I'll check the brothel. There must be at least one shapeshifter there."

Griffin and I share an amused look, having no words in response to the delusional male babbling to himself. Until Kace shouts over his shoulder, "And we'll live happily ever after… because I'm fucking amazing!"

Unsure if he's trying to convince us or himself, but already knowing it's best not to encourage him, we silently follow the ridiculous fae back to the city gates.

At the sound of the creaking door, all conversations cease and the room falls silent.

Pausing over the threshold, I look up and see every pair of royal eyes staring back at me. Grumbling a curse, I quickly shut the door and round the large oval table centered within the room, barely taking notice of the dark oak, honeycombed walls, the unlit

Gods Light sconces arrayed between the black and gold stitched tapestries, the Kings Council crest stitched within, and the view of the two moons through the floor-to-ceiling, arched windows.

Instead, my head remains high as I make my way toward the Cascadonian heir.

It took me much longer than I initially planned to return from patrol, and once I did finally arrive back to my chambers, the sun had already begun its daily descent. In no state to appear before royalty, I quickly washed and dressed, but by the time I left my rooms, it was already past time for the Kings Council to begin.

Once I'm seated, the silence ends and the royals return to their previous discussions. Chatting and laughing in all their finery and jewels, it appears my lateness is already forgotten.

Queen Celene of Arcadia tosses her head back, laughing. Her long black hair is pulled back into a sleek ponytail, and her flickering copper and starlight jewels illuminate her brown eyes and tan face.

Wearing a slinky black, form-fitting dress, it looks like something one might wear to a brothel, but judging by the quality of fabric and copper gems stitched within, it's not a gown even the highest paid courtesan could possibly afford.

Kace wasn't mistaken in her seductive beauty, but she's also just as dangerous as I insinuated, if not more so. The Shapeshifter Queen is intelligent, calculating, and just as lethal as the predatory black panther she often favors.

I chuckle to myself when I see the besotted expression on the face of the monarch with whom Celene is speaking. The Nature immortal of Ravaryn, King Elidyr, watches Celene as if he's moments away from professing his undying love. His flowing green tunic matches the forest green of his eyes and the emerald and starlight jewels accenting his face.

An ally of Cascadonia, Elidyr has always been one of my

favorites among the monarchs. Most rulers tended to ignore my presence, but he was always kind and playful with me, even as a child. He's a good male and an even better king.

The male seated at the opposite end of the table, King Olivier of Egralong, couldn't contrast more to Elidyr. Olivier is as stoic as ever, with his razor thin, black hair and the menacing scar slicing down through his eyebrow, past his orange topaz and starlight jewel, to end beneath his eye.

The sensible ruler is underdressed compared to the others, wearing an all-black tunic and matching leather trousers, but that's not unusual. The Fire King tends to gravitate towards practicality rather than the frivolous. Olivier may seem harsh with his curt and blunt speech and apathetic manner, but he's honest and fair, and always does what's in the best interest of his people.

There's not a soul alive who can say the same about the king seated beside him.

To some, King Luthais of Raetia is considered attractive, as most immortals are, with his blonde hair, charming smile, and lean, fit build. To others, the arrogant Air immortal is a vicious snake. But whereas Celene's lethality is only in response to those dense enough to threaten her or her people, Luthais is cruel and brutal, evidenced by his own citizens' comparison of him to the Savage King himself.

Passing my gaze over the oak table, I find the lone empty chair that hasn't been used since before the Breccans attacked. King Rainier of Brecca was the last man to be seated in that chair, and he'll be the last human to ever grace this table.

I grind my teeth at the sight of the Savage King's empty chair, thinking of all the pain and death he's caused for so many. Myself included.

After the Battle of Brecca was extinguished and their King was killed, Queen Adelphia, along with the other rulers, cut off all trade and communication with Brecca. All men who were captured were immediately executed for their treasonous acts, but unfortunately a few escaped.

Baffled by their newfound strength and their ability to neutralize our magic, all members of the Kings Council prepared for war against the aggressive humans, but all plans were waylaid when *they* arrived.

When the first Soulless came through the Cursed Woods, we weren't sure what they were. Some believed them to be ill, but only when the first person was bitten and they turned themselves, did we realize what they were: Demons.

Immortals and fae, as well as our human inhabitants, fought and died as they hacked, stabbed, and burned the creatures, but they still kept coming. It took many deaths to realize that the only way to kill the creatures was to stab it in the heart or brain. Then they came in waves.

It was a frightening time for our kingdoms, not knowing where these demons came from or how they came to be, until we noticed the lone living creature amongst the undead. The man was a human, stronger and faster than any immortal, and he carried the Goddess of Death's mark upon his cheek, a swirled rune filled with ruby flecked, black shadows.

Seeing Death's rune marking his cheek, we realized then that even though King Rainier had lost the Battle of Brecca and didn't hold up his end of the goddess' bargain, Desdemona had still chosen to grant her Gifts to Brecca.

But a Cursed Gift it was.

With glowing crimson eyes and extended fangs, the Gods Cursed man was more powerful than any being we have ever encountered before as he wielded his Death Shadows without recourse, killing dozens with a single flick of his wrist.

He commanded his troops of Soulless and he, too, barbarically drank the blood of an immortal. And once the Cursed bled him dry, we watched in horror as the immortal's discarded, twitching corpse transitioned right before our eyes into a feral Soulless.

Nothing we did to the Gods Cursed would kill him. Not even when we stabbed him in the heart or brain like we did his Soulless slaves. At this point, having no way to attack or defend against the Cursed, our outlook was bleak. Until, to everyone's astonishment, the Gods Cursed eventually just left, unharmed and of his own accord, leaving behind dozens of Soulless.

We then destroyed all the remaining Soulless, and when it appeared as if the attacks had ended, we built our walls and fortified our defenses.

Fortunately, we've seen less than a handful of Gods Cursed in the last thirty-four years. They don't venture far from Brecca, and besides those who call the Mandala Mountains and the Cursed Woods home, Soulless attacks are few and far between. That's why today's events are so alarming. The frequency and numbers of the attacks could be a precursor to change. A change that won't bode well for anyone.

Sensing the frosty gaze boring into the side of my cheek, I glance in the direction of the hosting monarch and realize my error.

Queen Adelphia of Cascadonia sits regally in her crystal throne-like chair at the head of the table. Garbed in a teal and gold stitched gown, her long blonde hair is partially pinned up with small braids intertwined throughout.

With high cheekbones, porcelain skin, and pale green eyes, she's considered gorgeous even amongst our attractive race. And judging off the Water immortal's scowl and her illuminated aquamarine and starlight jewels, she clearly has no intention of forgiving me.

Should've come directly from patrol, covered in Soulless blood.

After staring at me long enough to convey her displeasure, she returns her attention to the adjoining royals.

Theon leans into me, ducking his head to whisper in my ear. “You're late.”

“I'm well aware.”

“She's furious.”

I snort. “When is she not furious with me?” Staring at the center of the table, I set my elbow on the armrest and rest my chin in my palm, partially shielding my lips. “I ran into trouble during patrol.”

“You shouldn't have scheduled yourself the same day as a Kings Council,” he says, shaking his head in exasperation. “You shouldn't even be patrolling. You're the Captain of the Guards. Delegate.”

Ignoring the Prince’s reprimand, I peek at him out of the corner of my eye. “There was an ambush.”

He stiffens, his brows pinching. “That's the fourth time this month.”

Nodding my head, I notice the royals’ discussions beginning to taper off. “Did you speak with her?”

Sighing, Theon leans back in his chair and turns away, avoiding my gaze. “Yes.”

When he adds nothing more, I press, “Well?”

“She's not planning to touch on the topic today,” he grudgingly admits, eyeing me with a dubious expression.

“Why the fuck not?” I snap.

“Lower your voice,” he warns, his dark green eyes anxiously bouncing from one ruler to the next.

Noticing I’ve caught the attention of the rulers nearby, including Queen Adelphia herself, I inhale a deep, calming breath.

“She thinks it makes us appear weak,” Theon says. “She won't look weak in front of the other monarchs.”

I scrub my hands over my face. "I don't care how it makes us look. They have to prepare." Gesturing to the royals with a jerk of my hand, I hiss, "How can they protect their people if they're not even made aware?"

"I agree with you," he says in a soothing tone, patting my arm. "But she won't change her mind." Shaking his head, he returns his gaze forward, dismissing me.

Frustrated, I listen to the tedious discussions of the Kings Council. Not of defenses, trade, or even the welfare of their people. Oh no, the most powerful beings of Vanyimar gossip about gowns, balls, and limber new mistresses. Not a single topic of substance.

Temper spiking with each moment that passes, I have no more shits left to give when everyone stands to their feet, signaling the end of the meeting.

"I'd like to bring a matter to everyone's attention."

They pause halfway out of their chairs and stare, blinking slowly. I can only assume their surprise is due to the fact that I've never uttered a single word during these meetings, but I could be wrong.

Queen Adelphia hasn't moved to stand, but at my words her back stiffens and her head slowly swivels in my direction. "I believe we've covered every topic scheduled today," she bites out.

I highly doubt which king is fucking which servant was a scheduled topic of discussion.

"I'll have to insist." Based off the storm brewing within her gaze, if there weren't others present to witness it, I have no doubt she would've blasted me with a wave of water, shattering my bones and pulverizing my organs in the process.

Dismissing her without a second thought, I return my attention forward, waiting patiently for the monarchs to return to their seats and all eyes to focus on me. "When I was on patrol today, me and two other guards were ambushed by a group of Soulless."

"That's not uncommon," Queen Celene of Arcadia says, her lips turned down into a confused frown. "Your borders are pressed up against the Cursed Woods. Your people hunt there regularly."

Tapping my finger on the armrest, I pause before adding, "There were eight of them."

Ravaryn's King Elidyr startles and his eyes widen. "Eight?"

I nod. "Not only that, but four of them appeared to be newly dead."

The rulers glance between each other, concern radiating from them until booming laughter draws all our gazes.

"How can you tell they're *newly* dead?" King Luthais of Raetia says on a lingering laugh. "Dead is dead.'"

"They were in an early stage of decomposition," I reply, careful to keep my tone neutral in spite of my rising anger. "Unlike the Soulless we more commonly encounter."

Elidyr rubs his jaw. "That is unsettling."

"Have there been any disappearance within your kingdoms?" I ask. "Any new attacks we've not been made aware of?"

All shake their heads in answer.

Luthais crosses his legs, lounging back in his chair with an arrogant smirk. "It's obvious they came from Brecca."

Annoyed, I clench my hands into fists, but my expression remains impassive. "Their clothing wasn't that of the humans. The creatures appeared to have originally come from one of our kingdoms."

Luthais arches a brow. "You're basing this off their clothing?"

"It's unlikely they undress themselves before they're killed," Celene says with a roll of her eyes, just as irritated with the insufferable immortal as I am.

"Of course not," he replies, pasting on that charming smile. "But I imagine their clothes were dirty and worn. One couldn't possibly be able to determine which kingdom they came from based off such little information."

"It's an issue we need to address," I snap, at my wits end with the fool's attempts to undermine me.

Elidyr leans forward and places his clasped hands on the table. "What do you propose we do?"

Relieved to move this discussion forward, I direct my answer to him.

"More patrols, fortify our defenses, and notify the people." Bracing myself, I inhale a long breath through my nostrils and say what I know will be the most difficult for the rulers to accept. "I also recommend sending a scouting party up the Mandala Mountains."

A strained silence thickens the air as they all stare at me in shock.

"That's a dangerous task to undertake, based on such scant information," King Olivier of Egralong says, his face betraying no emotion.

Feeling as if foreboding claws scrape across my neck, I straighten in my seat and meet each of their gazes. "The frequency of attacks are increasing and the Soulless are adding to their ranks. Possibly from our very own citizens."

Stabbing my finger onto the oak table, I continue.

"I believe the Gods Cursed are planning something, and we need to know what that is. They have been quiet for too long, but why is that?" I ask, resting my arms on the table and clasping my hands together. "They hate us just as much as we do them, and with no known way to kill them, they may as well be indestructible. They could slaughter us all, yet they've done nothing."

Shaking my head, my lips flatten to an angry line.

"No, that's not right. They've been waiting. Plotting. But plotting what?" I meet each pair of eyes as I add to the gravity. "We must search for these answers, or else I fear the bloodshed will be one from which we won't recover."

Silence reigns while they ponder my words.

"Where was this ambush?" Elidyr asks. "The one from today."

"Practically at our gates."

"So close," Celene mumbles, her fingertips pressed to her lips.

Hope rises in me as I watch them consider my plans, only for it to quickly dwindle.

"I commend you on your dedication to your position," Luthais says in a tone thickened with sarcasm. "But the Cursed haven't been seen nor heard from in over thirty years, besides the occasional Soulless attacks that are quietly quelled. Why would I send my people across the border when I know it would not only be a death wish, but would most likely provoke the Gods Cursed?"

I open my mouth to speak, but he barrels on.

"Regarding the matter of how close they are to your gates… I would assume that to be an isolated security issue within your own kingdom."

I stiffen, offended he would assume my guards are inadequate or lacking in any way. "There are constant patrols, and my guards are highly trained."

"I'm sure they are." He dismisses me with a regal flick of his hand. "This very well may be simply an unusual occurrence. Or…. it may be due to a larger issue."

"Your meaning?" Adelphia asks, her tone laced with tightly leashed anger.

Luthais exhales a long, dramatic sigh.

"I'd rather not say, but as a friend of Cascadonia, I'd be remiss if I didn't. When there is instability or *weakness* within a ruling party, oftentimes that reflects in their citizens." His lips slowly curve into a snide smirk. "The guards are *your* people, are they not?"

Fuck! She's going to lose her shit.

If I thought Queen Adelphia was furious before, I couldn't have been more wrong. Eyes searing King Luthais with her wrath alone, jewels blazing, palms glittering teal—*Stars save us, she's going to kill him!*

She barely restrains herself before saying menacingly slow, "There is *no* weakness in my kingdom."

The fool is either daft or delusional if he can't see she's moments away from fileting him alive when that smirk widens.

"Of course, Adelphia, of course! But if your people are having difficulty controlling such a simple matter, there must be an even greater issue at heart. And you are their ruling monarch."

Feeling her wrath as a tangible entity, I'm both dreading and hopeful for his certain death. Until the pressure lessens with Olivier' s commanding voice.

"I'll take into account the information provided. More patrols and fortifying defenses is practical advice, but based on what little I've heard today, I won't be sending my people on such a dangerous excursion that could possibly incite the Gods Cursed. Not without more evidence."

Feeling both helpless and furious at the people who are oath-bound to protect their own, I clench my jaw and tighten my grip on the armrests of the chair.

"Your people need to know."

"That would cause unnecessary panic," Olivier replies, unflinching from my gaze. "Prove to me the situation is as dire as you say, and we'll plan accordingly."

My orange topaz and starlight jewels suddenly flare of their own accord. Scenting smoke, I glance down at my hands gripped tightly around the armrests and find my palms glittering with orange flames. Slowly unfurling my fingers, I release the chair and attempt to dampen my anger, but I'm met with minimal success. Olivier continues, taking no notice or care to my volatile state.

"Until then, I'll make the changes I previously stated. Now, if that's all for today..." He pushes back his chair, the wooden legs scraping across the floor as he rises to his feet. "I have other business to attend to."

Giving Queen Adelphia a single, brusque nod, he strides to the door before leaving the room altogether.

The others stand, whispering goodbyes and well wishes before they follow behind Olivier. Elidyr gives me a sympathetic smile as he passes and Theon squeezes my shoulder before he pushes back his chair and exits the room.

I remain seated, fuming. Sucking on my teeth, I push off the table, all but knocking my chair back as I rise to my feet. It's only when I turn to leave, that I realize I'm not alone.

"Sit. Down," Queen Adelphia orders.

Godsdamn it!

Having no patience for her castigation, I plop myself unceremoniously back into my seat.

"You disobeyed me."

Hearing the angry timbre to her tone, my gaze darts to hers and I finally see how apoplectic she is. Usually, I would take steps to appease her, but she's not the only person livid at the moment.

She rises from her crystal throne, her heels clicking and gown whispering across the polished floor as she moves towards the spirits, pouring herself a drink. With her back facing me, she lifts the crystal tumbler to her lips and sips in silence.

"Theon already spoke to me about your concerns," she says after several minutes, whirling to face me, "and I decided we would keep this matter private until I could assess the situation further."

"The attack today escalated the severity of the situation," I argue.

With glass in hand, she glides around the table, every step graceful and regal. "You should have spoken to me about it beforehand. You don't have the authority to speak of such issues without my consent." She arches her blonde brows disapprovingly. "Did I give you permission?"

"There was no time," I bite out, refusing to cower beneath her arctic stare. "I came directly from patrol."

"Your attire and lateness suggest otherwise." Pursing her lips, she wraps one arm around her waist, the other raising her glass half handedly near her cheek. "Regardless, I ordered you to keep quiet on the matter. You did not. Not only that, you spoke when the only people allowed to speak during the Kings Council are royalty and their *heirs*."

Hearing the click of my jaw as I grind my teeth, I remind her, "I have royal blood."

"How could I possibly forget *that*?" she sneers, but only for a moment. For in the next, her expression falls, her gaze roaming my face. "You have his face, you know. Not an exact replica, but near enough." She takes a sip of her drink, glowering at me over the rim. "Especially your eyes. When I look into your eyes, all I see is *him*." Curling her lip, she tosses her head back, draining the contents of her glass.

I'm well aware you rarely ever look at me, and when you do it's with hatred and derision.

She ambles toward the window, peering out at the two moons in a now darkened sky. "Increase the patrol and get a handle on the situation. I will not be thought of as weak."

Recognizing my dismissal, I bow with a visible sneer and say with as much venom in my voice as she offered to me, "Of course, Mother."

Turning my back on her, I stride towards the door and open it. Just as I'm stepping over the threshold, but before I shut the door behind me, I hear her parting comment.

"And Captain? If you ever disobey me again, I'll strip you of your command and banish you from the palace."

CHAPTER 2

LENA

Shielding my eyes from the retreating sun, I scan the colossal white wall surrounding the entirety of Cascadonia's capital city. With pristine white graphite rising several hundred spans high and a massive iron gate embedded within, the circular wall enshrouds all of Seboia in a blanket of stone. An impenetrable fortress no soul would dare to venture into without invitation. Unless, like myself, you had no other choice.

"It's so tall," Zander says from atop his brown stallion, his green eyes widened in awe. With shoulder length blonde hair, a large muscled build, and a single copper jewel beneath both brows and a starlight jewel at the corner of each eye, there's no other way to describe the shifter male as anything but gorgeous. Even while he gapes at the monstrous wall like he's no more than a drooling simpleton. "I can't even see the top."

"It looks like a prison," I grumble.

A stone prison. A dungeon. A tomb. I haven't even stepped foot within the city and I can already feel the walls closing in on me, burying me alive.

Lungs constricting at the thought, I search in vain for the peaks of the Mandala Mountains I know lay beyond, but I find neither that nor the heart of the forest the city is nestled within. Only when I tear my gaze from the stone city to the border where Cascadonia ends do I find where the forest begins.

Filled with oaks and maples topped with rust-colored leaves, the thousands of years-old trees shelter the forest as far as the eye can see. A breeze slips between their branches and the leaves rustle in delight. The wind picks up, a whoosh sounding in my ears as the gale reels the branches back with its might, the canopy parting with open arms to reveal the lush brush carpeting the forest floor, an invitation to bask in its peaceful embrace. But the woodland's welcome is deceptive. Trickery. Its beauty is nothing but an illusion to disguise the dangers that lurk within.

The Cursed Woods.

I've heard quite a few tales about the forbidden forest and its Soulless inhabitants. Squinting my eyes, I search through the wide trunked trees for its fabled residents, but find nothing besides fallen leaves and broken branches. I hum to myself, finding it odd not to find a single one of the Gods Cursed's creations when on our travels here, they refused to give us a moment's peace. We tried our best to avoid them, but the mountains and forest we passed through on our travels here were crawling with them. At least they were, until we were about a day out from Seboia and the Soulless just disappeared. The suddenness of it was jarring. One moment we were surrounded by the demons, the next, they were gone, seemingly vanished into thin air. It's as if there was some invisible border we breached that they could not cross.

We already had to be watchful of the guards once we neared Cascadonia's borders, but we were doubly so considering the Soulless' unusual behavior. Between that and the patrolling guards, we were all on edge when we reached the outlying village. Fortunately, we were able to sneak in without the guards detecting our presence, and our story was accepted without question. Another stroke of luck, as I doubt they'd be as welcoming to a party traveling from Brecca.

Returning my gaze to my fellow companions, I can't help but laugh at the diverse expressions crossing their faces.

Amara's whiskey-colored eyes watch the awestruck shifter in wide eyed bafflement. The lean but muscular woman with brown, chin length, angled hair sits atop her massive black stallion. Wearing a black leather vest and matching trousers, she could easily be mistaken for a warrior goddess. That is, if you didn't notice the anomaly of the singular starlight jewel beside only one eye.

A horse nudges my own as its black-haired owner stares at Zander, annoyance twisting the swirled marking on his pale cheek. Wearing a royal blue tunic beneath a black leather vest and matching leather trousers, there's not a spot of dust on Tristan. Unfortunately, the rest of us can't say the same. Covered head to toe in dirt, dust, and whatever other ungodly substances the forest excretes, I'll be scrubbing myself for weeks to rid myself of this stench.

Tristan's brown eyes veer to me, and I laugh even harder when he gestures between Zander and me as if I could possibly move us along quicker. He may get frustrated with the curious, silly male, but I find him to be highly entertaining.

Lips turning down into a frown, Tristan trots his brown stallion up beside Zander's, peering up at the object of his fascination.

"Well," Tristan shrugs, "it is a wall."

"But how did it get so tall?" Zander asks, unmoving from his position.

"It was built that way," Amara says slowly.

Blowing out a raspberry, Zander's irritated gaze snaps to hers. "Of course it was built that way, but how?"

"You act as if you've never seen a wall before!" Amara shouts, tossing her arms up.

"Not one *that* tall." He jabs a finger outward. "How did they even build it?”

Knowing this discussion could last for eons, I glance down at my hands covered from knuckle to forearm with my leather vambraces, and pull the reins to signal to my white mare to continue on the dirt road toward the city gates.

“Probably by using those with strong Nature and Air Gifts,” Tristan explains, now trotting his black stallion beside mine, the others following on his other side.

“They'd have to lift the rocks all the way to the top and float someone up just as high.” Zander shakes his head. “No one from this land has enough power to do that. And who would want to? No one willingly.” He bobs his head, reconsidering. “A slave would, of course. They’d have no choice.” He sucks in a breath, his green eyes widening. “Do they have slaves?”

Amara groans. “Vanyimar outlawed slavery generations ago and we’ve not heard even a whisper of them acting otherwise. So what would make you think that this kingdom would defy this law?"

“Because no one sane would be willing to fly that high!” Zander sputters. “They'd have to force them. I bet they have slaves.” He looks at me, his lips curling downward into a pout. “Do they, Lena?”

He looks like a wounded puppy.

“I doubt it,” I reply, my heart beginning to drum beneath my breast the closer we get to the gates.

“I hope not. I’d make an awful slave,” he notes.

“I think you’d make a wonderful slave,” Tristan teases. “You're strong and can shapeshift. They could use you as a mule.”

Zander gasps. “I would never shift into a mule!”

“No, he's too pretty for that.” Amara smirks. “They'd make him a whore. With your good looks, you'd be a favorite.”

Zander places a palm to his chest, appearing as if he might

shed a tear. "Aww, that's sweet."

Amara blinks slowly. "Fuck, you're stupid."

"How dare you?!"

"He's not stupid," I toss over my shoulder. "He just didn't hear anything besides he's too pretty."

"Thank you, Lena," Zander says with a haughty raise of his chin.

Sweat dots my brow when we reach the arched iron gate. My breathing becomes labored as we pass beneath the stone archway. A desperate longing urges me to join those rushing past us with the slowly darkening sky. I glance warily at the wall to my left, then to my right. My breaths become harsher as I imagine the white walls contracting around me, suffocating me, inching towards me until I'm pinned in like the rest of these fools.

Like a pig to a slaughter.

Feeling as if I'm a hair's breadth away from snapping, I squeeze my eyes shut and drop my head back. Staying that way for a long moment, I finally slide my lids open and breathe a sigh of relief once I see red, orange, and pink brushes painting the vast sky above.

Not entirely caged.

Once my heart begins to slow, I return my attention forward and my gaze veers to the guards loitering ahead. Slowing, I reach for the hood of my cloak and tug it over my head to shield my eyes and the top half of my face, hoping the act will draw less attention to ourselves.

The guards laugh and jest with one another, but their eyes remain vigilant in their inspection of each person leaving and entering the city. One guard's stare drifts towards us. When his smile turns into a frown and he begins striding towards us, I know he's going to be an issue.

Tugging at the hem of my hood, I check to make sure that my

face is properly concealed, then pull ahead of the others. Careful to keep my eyes downward as I inspect the jewels near the corner of the guard's eye, I try to recall the differences between races in this land.

This guard has jewels near the outer corner of his eyes, so he can't be a human because they aren't born with them. Neither can he be fae, since his ears aren't sharpened and he doesn't have the same jeweled markings known to their race, a single-colored jewel at the outer corner of both eyes. With rounded ears as well as an aquamarine and starlight jewel near the corner of each eye, I confirm he's an immortal. Or judging off the aquamarine jewels, he's more precisely a Water immortal. Which means he's not gifted by the gods with only a single Gift like the fae, but is blessed with the primary four: Nature, Water, Fire, and Air. The aquamarine jewel signifies his Water power as his most dominant Gift.

Grateful I don't have to deal with one of the less common shifter immortals' heightened senses or even a shifter fae, I command my horse to a stop once the guard is only a few paces away.

"Are you citizens of Cascadonia?" he asks, glancing at each of us in turn.

I shake my head. "No, just visiting."

He squints and ducks down, attempting to peer beneath my hood. My knuckles whiten around my mare's reins in response.

"Why is your hood up?" he asks, suspicion lacing his tone as he ducks lower. "Is there a reason you don't wish to show your face?"

"My only wish is to not look upon yours," I snap without thought.

His face hardens and he straightens. "Remove your hood."

So much for not calling attention to myself.

Jaw hardening, I jerk my hood back. My fingers rip at my

wavy, raven locks as they unfurl from my cloak, and I brace myself for his reaction as I slowly lift my gaze to his.

His eyes widen and he sucks in an audible breath, immovable as his gaze sweeps across my face. My lips, my cheeks, my eyes, the strange markings dotting my brows and eyelids.

Gasps sound behind him as the other guards finally take notice of my unusual features and I stiffen even more. My skin crawls at their oily, perverse thoughts.

"Happy now?" I ask, baring my teeth in a smile.

His throat bobs on a swallow. "Yes…I'm…uh… very pleased."

Amara stills off to the side, her lip curled in derision as Zander and Tristan's horses trot up beside my own.

"You'll find no pleasure here," Tristan says, his tone cold and threatening.

The guard snaps out of his stupor and sneers at Tristan. "What's your purpose?" the guard asks, returning his attention to me.

My horse stomps her foot, impatient with the male preventing her from enjoying her dinner and a good night's sleep in a stable.

"She and I are here to form trading agreements," I reply, nodding towards Amara. "We hired these males as our escorts."

The guard peers around me, seeing only wagonless horses. "What are you trading?"

"Leather."

"Leather?" he asks, his features twisting into puzzlement. "You're trading leather? In Cascadonia?"

Perplexed by his confusion, I nod my head slowly in answer.

The guard stares at me for several moments, then tosses his head back, roaring in laughter. His fellow guards quickly join in.

Zander leans into me and whispers loudly, "Are they all mad?"

"Maybe they don't know what leather is?" I offer, but it's highly unlikely when they're all garbed in black and teal trim uniforms, comprised entirely of leather.

"I bid you good luck," the guard says with a lingering chuckle, wiping tears from his eyes. "Do you carry any weapons on your person?"

That's a foolish question. I think Zander's right. They're deranged.

Amara gapes at him in surprise. "Did we travel across the continent with weapons? When there's murderers, bandits, and thieves on the road?" Her expression sobers. "Of course not."

I sigh. I have very little patience left from traveling for weeks on end, but I apparently have more than Amara. "Yes, we have weapons."

The guard's eyes glimmer. "You'll have to turn them over."

What the fuck?

"No," Amara says before I can.

"Citizens are the only beings permitted to carry weapons within our walls. All visitors must be relieved of weaponry before entering the city," he says, as if he's reciting a commanding officer's words.

"I've already entered your city with a weapon," Amara points out. "So it seems you've already broken your laws."

He narrows his eyes at her and I suppress a chuckle. "What about humans?" I ask. "Does that rule apply to them?"

"*Especially* them," he sneers.

I narrow my eyes at the bigot and wonder how hard a kick to the face should be to knock the prejudice out of him. Aware that we must get past these gates, I attempt to control my anger, while wishing I had stashed my obsidian and starlight daggers in the forest along with our more unusual weapons. Swallowing thickly, I order, "Turn them over."

"No fucking way!" Amara shouts, her stallion neighing in agreement. "No one touches my weapons. Ever. What if I need to use one?"

"You won't," a guard says, standing beside Amara's stallion with raised arms, waiting to receive her weapons. "The guards will protect you."

A deranged smile crosses her face as she lowers her head near his, speaking in a sickly-sweet tone. "Oh, honey. Look at me. Do I look like a woman who needs someone to protect her?" Straightening atop her stallion, she adds with a crinkle to her nose, "No, I'll not give up my weapons to the likes of you. You'll chip it or smudge it with your greasy, thieving fingers."

Frustrated, I look at Amara. "Just hand it over, Amara. We're not getting in if we don't."

"We can get in," she promises, sweeping a thoughtful gaze atop the wall.

"Oh, yes," Zander agrees. Hands on his hips, he examines the wall. "They have many weak spots. We could wait until nightfall and then come through there." He points up and to his right. "Or there." He swings his pointer finger to the left and down. Swinging his finger a bit more to the right, he chuckles. "Frankly, we could just walk in there while it's still daylight."

"Not when you just told them all your plans," Tristan says dryly.

"Amara," I say, my tone laced thick with command.

Furious, she remains unmoving as she glares at me. After seeing I won't be swayed, she grumbles a curse and drops down from her horse, jerking her weapons free. Her bow, a sword, an axe, and then dagger after dagger after dagger. She shoves them all into the waiting guard's chest, earning his grunt and the satisfaction of seeing his knees bow beneath the weight. Tristan, Zander, and I quickly do the same.

As I'm passing my last dagger to a silent guard, their leader tries my patience more.

"We'll have to pat you down."

Irritated, I narrow my eyes at the asshole as I whip my arms outward and widen my legs.

The silent guard kneels at my feet and slides his hands slowly up my calves. His movements start out clinical, but they all too quickly become familiar. His fingers knead and rub, exploring in a predatory manner as he slides upwards.

I'm about to lose my shit when the pervert's fingers splay out as they near the apex between my thighs, but Amara's sinister voice beats me to it.

"Squeeze my ass one more time and I'll cut your balls off."

My pervert's hands instantly still. When he looks up to meet my wrathful gaze, I bob my head towards Amara. "What she said."

Swallowing thickly, he stands with trembling hands and begins unclasping my vambraces.

"What could I possibly hide in there?" I snap. "A needle?"

He jerks his hands back and scurries away.

The leader remains impassive, uncaring of his guards' attempts to molest us, and steps aside, allowing us entry. Tugging on my horse's reins, I curl my hands into fists as I walk past, my nails gouging crescent shapes into my leather clad palms as I restrain myself from lunging at the guards. But if I do that, then the others will join in and we'll kill every last one of them. I can't imagine them allowing us entry after that. So I bite my tongue, blood pooling into my cheeks as I imagine it's their blood I'm tasting.

I'm almost past the guards when I see the lone male who chose not to laugh with his brethren. "Is there a stable nearby?" I ask. "A pub?"

"There is." His brown eyes glance up over my head and he cups his hands around his mouth. "Trip!" he calls out, waving a brown haired fae youth towards us. When he reaches our side, the guard asks him, "You heading to the pub?"

Trip nods.

"You mind taking these folks?"

"No problem at all!" Trip says, passing his gaze over our horses. "Right this way. We'll stable your horses and then head there."

Following behind the youth, we pass by a few off-duty guards playing dice when the jubilant Nature fae says, "You must be starving! You're in luck. They're serving mutton pie tonight." He glances down at me with a big, toothy grin, and I take note of his mop of red hair and homespun tunic. "It's the best in all of Vanyimar."

At the mention of food, Zander slaps the reins of his horse against Tristan's chest and squeezes between me and the boy, all but shoving me out of the way in the process. "Show us the way, my young friend," Zander says with a beaming smile, tossing his arm over Trip's shoulder. "I'm absolutely famished, and mutton pie sounds fantastic."

In sight of the stables, I shake my head as I watch Trip and Zander chatter away while Amara trails behind at a more sedate pace.

"Did you notice the way they spoke about humans?" Tristan asks.

"How could I not?" I reply bitterly, watching the other three open the wooden door and enter the stable.

"That could make things more difficult for us."

Choosing not to dwell on the guards, I pat Tristan's shoulder and smile "Probably, but don't concern yourself with that just yet. If an issue arises, we'll handle it. Just worry about our objective."

A teasing smile crosses his face. "Trading leather?"

I laugh. "Of course. Trading leather." Then we walk our horses towards the stables for a much-needed meal and a good night's rest.

CHAPTER 3

DARIUS

Ale, smoked meat, and the scent of unwashed bodies saturate the air, permeating the oak beams that rise up the vaulted ceilings and wafting across the numerous banquet tables scattered throughout The Quiet Harpy. Fae laugh and shout, mingling with humans with bloodshot eyes and tattered clothing while gossiping females in billowy gowns stroll past, their heeled shoes adding their own contribution to the countless scratches decorating the wood floor. All walks of life fill the pub, from wealthy nobles to impoverished humans. All are illuminated by candlelight as they gather to drink a pint once the two moons have risen. Even bastard princes such as myself.

Tossing my head back, I drain the last foamy dregs of ale before placing the empty tankard down to the view of Mona, the namesake to The Quiet Harpy herself, who eyes me from behind the bar. Arms folded, the brown-haired Water fae says nothing to me as I double tap my knuckles against the worn bar. Without even a nod in response, she turns toward the barrel and pours me another pint.

Mind churning over the events of the day, my gaze drifts across the room, unseeing over the pub's patrons until I spot Kace seated at a table near the cool hearth, unaware of my arrival due to the female's cleavage into which he's currently burrowing.

Smirking, I turn back to a new pint of ale. Mona is already at the other end of the bar, eyeballing another. I raise my drink, prepared to drain every last drop, but I'm interrupted before the liquid gold can touch my lips.

"Hello, my prince."

Peeking out the corner of my eye, my mood sours even more when I spot a beautiful blonde haired Air immortal smiling down at me with a predatory glint to her eyes.

"Danya."

"You look dreadful, my prince. Brooding here all alone." She pouts. "Allow me to help you relax."

"I'm not in the mood," I reply, staring straight ahead at the wooden barrels.

Never one to be dismissed so easily, she places a crimson nailed hand upon my upper thigh, my cock instantly shriveling at her touch.

"I can get you in the mood," she purrs.

Wanting nothing more than to enjoy my solitude before I head to my own bed, *alone*, I turn to tell the female exactly that when another more welcome voice reaches my ears.

"Leave."

Turning toward the sound, I find the blonde-haired, green-eyed Fire immortal who looks so much like our mother, glaring at Danya. Unlike our mother, her hair is styled in a messy topknot that I doubt has seen a brush in days, and is dressed in trousers and a tunic that's spotted in soot. Typical attire for Seboia's very own Blacksmith Princess.

"We're having a discussion, Aurora," Danya hisses, jerking her hand from my thigh.

Exhausted with arguing for the day, I return my gaze forward and allow my sister to handle the annoying female while I swig from my drink.

"Go prey on someone else," Aurora snaps. "He's not interested."

I hear a gasp, then the click of Danya's heels as she retreats from the snarling princess.

"Why does she even come here? She opens her legs for anything with a pulse. Better suited to the brothel, if you ask me," Aurora grumbles, seating herself on the stool beside me. "At least there she could be compensated for it."

"Her father might take issue with that."

Huffing, she waves down Mona. "Yet, I doubt he'd be surprised. I can't believe you fucked her."

Blowing out an exasperated breath to the statement I've heard too many times to count, I groan, "It was one time, Rory."

Rolling her eyes, she raises her newly acquired pint. "One time too many. I hope it was worth it."

It wasn't.

Aware of the nobleman's daughter's penchant to fuck anyone who could possibly raise her station, as the son of the Queen – legitimate or not – I knew to stay far away from the ambitious female. But one night after too many pints, I caved and took her to bed. I honestly recall very little of the night, but although she was pleasant to look at, what memories I did manage to retain were otherwise unremarkable and bland.

My hand would have been a more enjoyable outlet and at least in that instance, I wouldn't have to endure her constant nagging for a repeat, and Aurora wouldn't feel the need to constantly remind me of my error in judgment.

The stool on the other side of mine scrapes across the floor before Griffin seats himself.

"The meeting?" he asks, never one to mince words.

Cursing internally, the words sit at the tip of my tongue, but

I'm relieved from answering when a commotion catches our attention. Turning to face the disruption, I find a smiling Kace racing towards Aurora, his arms raised as if in embrace.

"My love! How I've missed you so!"

Aurora cocks her head to the side, watching Kace with an almost placid expression. But once he reaches her and begins to wrap his arms around her shoulders, she slaps her palm to his face with a loud smack, curls her fingers around his head, and tosses him across the room.

Kace screeches his displeasure amid his impromptu flight.

Sprawled atop splintered chairs and a flattened table, Kace's face contorts into fury as the pub breaks out in laughter. "What was that for?!"

Aurora jolts out of her chair, pointing. "You've had your head between *that* female's tits the entire night." She wrinkles her nose. "I don't want you slobbering on me with tit sweat all over your face!"

Kace dusts himself off and storms towards her. "She doesn't have tit sweat!"

Nose to nose, Aurora curls her lip. "I can *smell* it on you."

Shaking my head at the strange duo, I curse Griffin, ever the mediator, when he shoves fresh tankards of ale to both their chests.

Never ones to waste a pint, they give each other one last parting glare before tabling their argument for another time.

"What happened at the meeting?" Griffin asks, returning to our earlier discussion.

"Oh! I heard all about *that* debacle," Aurora chimes in, planting herself on the edge of the stool beside me.

"How would you have heard that?" I ask. She says nothing, but her single arched brow is answer enough. "Theon gossips too much." Narrowing my eyes, I add, "You both do."

"Well?" Kace asks, his blue-eyed gaze bouncing between me and Aurora.

"They're not going to do anything," I admit.

"Why the fuck not?"

Gritting my teeth, I attempt to stifle my anger as I recall the cowardice of the Kings Council. "I didn't provide enough *evidence*."

Griffin scowls and Kace tosses his hands up, balking.

"Oh, yes," Aurora says, fiddling with the wooden handle of her tankard. "Adelphia was quite displeased with you." She sips from her pint, licking her lips as she lowers it. "Heard Mother dearest gave you quite the tongue lashing."

"Did Theon eavesdrop at the door?" I snap, slapping my tankard against the rail. "No one else was in the room!"

Her lips spread into a wide, unabashed smile as she nods enthusiastically. "Of course!"

"What did your mother say?" Griffin asks.

Tearing my gaze from my nosey sister, I expel a mirthless laugh. "She threatened to strip me of my command and banish me from the palace if I ever disobeyed her again."

"What. A. Cunt."

"Kace!" Griffin scolds, lips slashed in a disapproving line.

"What? She is!"

"She's your queen," I respond neutrally.

"Okay, she's Queen Cunt." We all groan at his response and he shrugs. "What? You know it's true."

"Yes, but you don't say it in public," Griffin says on a sigh, weary of the fae's foolish habit of not guarding his words.

"What's she going to do? Torture me? Kill me?" He scoffs, swigging from his ale.

"Kill? No," Aurora replies, slowly shaking her head. "Torture and maim? Absolutely. Killing those who are only verbally opposed to her reflects poorly with the people."

"How magnanimous of her," Griffin states dryly.

"I'm actually surprised you all thought the Kings Council would be willing to act against Brecca," Aurora says, bobbing her crossed legs as she leans back against the bar.

"And why would you think that?" I ask.

Drumming her nails on the rail, Aurora watches us for a long moment before placing her tankard down and clasping her hands in her lap.

"The rulers on the Kings Council like to believe they're the most powerful beings on the continent, but they're not. The Breccans are, with their Gods Cursed and army of Soulless. They know this, you know this, everyone does," she says as she twirls a finger, gesturing toward the patrons of the filled pub. "Yet we all act like we forced them to retreat, even though we all know we didn't. They slaughtered hundreds of us within minutes and walked away. Not because we defeated them, but because they chose to leave." She shakes her head, scoffing. "And you wonder why they won't pursue an enemy that could exterminate every last one of us? They won't do a godsdamn thing unless given no other choice."

"I gave them evidence," I remind her.

"You gave them evidence that was easily dismissed." She pats my leg. "You need to give them facts that are irrefutable."

I rub the scruff along my jaw, processing Aurora's words. This task was already a difficult one to begin with, but considering this, I realize how much more complicated it is if the rulers aren't even willing to consider the possibility of Brecca's return.

Tossing back the rest of his pint, Kace slaps his empty tankard on the bar, the noise jarring me from my thoughts. "I'm weary of all this talk of doom and gloom. We must raise this male's spirits!"

He claps me on the back, waggling his brows. “What you need is a beautiful female to fill your bed.”

“No.” Eyeing Mona down the bar, I nod and stand, tossing a few coppers on the counter.

“Don't be like that,” he chastises, scanning the crowd. “Not many favorable options at the moment, I’ll admit,” he mumbles before his eyes light up and he whips his gaze to mine. “I know what we can do. You can join me at the brothel!”

“No,” I repeat, nudging him out of my path.

“Why not?” Tossing his arm over my shoulders, he tugs me to his side. “There’s plenty of females there willing to deal with your dour mood. If you pay them enough,” he adds unrepentantly. “Now, there's this new shapeshifter there. She can’t shift only her throat, but…” Kace’s eyes suddenly widen, his words drift off, and his jaw drops along with the arm he tossed over my shoulder. “Dear gods.”

Frowning at the awestruck fae, I search for what has rendered him speechless, but as I scan the pub, I find nothing of note. Not until I catch sight of the vision walking through the door of the pub and I freeze, stop dead in my tracks as my world, this realm, my entire existence condenses to her and her alone.

They say my mother’s beauty could rival Uriella, the Goddess of Light herself. But not my mother, not a goddess, nor any other creature can hold a candle to the female woman who just walked into the tavern. She’s breathtakingly gorgeous with long, wavy black hair; golden, sun kissed skin with high cheekbones; and a red, heart-shaped mouth that will be the object of my fantasies for as long as I take breath. Yet, what truly makes her beauty so astonishing, to forever have no equal, is the unique color of her eyes. Almond-shaped, with full, black lashes sweeping above orbs the same deep, dark shade of amethyst, they gleam even more brilliantly than the coveted violet jewel.

Trip escorts her along with three others towards the center of the dining area, but all I see is her as I peruse her muscular, yet curvy frame. I force my gaze to pass over the plump breasts contained in a brown leather vest, but my gaze stutters on its path once spotting her partially bare abdomen, imagining how I would sell my soul to lick beneath the seam of her vest to the slip of golden skin she's left exposed below. Trip pulls out a chair for her and as she seats herself, I'm unable to stifle a groan when I see the burgundy leather trousers that hug the globes of her tight ass.

I'm completely gobsmacked by the divine creature and her bewitching beauty. My heart races, my palms are sweaty, there's a ringing in my ears, and my dick has swelled to half-mast. I can't move, can't breathe, can't think. My entire being is focused on her and her alone. There's nothing I'm not willing to do to make her mine.

"She's mine," Kace breathes.

My palms instantly flare, glittering orange as a visceral, blinding rage previously unknown surges within me. "Don't. Touch. Her."

Kace's gaze darts to mine in surprise, his eyes widening momentarily before dropping his gaze altogether, jerking his head in assent.

"I think Darius found his bedmate *all* on his own," Aurora says with a smile in her voice.

Returning my attention to the captivating female, I find her and her companions already seated and Trip heading in our direction.

I adore Trip. The young Earth fae has had a similar upbringing to Kace and is just as determined to change his lot in life. He wants to be a warrior, not for the glory, but to protect others. Being that he's too young to join the Guard and lacks a father figure to teach him, we've taken him under our wing and alternate as his trainers. His infectious smile and sweet personality even softened the Harpy herself and managed to get himself a job here where very few were able to do so.

Like I said, I adore Trip, but I can barely comprehend speech at the moment, let alone be polite. I demonstrate this lack of control when Trip passes by and I snatch him up by the arm. "Who is she?"

Trip's signature smile spreads across his face. "She's pretty, isn't she?"

Trip snickers at my silence and Aurora joins in, but quickly composes herself with a motherly warning. "Trip."

"Don't know." He shrugs. "I was walking past as they entered the city and one of the guards asked me to escort them here. They're nice, though." Thumb gesturing over his shoulder, he pulls from my grasp. "They said they're hungry, so I'm going to grab them some pie and ale. They look like they've been traveling for a while."

He turns to leave, but when Aurora lunges forward and grabs a fistful of his tunic, he stumbles over his feet.

"We'll take the ale!" she shouts, then shoves him away. Grabbing four pints from the bar, she smacks two to my chest, sloshing ale over the rims to drip down my vest, before doing the same to Griffin. Then, with an impish smile, she loops her arm through mine and pulls me toward the newcomers.

The female and her companions have their heads huddled together, speaking in hushed voices, but as we near their table they pause their discussion to peer up at us. When the mesmerizing creature meets my gaze, that same paralysis from before overcomes me.

Fuck me, her eyes practically glow from this distance.

"We noticed you when you came in and thought we'd introduce ourselves. I'm Aurora, and this is Darius, Kace, and Griffin," Aurora says, pointing at each of us in turn.

The female's amethyst eyes drift towards Aurora, freeing me from her snare. "I'm Lena and this is Amara, Tristan, and Zander," she says, nodding toward each of her companions.

"It's a pleasure," Aurora replies, but I barely comprehend her words once hearing Lena speak.

She has a raspy voice with a strange accent. It's rough and throaty, yet surprisingly lyrical. My body instantly responds to the seductive sound, my dick straining at the leathers as I imagine the raspy moans she would make while milking my cock.

"May we join you? We've brought ale." Aurora bumps my arm with her shoulder, reminding me that I'm still clutching their drinks against my chest. I pass the pints to the two females, while Griffin does the same for the males.

"Of course." Lena nudges the empty chair I'm standing in front of with her boot, sliding it across the floor in invitation. Spellbound by this sensuous creature, I drop down into it without breaking her gaze.

"You're pretty," Kace says in a dazed voice. "Like, *really* pretty."

Hearing the wonder in his tone, I tear my gaze from Lena and my clouded thoughts instantly clear when I see him. Still standing, still awestruck, and attempting to catch flies with his gaping mouth.

Uriella's Light, I hope I don't look that ridiculous.

"Sit down," I bark, angry at myself more so than him for my own foolish behavior.

Quickly doing so, Kace scurries to the seat beside Griffin.

"You've got a bit of drool right there," her companion Zander says, tapping his chin.

Kace slaps a hand to his face and wipes vigorously. "Did I get it?"

He nods with a smile, then claps Kace on the back. "All gone. Don't worry! You're not the first male to drool over her." Zander leans into Kace and whispers conspiratorially, "It's a common reaction to our lovely Lena."

They both laugh at the females' answering scowls until Griffin smacks Kace on the back of the head.

"Ow! Whatd'ya do that for?!"

"Stop talking," Griffin says to Kace, then adds to a snickering Zander, "Both of you."

"So," Aurora says with a roll of her eyes. "Where are you all from?"

"An outlying village on the Cascadonian border," Tristan answers in a clipped tone, clearly unreceptive to any follow up questions.

"Oh, okay." Aurora's eyes round in surprise. "What brings you to Seboia?"

"To broker trade deals," Lena says, throwing a scowl at Tristan.

"What are you trading?" Griffin asks.

"Leather."

Griffin and I share a confused look.

"In Cascadonia?" Griffin asks, his brows pinched.

Differing shades of wariness pass over the foreigners' faces as they all nod their heads.

Cascadonia is known for our leather. We make everything from clothing to armor with it. Besides a repair shop, no other kingdom even has leathersmiths. Due to laraks only being found in the Cursed Woods, and no other kingdom having quick access to the forest, nor the animal, no one even attempts to compete with us. No other creature can produce such a high-quality product. This isn't just common knowledge; it's ingrained within all citizens of Vanyimar. For someone to come to Cascadonia, to Seboia in particular, to trade leather, is not only laughable, but mildly offensive.

"That's nice," Aurora says as if it's anything but. "Are you leathersmiths yourself?"

Lena shakes her head. "I'm just brokering deals, and they're escorting me. My uncle's the leathersmith."

"Smart," Kace says with a thoughtful bob of his head. "Twice as many coppers sending a pretty face."

Griffin glowers at Kace, but he ignores him as he places his elbow on the table and rests his chin in his palm, watching Zander with the same adoring smile he gave Lena moments ago.

"I'm sorry to stare, but you're a very handsome male."

"Thank you," Zander replies with a smug smirk, flipping his silky blonde hair over his shoulder.

"The ladies at the brothel would just eat you up. Have you been?"

"Not yet. We just arrived."

Kace sucks in a breath, staring at him like he just admitted to murdering a litter of puppies. "That's no excuse." He nods to himself. "We'll head there on our way out."

"Aww, how welcoming!" Zander's eyes light up, and he leans over the table to peer at Lena with a smile that stretches his cheeks from ear to ear. "Look, Lena. I've found my very own escort to the brothel."

"Kindred souls, I see," she replies with a fond smile.

Kace continues to worship Zander while he chats with Lena, but then the adoration suddenly dims in his eyes, the corner of his lips turning down into a frown.

"Your jewels are different. Handsome," Kace reassures him

with a tight smile, "but different from other shifters." Kace leans in closer to Zander and squints up at the two copper jewels beneath the Shifter immortal's eyebrows, his gaze narrowing even further when it veers to the lone starlight jewels near the outer corner of each eye. "That's strange," he mumbles, but as he says this, I now see that Zander's not the only one who seems strange.

Tristan seems normal enough. A human with cropped black hair, ivory skin, and dark brown eyes. The only characteristic that may seem abnormal is the silver swirling scar covering the entirety of one cheek. But scars are common enough, even if this one is shaped oddly. But whereas Tristan is human and Zander is clearly an immortal shifter, even with his strange jewels, Amara is an enigma. With chin length brown hair, whiskey-colored eyes, and tan skin that's long lost the suppleness of youth, common for a human woman in her early to mid-thirties, everything about her screams she's human. All but for the singular starlight jewel near her left eye.

Baffled, I lean back in my chair, searching and finding several peculiarities.

Amara and Lena are wearing trousers when, with my sister being the exception to the rule, females rarely wear anything besides dresses. I would normally shrug this off. I'm sure there are plenty of women and females outside Cascadonia who prefer trousers over dresses, but they wear fighting leathers similar to what our guards wear. Females aren't guards and they're certainly not warriors, but their attire suggests otherwise.

Zander, Tristan, and Amara also have the same lilting accent that Lena possesses; one I've never encountered before, even on my vast travels throughout the continent. And although both Tristan and Amara seem human and unassuming, that appears intentional. A distraction from the almost deadly air surrounding them, surrounding all of them. Their clothing, accent, and demeanor all point in the direction of them being hired mercenaries or warriors. But that can't be, since after The Battle of Brecca, no kingdom would allow a human to enter into such a violent profession.

"What are you?" Kace asks, his eyes darting from one person to the next.

"Kace!" Aurora hisses through clenched teeth.

"What? It's an honest question!"

"It's rude," she scolds, even as she swivels to face their group once again, silently waiting for their response.

Unsure if their behavior is comical or embarrassing, I shove the thought aside and instead return my gaze to Lena, searching for the colored jewels that signify her most dominant immortal Gift. But as I look at the spot near the outer corner of her eye where the jewels we're born with are placed, I'm shocked to find nothing.

She's human.

I'm completely dumbfounded to find not one jewel. How can that be? How can she not have any? Humans aren't this attractive. Not even an immortal. It's simply not possible that she's human.

I narrow my eyes, searching for a jewel hidden somewhere, but all I find are small, dot-shaped scars, only a shade darker than her skin tone, the markings staggering across both eyelids, all the way to her hairline and partially beneath her brows. Scanning her from head to toe, I notice they begin again at her shoulders, loop around her arms, and eventually disappear beneath her leather vambraces. I don't see more markings past that, but I imagine more are hidden beneath her clothing.

"Your jewels, or lack thereof, are nothing I've ever encountered before," Kace notes shrewdly, gesturing towards their group with a wave of his hand.

As if choreographed beforehand, their entire party's features clear of all emotion and they slowly straighten in their seats, hardly blinking as they stare at Kace.

"Is that the mark of a lesser god?" Kace asks Amara, reaching out to touch her starlight jewel.

She scowls at the offending appendage and smacks it away. "Lesser gods?"

"That's right," Kace replies, shaking his finger with a wince. "Immortals and fae are usually only Gifted by the primary gods, but occasionally they can receive an additional Gift from one of the lesser deities. The Sight, Wards, Healing, and so on, but those are rare."

"Quite educational," Tristan says dryly, nursing his pint.

The fool preens at the "compliment" before returning his attention to Lena. "Well?"

She shrugs. "We're people."

Squeezing his eyes shut, Kace pinches his nose. "We're *all* people. I mean-"

"Leave it be, Kace," Griffin cuts him off, shaking his head.

"But…" Kace begins to argue, but then his words trail off as he finally takes notice of the foreigners' glares and the warning hidden beneath.

Kace pastes a smile on his face and slaps a palm on the table hard enough to rattle our tankards. "Mysterious. I like it! I bet that works wonders with the females." Mumbling, he adds, "I should try to be more mysterious."

"You'd have to stop wagging your tongue to become mysterious," Griffin states dryly.

Kace peers upward, tapping his chin. "That would be a lost cause then, wouldn't it?" Sighing, he slumps in his chair. His dour mood saps away all the jovial energy, leaving us with no escape from the tense air still radiating from them.

I don't believe this exchange could possibly get any more awkward.

Readjusting in my seat, I clear my throat. "How long will you be visiting?"

Lena watches Kace for another long moment before returning her gaze to mine. "We don't have a set timeframe, but not too long," she answers vaguely, her amethyst orbs leisurely trailing me from head to toe. "What do you do?"

"I'm Captain of the Guards," I reply, grateful for the change of topic. "Griffin is my second, and Kace is my third."

She stiffens, her face hardening with a cold glare of which my mother would be envious. "Is that so?"

Brow furrowed, I look to the other members of her party, all leering in my direction. The menacing silence thickens with each moment that passes as I gauge their reaction.

I stand corrected. It can *become more awkward. Excruciatingly so.*

Amara folds her arms over the table and ducks toward me, a demented smile stretching her cheeks. "Tell me, Captain, are your recruits trained to molest weaponless females? Or is that just common practice?"

I stiffen. "What the fuck are you talking about?"

"It seems your guards enjoy taking liberties without permission," Tristan says with an air of nonchalance, but his eyes flash with a promise of violence.

It takes a moment to process what he said, then another to wrap my head around the thought that my guards, the guards I trained, the guards I recruited, would do something so vile. So repulsive. When I finally do, rage whips through me. Blazing a path down my arms, my legs, billowing within my chest, it surges into a wildfire and douses me in its flames.

Baring my teeth, I slap shimmering orange palms down onto

the table and stand, hovering above Lena. “Did they touch you?” I ask her, wrath hoarsening my voice.

“One of them squeezed my ass,” Amara says, disgust evident in her tone.

My anger spikes with her admission, strong enough that my trembling arms vibrate the table. But I refuse to remove my gaze from Lena’s as she searches my eyes, saying nothing as the flames within me heighten with each moment that passes.

“Did. They. Touch. You?”

Black smoke curls between us and she glances down at the scorched wood beneath my palms.

“I'm pretty sure he was touching me when he was rubbing near my cunt.”

Kace snickers. “A woman said cunt.”

She breaks my gaze to scowl at the dumbass. “I have one, don't I? I should be able to use the word.”

They touched her! They fucking touched her!

My vision turns hazy, my world becomes red, and the ringing in my ears is deafening as I think of the males who dared to touch *her*, imagining how I’ll burn the fuckers to ash after I rip them apart with my bare hands.

They touched her! They touched *her!*

Kicking back with a snarl, I barely comprehend the sound of cracking wood with the fury whooshing through my blood, only able to focus on avenging Lena as I whip away from the table and charge towards the door. But I've barely taken a step when I feel a warm shock from the delicate, vambraced hand wrapped around my forearm, reining me in from my murderous rage in an instant.

Similar to the feeling of electrically charged air the instant before lightning strikes, a mild shock radiates down my arm with a pleasant warmth. Stalling my steps, I follow Lena’s hand back up to her face and find her heart-shaped mouth tilted in a small smile.

"No, he didn't touch me," Lena says softly.

"You said he touched your cunt."

She walks her fingers down my arm to clasp our hands together, her touch humming beneath my skin long after it's gone. "He didn't make it that far. Come." She tugs on my hand. "Sit back down."

As I stare down at her, my anger conflicts with this new, foreign need to please her. But as I recall the reasoning behind my rage, I squeeze her hand in apology. "I have to handle them. My guards can't be assaulting women."

She shrugs one shoulder. "I'd wager they're already off duty by now. You can maim them all tomorrow. I promise." Unwilling to cede, she circles her thumb on the top of my hand. "Sit. I'll buy you another drink."

Reluctant to deny this woman anything, I allow her to pull me down to an unbroken chair someone has already replaced, my gaze boring into hers the entire path down.

"What about me?" Kace whines.

Lips stretching into a blinding smile, she laughs. "I'll buy a round."

Fuck! That laugh. So throaty, uninhibited. Seductive. It takes all my willpower not to reach across the table to smother those pillowy lips with my own and taste that sexy rasp. Grimacing, I readjust myself in an attempt to conceal my throbbing cock currently beading with my seed.

"Don't worry, Darius." Amara chuckles, misinterpreting my grimace. "Your guards won't be coming near us anytime soon. Males tend to think twice after you threaten to cut off their balls."

"Ach! Females use that one too often," Zander declares, sliding his empty tankard to the other end of the table. "You threatened that very same thing on the way here."

"I hear it on a daily basis," Kace adds with a proud lift to his chin.

Amara considers Kace thoughtfully. "You *do* seem like the type of person I'd castrate."

"You mean the type of person you'd *threaten* to castrate. You forgot threaten."

"No I didn't," Amara deadpans.

Kace slowly arches away from her, bending over the back of his chair as he eyes Amara warily. "You're a bit terrifying."

The first joyful smile I've seen from her spreads across her face. "Thank you."

"On that note," Lena says, "I think I'll get that round."

Pushing off the table, Lena stands and I watch her glide away, enthralled by the intoxicating sway of her hips, her confident bearing, and the graceful way she slips between the crowd, every part of my being completely entranced by her. Until I notice the countless male heads swiveling in her direction, watching her just as closely as I am.

"Stop glaring," Aurora whispers, pressing her shoulder against mine.

"I'm not glaring."

She laughs. "Yes, you are."

Turning to face my annoying sister, I glare at her.

She laughs even harder. "Now you're glaring at me!"

"Shut it, Rory," I growl. "I'm not glaring. I'm just looking… angrily."

"You like her," she says with a shocked gasp, as if she can't believe it herself. "You actually like her. The great Captain not only likes someone, but she's a foreigner, to boot!"

I shrug. "She's gorgeous."

"It's more than that." Aurora cocks her head to the side and watches me with a pleased smirk. "You've never been addled by a pretty face. You're glaring at any person who so much as looks in her direction. Feeling protective, territorial. I can see it." I shake my head, but she cuts off the motion with a swipe of her hand. "I'm halfway in love with her myself. She's beautiful and fierce. I can see the appeal."

"I don't know anything about her," I reply, rolling my shoulders, feeling a strange itch form between my shoulder blades, prickling along the shadows marking the entirety of my back.

"You won't, either, if you don't take the time to get to know her." She puffs out an irritated breath, stray wisps of blonde hair whisking out of her face.

She makes it sound so simple. That if you give away a part of yourself, it's to be expected that someone will keep that piece of you safe. But she's not a bastard. The product of a rape, no less. As a legitimate child, she'll never understand the difficulties those of us face just by existing.

Trust never has and never will come easily to me. People have always treated me poorly due to my bastard status. For the few who didn't, they often only befriended me in an attempt to gain status. But that's just for the males. Females, on the other hand, are even more cruel. One time too many, I've developed feelings for a pretty face, only later to learn their duplicitous motivations. Those experiences left me with very little faith in their gender. Human, fae, or immortal. As a result, I rarely seek out the opposite sex, and it's not something I plan on changing anytime soon, if ever. Even for the sinfully wicked beauty that is Lena.

It's sexual, nothing more.

No longer interested in listening to Aurora's fantastical ideas, I dismiss her, ignoring her high-pitched growl as I return my attention to Lena.

Lena drums her fingers along the counter, patiently waiting for our drinks with a placid expression. But that expression quickly sours when a male squeezes in beside her, lowering his head to whisper in her ear. She says something to him that I'm unable to make out at this distance, but judging from his reddening face, it wasn't flattering.

Undeterred, he presses into her side, aligning his body with hers. And when he places a palm on her ass and squeezes, that same protective, possessive streak that Aurora accused me of, and which I vehemently denied, swells within me and I spring from my chair.

"Sit the fuck down."

I snap my head around with a snarl, eyeing Amara with a withering glare. "He's touching her."

She stares back defiantly, her arm tossed lazily across the back of her chair. "He won't harm a hair on that perfect little head of hers. She doesn't need a hero. She can take care of herself." Eyes boring into mine, Amara tilts her chair back, teetering on its back legs. "I saw you two eye-fucking each other all night. If you ever want a chance with her, I suggest not treating her like a maiden in distress."

"She is *nooo* maiden," Zander says, followed by a loud smack. "Ow!"

"No more talking," Tristan orders.

Amara ignores them, continuing without pause. "Some can't see past their dicks to the predator in their midst." Amara jerks her head in Lena's direction, a sinister smile slowly lifting her lips. "And Lena will never be prey."

Fighting my instincts, I ball my hands at my sides and try to calm the rage distorting my vision, to douse the fire thumping within my veins as I search for the male deep down who I know is capable of rational thought.

"It *can* be difficult to see past our cocks," Kace offers.

"They're quite the demanding appendage when roused by a pretty face."

"I know, right?" Zander agrees. "One time, there was this female who was just begging to suck my cock. Who am I to deny her? Anywho! She was gorgeous. Great tits, amazing ass, and gods, I could smell the lust bleeding from her-"

Kace sighs. "She sounds lovely."

"But… all I could see were these wet, plump lips that the gods made specifically to suck my dick. What I *should've* been looking at were her razor-sharp teeth."

Kace gasps in horror. "Oh, no!"

"Oh, yes," Zander solemnly replies. "That was a Gods Blessed predator if I ever saw one."

"Shut the fuck up," I order without removing my gaze from Amara's. Choosing to accept her advice, if only for a moment, I swallow as if broken glass is trickling down my throat and return my attention to Lena.

Lena lets her arms fall from the counter and slowly pivots to face the unwelcome male. Hands on her hips, she peers up at him as he speaks, saying nothing in response. After watching him for a handful of moments, she swivels only her head and meets my gaze across the pub. Seeing the ice-cold tundra swirling within her eyes, I'm about to say fuck it to Amara's advice when a brash smile suddenly appears and she winks, right before she grabs the male's balls and twists.

The male drops to his knees with a yowl, attracting the attention of every patron in the pub.

"Oh, does that hurt? Oh, poor baby, I bet it does," Lena coos in mock sympathy, bent over him with her fingers gripped tightly around his balls.

He scrabbles at her wrist to remove her hand, but she clenches tighter and he falls to all fours with a strangled yelp.

"No, no, no," she tsks. "That won't work. I'm quite a bit stronger than I appear." Crouching beside his drooping head, she raises a single finger of her unoccupied hand. "Now, I believe I said no to your advances, and I assumed it was implied that I didn't want to be touched, but I apologize. I must not have made myself clear." She lowers her lips to his ear, all but spitting venom. "*I don't like to be touched.*"

She expels a drawn-out sigh and shakes her head. "Now, I'm going to let go of that little worm you call a cock and hopefully you'll lose the ability to ever harden again. Wouldn't want you to create anymore little assholes." She crosses her fingers with a wide smile. "Here's hoping! And you will *never* touch another female without their permission again. If you do…" She twists again and every male in the bar groans. "I'm going to find you. And when I do, I'll remove the appendage that seems to be the source of all your difficulties." She pauses, allowing her threat to fester before adding, "Lest you forget this unfortunate event…" She pinches her fingers shut around him and he vomits all over the floor. "Let that be a reminder."

Lena releases the vile male and he slumps to the floor with a groan. Paying him no mind, she stands upright and regally stares down the crowd as if she's the living embodiment of an avenging goddess delivering her wrath. Awestruck, the pub watches her in hushed silence until they break out into applause, Lena laughing and smiling with all her admirers.

"I think I just came a little," Kace groans.

"Another common reaction to our lovely Lena," Zander boasts.

Mona smiles at Lena – *I didn't think she could smile!* – and passes her a tray of full tankards. Lena makes her way back toward us and I'm unable to restrain myself any longer, meeting her halfway and grabbing the tray from her.

"You had me worried there for a moment," I say, my jaw aching from the smile stretching my cheeks.

"I can take care of myself," she chides gently.

I laugh. "That's quite apparent."

Looking up at me, her eyes crinkle and her smile widens. Her expression shifts, softening into something akin to affection.

At the sight, I feel that itch begin to spread, traveling up over my shoulders and down my lower back. Inhaling a deep, calming breath through my nostrils, I attempt to convince myself that my eyes are playing tricks on me, that I'm imagining the emotion behind that look.

Until I'm suddenly smacked in the face by Lena's intoxicating scent.

I don't know if I missed it earlier because there are too many beings or too many competing scents, but I'm shocked to just now notice the alluring perfume that's all Lena. My dick hardens to stone as I breathe in another long whiff, catching vanilla, cinnamon, and a hint of cherry. The sensual, sweet, and a little tart scent complements the enticing female before me perfectly.

That's not helping! Would she taste the same if I buried my face between her thighs?

My nostrils flare as I try to wrangle control from my raging cock. But at this point, it's weeping its fury at me and I'm helpless at diminishing its rigidity. That is, until Lena verbally tosses a bucket of ice water over me.

"Did you just sniff me?" she asks, biting her lip to stifle a laugh.

I glare at her. "No."

My cock hasn't been completely tamed, evidenced by him twitching towards her when she chuckles huskily.

"You definitely did."

"I'm thirsty," Kace whines.

"Where's my ale?" Zander demands.

Grateful for once to be surrounded by these half-witted males, I turn my back on Lena and stride towards our table as I debate the quickest way to get her into bed. Because she *will* be in my bed one way or another, there's no mistaking that. The only question is when. For if it's not soon, I fear this enchantment she's cast upon me will forever alter me.

And that, I cannot allow.

CHAPTER 4

LENA

Standing on the porch of The Quiet Harpy, I cradle the hanging lantern within my palm. My thumb brushes along the complex curls of black iron that cages the rippling, orange flames, studying the sparkling strands of gold woven within.

Darkness and Light.

Outlined in a shimmering blue ward, the blaze writhes to a song only it can hear as it reels the hovering ward into a seductive dance. In the ward's pursuit, they curl, twist, and twine. To and away. Again and again, as they attempt to mold itself to the other. Never stopping, never touching, the Stars-crossed lovers could be mistaken for Uriella and Azazel themselves, pining and desperate for one another, but destined never to be.

Paying homage to the gods in the design of a lantern.

I snort at the thought, only to smother it once I hear the creak of wooden steps. "What is it?" I ask, stilling my gaze on the ill-fated lovers.

Skin crackling with his nearness but hearing no response, I spin away from the peculiar magic, but all I see is black. A black leather vest and black tunic molded to the heavily muscled chest of the Fire immortal currently blocking the light of the two moons.

Darius is huge, abnormally so, compared to the beings of this land. I reluctantly drag my gaze from his chest and follow up… up… up, passing his thickly corded neck to the handsome face even the gods would bow down to.

Meeting his square-cut jaw and full lips, it takes a large amount of willpower not to scratch my nails through the scruff along his jaw, imagining the burn it would leave between my thighs.

Tilting my head back even more, I pass his straight nose to the burning, glacial blue eyes that bore intently into my amethyst ones. The burn of his gaze sears every place it touches, as well as every place I wish he would touch.

The intensity of his gaze alone would intimidate a lesser female, but I hold my stance and try not to squirm in a fruitless effort to lessen the need currently glistening the lips below my waist.

It's not just his eyes that are intense; it's all of him.

The sharp mind behind those blue orbs. His severe silence. His tall, muscular build. I'm convinced that if I were to spend enough time with him, I would develop a crick in my neck. His fierce protectiveness makes me squeeze my thighs together in remembrance of his volcanic reaction to the thought of me being touched.

His power. My gods!

His power and strength is an almost tangible entity in itself, thickening the air with his presence alone. It's savage and primal, crippling in its potency. So much so, I find it difficult to breathe with him near.

"It's Gods Light," he says in that gravelly voice of his.

Of course it is.

Passing my gaze over the ward encapsulating the roiling flame, I use Kace's words and ask, "I thought it was rare to have Gifts from the lesser gods?"

Lesser gods. Ha!

I stifle a snort.

They aren't lesser gods. If anything, they're more powerful. More dangerous. Their powers just haven't manifested in many bloodlines. How the Seboians classify and worship the gods makes my stomach churn at their naivety.

He says nothing as his intense stare bores into mine.

If I hadn't spent the last several hours with him, I would think he didn't hear me. But I see the wheels churning in those brilliant eyes and know he rarely speaks without thought.

Leaning my hip against the railing, I wait patiently for his response. It's not long before a slight crease appears between his brows.

"Common enough to have trinkets such as these, and access to Gifted healers." His frown becomes more pronounced. "Have you not seen one before?"

Evading his question, I step off the porch and look to the others walking ahead of us, paired off and chatting as if they're all long-lost friends. I smile at the sight of them laughing and teasing one another. Mixing, mingling, ingratiating themselves.

Inwardly nodding to myself at the thought of one task complete, I peer down at my boots striding across the cobbled street.

When we entered the city, there weren't any visible buildings near the guard station. Along with that and in need of a filling meal, I didn't have the wherewithal to take stock of my surroundings, but now it's impossible not to take notice.

The cobbled street is four wagons wide. Grey, white, and cream-colored stones twinkle beneath the light of the two moons from the large, uncut gems embedded intermittently into the stone of the street.

The streets are clean and well-tended, lit by Gods Light lanterns attached to tall, black iron poles. The shops lining the street are either darkened by the late hour or lit by flickering Gods Light, built with a blend of curving oak woods, white stone, and for the wealthier businesses, several uncut gems.

You can see the presence of Nature magic in the flowers blooming near entryways and the greenery crawling up the sides of the buildings. It's magical, beautiful. Their wealth is present everywhere; I wonder if the other kingdoms are just as prosperous.

Dropping my gaze, I study a blue sapphire beneath my boot.

It's larger than my fist and I'm just stomping across it as if it's nothing more than dirt.

I wonder how they are so blessed.

A sense of foreboding fills me as I think of how these beings worship the gods and how everywhere I look I see the gods' touch. Their wealth. The gems beneath my feet. The lanterns with their swirling black and gold.

Even the people themselves are a likeness of the gods.

Tilting my head back, I squint at the blinding, white stone wall that encases the entire city. Built for protection, but all I see is a cage.

The gods' hands are most prevalent there.

"Your city is quite beautiful," I say, attempting to fill the silence.

"It is," he replies, scanning his surroundings with a bland expression, as if he's grown accustomed to its beauty.

Lowering my head at a tilt, I draw his gaze to mine.

"It truly is. I've seen many cities, and it's rare to find one maintained as well as yours. A nighttime stroll is much more pleasant when you're not dodging horseshit."

He laughs, the sound deep and guttural. "That probably has more to do with the ban on traveling by horse."

"Really?"

He nods, his voice darkening as he slides his thumbs into his belt loops. "Unless you're the Queen."

Feet stuttering to a halt, I fold my arms over my chest and study him, searching for any indication that he's joking. But I don't find laughing eyes or a teasing smirk, only hardened lines and thinned lips.

"That's horseshit," I say on a scowl.

Boots scraping against stone, he slows to a stop, his brows knitting together. "Not really."

"You don't see anything wrong with that?"

Darius shakes his head.

"She's the Queen. That affords special privileges."

"A privilege that citizens paid for with coins from *their* pocket, not the Queen's. They should be able to use the street however they see fit."

Stepping towards him, I jab a finger into his chest.

"Whether that's by riding in fancy carriages or on horses that shit all over the street."

"It's also a security issue," he says, his words muffled as he peers down in bafflement at my finger nestled between his pecs.

I scoff. "A security issue?"

"It's more difficult for her protection detail to travel on foot," he answers diplomatically.

Arching a brow, I point up ahead. "I don't see Aurora with a horse or protection detail."

His brows knit further, staring at me as if I'm the illogical one. "Aurora's not the Queen."

No, just the perfect hostage. I could snatch her up right now if I wished.

Pursing my lips, my hair whips over my shoulder as I whirl around and continue forward, bitterness powering my legs and hatred clouding my thoughts at the discovery of another land ruled by those who only serve themselves.

Gods, immortals, Queens, even the Stars, to a certain degree, are all the same, regardless of where they originate. Greedy, self-serving, power-hungry entities.

They take and take and take, depleting their resources to ash and bones, giving no thought or care to whose blood they spill in doing so. Whose lives they destroy.

Some, if not most, even revel in it.

Movement catches my eyes and my lips twitch when I see Tristan smack Kace upside the head, reminding me that it's probably not in my best interest to get all pissy with an immortal. The Captain of the Guard, no less, and my only source of information at the moment.

Blowing out a steadying breath, I give Darius a tight smile.

"She must have quite a few enemies if she can't even take a walk without guards."

"That's the life of a monarch," he says as if he's the monarch himself. "There will always be those who oppose their rule."

On a humorless chuckle, I say, "Of course they do. She's not willing to abide by the very same laws she enforces. Why should they? It's hypocritical."

His shoulders lift in a dismissive shrug. "Nevertheless, she's still their Queen."

"Doesn't make her deserving of her throne."

Blue eyes coolly assess me as if he can't fathom someone speaking of their Queen so boldly, staring wordlessly at me like Tristan does those puzzles he's so fond of.

That is, until a small blonde female smacks into his chest, molding to his body and hugging him around the neck.

He grunts on impact, but then he smiles, raising his arms to snake around her waist.

Aurora giggles into his neck, squeezing him tightly. When she pulls back to place a sweet, affectionate kiss on Darius' cheek, my puzzlement quickly shifts to a roiling in my stomach.

They're together?

Eyes darting between the two lovers, my chest tightens in realization. Unsure if I want to curl into a ball and sob or tear the offending limbs from her body, I instead stand paralyzed, helpless to endure the horror of how I could have so grossly misread their relationship.

"You're not coming home tonight," he says, not as a question but a statement.

Aurora skates her palms down his neck to grip his massive shoulders. "I'm going to sleep in the loft above the shop."

"Again?" he asks, still fucking holding her.

She nods.

How did I not see this?

Aurora drops down to the street and pivots to face me, completely unaware of my devastation.

"You'll be coming by the shop in the morning, won't you? With Amara?"

It doesn't matter if he's taken. That's not why you're here, I chide myself.

Disappointed and embarrassed by my own flaunting behavior, my words lodge in my throat, but I still manage to give her a jerk of my head.

A bright smile crosses her perfect little princess face that I instantly wish to slap off before she wanders away, moving towards a shop with a sign above labeling it Rory's Swords and Daggers.

"She won't be pleased," Darius calls out.

With a wicked smile, Aurora turns to face us, but continues

walking backwards. “When have I ever wished to please her?” She laughs. “Goodnight, little brother.”

Brother?

Breath hitching and heart quickening, I recite her words over and over in my mind, taking much longer than I would admit to determine I didn’t imagine it.

Aurora points at me in warning. “Don't eat the inn’s porridge.” She shrugs, then drops her hand. “Unless you enjoy having the shits.”

Tension easing at the knowledge that they're siblings, I laugh in relief. “Not especially.”

Spinning towards the shop, she skips onto the side street and tosses a wave over her shoulder as she opens the door before disappearing from sight.

“Sister?” I ask, biting my lip.

“Unfortunately,” he grunts, but his words are diminished by his dimpled smile.

I've always been a sucker for dimples.

Basically chewing through my lip at this point, I release it with a pop.

“Then that would make you a prince.”

His face shutters instantly. Snapping his gaze from mine, he continues toward our companions, but his strides lose their previous leisure.

“No, just a Captain.”

Hastening my steps to match his, I frown. “Are your parents royalty?” When I realize he doesn't intend to answer, I press, “Are they?”

“Yes,” he admits through gritted teeth.

I'm all but running at this point to keep up with his long strides, and I grip his forearm to slow his gait. “I believe that makes you a prince.”

Ignoring the physical hum from our contact, I retain my grip but take a step back when he rounds on me and snaps, "I'm a bastard!"

Meeting that challenging stare, most would see only irritation and anger. But when I search his eyes, I see the pain and hurt such a word can cause. The scars of ill treatment and the acceptance of what others labeled him as.

My daily vocabulary consists of many nasty, vulgar words, but bastard's not one of them. Children are born pure and innocent and have no say in how they were born or to even be born at all. How anyone can judge another person by the actions of their parents, at how they were conceived, is bewildering.

"And?"

He opens his mouth to speak but quickly shuts it. "I'm not legitimate."

"I know what a bastard is, thank you." Placing my hands on my hips, I step closer towards him. "Do you have royal blood?"

Silence.

Unwilling to cede, my brows arch. Waiting for a response. Demanding one.

Hands tightening into fists, his orange topaz and starlight jewels flash as he grudgingly admits, "Yes."

"Then that makes you a prince. Being a bastard doesn't change that, and don't call yourself that," I chastise, swatting his shoulder.

His eyes still burn with anger, but I see the surprise glinting beneath.

"It's what I am."

My boots clack against stone as I take another step closer to him. Leaving barely a breath of space between us, I can feel the heat of him blasting into me. His very essence coils around my arms and legs, blanketing me in its warmth as I drop my head back and stare up at him.

"It's a derogatory term for how you were conceived, which has no bearing on who you are. It's intended to wound, and you labeling yourself as one gives others permission to do the same. Don't allow others to wound you. Don't be a victim."

His nostrils flare and his biceps bulge, and I see the veins throbbing in his thick neck as he bares his teeth. "I'm not a victim."

"No, you're not," I whisper. "Don't let them mistake you for one."

The strain coursing through his limbs doesn't lessen, but the lines bracketing his lips soften, his eyes bouncing between my own as we stare mutely at the other. "He's right, you know."

Confusion flickers across my face. "Who?"

"Kace."

I bark a laugh. "I find that unlikely, but what do you think he's right about?"

"You're beautiful," he says reverently.

I am beautiful and I'm well aware of it, so I'm accustomed to admirers from both genders. Yet, although it can be convenient when needed, more times than not it attracts those with more sinister intentions.

Intentions that are most definitely not welcome and have been the source of much suffering within my life. So much so, I've often wished to trade my face with another.

In one of my darker times, I went so far as to take a knife to my face, carving several jagged lines all the way to the bone in an attempt to rid me of my curse. If I was ugly, if no one wanted me, they wouldn't hurt me. But I healed too quickly and the scars didn't hold. All I was left with was a lingering pain and a blood-stained gown.

I've learned to accept that my looks are a part of me, but I can't say that I'll ever hold more than a begrudging acceptance that the Stars damned me with a face others are incapable of seeing past to who I am within.

But with Darius, I feel like he sees more than a pretty face. As if his searing gaze can scorch through flesh and bone all the way to the core of my soul, discovering the person I truly am. Which is absolutely ridiculous.

He doesn't know me, can't know anything about me. But I can't suppress the all-encompassing warmth I feel at the thought of actually being seen. Or the warmth of the blush filling my cheeks.

An unfamiliar shyness envelops me and I drop my chin, peering down at my feet as I chew on my lip. Powerless at keeping my gaze away for long, I lift my head after only a moment, and my breath catches at the sight of his dimpled smile.

His attention veers to where I drag my teeth over my lip and his smile slips, tightening as he clenches his jaw. Eyes glazed over in lust, he stares into my amethyst ones, piercing me with a gaze filled with so much need. So brutal, so feral, he looks as if he's moments away from devouring me whole.

Feeling the heat of his breath caress my face, I inhale a deep breath and instantly regret teasing him for sniffing me. All I want to do is slip beneath his vest and tunic and burrow my nose into that powerful chest.

The scent of cedar, smoke, and male musk has me shutting my eyes and inhaling slowly, savoring the raw essence that is Darius. Curling into him, I feel the power of him singeing me, crackling along my skin and humming within my blood.

My breaths become harsher; my pussy pulsates and my nipples pebble at the friction of my heaving chest brushing against his own.

Opening my eyes to mere slits, I find his blazing into an inferno, melting me to my very core as he dips his head, slowly lowering his lips to hover above mine. Not yet touching, I can taste his breath roll across my tongue as well as feel his erection bobbing where he's pressed against my belly.

When his nostrils flare, his eyes flash and his cock prods deeper against me, digging in search of that promised moist heat. And when a growl rumbles within his chest, the vibrations shudder through me and a whimper escapes me at the realization he can smell my desperation for him pooling between my legs.

"Lena!"

It takes me a moment to realize that someone's calling out to me. When I do, I do the only logical thing that any red-blooded female would do. I tune the voice out and instead arch against Darius, waiting for the touch of his lips. Needing it.

"Lena," Amara whines.

Darius glances to the side, then back. I see the heat begin to bank in his eyes.

"Just ignore her," I whisper. "She'll eventually go away."

He chuckles and I feel my pussy's grief when he backs away.

Amara tugs on my arm, shaking it. "Lena!"

"What?" I snap, rounding on the dense woman.

"Look!" She points behind me.

I glare at her and she shoves at my shoulder, shaking her finger on the opposite hand.

Growling in frustration, I place my hands on my hips and turn to look at what's caught her attention.

It's a building. A godsdamn building.

The structure is constructed of a mix of arched woods and white stone, similar to all the other shops in Seboia, if not triple the size. But the patrons themselves are an altogether different matter. Females and males laugh, smoke, dance, and caress all types of beings.

Leaving very little to the imagination, they're all dressed in clothing that is basically nothing more than ribbons wrapped around their genitals.

Although I'm not sure why they even bother. Their nudity is visible beneath the sheer, colorful fabrics, the jewels and metal disks stitched within clinking together as their masters participate in all manners of sexual and deviant activities.

Activities I would be enjoying at the moment if not for the annoying brat standing beside me.

"Yes, Amara, it's a brothel," I bite out. Narrowing my eyes, I debate whether I can run away fast enough after I kick her in the cunt.

Probably not. She's fast when she's pissed.

Having about as much patience as I do at the moment, Amara rolls her eyes while placing both hands on the sides of my head and jerking it up.

"Godsdamn it, Amara!" I shout, smacking at her hands, but she holds tight, refusing to let go.

Feeling as if my head has been torn from my shoulders and already knowing Amara won't be satisfied until I do as she asks, I let my arms fall to my sides and focus my gaze on the object of her fascination.

I jolt.

Painted in the same white as the stone of the building, a tall, rectangular sign hangs suspended above the brothel. But it's not the sign itself that surprises me; it's the letters artfully scripted in a metallic, caramel color.

"Maiden's Eye Pleasure House," I read, scrunching up my nose. "What kind of name is that?"

"Right?" Amara chuckles, her eyes widened in bafflement.

"It's horrible." I laugh along with her.

"I think it's a lovely name," Zander defends.

"No." Tristan shakes his head, the disdain evident in his tone. "It's appalling."

"Not one of the Madame's brightest moments," Griffin adds.

A strangled, keening sound comes from Kace.

"Never speak poorly of the Madame! We're Gods Blessed to have such an upstanding citizen. Seboia would be bereft without her."

"Or husbands would be forced to fuck their own wives for once," Griffin retorts.

Darius ducks around me to look at Kace. "You only say that because she gave you your own chambers."

"Your own chambers?" Zander gapes.

"Oh, yes. A sitting room, a bed large enough for a dozen females. There's even a swing! It's magnificent, fit for royalty."

"I haven't ever received my own chambers," Zander mumbles, toeing a rock with his boot.

Except for the whole suite of rooms he has back home. With a bed that can and has *fit over a dozen females. A story he's repeated to me numerous times over the years, in excruciating detail.*

"Do you have a room there?" I ask Darius, followed by an immediate wince, regretting my jealous words almost instantly.

An arrogant smirk tugs at his lips.

"No, I tend to be a bit choosier with my bedmates."

The heat of a blush spreads through my cheeks and I turn my back on that knowing gaze, instead directing mine to a confused looking Amara.

"Do they pretend to be maidens?" Amara asks, scratching her head. "Like role playing?"

"I bet the local virgins go there to be deflowered," Zander says, hands on his hips. "You know, have a trained professional teach them the pleasures of the body."

Amara shakes her head.

"The first time is never pleasurable."

"Just an awkward, painful experience followed by an overwhelming sense of disappointment," I say, to which Amara cackles.

"I would make it quite pleasurable for you, my lovely Lena," Zander says, waggling his brows.

I chuckle at his teasing just as a low growl rumbles beside me.

Gaze drifting to the owner of that growl, I find a furious Darius glaring daggers at Zander.

Godsdamn, I bet he growls when he fucks.

Forcefully shoving aside the thought of how pleasurably that growl could rumble against my clit, I pry my eyes from Darius when Amara says, "I guess I can understand the reasoning behind maiden, but the eye? And tears?"

Gaze swinging back to the sign, I find a drawing of exactly what Amara described, an eye shedding a lone tear.

"It's a pussy," Kace says matter of factly.

"What?" Amara asks.

Cocking my head to the side, I squint up at the sign, wondering how an eyeball could possibly resemble a cunt.

"My pussy sure as fuck doesn't look like that."

Darius and Amara both laugh.

"It's a pussy weeping with pleasure," Kace says as if it's obvious, then sighs dramatically. "It's a common issue for me."

"Or crying from dissatisfaction," Amara quips.

Kace gasps.

"Don't listen to them," Zander says, narrowing his eyes on Amara as he rubs Kace's back. "You're a very handsome male. I'm sure you make all the women weep with pleasure."

"That's kind of you to say," Kace replies, patting above Zander's bulging pec. "You're quite handsome yourself."

Zander puffs his chest out, preening.

"There's two of them," Tristan says, and I laugh at the look of horror on the normally stoic man's face.

Kace tosses an arm across Zander's shoulders and tugs him to his side, heading toward the brothel.

"Let me explain the basics."

Wholly engrossed in his words, Zander nods earnestly.

"Tally, Milly, and Vita are always good for a spin, but you're going to want to avoid Elva for the next few weeks. Unless you don't mind having a rash on your… Ladies!" Kace's arms whip up, his words trailing off. "I've brought a friend."

All the courtesans cheer and throw themselves at both males, peppering them with kisses.

There really are two of them.

Shaking my head, I look at a chuckling Darius, who appears just as amused as I am by our absurd friends.

"There's the Early Bird Inn." He motions with his head towards a building that looks to be quite older than the ones surrounding it.

I scrunch up my nose when I see it.

The Early Bird Inn is one of the few structures I've seen that wasn't built with this kingdom's signature white stone.

But while the lack of stone ornamenting the pub and a few of the other shops was a conscious choice rather than a lack of coin, the two-story inn constructed of all dark wood may not be able to say the same.

With its fraying wood, missing shingles, and a dilapidated wraparound porch, its neglect is more than apparent. It's the first building I've seen since arriving in Seboia that hasn't been pristinely maintained.

"An inn across the street from a brothel." I snort. "That's convenient."

Darius chuckles. "Lords love visiting Seboia. Their wives, not so much."

We share a smile, following behind Amara and Tristan as we silently make our way towards the inn, but my smile lessens the closer we get. Palms sweaty, heart galloping, I trail behind Amara and Tristan up the stairs.

The rickety porch voices its protest with creaks and groans as it struggles to bear our weight.

Tristan opens the door, a bell tolling his arrival as he and Amara disappear inside, while I turn to face Darius who's still loitering at the bottom of the steps.

Without looking in his direction, Darius waves Griffin on and we both listen to the sound of his retreating boots as we stare wordlessly at one another.

A niggling of doubt suddenly creeps in, its warning strengthening in volume the longer I stare into those glacial blue eyes. I'm not sure why. It's not like I'm a stranger to casual sex.

Far from it, actually.

It's the only way I *do* have relations. Although, now that I think about it, that could be the reason why, as I doubt anything involving Darius could remain casual.

I wipe my sweaty palms on my leathers, slickening the supple hide as trepidation rears its head, churning in a whirlwind along with the doubt and fear.

Fear that he is someone I won't be able to forget, not easily, at least, as is the case with any male I've bedded in the past.

Because I have to forget him. I have to forget everyone.

Still, I can't help but hesitate, wondering if one night could scratch the itch of what I know will be a long, sweaty night that'll leave me sore and walking bow-legged the following morning, yet supremely satisfied.

"Well…" I clear my throat. "It was an interesting night."

"It was."

His burning gaze searches mine and I see my own reluctance reflecting back at me, as well as the obviousness of my hesitation when a soft smile tilts his lips.

"Goodnight, Lena."

Disappointed but knowing it's for the best, I reply quietly, "Goodnight, Darius."

Ignoring my need, I turn away while I'm still capable and listen to the chime above the door as I open it and the groans as it slams shut.

Shutting my eyes, I drop my head back onto the wood as I try to convince myself and my deprived cunt I made the right decision.

A disconcerting thought suddenly enters my mind and my eyes snap open. Diving towards the window, I pay no mind to the moth-eaten curtains as I peek out into the night.

My chest expands and my breaths halt in my lungs as I watch Darius and Griffin walk side by side down the street.

One step. Two steps. Three steps.

Then I exhale in audible relief when I see them pass by the brothel without stopping.

"What are you doing?"

I squeak, quickly jerking the curtains shut. "Nothing."

Amara eyes me suspiciously, dust drifting around her head from my violent handling of the curtains. Whiskey eyes wander towards the window, and I mutter a curse when she reaches out and peels back the swaying curtains.

She glances back at me over her shoulder and I wince when I see her evil smirk. "With the moon-eyes he had for you all night, I doubt he'd be willing to risk his chances with you to spend the night with a whore."

Normally, I appreciate how observant she is, but at the moment it pisses me off.

"Shut up."

She laughs as I stomp past, but it morphs into a howl when I snap my arm out and punch her in the tit.

Running away, I laugh maniacally as she screams, "Fuck, Lena! That hurt!"

CHAPTER 5

DARIUS

Shops are darkened and the streets are free of pedestrians. The only noises that can be heard are the waning sounds of the brothel and the thunk of mine and Griffin's boots scuffing against the jeweled stone street.

Peering down at my feet, I inspect the gems littering the stone road. I've never paid much mind to them before. The other kingdoms are similarly grandiose and I thought it to be quite common, but judging off Lena's reaction, that might not be so everywhere.

Lena, Lena, Lena.

It was physically painful to leave her on the inn's doorstep untouched, but I could sense her hesitation. Could practically see the wheels churning in those amethyst eyes of hers. I'm unsure as to why. She showed no such reservations throughout the night, but something gave her pause. Based on her reaction to me, I'm quite confident I could've convinced her otherwise, but I sensed that would be a mistake.

There's something special about her, something unique. Yes, she's extraordinarily beautiful, but there's so much more to her than that. Her mind and the way she thinks is completely foreign to me. It was mind-boggling how flippant she was with my bastard status, actually offended on my behalf that I applied the word to myself. I've never met another who didn't find being a bastard something to be ashamed of. Even those who treat me no differently than others never spoke out against society's stigma for those such as myself.

But not her. She had no issue voicing – rather loudly – how illogical it is to scorn those with no choice on how they were conceived. So convincing, she made me feel a fool for ever believing otherwise. She spoke her mind and offered no apologies. Even her thoughts of the Queen weren't censored. I'm unsure if I admire her for her brazen impudence or fearful for her.

I chuckle to myself, imagining the reaction Adelphia would have to her. Lena is clever, feisty, and can banter with the best of them. Adelphia may very well meet her match in her. Or kill her. The thoughts Lena expressed definitely lean more towards traitorous. My mother doesn't usually kill those who verbally oppose her, but that's only in regards to her own people. A foreigner is an entirely different matter. I suspect the Queen would have no conundrum killing a non-citizen.

Stepping outside its perimeter of detection, a Gods Light winks out just as another flares, illuminating our steps. Haloed beneath the flame, Griffin's glimmering sapphire and starlight jewels draw my attention to the Air immortal's creased brow.

"What did you think of them?" I ask.

"Hmm… I'm not sure."

A breeze streams past, chilling my cheeks and sweeping strands of black hair into my face. Unraveling the leather strap on my wrist, I tie my hair back, waiting for Griffin to continue. But when I peek out the corner of my eye, I find him staring straight ahead, appearing as if he has no intention of expounding.

"Meaning?"

He shrugs. "Meaning, I'm not sure."

Aware that he can stew indefinitely, I slow to a stop and pivot towards him, a command in itself.

Rubbing the back of his neck, he turns to face me. "I'm not sure how I feel about them."

That's understandable. I'm having conflicting thoughts myself. More specifically about Lena, but I doubt that's what he's referring to.

"How so?"

Placing his hands on his waist, he begins to pace. "I don't think they have any ill intentions toward us, but there's something… *off* about them."

When I stare blankly at him, he explains, "For instance, their race. I have no clue what kind of beings they are." Raising a hand, he counts off on his fingers. "Their party consists of a woman who looks like a goddess, but is apparently human; a mortal with strange scarring; a shifter with abnormal jewels; and a being who's either fae or immortal, but only has a singular starlight jewel." He stops midstep, facing me with thinned lips. "And they never actually confirmed what race they are, did they?"

Rubbing along my jaw, I consider how odd that is. All races are born with certain traits that are easily identifiable at a glance. Being unable to distinguish a person's race based off their appearance is unheard of.

I nod, impressed by Griffin's astuteness. "Did you find out what kingdom they're from? How they came to know each other?" Their relationship is too intimate to simply be hired escorts, as Lena originally stated. They must have known each other prior to their travels.

"No." He shakes his head. "They evaded all questions about themselves. Expertly, I might add. They were very strange." He gauges my reaction before adding, "All of them were, Darius."

Lena most of all.

"Lena behaved as if she's never seen Gods Light before." I glance up at the flame at the top of the iron pole. "It's readily available to even the poorest citizens. It's not possible for her to not have come across it." Shuffling through my memories, I'm able to pick out several odd reactions from her. "She ogled the jewels in the street as if it was excessive, an uncommon luxury. I don't know of any kingdom that doesn't use gems ornamentally."

"And they're here in Cascadonia, of all places, to trade leather," Griffin says, his lips set in a grim line.

Now that my mind's no longer muddled by Lena's presence, I can think not as a lust-filled male, but as the acting Captain of the Guard, to detect the details I normally wouldn't have missed. The things they said. The way they look and act. Even their accent is nothing I've ever encountered before, not even remotely similar. With a clear head, I can see the oddities and the suspiciousness of their group for what they truly are.

A possible threat.

"Did you read them?" I ask gruffly, internally cursing myself for being so blind.

It's rare for a fae or immortal to be Gods Blessed with an additional Gift, but it does occur. Those who can Heal, have the Sight, or the ability to draw Wards are highly sought after, a boon to any kingdom. When these rare Gifts manifest, most are ecstatic to pledge their services to the crown. But, on occasion, there are those who choose to carve a different path in life. In those instances, they face immense pressure to pledge their services to the crown. If that doesn't work, they're ultimately forced to enlist for 'the good of the kingdom'.

Griffin himself is a Gods Blessed. He's an empath who can also see a person's aura. Griffin's father, one of my mother's most trusted advisors, was thrilled to discover his only child manifested not just one, but two Gods Blessed Gifts. But he also wished for Griffin to have a choice in what direction his life would take.

In an attempt to protect his son, Griffin's father retired from

Adelphia's service soon after his son's Gifts developed. Griffin's mother passed during labor, leaving a babe without a mother and a father widowed, so it wasn't suspicious for him to do so. Once he was able to distance himself from the court, he sheltered Griffin the best he could, keeping his additional Gifts a secret and teaching Griffin to do the same. Besides Aurora, Kace, and myself, Griffin has never confided in another.

Scrubbing his face, Griffin blows out an uneasy breath. "That's where I'm most confused."

"Elaborate."

"Reading Tristan, Zander, and Amara, I saw that they are good, honorable people," he replies factually. "They're strong and willful, yet compassionate beings. Everything that makes up a good soul is present in them."

I notice he doesn't add Lena to the list of good, honorable people. "But?"

"It's difficult to explain." Griffin drops his head back and stares up at the night sky, the light of the moons making the harsh lines on his face appear even more severe as he collects his thoughts. "When I read someone with my empathic Gifts, I feel an echo of what they do, but with auras, emotions emerge differently. They're visible."

He blows out a frustrated breath and scratches the crown of his head. "A person's aura appears as a single color. It's always present, and the color itself is a direct reflection of their soul. But on occasion, if that person is feeling a strong enough emotion, a separate color can manifest. One that represents that particular emotion, cloaking their soul's aura as if it's a lace veil."

Griffin shakes his head, trying to find the right words. "But with Tristan, Zander, and Amara, their auras are different. They don't have just *one* color that represents their soul, they have several. I've never seen that before. Sometimes a person's aura will lighten or darken, but it never changes to a different color altogether, and they definitely don't gain an additional one. I didn't even know it was possible." He pauses, worry contorting his features. "It's almost as if who or what they are isn't the same as us. That their very makeup is different from ours."

A thousand questions bounce within my mind, one popping up before another rears its head. But before I can voice any of them, Griffin lays another riddle at my feet.

"But even if I find that to be odd, that's not what's most concerning." Griffin meets my eyes. "There's a darkness to them."

I stiffen. "Darkness?"

He nods, tonguing his cheek. "Darkness marks everyone, whether it's the death of a loved one, the pain of heartbreak, or the lingering guilt of killing another. Even if it's only in defense. But darkness can also represent cruelty, maliciousness, or even evil." Curling a lip, he rubs the tips of his fingers together. "When it does, it feels thicker, almost sludge-like."

A knot forms in my chest, coiling tighter and tighter with each passing word. "And with them?"

"Everything that they are is shrouded in darkness. Not evil or maliciousness," he quickly adds, "but by torment, fear, and death. Especially Lena. Hers is…" His expression twists, contorting into agony as his voice hoarsens. "The magnitude of it is incomprehensible." Griffin pauses for a moment, then clears his throat, the strain lining his face relaxing for all but the creases near his eyes. "Your mother has a similar darkness to her, but it's only a fraction of Lena's."

I start to wonder what could possibly have caused Lena such pain, what must have happened to her if it's comparable to my mother's, but I quickly cut off that train of thinking.

She's not my concern. Only my kingdom.

"What about Lena?" I ask. "How does her aura feel?"

Eyes widening, Griffin laces his hands on top of his head. “Lena's is baffling. Her aura is completely different from ours or even theirs.” He barks a laugh, bending over at the waist. “Gods! I've never felt anything like it. I’m not even sure I can describe it properly. Her soul…it’s this bright white light, almost blinding in its intensity. So innocent and pure. It’s extraordinary. Not only that, she doesn't have only a few colors, but *all* of them. Red, blue, black, gold, and any other color you could possibly imagine. Constantly flashing and flowing like a hurricane around this blindingly white ball of light that is her soul. It’s unfathomable. Breathtaking.”

He presses the flat side of his fist to his mouth, shaking his head in awe. “She truly is special,” he says quietly. Hands falling to his sides, he stares off into the distance, eyes glazing over in wonderment. “Her presence alone draws everyone in. You feel this desperate need to be near her. To touch her. Even if others don't have my Gifts, they can feel what I do to some extent. I doubt I'll meet another like her within my lifetime.”

Glaze clearing, he steps towards me, his brown eyes blazing in earnest, shaking steepled fingers near his lips. “But that's what's so alarming. So dangerous. The way her friends hover around her. It's as if she's the sun and all her companions gravitate towards her, worshipping her. They'd lay down their life for her and it feels like…” He hesitates, throat bobbing on a swallow. “Like they’re preparing to do so. Like it's inevitable.”

Placing a palm on my shoulder, he grips tightly. “What I feel strongest in all of them is their strength, conviction, and righteousness. It's alarming because I usually only see this combination from warriors in the midst of combat.” He pauses, his eyes burrowing into my own, trepidation flashing beneath. “It feels as if they're in a war, and I fear Cascadonia may be their battleground.”

“That's reaching a bit, don't you think?” Prickles of unease skitter down my spine, but I try to brush off his warning. I understand to an extent how Griffin's Gifts work, but not being intimately familiar with them makes it difficult to grasp the direness of his words.

Lips tightening, Griffin inhales a long breath through his nostrils, chest expanding as his arms fall limply to his sides. "You asked my opinion and I'm telling you. We don't know anything about this woman. Who she is, what she is, or what her motivations are, whether they're good or bad. How easy do you think it would be for her to sway people to her line of thinking? Not difficult at all, I'd wager." He barks a humorless laugh, swiping his hands through his hair. "That's a lot of power for one person to hold. Too much. It's a bit frightening."

"What do you think their purpose is?" I ask, that knot in my chest twining even tighter, fraying at the edges. "You said you think they've dealt with something traumatic. Maybe they're hiding from someone? Or escaping?"

"Or both?" He shrugs. "Regardless, they're here for something, and it's not to trade leather. With how secretive and mysterious they are, it leads me to believe it can't be good for Cascadonia."

"But you said they're good souls," I remind him, grasping at anything that'll lessen the gravity of the situation.

"Yes, but good people can do horrible things if they feel it's for the right reasons." Watching me roll my shoulders forward to ease the sensation in my chest, a brittle smile crosses his face and he slaps me on the back. "I don't think they're a threat to us or that they're here for malicious reasons, but I do believe their presence alone might signify a chain of events that are."

I shrug off his hand, turning my back on him to stare up at the starlit sky, wondering how I could have missed so much. How I could've allowed my judgment to become so skewed all because I felt more than an ember of attraction to someone.

I chuckle bitterly to myself. Of course the Stars would tempt me with such a vixen, knowing she'd be the worst possible choice. Thank the gods I regained my wits before we went any further. If I allow this foreigner to get close to me, possibly even giving my trust in the process, it could have disastrous consequences for not just myself, but for all of Cascadonia.

Disgusted with myself for allowing my emotions to get the best of me, I recall Amara's words of how most males can't see past their dicks to the predator in their midst. Maybe that's accurate for most, but I sure as fuck won't be one of them.

CHAPTER 6

LENA

No sight.
No scent.
No sound.

Only the complete absence of light. Only the fluid touch of the all-consuming blackness flowing beneath me. Inky liquid spills over me. Its obsidian ribbons glide across my skin, slinking through my hair, and trickling over my face and torso to snake around my arms and limbs, enveloping me. Cocooning me. Shielding me from the burdens that only light can bring.

"Wakey, wakey."

The blackness shudders, contracting. The veil I'm swaddled in ripples on a glassy sheen.

A moment passes, then it stills, seeming to breathe a sigh of relief as it loosens its hold. I allow my limbs to relax as I sink back into its slithering embrace.

"Wakey wakey," the distant voice coos again, followed by a tap, tap, tap on my nose.

Tremors wrack through the blackness and it roars its wrath. Fractures form and spread, beams of light spearing through the cracks webbing along the veil. Waves wash over me, slipping into my eyes, nose, and mouth, leaving me no choice but to flee,

Nose twitching, I battle the grogginess of sleep and lift my heavy eyelids. Squinting against the bright light, I wait until my eyes acclimate to the brightness. When they do, I find a heavily muscled male crouching beside my sleeping form.

The cobwebs of sleep instantly receding, I slip my arm out from beneath the blanket, raise my flattened palm cautiously slow… and smack him in the ear.

“Ow!” He collapses to the floor, clutching his ear. “Lena, It's me! Zander!”

“I know.”

His arms fall limp to the floor and he purses his lips.

“Is Amara awake?” I ask on a yawn, hoping to redirect his attention away from me so I can embrace the darkness once again.

A saccharine smile, so full of naivety, spreads across his face. “Not yet.”

Standing, he rounds my twin-size bed and creeps towards where Amara is sleeping beneath the lone window.

How he's not aware he's walking the plank is beyond me.

Too lazy to follow him, even with my gaze, I shut my eyes and enjoy the warmth of morning light heating my cheeks as I tug the woolen blanket up to my chin, burrowing into the scratchy fabric. I wait for the inevitable.

Hearing the creaks of the floor halt with his steps, an evil smirk quirks my lips.

“Wakey wakey. It's a beau– *Ow*!” he yowls. “She bit me! You fucking bit me! Why do you always have to bite?!”

“Stop waking me up like that and I'll stop biting,” Amara replies groggily.

“Vicious little creature,” he mumbles.

Rolling to my other side, I find Zander sucking on his finger while glaring down at where Amara is snuggled up in her bed.

Always quick to forgive, he releases his finger with a pop and smiles brightly as he makes his way toward the door.

“It's a beautiful day. The sun is shining. Birds are singing. It's time to seize the day!”

We both stare blankly at him and he huffs while opening the door.

“I’ll leave you two ornery females to dress in private.” Stepping over the threshold, he murmurs, “Must be that time of the month again.”

Amara quickly snatches a figurine off the bedside table and whips it at his head.

His eyes widen and he squeaks as he slams the door shut, leaving the statue to shatter against the wood.

I wonder if I’ll be charged for that?

If anything, Amara should charge the innkeeper for relieving her of such a frightful piece. Frankly, it was a bit terrifying sleeping next to the doll-like figurine with a demonic smile.

I swear its ungodly eyes were cataloging every one of my weaknesses, imagining all the ways it could murder me in my sleep.

Unable to hold that porcelain stare for long, I spun its face towards the wall several times throughout the night, but every time I reopened my eyes… there it was. Watching me.

The first time I woke and saw its creepy doll eyes, I swear I peed a little. At that point, I debated hiding it beneath the bed, but then I thought of how it would stare up at me through the mattress and that concerned me even more.

Holding onto the mantra that one should never take their eyes off the enemy, I thought it best to keep it within view.

Praying to Azazel himself that the evil doll won't resurrect itself, I watch the porcelain pieces skate across the wooden floor of the tiny room.

When the remaining slivers pass the cool hearth and tattered privacy screen to clank against the lone wardrobe, my fear lessens and I determine its regeneration unlikely.

Stretching my arms above my head, I say, “I slept like the dead.”

Even if the bed is lumpy and smells of mildew.

“I did, too.” Eyes twinkling in mirth, Amara smirks. “After you finished twiddling yourself, that is.”

I choke on my spit. “I was *not* twiddling myself!”

She laughs. “I heard you.”

How did she know? I barely made a sound!

“You were asleep,” I accuse. “Snoring!”

She shrugs, her shoulders lifting past the blanket’s frayed hem.

“You're noisy when you play with yourself. You make these soft little whimpering sounds.” She cackles. “I was just waiting for you to scream, ‘Darius, oh, Darius!’”

Able to see the humor even in the face of my embarrassment, I chuckle along with her and roll onto my back, staring up at the peeling wood of the ceiling.

Amara isn’t far off in her assessment.

I had to bite my lips to stop Darius’ name from rumbling past them. Watching him walk away, I assumed the need would lessen with distance, but unfortunately he consumed my thoughts.

I would've normally found a bedmate or at least waited to touch myself until I was alone, but my reaction to him was too intense to ignore.

I sigh. “It's just been too long.”

Still smiling, she says, “I bet Darius could help with that.”

I’m sure he could.

The memory of his cock pressed against my belly flashes before my eyes, but I quickly kick it aside. My reaction to him may be intense, unusually so, but that's not why we're here, and such emotions could be dangerous.

Not only for myself, but for him as well.

Best for me to steer clear of him and allow whatever flame he kindled to wither and die.

"Not him. Someone who's a bit less… memorable."

"With the way he was glaring at any male who glanced in your direction, I'd wager you'll have a difficult time finding a willing partner."

"Hmph."

We lay there silent for a time, lost in our own thoughts.

When enough time passes without a sound, I begin to suspect Amara has fallen back asleep until she suddenly whips the blankets off and springs to her feet.

"We're going to Aurora's shop today!" She lunges towards me and grips my shoulders, shaking me violently. "Get up, get up, get up!"

With one last shake, she races toward her trunk and flips the lid.

I grunt and tug the blankets over my head.

"I know we can't carry weapons here, but maybe Aurora will let me touch one," Amara prattles over the sounds of rustling fabric as she rummages through her trunk. "Or hold one! Just for a second. I miss my blades."

She whimpers, then sucks in a gasp.

"Maybe I'll just take one? Slip it into my boot? You know… just a small one," she says, as if stealing something small isn't considered theft.

"Yes, because that would endear us to the princess," I reply dryly, my voice muffled beneath the blanket. "Stealing from her."

"I wouldn't *steal* it. I'd just take it and hide a few silvers for her to find at a later time. I'll even leave an extra coin or two!"

I laugh at what I like to call 'Amara logic' until I hear the latch of her trunk and the silence that follows, feeling those whiskey eyes drilling holes through the blanket.

"What are you doing? Get up!"

I tuck tighter under the fabric. "Five more minutes."

"No fucking way!"

I hear two pounding stomps, then a brush of cool air as Amara whips the blanket off me.

"Hey!" I snatch at the blanket, but she jerks it outside my reach.

Ducking her head slowly near mine, she bares her teeth. "Get. Up. *Now*."

"No!"

Folding my arms over my chest, I fall back on the bed and shut my eyes, determined to ignore the psycho. A sigh of relief passes my lips once I hear the sound of her retreating steps. But knowing how obsessed she is with blades – and that she's a fucking sociopath – I should've realized that was too easy. But I don't, so when she punches me in the cunt, I'm taken completely by surprise.

"Aaaah!"

"I thought you'd be extra sensitive down there with all the rubbing you did last night," she cackles. "Now, get dressed!"

Cupping my mound, I shout, "Fuck, Amara! That hurt!"

Placing my foot as gingerly as possible on the wooden step, I wince at its loud groan. My chest tightens as I wait for the crack of wood that will ultimately lead to my body falling through the broken boards. I'm not even sure how Zander made it up here.

The tiny stairway is so narrow my shoulders brush against the walls, and the ceiling so low my hair snags on it. With Zander being twice my size, I'm positive he'll have to walk sideways and hunch over.

A sigh of relief passes my lips as I step off the last step onto the first floor, but then my nose crinkles as I scan the room.

Uneven rectangular tables with mismatched chairs fill the gloomy space. The oak walls are cracked and discolored. The floor is crusted with dirt. Moth-eaten curtains are pulled back in an attempt to allow sunlight to stream through, but the filth smeared across the paned windows obstructs its path.

There's even a stifling mugginess to the air. The only appealing aspect to the room could be the cold hearth, but I suspect the mountain of ashes at the bottom makes it more of a fire hazard than an aesthetically pleasing addition.

Last night I'd hoped the inn would look more appealing by day, but clearly I was wrong. It's not the worst lodging any of us has stayed in. Far from it, actually.

I was just surprised to see how neglected it is in comparison to the rest of Cascadonia. Even the shops that appear less profitable than others seem luxurious compared to some of the other towns we've traveled through, so I doubt the only inn within this caged city is struggling financially.

No, I suspect the neglect has more to do with the female standing behind the bar, eyeballing me as if I'm a bug she'd like to squish beneath her foot.

Since arriving in Cascadonia, I haven't seen any beings that aren't attractive. Even those who aren't to my taste were appealing in one way or another. But by the looks of Lottie, I'm guessing that trait wasn't passed down to her.

With her pale sunken cheeks, rail thin body, and limp brown hair pinned at the nape, I suspect the Air fae doesn't have many suitors knocking on her door. It's not that she's ugly; she has a willowy beauty that I'm sure is alluring to many. It's more that her dour resting-bitch-face lowers the appeal of an otherwise simple attractiveness.

Amara steps off the last step and we move deeper within the room, Lottie following our every step with narrowed eyes.

And I assume that expression sends any remaining suitors running in the other direction.

Our chairs skid across the floor as we sit across from Zander and Tristan. I instantly reach for the steaming mug of coffee waiting for me. Raising the cup beneath my nose, I shut my eyes and inhale the nutty aroma, savoring the feel of the rising steam moistening my cheeks.

Taking a cautious sip, I allow the bitter flavors to roll across my tongue, washing away any remaining grogginess.

Amara scrunches her nose. "How can you drink yours black? Ugh."

Tristan passes two small bowls toward her and she proceeds to dump half the cream and practically all of the sugar into her mug. Stirring with a spoon, the liquid overflows onto the saucer.

Zander chuckles. "What I don't understand is how someone so bitter can drink something so sweet."

Amara drops her spoon to the table with a clank, her lips set in an angry line.

"I'm not bitter. I'm sweet. Sweet as fucking pie! Just the other day, when that male tried to rob me, I wanted to kill him, but did I? No. I just broke his arms and legs."

Tristan arches a brow over his brown, almost black eyes.

"I'm sure he was quite appreciative of being wounded and stranded in the middle of the wilderness with no means of defending himself."

Amara snaps her fingers, pointing at him. "I know, right? I

gave him hope. A chance to live. If I had killed him, he wouldn't have had that opportunity now, would he? If that's not sweet, I don't know what is."

"Sweet as pie," I echo Amara's words, but my sarcastic tone doesn't seem to register with her as she emphatically nods her head.

The heated mug warms my hands as I lift it to my lips, but before I can taste it, I notice another more potent scent overshadowing the nutty aroma.

Glancing at Amara and then Tristan, I easily dismiss them as the source, but when my gaze lands on Zander and I notice his disheveled state, I lean over the table and inhale a deep sniff. Only to stifle a gag when I'm instantly accosted with the overwhelming stench of horse and body odor.

"Zander, did you *forget* to bathe?" I ask, arching away from the offending smell.

Amara groans, slapping a palm to her forehead. "Please tell me you didn't force those poor females at the brothel to endure your beastly stench? They deal with enough shit as it is!"

"Of course, I bathed," Zander replies with an indignant raise of his chin.

I gesture to his clothes with a wave of my hand. "Then why are you in the same filthy clothes you had on yesterday?"

Folding his thick arms over his chest, he glances down at his soiled tunic. "Because all my clothes are dirty, and the brothel didn't have anything large enough to fit me."

"You could wash them," I say slowly, wondering how he can handle the smell with his heightened shifter senses when I barely can.

He cocks his head to the side, looking at me as if I've grown another head. "That's a female's job."

Amara and I stare at him in silence as we process his words.

Once I've come to the conclusion that, no, he didn't misspeak and yes, his words are offensive, I snap my arm out and twist his nipple.

"Aaaah!"

"That was completely warranted," Amara murmurs. I nod in agreement.

Tristan pinches his nose. "Remember what we talked about? About thinking before speaking?"

Grimacing while rubbing his nipple in a circular motion, Zander's gaze darts to the ceiling and we wait patiently for his words to click. After a few minutes, his eyes widen and his mouth shapes into a silent O.

"Oh, yes. I can see how that was interpreted. Point taken. Anywho, most of my clothing is worn beyond repair and in need of replacing."

Folding his arms on the table he leans forward, his expression becoming somber as he speaks in a hushed voice.

"I figured I'd purchase a few items at the market. Meet with some of the locals. See what this city's busybodies are talking about."

When passing through any town, our first task is to ingratiate ourselves with the people. With Amara having very little patience and my personality considered too abrasive for most, that task usually falls to Zander.

Using only his natural charm, he's quite gifted in loosening tongues, whether that's by befriending a chatty male at the local tavern or from the female workers at the brothel. The brothel is usually his main source of information since males tend to not hold much regard for whores and more often than not indulge in ill-advised pillow talk.

Even so, respect and sufficient coin go a long way, and Zander is a master at using both to his advantage.

But in the rare instances Zander has difficulty garnering this information, we then employ Tristan's more subtle skills. With his unassuming appearance and knack for fading into the background, most are oblivious to his stealthy presence.

How he manages to slink within earshot to the most private discussions has always baffled me. I can only assume he was an assassin in a past life.

"That'll work, but don't lay the charm on too thick," I say, recalling some of the citizens' almost hostile reactions to us. "These beings are a suspicious lot."

"With good reason," Tristan says. "They've lost a lot more than other kingdoms."

"And a lot less than others," Amara murmurs, staring unseeing down at the table.

My chest begins to throb in tune with my heart, and I reach over and clasp our hands together, squeezing until she meets my gaze with a sad smile. Offering her a small smile of my own, I pat her hand before redirecting my attention to Zander.

"Go ahead and work the market. See what information you can glean, but back off if anyone becomes suspicious. I don't want them asking too many questions."

Drinking the last sip of the cooled coffee, my gaze wanders to Tristan.

"Amara and I have to go to Aurora's shop today. Why don't you tag along with Zander?"

Tristan glances down at the table and shuffles awkwardly in his chair, an uncommon reaction for our usually unflappable partner. "I thought I'd accompany you and Amara today."

With a raise of a black brow, I urge him to elaborate.

Regaining his usual stoic expression, he crosses one leg over the other and clasps his hands in his lap. "I think Zander will gain more information without my presence. Cascadonians don't seem overly fond of humans."

His lips tighten in distaste, which I more than share, before he gives me a knowing look.

"Besides, you and Amara can chat with the princess while I search her shop."

Agreeing with his thought process, I jerk a nod in the same moment I hear the slide of slippered feet. Pausing our discussion, I glance up at where Lottie loiters at the edge of the table, holding two bowls.

Without a word, she glowers down at us and tosses both bowls towards me and Amara. The bowls clatter and spin across the table, slopping porridge all over the sides as she turns her back on us and stomps back to her spot behind the counter.

"She really doesn't like us, does she?" Tristan asks with a curl of his lip.

Amara bends forward and sniffs warily "You think she poisoned it?"

"Probably," I reply, my stomach churning at the sight of the blackened yet white, undercooked chunks.

Zander clasps my hand with his and tugs me out of my seat. "Come on. There's a pastry cart right around the corner. I think I even saw a banket."

Perking up at the thought of the delicious almond pastry, my stomach begins to slow its revolt as we all stand and stride towards the door. Lottie tracks our every step with a smug smirk, her sharpened ears twitching in amusement.

Starving and at my wits end with the unsavory female, I wait until I'm only a few paces away and then lurch toward her with a hiss, snapping my blunt teeth within an inch of her face.

She shrieks and stumbles backwards and Amara and I laugh as we trail behind the others.

At the tinkle of the bell above the open door, Tristan exhales a long-suffering sigh. “Can't take you two anywhere.”

Amara and I share another smirk and I reach for Tristan, wrapping my arms around the back of his neck and dragging him down for a loud smack of a kiss on his marked cheek.

“You know you love us.”

CHAPTER 7

DARIUS

Surrounded by gray slate in a minimally adorned room, I ignore the clash of steel on steel from the outdoor training grounds below where I sit behind the desk in my private office in the tower of the Guards Base. Griffin and Kace stand silently beside me, their thoughts as turbulent as my own as I glare at the iron knob attached to the lone wooden door, willing it to move with my thoughts alone.

Frustration mounting with every moment that passes without a knock to my door, I roll my neck in a futile effort to release the tightening in my neck, my mind wandering to the events of the night prior.

After Griffin voiced his suspicions of Lena and her companions last night, I spent the entirety of the walk back to the palace castigating myself for my blindness. By the time I finally arrived in my chambers, I fell into bed exhausted, but my mind refused to succumb to its body's needs. Thoughts fixated on the mysterious woman to the point of obsession, I replayed every detail of our encounter. Every smile, every change of tone, every finger twitch, in an attempt to catalog and decipher the words she said, and most importantly, the ones she did not.

Thoughts swirling with question after question, I tossed and turned throughout the night. When I eventually did manage to sleep, she plagued that realm as well. With dreams filled with silky black hair, tan smooth skin, and brilliant amethyst eyes, my suspicions fell to the wayside as I envisioned every filthy way I'd feed this irrational craving for a woman I know nothing about.

By the time dawn's light began to flood my chambers, I felt as if I had just shut my eyes.

Stumbling from bed with a sluggish mind and bloodshot eyes, I proceeded to dress with a stiff cock that refused to soften despite my relentless ministrations. With how poorly the day began, I should have foreseen its downhill trajectory.

Griffin, Kace, and I arranged to meet first thing this morning to question the guards who had assaulted our mysterious visitors. Even though Lena and her friends fed us nothing but half-truths, we all agreed their recounting of the incident was too sincere to have been faked. In this matter, her intentions for Seboia are inconsequential.

No one, whether friend or foe, deserves to be touched without their permission. But my determination to weed out the culprits has been thwarted at every turn. Each guard we've interviewed so far not only strongly denied the accusations, but had no recollection of any outsiders entering the city.

Normally in this type of situation I would believe the words of my guards and backtrack to the accuser, but Trip – who doesn't have a dishonest bone in his body – specifically said a guard asked him to escort them from the entrance. I could assume the guards forgot, but Lena isn’t someone you could simply forget.

After much thought, the only plausible explanation I can come up with is that my guards are lying.

Hence my irritation at having to wait over an hour for one of the last remaining guards to grace us with his presence.

A double knock at the door interrupts my turbulent thoughts. “Enter.”

At the turn of the knob, a large, brown haired and brown-eyed shifter fae enters the room. “Captain,” he says in greeting, then nods to both Griffin and Kace. “Commanders.”

"Sit, Ajax," I command.

The boy, only a few years past manhood, pauses at my clipped tone before calmly shutting the door and seating himself in the chair before my desk. "What did you need to see me about, Sir?"

"When you were on duty yesterday, do you recall a group of foreigners entering the city? Their group consisted of three humans and an immortal shifter. They are…" I pause to peer up at the ceiling, searching for the words to best describe the strange party. "They may have seemed a bit odd. Especially the two women."

He chuckles. "I remember them."

Having no patience left to give, I get straight to the point. "Were the women touched inappropriately?"

His eyes drop to my chest, throat bobbing on a swallow as he speaks in a hushed tone. "Yes, Sir."

Clenching my jaw, I ask through gritted teeth, "Did *you* touch them inappropriately?"

His head whips up. "No!"

"Did you attempt to stop the others from violating them?"

"No."

"Did you plan to report this behavior?"

"No."

I stiffen. "Why the *fuck* not?"

He shrugs, his brow pinched. "They handled them just fine on their own."

Wrong answer.

Palms glittering orange, I summon a strand of fire. The flamed thread winds between my fingers as I flatten my palms on the desk and stand. It untwines, slithers down the back of my hand, then races across the desk towards Ajax.

Rising up until it's only an inch from his face, the flame curls into itself and sputters a hiss. A viper preparing to strike.

Ajax warily arches back into his chair, his copper jewels flickering as his gaze hones in on the flamed serpent.

"Your duty as a guard is to protect. Even in the event your skills are unnecessary," I growl. "Yet you did nothing as your fellow guards attempted to *molest,*" my lip curls in a sneer, "unarmed women, and you had no plans to report it."

Bending my arms, I lower my head to his.

"What kind of guard does that make you? What kind of *male*?" I allow the insult to fester before adding, "You may not have participated in the act, but you're just as guilty as the guards who did."

He shows no reaction, his brown eyes bouncing between my furious ones. Searching for what, I don't know, but I don't give a shit either.

Ajax finally speaks. "May I speak frankly, Sir?"

I nod slowly.

He squares his shoulders. "I have reported this type of behavior before. Multiple times. Yet, the guards have never been reprimanded." He shrugs. "I assumed this was acceptable behavior."

Surprised, I straighten. Breaths ripping from my lungs and my heart thumping against my chest, I feel the surge of blood rushing to my head and my temples begin to throb.

Ajax pays no mind to my reaction and continues without pause. "As for allowing such a perversion to take place within my presence? I don't. I was ready to step in when the women handled it themselves." He chuckles. "And they did so beautifully."

Sucking on my teeth, I plop down in my chair, rubbing at the scruff along my jaw. Disinclined to admit my ignorance, but acknowledging to myself the fae deserves the truth, I bite out, "I haven't received any of your reports."

He snorts. "Figures."

Opening a drawer, I pull out a few sheets of parchment and slide them across the desk. "I need you to write down every instance a guard's conduct was abusive, as well as the names of those who sanctioned these activities."

Ajax shuffles forward to the edge of his seat. "Of course." Grabbing a quill, he dips it into the inkpot and begins to write.

Mind cycling from one thought to the next, I drop my head back on the chair and allow the scratching of quill meeting parchment to clear my thoughts and, hopefully, quell my anger. Or at least lessen it.

I've always been what others might say overly aggressive, quick to anger. My mother says it comes from my human half, while Aurora believes it's from all the fire in my blood.

They're both wrong. It's a Gods Blessing.

Necessary tools bestowed by the gods themselves to a child who was destined since conception to be despised. Armor forged from anger gave me the strength to emotionally survive in a world inhospitable for a half-breed bastard such as myself, and aggression gave me the power to dominate those who refuse to accept me as I am.

Strength and power are the only deterrents in this world, and mine is unparalleled.

In more ways than one.

Opening my eyes to half mast, I find Ajax still scribbling away. Reaching forward, I grasp the file I was reading before his arrival and flip it open, scanning past the charcoal drawing of Ajax's likeness until I reach his test scores.

Magics: Highly Gifted

Sword work: Exceptionally Gifted

Hand to Hand Combat: Exceptionally Gifted

Archery: Moderately Gifted

Blade Combat: Exceptionally Gifted

Analytical Thinking: Profoundly Gifted

His scores take me by surprise. Very few immortals have ever tested as well as him, and never has a fae. He even received the best possible score in Analytical Thinking. Besides myself, the only other person alive to have received it is Griffin.

He should've been promoted ages ago. Why wasn't I notified of this?

Scanning the rest of his file, I see he's requested to be transferred on multiple occasions due to altercations between him and other guards but was denied each time.

Dropping my gaze further down the parchment, I grind my teeth when I discover the number of times he's been sent to the whipping post as punishment.

In several of those instances, he received more than ten lashes. I've rarely issued such a severe punishment, typically assigning no more than five lashes at a time, yet he's received double that on multiple occasions.

The crisscrossed scars slashed across my back twinge in remembrance of my own floggings. I roll my shoulders, searching for the name of the superior officer who signed off on these reports.

Lieutenant Jareth.

A growl rumbles through my chest at the sight of his name. Although I can't say I'm surprised.

"Here," Ajax says, his arm extended with the completed report.

With a growing suspicion, I snatch it out of his hand and skim through its contents, searching for the names of the commanding guards with whom he filed his reports. I bite out a curse when my suspicions are confirmed.

All under Jareth's command.

My stomach flips onto itself as I wade deeper into his statement, churning faster and faster as I learn of occasion after occasion of the guards' mistreatment of our people until it's nothing but a wild, acidic roil.

Feeling bile rise in the back of my throat, I swallow convulsively but force myself to continue, to read every depraved act in which my guards participated. To channel my disgust into a white-hot rage, blistering my lungs and scorching my veins.

Reading the last incident, my fury peaks and my palms burst into flames at Ajax's retelling of Jareth torturing a child. A human child. Even immortals and fae who despise humans would never torture someone so young.

Tossing the report onto the desk before it can ignite, I grip the arms of my chair and attempt to restrain myself from hunting down each and every culprit Ajax listed. But then an image flashes before my eyes. A glassy eyed, screaming Lena struggling to fight off my guards.

Rage blazes into me, razing through my heart and lungs, igniting my blood. My biceps bulge, veins thicken and throb, and my nostrils flare as I inhale the rising smoke from the crackling and inflamed wood where my shimmering palms burn and splinter the arms of the chair.

"Sir?" Ajax asks, fear tightening his lips and the creases near his eyes, but he still boldly holds my gaze.

It's his fear that begins to calm me, slowing my breaths and cooling my blood. Not completely, but enough to where it's more manageable. Because it's not Ajax's fear I want. It's Jareth's and every other male like him.

Exhaling a steadying breath, I say, "You've done well, considering the circumstances."

Ajax's eyes widen. "Thank you, Sir."

"I know all of this," I wave my hands over the desk, "has

affected you negatively, but I'm afraid it'll continue to do so. But know this: every male you've listed will face the consequences of their actions. I have no intention of releasing your name, but it'll be obvious that you were my informant."

He smiles. "I'm not concerned."

"The backlash could be severe," I warn.

He laughs, swiping his hands through his hair.

"I don't care. Do whatever it is you need to do to fix this, and I'll take any repercussions gladly."

Liking him more and more with each passing second, and suspecting that he could do great things if under the proper tutelage, an idea crosses my mind.

Choosing not to dwell on it too much, I decide to trust my instincts.

"Ajax, I'm removing you from your unit. Once you leave here, you're to go directly to the barracks and transfer your possessions to the Commander's quarters. From now on, you'll report only to Commander Griffin or Commander Kace. "

Shock crosses his face before it quickly twists into a scowl. "With all due respect, Sir, I didn't become a guard so others could protect me. I became one to protect others."

"And *I* don't recruit guards that I have no intention of protecting." Seeing his dubious expression, I add, "But that's not the only reason. You should have been promoted long ago. Since your skills exceed anyone below a Commander, this would be a more beneficial assignment."

He eyes me for a moment longer before giving a reluctant, "Yes, Sir."

I nod his dismissal and he stands, heading towards the door. "Ajax?"

He pauses over the threshold and glances at me over his shoulder.

"Tell Lennox I wish to see Lieutenant Jareth immediately. He's to collect him himself."

A smirk quirks his lips. "Yes sir."

When the door clicks shut, I slam my palms down on my desk, the inkpot toppling over from the impact. I pinch the bridge of my nose and slouch back in my chair, the cindered arms crumbling with the motion.

Kace reaches for the report. Eyes sweeping across the parchment, his expression darkens the more he reads.

"Son of a bitch!" he snarls, passing the document to Griffin before pressing his knuckles into the desk, his brown hair slipping past his shoulder to partially shield his face. "I don't give a fuck whose blood Jareth shares. I'll strangle the piece of shit!"

Gripping the edge of the desk, he hangs his head.

"He burned a Godsdamn child. Branded him like cattle." Shoving off, he clasps his hands on the top of his head, his emerald jewels flickering as he shakes his head in disbelief.

I say nothing in response.

"He's right, Darius," Griffin says, tossing the statement onto the desk. "This can't go unpunished."

"I know."

At another knock at the door, both males expressions clear of all emotions and resume their positions beside me.

"Enter."

A guard cracks the door open and peeks inside. "Captain, I have Lieutenant Jareth here as you requested."

"Bring him in."

Lennox opens the door further and turns to the side. When I see the cocky motherfucker strut like a peacock into my office, I feel nothing but loathing.

With a practiced smile, Jareth raises both arms in greeting.

"Captain! How kind of you to request my presence. It's been too long, old friend."

Disregarding protocol, he seats himself without permission in the chair Ajax just vacated.

"I was just telling Theon the other day how you haven't been to court in ages." He chuckles, an arrogant, breathy sound that raises my hackles. "Of course, he mentioned how you despise such events, but I told him that's no excuse for avoiding your friends."

Friends, my ass.

Wanting nothing more than to knock that ridiculous smile off his face, I instead study the entitled little shit who tormented me throughout childhood and all the way into adulthood.

Even when I eventually began to transition into manhood and grew stronger and more powerful than him, he still believed I'd be willing to take his shit. But after beating him within an inch of his life, he realized his old tactics would only result in pain and embarrassment.

My mother was furious with me for walloping the son of one of the highest members of court, and it took weeks to recover from the lashings I received as punishment, but I have no regrets.

Unable to forget his humiliation at my hands and incapable of besting me in strength or power, Jareth had to find more creative ways to dole out his cruelty. But cruel he is, even if it isn't as obvious to those who didn't know him as well as I do.

Knowing full well he never grew out of his habitual need to terrorize those more vulnerable than him, I knew he wouldn't be a good fit for the Cascadonian Guards. Which is why I denied his application.

His father – Lord Kanus – caused quite a scene when he stomped into my office demanding I reverse my decision. When I refused, I have no shame in admitting I howled in laughter at his shocked expression. After all, he's just as awful as his son, if not more so.

I thought the issue was resolved when Kanus stormed from my office, sputtering profanities the entire way, but I should've known they wouldn't accept my rejection gracefully.

After I dismissed her father, Princess Kiora went to her husband – my brother, Prince Theon – and demanded he give Jareth entry. Theon, always overly indulgent to his bitch of a wife, went over my head and ordered the processing of Jareth's application. Even going so far as promoting him to Lieutenant despite my protests.

From the moment I was forced to authorize Jareth's enlistment, I knew he would be an issue. But I never thought it would get this far without my knowledge.

"Jareth, this isn't a social visit," I bite out. "I've recently received some serious allegations against you."

"These allegations are…?" he asks, seeming unsurprised.

Leafing through Ajax's statement, I list off all his crimes.

"Mistreatment of guards under your command. Falsifying reports. Whipping a fae without cause. Sexually assaulting females and women."

Losing my composure, I clench the parchment tightly, crinkling it as I growl.

"Burning and branding a human child with your insignia ring. *Disfiguring* him for life." I slap the parchment onto the desk and grit my teeth. "Basically, participating in all types of illegal activities when your sole purpose as a guard is to uphold these very same laws. A male within my command is supposed to be a protector for *all* the people, including fae and humans, but is instead terrorizing and striking fear into our most vulnerable citizens."

"You've always been so righteous," he mumbles. He crosses

one leg over the other and adopts a bored expression. “These accusations are false, and I'm deeply offended.”

“I doubt that.”

“Who made these ridiculous allegations?”

I remain silent.

With an audible sigh as if this whole conversation is nothing but an inconvenience, he says, “I have a right to know who's slandering my name.”

“Only if I wish it,” I state coldly. “And I don't.”

Jareth narrows his eyes. “I'll find out one way or another.”

Disregarding his threat, I carry on.

“These charges cannot go unpunished.”

His expression hardens to stone, searching my eyes for mercy or weakness. I can see the exact moment he realizes he won't receive any. He sits back in his chair and relaxes his posture.

“You have no proof.”

I smirk. “I don't need any.”

The dumbass really must believe he's untouchable because he huffs a laugh, a taunting smile spreading across his face.

“Oh, pray tell, your high and mighty bastard prince, what punishment will you give me?” He places a palm to his chest. “I am brother by marriage to the heir to the throne. His wife’s *adored* brother.”

“Theon is not yet King, and your sister not yet Queen. They have no power over my decisions.”

Jareth’s face reddens and I stifle a smile as I nod to Kace. He walks to the door and cracks it open, whispering to the guards stationed out in the hall.

Once the whispers cut off, Kace resumes his position beside me and Jareth’s face drains of all color when he glances over his shoulder, seeing three guards along with Lennox file in behind him.

Tone cold and unyielding, I sentence, "Lieutenant Jareth, you will pay three months of your earnings to all your victims."

His mouth pinches and I hold in a laugh at his outraged expression.

"In addition to any expenses for those with extensive health related issues, including lost wages as a result of your assaults."

"I'm not paying shit!" he spits venomously. "This is absurd. I never touched an immortal. And no one gives a fuck about the fae or humans anyway." His gaze purposefully swiveling to Kace, he sneers, "They're filthy and pathetic. No better than animals."

I slam my hands on the desk and Jareth blanches, cowering into his seat as I rise slowly to my feet, lowering my head towards his until we're almost nose to nose.

"The only pathetic creature in this kingdom is *you.* You're weak, narrow minded, and cruel." I express every ounce of loathing and disdain I have for the cowardly male with a sneer. "You're worth less than the shit I scrape off my boot. Nothing but a piss stain on this great kingdom."

I grip the desk with all my might, listening to the crack of wood as I crush the edges of the thousands of years-old oak.

"I'm tempted to kill you myself."

And I would without a second thought if he was anybody else.

Watching him as I slowly lower myself back down to my seat, I clasp my hands together with a smirk.

"Lastly, you'll receive ten lashes before being imprisoned for a minimum of a fortnight."

Regaining some of his courage, Jareth's face turns to scarlet, the vein in his forehead thumping in tune with his rage.

I jerk a nod, a silent command to my guards, and Kace, Griffin, and I watch in silence as they close in on him.

Jareth's head swivels toward the approaching guards, his glare quickly turning to panic.

As Lennox reaches for him, his eyes flash and he suddenly shoots to his feet, raising blue, glittering palms and blasting a shot of air at us… only for his power to be swept up in the cyclone of air that I summoned a split second before he attacked.

Arms extended, chest heaving, and his face dripping with sweat, Jareth fights tooth and nail against the raging winds I conjure while my breathing remains even and steady, almost bored.

His power battles pitifully against my own and his hands glow brighter, desperately searching for his last reserves, until he can take no more and the power slips from his grasp. His palms dim and his hands fall to his knees, then his head bows as he gasps for air.

Remaining that way until his laboring breaths eventually slow, he then cautiously lifts only his head, eyeing me timidly.

Before he can utter a single word, I whip up a glittering orange palm and a braided rope made of fire streaks towards him, coiling around his neck all the way down to his feet.

Rising to my feet, I stroll towards Jareth until I'm only a finger's breadth away, glowering down at the pitiful excuse as he wails and sobs.

Watching him thrash against his binds that give him not an inch, seeing his skin char beneath the flames, my lips curl into a cruel smile, euphoria filling me as I relish in his suffering.

Unwilling to wait until he screams himself hoarse, I snap my palm shut into a fist and I suck the air from his lungs.

His screams cut off mid-shriek and the room silences all but the shuffling of his clothes as he grapples with his binds. Eyes widening, his struggles become more fevered when he gulps for air that will not come.

Instantly forgetting his pain, he focuses on the direst of issues: his body's need for oxygen.

"You may have thought yourself to be untouchable, but you're not. You mock how feared I am, but you seem to have forgotten why." I bare my teeth on a growl. "Why to corrupt assholes like you, my name is nothing but a frightened whisper. Why they would rather die at their own hands than dare to suffer my rage. Why they call me the *Gods Wrath*."

I wrap one hand around his throat, the fire causing me no pain as I squeeze.

"It's not because I can crush a skull with my bare hands, or that I could cut down even the strongest of warriors before they can even reach for their blade. That's not what terrifies them. It's my *power*, Jareth."

I raise my other arm. "Water." Water spreads beneath my hand on his throat, spiraling into a stream that crawls upward, encircling his head.

"Nature." Wood cracks as gnarled branches sprout from the floor to skewer through his wrists. His lips round on a silent scream, blood flowing down his forearms to drip onto the floor.

"Air." His shirt flaps, blonde hair whipping into the whistling winds as a tornado spirals around us.

"Fire." Glittering orange flames bloom within the tornado, the orange paling as the flames grow hotter and hotter, morphing into a monstrous beast of white-blue blaze, devouring the winds as it evolves into a twisting, raging inferno that can incinerate with a touch.

"You immortals boast about the strength of your power, but all I see is how fragile you are. How *weak*. You're feeble in your most dominant Gift, and barely have a speck of power in the others."

I laugh, a cruel, bellowing sound.

"Oh, how easy it would be for me to conquer you all." I squeeze his throat tighter and increase the heat, watching him squirm as an imprint of my hand slowly brands his neck. Being an immortal, he'll heal eventually, but not before all will see the shamed mark of his subjugation. “You see, I'm not dominant in just one.” My lips draw back into a snarl. “I’m dominant in *all.*”

When I see his dirt brown eyes roll back into his head, I return his breaths to him before he loses consciousness. Before he can make a sound, thorned vines sprout from my palm, slithering onto his face to twine around the lower half of his head. Roses and thorns bloom into his mouth, muting anymore of those pathetic sounds.

Gagged by roses, he trembles and cries while blood dribbles from where the thorns puncture his mouth and cheeks. Hearing a trickling sound, I peer down and see moisture spreading across the groin of his trousers, darkening where he's pissed himself.

“I'm the most powerful immortal that's ever existed,” I growl. “My power is absolute. Nothing other than the gods can match me. That means I can do anything I want to whomever I want, and there's not a being alive who can do a damn thing about it.” His trembling becomes more pronounced and his knees give out, the fiery rope bearing his weight. “It’s taking everything in me to hold back my flames. To not burn you slowly until you’re nothing but charred bones in vengeance for the boy you tortured.”

Reaching down, I yank off the ring he used to brand the child, passing it over my shoulder to Griffin, who plucks it from my grasp.

“Now you're going to stop your whining and crying, your empty threats, and you're going to cooperate. If not, I'd love nothing more than to kill you this very moment. The world would be a better place without you in it.”

He nods frantically and I turn my back on him, the twister dissolving as I stride back towards my desk and lower myself into my chair. To the view of Jareth's slumped form and bowed head, I flick my hand and the flamed rope and vines disintegrate into a spray of sparks. He slumps to the floor and the guards rush toward him.

Watching them drag Jareth's motionless body all the way to the whipping post, a barbaric elation fills me and my lips curl into a savage grin.

CHAPTER 8

LENA

Lips trembling and her eyes glassy with unshed tears, Amara places a palm to her chest and sucks in an audible breath. "It's…" She shakes her head with a watery chuckle. "I have no words. They're all s beautiful."

I snort. "You're such a drama queen."

She narrows her eyes. "Fuck off!"

My comments already forgotten, she moves further into the room, stopping to spin in a slow circle, whiskey eyes darting from one item to the next.

I pass my own gaze over the shop, seeing dirks, broadswords, short swords, scythes, and axes, as well as any other blade you could possibly imagine. All artistically displayed from ceiling to floor, covering every inch of available space on the white walls of Rory's Swords and Daggers. Near the back of the storefront, Amara looks like a kid in a sweets shop as she flattens her nose and both palms against the clear pane of the wrap-around glass casing, ogling some of Aurora's finer creations. Eyes straying past that, I find a hutch pressed up against the back wall, displaying her less lethal creations. Nails, horseshoes, and locks are scattered chaotically across its shelves, a stark contrast to the otherwise well-organized room.

Tristan brushes past me, poking his head through the archway off to the side.

“There's more in here,” he says, tossing a thumb over his shoulder.

Amara bites her fist and squeals in glee, and I laugh at the sight. It's comical how one of the toughest women I know can be brought to tears over a few blades.

If a suitor was to offer her gold and jewels, she'd gut the fucker for insinuating she was a whore who could be bought with trinkets.

But bring her a pretty sword or dagger, and she'd fall to her knees and have him cumming down her throat in less than a minute.

I don't know if Amara will ever drop her guard enough to fall in love, but if she does, one thing’s for certain. He'll have to come to terms with the fact that her first true love will forever be made of steel.

Off to the side of the hutch, a black curtain sways on copper rings in an entryway that I assume leads to a workspace. A slender hand draws back the black curtain and a beaming Aurora appears.

Draped in a soot-covered apron over dark leggings and a tunic, her hair is pinned in a knot atop her head, bouncing with her motions as she rolls up her sleeves and glides in our direction.

The princess clearly balks at traditional garb, but she could be wearing a burlap sack and still no one could mistake her for anything but royalty.

Clasping her hands together, Aurora quickly moves to greet us but stumbles and grunts when Amara throws herself at her, tossing her arms around Aurora in a crushing hug.

“Your work’s amazing.” Pulling back, Amara squeezes her shoulders. “I thought I’d come here and it would all be shit, but it’s not!” She steps back and punches the princess in the arm. “I guess princesses *can* do more than push out babies.”

Aurora shoots me a bewildered look as she rubs the soreness out of her shoulder. “Thank you?”

“No, thank *you*.”

Glancing at a silent Tristan leaning against the archway, I nod imperceptibly and he slips into the adjoining room as I join the two females.

"I'm so glad you both came!" Aurora says, clapping her hands. "I didn't know if you were just being kind or if you were really going to, but I'm so happy you did!"

She's adorable.

"Of course, we came, sweetie," I reply.

I didn't know it was possible, but her smile spreads further at my endearment.

"Come on back." She waves us over, walking backward. "I brought out a few pieces I've been working on."

Aurora and Amara race away and quickly slip past the curtain.

Following at a more sedate pace, I listen to the clink of copper rings as I slide back the black fabric, revealing an astonishingly large workspace.

The cavernous room is as tall as the front of the shop, but it extends much wider. The walls are made of the same gray slate I've seen from some of the older buildings in the city, and a burning forge is off to the side, connected to a chute that rises between massive wood beams all the way to the top of the cathedral ceiling.

A barrel of water is only a few paces away from the forge, placed next to an anvil that reveals its age with numerous dents and scratches. Metal tongs, hammers, chisels, and various other tools of which I have no clue of their purpose are scattered throughout the room.

I find both females huddled around a weathered wood table, inspecting a small dagger.

Rounding the table, I toss one leg over the bench and sit while I examine the array of weapons. Aurora has placed several daggers, an axe, a scimitar, and a khopesh across a discolored beige cloth.

You can see how Aurora's designs differ from a traditional blacksmith's work.

They seem lighter and more delicate, but no less deadly, and each one has its own distinctive, artistic twist. Not feminine, per se, just more visually appealing.

All her pieces are absolutely stunning and unique in their own right, but my eyes keep snapping back to the khopesh.

Lifting the sword, I twirl it as I inspect the hook of the steel blade. Deceptively slim, the blade appears as if it could barely cut through butter, but after applying pressure between my thumb and forefinger, it's obvious its thinness is deceptive.

The slim steel is stronger than most broadswords I've handled, and I imagine I could sever clean through a person's neck with very little effort on my part.

Placing my palms flat beneath, I bob it up and down, barely registering its weight.

Eyes downcast, Aurora pulls loose threads from the frayed cloth. "It's not complete. I'm still working on the hilt and I think I made it a bit too heavy."

I snort.

"If you made it any lighter, it'd disappear." Waiting until she meets my gaze, I smile. "Aurora, this is brilliant."

"You think so?"

"I do."

Flipping it end over end, I catch it by the hilt.

"It's well balanced, light, and the steel of it is surprisingly strong. It's extraordinary. You're very talented."

She blushes and averts her gaze, but I can see the pride in her eyes. "If you like that, you should look at this."

She reaches for the axe and lifts it up by its hickory handle, paying no mind to me or anyone else as she prattles away.

Tristan slips silently between the curtains without stirring a clink from a single ring. When I catch his gaze, he disappointingly, but unsurprisingly, shakes his head.

Unaware of Tristan's presence, Aurora taps the edge of the axe's blade as he falls in behind her.

"Now, to get this dark shade of purple, I wanted to use the forge, but the heat was too inconsistent. So, I quickly scrapped that idea and instead, I used my Gif – aaaah!"

Startled by Tristan's sudden appearance, she spins and swings the axe up over her head. As she arcs downward, Tristan, thankfully, has the wherewithal to seize the handle before it impales his skull.

I slap a hand to my mouth, smothering a shocked laugh, Amara doing the same.

Aurora freezes with the axe poised above his head, her expression that of horror.

"Uriella's Light! I almost killed you!"

That horror suddenly contorts into a panicked rage.

"You shouldn't sneak up on someone handling a weapon!"

Unfazed, he chuckles.

"I'll admit it was a close call. Here, why don't I take this?"

Aurora nods frantically and he pulls it from her grasp, his brown, almost black eyes sweeping over it appraisingly.

"What's this here?"

She looks at me with a confused expression.

"It's an axe. You cut things with it." She stacks fisted hands above her head and mimes slicing downward. "Like to chop wood, or to cut off someone's head, or-"

"Obviously," he cuts in dryly, extending it outward and spinning the handle. "Did you make this?"

Aurora nods.

"The craftsmanship is exquisite." Tristan steps back, mimicking a few practice swings before examining it more closely. "How much would you like for it?"

Her smile falls.

"Oh! Well… it's actually a commissioned piece," she says, then adds quickly, "but I'd be more than happy to create another one."

Adjusting his grip, he swipes a few more times before standing upright and passing it back to her.

"Please, I'd love to have one for myself."

"Of course! Do you have any special requests?"

Tristan strokes a finger along the hickory handle. Aurora watches him, intently following the path. When she sees me watching her, she bites her lip and blushes.

"No, I wouldn't want to disrupt your vision," Tristan says, dropping his hand to his side and stepping back. "Your work really is remarkable."

She smiles at his praise.

"Oh, no, it won't take anything away. If any of your suggestions did, I'd advise you differently."

Staring at the axe, he taps his chin and nods. "Alright, then." He scans the room. "Do you have anything to write with?"

Shuffling her feet, Aurora stares down at the floor.

"Maybe we could discuss it over dinner? Tomorrow night?"

Tristan lifts the cloth and pulls out a loose leaf of parchment hidden beneath.

"I wouldn't want to put you out like that. It'll only take a moment. If I could just find something to write with," he mumbles to himself.

Spotting a charcoal stick, he snatches it up and begins to write.

"Uhhh…." Aurora's mouth rounds as if to speak, but she can't find the words. Snapping it shut, her face pinches in determination. "It's no trouble at all. I insist."

Tristan is one of the most intelligent men I know, but when it comes to the female gender, he tends to be a bit dense.

Tristan's cheeks puff out and he blows on the parchment to remove charcoal shavings, passing it to Aurora with an oblivious smile. “No need. Everything I need is right here.”

“Thank you,” she mumbles, grabbing the vellum from him.

“Alura’s tits!” Amara rolls her eyes. “She's interested in you, you idiot.”

“You’re interested in me?” he asks Aurora, his brows knitted together.

Aurora curls an errant piece of hair behind her ear and nods.

Always so suspicious, he narrows his eyes. “Why?”

Amara slaps her head onto the table, and we both groan at his response.

“You seem interesting and you're attractive.” Avoiding his gaze, Aurora looks down at her hands while picking at her nails. “I just thought it could be fun.”

He stiffens, blinking rapidly. “Huh.”

Amara groans again, a long, drawn-out sound as she drags her hands across her face, comically stretching the skin of her cheeks.

I laugh and lightly smack her arm. “Stop it.”

Face resting between her palms and wide eyes she asks, “How can he be so oblivious?”

“He just isn't used to female attention,” I defend weakly. “He's always with Zander, and most females are too googly-eyed over him to notice how attractive Tristan is.”

He huffs, “I'm standing right here, you know.”

“We know,” Amara and I say in unison.

Blowing out an irritated breath, Tristan faces Aurora, his ears pinkening as his stare skims the top of her head. “Dinner sounds wonderful.”

Lifting her gaze, Aurora shows all her teeth in a blinding smile that he quickly mirrors. “Perfect.”

“Aww,” Amara coos. “They’re so cute.”

“Absolutely adorable.”

Tristan shoots us a glare and I lean to the side, whisper-yelling to Amara.

“I think we're embarrassing him.”

“Definitely.”

She raises a finger, drawing a circle in the air.

“See how red his face is getting? He looks like he's having a stroke.”

He growls and it finally hits me that we should probably stop talking.

The bell at the front of the store rings and boots thunk in our direction.

Aurora moves to greet the visitor, but when a large hand peels the curtain back and Darius walks through, she returns her attention to Tristan.

Ever since I left Darius last night, I tried convincing myself that he wasn't *that* attractive. That I had imagined this connection, this longing. But as soon as he fills the entryway and I meet those glacial blue eyes, I realize how wrong I was as every emotion I felt the night before slams back into me.

Heart racing with a hum that ripples beneath my skin, confusion and trepidation wars with desire as my pussy pulsates and swells from an irrational, almost animalistic need.

But along with that want, along with that raging desire, something else appears. Something that is neither wanted nor needed, something I could have never foreseen.

I suck in a shocked breath when a crackling sensation suddenly spreads throughout my chest.

Recognizing the feeling for what it is, helplessness and horror fills me as that sensation quickly roots and braids beneath my breast, twining into an electrified cord that suddenly springs out towards Darius, attaching beneath his chest.

A cosmic link. An unbreakable bond.

Well, it's unbreakable as far as I know since I haven't a clue as to how to break one.

That's not a question I ever thought to ask since all the bonds I've already formed with others were intended to be permanent. But with those, I chose to initiate them, whereas with this one, I certainly did not.

Never would have with someone I just met. But that's not even the most glaring difference between this connection and the others.

It's the feeling of arousal the tether blasts into me, strumming into my chest and electrifying my nerves as it travels until there's not a part of my body that's been untouched by the intoxicating, yet disconcerting sensation.

And I'm beyond grateful in this moment that I never had a similar reaction with the other links I've formed.

That would have made awkward dinner conversation.

A burst of laughter rips from me, an unflattering, panicked garble that has Tristan, Aurora, and Amara staring at me as if I've gone mad.

I swallow back the laughter and clear my throat. "I just remembered something funny."

They give me another confused glance, then return to their discussion.

Alright, it's not that bad. It's just a connection, nothing more.

I must have somehow initiated it without realizing what I was doing.

Another troubling thought suddenly enters my mind, piling atop this colossal mound of horseshit.

I shut my eyes, searching within myself for that hated, but vital iron cage, and sigh in relief once determining the bars are still intact.

So, I didn't lose control, thankfully, but it still doesn't explain how the bond came to be, and that's even more unnerving.

Wondering if Darius can feel the bond like I do, I flit my gaze to him and I no longer have to wonder.

Jaw locked and nostrils flaring, his lust-filled gaze burns into my own, searing me to my very core. When his fingers curl into the wood of the entryway, I can see the veins in his forearms thicken with restraint, and I know he feels it, too.

At least I think he does, until he drags his eyes towards the table and spots the weapons scattered across the top.

His face shutters and hardens, the flames in his eyes icing over. Pushing off the entryway, he stalks towards us.

"Outsiders are forbidden to carry weapons in the city."

At the sound of his gravelly voice, a zing travels straight to my clit and I inwardly whimper.

I guess I didn't imagine the sound of his voice, either.

"Piss off," Aurora says, slapping her hands to her hips. "They're just looking. Besides, it's nice to have someone appreciate my work."

He gives her an exasperated look.

"I appreciate your work. You know I do."

She scoffs.

"If you did, you wouldn't be in talks with Arcadia to replenish the Guard's weaponry."

Amara gasps and stabs the dagger into the table.

"How could you do that? She's your sister!"

Ignoring Amara, Darius folds his arms over his chest.

"I've told you, Rory. You don't have the staff to produce at the volume I need."

"And I told *you*, if I had a contract, I could hire help," Aurora retorts.

He rubs the back of his head, sighing as if he's had the same argument a thousand times before.

"I would if I could, but Mother wants Arcadia to be our sole supplier. It'll help strengthen relations with Queen Celene."

"Of course, she does," Aurora says bitterly, fiddling with the edge of a dagger's blade. "Just another one of her political games."

Slapping the dagger down on the table, she rounds on Darius.

"You know my work is better than theirs."

He lays an arm across her shoulders and presses a soft kiss to the side of her head. "Far superior."

If I hadn't been seated already, I would've swooned at the sight of the gruff male giving such tender affection.

"Hmph."

Aurora pouts for a moment, then glances up at Darius with her brows knitted together.

"What are you doing here, anyway? I thought you'd be stuck in the tower all day."

"There's a..." His words trail off as he glances at me stonily. "Situation."

I shuffle in my seat, uncomfortable with how cold his eyes are now compared to how they were just minutes ago. The lust within me, although still present, has lessened the longer the siblings have been speaking.

With the way he's looking at me now, it's practically nonexistent, even though I can still feel our link throbbing in my chest.

It's not real, I imagined it. Or I finally lost my godsdamn mind, which is quite plausible, if I'm being honest with myself.

"That sounds ominous." Aurora pulls away from him, concern marring her features as he drops his arm from her shoulders. "What kind of situation?"

He side eyes me before meeting her stare. “It's not something I wish to speak about in front of *outsiders*,” he sneers.

I inwardly jolt at the verbal slap. I know he doesn't know me or trust me and, truth be told, he shouldn't. But the way he said *outsider* was clearly slung as a barb. I wrack my brain for what I could've done to upset him from the time he walked in the door to now.

For anything that could excuse such rudeness, but I find nothing. Confusion and, ridiculously, a pinch of hurt sours my stomach.

Seeing the flat expression on Aurora’s face, I can tell I'm not the only one who perceived it that way.

“Well, it'll have to wait.” She turns her back on him, dismissing him in the process, and faces me, giving me such a sincere smile that I can't help but return it, regardless of my current emotional state. “I'm visiting with my new friends.”

Shoving aside Darius' comments, I ask Aurora, “Do you mind if I take a look around? I was hoping to stock up on a few items.”

“Go right ahead.”

“Are you daft?” Darius bites out. “I just said outsiders are forbidden to carry weapons.”

“I heard you just fine,” I snap, hurt and confusion swiftly morphing to anger. “I’ll purchase them now, but pick them up when we *leave*.”

“Asshole,” Amara mutters.

“Of course, you can,” Aurora says with a strained smile, pointing towards the curtains. “Head to the front and you'll see an archway on the right. That's where I stock the nicer items.”

I try to return her smile, but I'm sure it comes off more as a grimace. “Thanks, Aurora.” I toss my leg over the bench, refusing to look at Darius as I pass by.

As I draw back the curtain, I search for the bond that connects me to him, the bond I'm now sure more than ever is only a hallucination, and realize it no longer feels like a euphoric tether, but a weighty chain.

CHAPTER 9

DARIUS

"She won't be spreading her legs for you anytime soon," Amara says in a flat tone. "If ever."

Without a doubt.

Aware of my vulnerabilities to Lena's charms, I promised myself I wouldn't allow her presence to cloud my judgment any longer. With Griffin's ominous prediction and remembering how strange and secretive she and her companions are, I can't allow lust or attraction to blind me to the threat they may pose. No matter how intense that attraction may be.

But all promises were tossed aside the moment I spotted her straddling that bench. All I could think about was stripping her bare for her to straddle me just the same. Legs locked around my waist. Black rippled tresses draped over my chest. Pillowy red lips moaning my name. My hands warmed at the thought of squeezing her plump ass as I bounce her dripping cunt down on my cock.

Utterly transfixed, I saw nothing but her. Until I caught a glimpse out of the corner of my eye of Amara twirling a dagger. Libido doused at the sight, I tore my gaze from Lena's to the view of all these unknowns armed in the presence of my sister. How easy would it be for one of them to grab a knife and plunge it into her chest? Not difficult at all, given the situation. I wouldn't have noticed, and I doubt I would've reacted in time.

Lena’s effect on me is all-consuming and deeply unsettling. I hadn’t even spoken a word to her and she had already managed to suck me in with those bewitching eyes, the world disappearing for all but the two of us. For someone who’s unused to blundering, I’m furious at myself for failing so miserably.

Dragging my gaze from the swaying curtains, I turn to face the others, only to meet Amara’s cold glare. One ankle crossed over the other, she leans a hip against the table while dragging the tip of a dagger across her palm, eyeing me as if she wishes to gut me with it.

“Did I say I wanted to spread her legs?” I bark, both of us well aware I'm full of shit.

She scoffs, tapping the flat side of the blade to her temple. “I've got eyes, don't I?”

Aurora shoves my shoulder, drawing my gaze to her. “Go apologize.”

“For what?” I ask, purposely obtuse.

Hovering behind Aurora – a little too close for my liking – Tristan folds his arms over his chest and arches a single brow. “For being a dick.”

Stepping forward, I slowly lower my head over Aurora’s shoulder, staring him dead in the eyes. “I wasn't a dick.”

Tristan’s eyes flash in response, a thunder roiling within as he meets my challenging stare with one of his own.

Try it, cocksucker.

Meeting Lena, dealing with Ajax, all the drama with Jareth, and now this? It's too much. My mind has been an unmanageable frenzy of chaos, darting from one heightened emotion to the next for too long without reprieve, and I'm a hair's breadth away from snapping. My desperation for control pleads for a release that'll level me out, but that can only be achieved in one of two ways: Fucking or fighting. Since the only person I want to fuck is Lena and that's out of the question, a fight it is. Based on Tristan's expression, he's in need of one himself.

A shot of excitement shoots through my veins when I meet his hostile gaze that all but guarantees a dirty brawl. He's human, and normally I wouldn't entertain the idea, but the volatility roiling within me makes me consider an exception.

I'll just rein it in a bit.

But before I can lift so much as a finger, Aurora slaps her hands to my chest and shoves me back, expunging all thoughts of a fight in an instant. "You called her daft."

"It was an honest mistake."

Disliking my answer, Aurora plants her fists on her hips, skewering me with the same evil-eyed glare that forced me to confess all my deepest, darkest secrets as a child.

Born a half-breed, everyone assumed my human blood would dilute my immortal one, ignorantly believing my power would be weakened and therefore, I'd be an easy target. So, they challenged me and I answered. I fought, I bled, and I dominated every motherfucker who thought they could stand against me. Earning my rank through blood, sweat, and tears, my reputation of ruthless brutality was cemented with every victory, and whispers quickly spread of the merciless *Gods Wrath*. I took no part in fabricating the title, but I thrived under the potent moniker.

I was relentless and vicious, and as I aged, my power became more absolute, indomitable. For no one could stand against me. Anyone who dared is either dead or wishes they were. Which is why when I say there's not much in this world that scares me, it's the truth. But seeing my sister pissed off at me like she is at the moment? Well, she's a bit frightening, to say the least. Aurora may look small and meek, but beneath that mask of sweetness, she's a crazy bitch.

"Maybe, but you didn't need to insult her," Aurora retorts, poking me in between my pecs. "Go. Apologize."

There comes a time in every male's life when he realizes if he ever wants to keep his balls, he can't fold to every demand brought to him by the females in his life. With how loathsome the idea of apologizing to Lena is, it seems that time for me is now.

I square my shoulders. "I'm not apologizing."

Dropping her head back, Aurora meets my gaze with her narrowed one. "Yes. You. Are."

Gods, she's terrifying. Hold strong!

Ducking my head until we're nose to nose, I say with steel in my voice, "No."

Unused to my defiance, Aurora blinks several times in surprise before blowing out a defeated sigh, cupping my cheek.

Annnd that's how you put a female in her place!

Feeling pride as well as an embarrassing amount of relief, I don't hesitate in returning her now-saccharine grin as she brushes her fingers through my hair. Until her smile shrivels to puckered lips and she yanks on my ear.

"Fuck, Aurora!"

"That is *not* how you speak to ladies." She clucks her tongue. "I raised you better than that!"

I try to pry her fingers away, but her hand is like a fucking vice. Crouched above the floor, I whip my arms up in defeat. "I'm sorry! I didn't mean it!"

"Darius Lesdanas, you're going to march your ass out there right now and apologize to her, or so help me gods, little brother, I'll tell the entire court your dick is covered in sores!"

"Fine! Just let go!"

She twists my ear one last time and I yelp before she shoves me away. "Go. *Now*," Aurora orders, pointing toward the front of the shop.

“I’m not leaving you alone with them,” I reply, my narrowed eyes darting between the two foreigners while rubbing my ear.

“Darius!”

Enraged but not stupid, I force myself to turn away. “Fuck it, I'm gone!”

Whipping back the curtains, my boot steps echo throughout the shop as I hurriedly tromp past the door to the loft upstairs, the display case to my left, the white stone walls decorated with swords and daggers, only to slow my steps once nearing the archway when I hear something odd, something out of place and unexpected in a blacksmith's shop.

Cocking my head to the side, I try to identify the source, but it's too quiet for me to be sure. It's almost as if someone’s playing an instrument or singing, but the melody is muffled somehow, almost imperceptible. Careful to quiet my steps, I peer around the archway and freeze midstep, struck dumb at the sight and sound of Lena humming to herself.

Her tone is rich but sweet, with a melodic rasp that's elegant yet slightly rough. Her song has no words, but it doesn't need any. I can feel the pain and sorrow, made more so in Lena’s husky, lyrical voice. I've never heard the song before, but it resonates with me on so many levels. So much so, it feels like I've heard it a thousand times before. Heartbreaking, yet hopeful, I soak up every note. Hardly a moment ago I had no control over the swirling chaos within my mind, but listening to her voice now, my rage is dampened and my emotions level out. Calm and peaceful, it's as if her voice is a balm to my soul.

At the sound of Lena’s voice, that strange, corded sensation stretches taut, startling me just as it did when it appeared only moments ago. It snapped into place the moment I stepped into Aurora's workshop, but at a loss for what it is, why it is, or even how it came to be, I smothered the damn thing. But being so close to Lena now, it bites back with a vengeance, refusing to be ignored. My anger is subdued, barely present within her proximity, but flowing within the mysterious tether, I detect a muted echo of sadness and hurt that's unfamiliar. It feels similar to my own, yes, but more feminine and tragic. Soul wrenching. A raw, deep darkness from an old, but mending laceration that something – or someone – has reopened, and it now bleeds anew.

Unaware that she's being watched, Lena's hips sway to the song as she sweeps her palm across a copper sword. It seems inconceivable, but seeing Lena's somber expression, seeing that heart wrenching pain cloud her amethyst eyes, I know these foreign emotions belong not to me, but to her.

I chuckle to myself and shake my head.

Gods, I sound insane. Feeling someone else's emotions? It's ridiculous, not to mention impossible.

Lena raises to the tips of her toes, reaching toward a stiletto displayed on the wall, but as she moves to touch it, I catch the exact moment she notices my presence. Her hums trail off, her back stiffens, and her hand freezes below the dagger. She glances at me over her shoulder and my stomach drops at her look of cold indifference before she returns her attention forward, silently dismissing me.

Guilt balloons at her chilly response. Without my anger shadowing it, I detect another emotion. Regret.

Inwardly cursing her for eliciting another unwelcome emotion, I clench my jaw and step fully into the room. "I apologize if I was rude."

With her front facing away, she barely acknowledges my presence, brushing her fingers across the dagger's hilt. "What do you mean *if* you were rude? We both know you were."

Of course I'm aware; it was intentional. But I'm not going to admit that. Neither will I mention how rude it is for her to question me on my apology, which I think is quite generous of me, given the situation.

"I'm sorry," I grind out, expecting my apology, my *repeated* apology, to be the end of that. But at her lack of response, I can only assume it's not.

Dropping her hand, she spins to face me, finally giving me her sole attention. "Did your sister force you to apologize?"

"No," I lie. She arches her black brows, watching me with a knowing stare that's uncannily similar to Aurora's. Rubbing my forehead with my fingertips, I glance back at the archway and debate leaving altogether. But I quickly dismiss the thought, knowing Aurora will send me right back in.

This infernal woman just can't make this easy on me, can she?

"Yes," I admit, feeling like I'm swallowing broken glass.

"In that case..." She smirks. "I don't accept."

I open my mouth to speak, but taken aback at her refusal, I snap it shut, unsure how to respond. That's not a *normal* response. When someone apologizes, you accept it. It's just...what you do. Compulsory. Automatic.

I fold my arms over my broad chest. "What do you mean you don't accept? You have to."

"Do I? Hmm..." Lena feigns a thought, then shakes her head. "I don't believe I have to do anything."

"It's the polite thing to do."

She laughs, a husky, sensual sound. "When did I ever give you the impression I was polite?"

Seeing her mask fall to humor, I can't help but share in her amusement as I shake my head at our ridiculous conversation. "Most say thank you when someone apologizes."

Her smile spreads wider. "If it's sincere, yes, but yours was not. If I'm going to thank anyone, it'll be Aurora."

Grinning from ear to ear, I toss my palms up, conceding defeat.

I can see this isn't a conversation I can win. I'm guessing that's quite common for the witty woman. With eyes glittering with mischief, she reaches across the round table centered within the room and grabs a garishly jeweled push dagger. Touching the tip of the blade with the pad of her finger, she grimaces at the useless weapon and places it back down.

Noticing the pile of daggers she's set aside, I slip my thumbs into the pockets of my trousers, rounding the table to stand beside her. "What does someone who trades leather need with all these knives?"

Her smile slips, and she drops her gaze from mine as she leans over the table to retrieve a dirk with a simple, leather-bound hilt. Hair slipping past her shoulder, it curtains her face and I itch to touch it until she lifts one vambraced hand to curl the raven locks behind her ear. "Normally they wouldn't, but I travel quite a bit. There's no shortage of males who fail to understand the word no." She flips the knife end over end and when she catches it by the hilt, a sinister smile curls her lips. "I'd be foolish not to take the necessary steps to protect myself."

Watching her flip the dagger as if she's done it a thousand times before, I realize I've uncovered the real reason why females were never allowed in the Guard. Not because they're incapable, but because males are incapable of controlling themselves at such a sight. I never thought a woman handling a dagger would be erotic, but judging off the way my dick perks up at the display, it appears I'm wrong.

Internally scolding myself, I clear my throat along with my thoughts. "Isn't that why you hired Zander and Tristan? For protection?"

She rolls her eyes. "Yes, but why would I depend wholly on someone else? I've got two hands, two arms." She waves the point of the dagger in my direction. “They're just as capable as anyone else to wield a sword or raise a knife.”

“I can see that,” I smirk, bemused by the feisty woman. “Where is Zander? Not much of a protector if he’s not near you.”

“Are you trying to say I'm not safe with you?” she teases.

“Hmm, no.” I feign consideration before motioning towards the dirk. “But after seeing your skills, I suspect I'm the one who's unsafe.”

Lena laughs, adding the dirk to the pile. “Zander went to the market. He's in need of fresh clothing and according to him, only females wash clothes.”

A loud guffaw rips from my chest, surprising me just as much as her. “Gods, he didn't actually say that, did he?” Swiveling to face her, I seat myself partially on top of the table, curling my fingers over the edge.

“Basically, word for word.” She giggles, an innocently sweet sound that's otherwise contradictory to the formidable woman I’ve only begun to uncover. It's alluring and intriguing, unfortunately endearing me to her even more.

“And how did that go over?”

“I twisted his nipple,” she replies, her expression deadpanned.

Shocked, I suck in a breath before howling in laughter. “He's lucky that's all he got!” I say between laughs.

“To be honest, he should be thanking me. I thought Amara was going to stab him.” Her eyes widen. “All she had was a spoon, but she's very creative when she’s feeling stabby.”

At the thought of an angry Amara stabbing an unsuspecting Zander with only a spoon, I laugh even harder, clutching my stomach and widening my legs as I drop my head between my thighs.

Uriella’s Light, I don't remember the last time I laughed that hard. If ever.

Laughter tapering off, I slowly straighten and lift my head. My laughter cuts off when I notice that Lena has stepped closer, standing practically between my thighs. Her nearness is unexpected, surprising even, but that's not what causes my mouth to dry out or my heart to stutter in my chest. It's the look in her eyes.

Amethyst orbs filled to overflowing with adoration and blatant raw affection. Both sentiments, so profound, so devastating, it feels like a boulder has slammed into my chest and I can't suck in the air needed to take a breath. No one has ever looked at me that way. It's not even something I dared to wish for, knowing full well it's something I'd never receive. So warm and tender, it's as if she sees into my soul and found something good. Something desirable. Like I'm worthy of more than what life's given me. Worthy of someone like her.

She blinks, her cheeks flooding crimson as she startles herself back into the moment, finally becoming aware of where she's positioned herself. She moves to take a step back, attempting to put space between us, but she's halted when I snatch at her wrist, holding her in place as I try to come up with a plausible explanation as to why I can't let her go. Unable to do so, I grip her tighter and instead change the subject, hoping she doesn't question me further.

"So, Zander went shopping," I say. "And you didn't join him?"

Her lips lift into a knowing half smile, but she doesn't try to remove my hand. "Oh, no."

"No? Don't most women like to shop?"

Her smile falls and she spears me with a droll look. "Do I look like someone who likes to shop?"

"For weapons," I add quickly, realizing my error.

"Yes, well, that's why I'm at a blacksmith's shop and not the dressmaker's," Lena says dryly, before her eyes dart away from mine. She chews on her lip. "I probably should have gone with him and stocked up on a few provisions, but I'm not a big fan of crowds."

"Too many admirers," I tease, rubbing her hand with my thumb, the feel of her silky skin soothing me along with the warmth of her leather vambraces.

"Unfortunately," she mumbles to herself, blowing out an uneasy breath. "No, that's not why." She shuffles awkwardly and I force my legs to remain still when her hip brushes against my inner thigh. "Being around that many people at once can be a bit much. Not that they appreciate my presence anyway." At my blank stare, she explains, "I can be a bit blunt. It's off putting to most." She shrugs.

"That's because most people are liars," I reply, my mood darkening at the thought of anyone treating her less than what she deserves. "They can't stomach someone exposing their truth for all to see."

Cocking her head to the side, she eyes me quizzically. "You believe someone to be a liar, simply because they keep secrets?"

"Omission and lies are one and the same, both an act of betrayal." There's never one without the other, and I've experienced too much of both to ever think any differently.

Lena watches me with eyes no longer soft or affectionate, but disappointed, perhaps even sad. My assessment is confirmed when I feel an odd twinge down that link, traveling from her to me in what I now suspect to be some sort of bond between us.

"What if they only do so to protect someone?" she asks, her voice thickening with a more pronounced rasp. She tugs her hand from mine. "Is it a betrayal then?"

"It doesn't matter the why, just that they do." Feeling a strange emptiness from the loss of her touch, I readjust myself against the table, her body swaying in tandem with mine. "How can you trust someone who's dishonest with you?"

"You earn their trust first, and they'll reveal it to you in their own time."

I scoff, surprised at how such an intelligent woman could be so naive. "That's not good enough."

"It should be." Smiling softly, she looks at me as if I'm the naive one. "You aren't entitled to someone else's truth; neither are they to yours."

We stare at one another, neither of us willing to give in to the other until Lena shakes her head with a roll of her eyes, smiling.

"And now you can see why some find my bluntness to be an acquired taste." She chuckles, I along with her, but it trails off when I see her slide her palms along her backside, slipping her fingers into her back pockets, unconsciously jutting her chest out in the process.

Since entering the room, I've been careful to keep my gaze from drifting below her neck, but when her tits bounce with the motion, my eyes helplessly swerve in their direction.

Fuuuck!

Mouth watering, I watch her chest rise and fall with her breaths, her vest slowly slipping lower with the motion to reveal more of those circular shaped scars. Small dots stagger from between her cleavage to rise up and outward to shape the swell of her breasts like she draped a strand of skin-colored pearls artfully across her skin. And I have to bite my tongue to refrain from licking every last one.

Realizing I've been ogling her for an indeterminable amount of time, I tear my gaze from those perfectly plump tits and speak in a tone more gravelly than usual. "Have you formed any trade contracts since arriving?" I ask, already knowing the answer to that question, but it's the only thing I can think to say while the image of her breasts is still seared into the forefront of my mind.

"Oh!" she says, obviously startled by the change of subject.

"None, actually. Although, I'm sure that's more a reflection of my people skills than the leather itself."

"Or it could be because you came to Cascadonia to sell leather," I say, followed by a grumbled curse, realizing my own social skills are a bit lacking at the moment.

Lena shrugs. "And?"

Does she really not know? How can she not?

"Cascadonia is the only supplier of leather for all of Vanyimar," I say neutrally, even though her lack of knowledge is baffling. "None of the other kingdoms even have leather workers, besides a few repair shops here and there."

Her eyes widen and she places a hand on my thigh, curling her fingers into my trousers. "Is that why everyone acts so strange when we tell them what we trade?"

That, and your beauty can befuddle even the strongest of males.

"That's exactly why."

"That explains that, at least." Frowning, she peers upward, mumbling to herself. "Jathro should have done more research before sending me here."

"Jathro," I say, his name tasting like ash on my tongue. "A lover?" I hiss through my teeth, flames suddenly flaring from my palms as I clench the table, wood smoldering on a crack between my grip.

Eyes widening at the sight, she steps further between my thighs, snatching my hand up before I can stop her. Shocked, I jolt back, smothering the flames instantly as I try to pull from her grasp, but she holds tight.

"My brother," she says gently, clasping her hand with mine. "The leathersmith."

Hissing a curse, I pry her hands from mine and unfurl her fingers, sure I've burned her all the way to the bone. But I'm shocked to find not a single mark marring her skin. Even her vambraces are untouched, the texture unblemished as I stroke my finger along her palm. Slowly tracing along the lines of her skin, my concern morphs to fascination as I absorb the feel of her small, smooth hands splayed within mine. She laces our fingers together, braiding and twining one finger with the other. Her tender touch fills me with a sudden warmth, fanning the flames within.

"Does this mean you'll be leaving soon?" I ask, my voice guttural, grating against my throat.

She watches our clasped hands dance with one another, just as enthralled as I am. "Not yet. I came all this way. May as well try."

"Is there anyone waiting for you back home?"

She lifts her glazed gaze to mine and swallows thickly. "My brother."

Locking my jaw, I hiss through clenched teeth, "I'm not talking about a brother."

She says nothing as she watches me, beguiling amethyst eyes boring into my blue ones as she steps closer, swaying into me as she places both hands on my upper thighs and whispers, "No."

That single, breathy word rams into me like a sledgehammer, battering my control. I inhale a deep breath through my nostrils in a last-ditch effort to control myself and I'm instantly bombarded with the scent of vanilla, cinnamon, and cherry. My cock has been twitching throughout our entire encounter, but when I smell the scent that's all Lena, it hardens to steel.

Heart stampeding within my chest, I watch the purple of her eyes begin to glow with desire as she arches against me and licks her lips. At the thought of gliding my cock between those red, juicy lips, my blood begins to boil and my dick rages against its leather prison as my whole body tenses and prepares to pounce.

Palm slipping off the table, I reach for her hips where that small patch of bare skin is displayed between her vest and trousers, but a troubling thought suddenly slices through my haze of desire, freezing my hand midair. Slowly curling my hand into a fist, it visibly trembles as I draw back from her.

Ignoring the physical pain of retreat, I ask, "Your brother owns the leather shop?"

Her breathing is erratic and her eyes are glazed over in lust, but a line appears between her brows. "Uh, huh," she mumbles huskily.

A wave of ice spreads through my veins, successfully dousing any remaining lust. "The other night you said your uncle owned the leather shop," I state coldly. "Not your brother."

At my statement, her eyes instantly clear and an emotionless mask slips into place. "Did I?" she asks blandly.

Fucking liar.

Neither of us speaks as I glare into her apathetic eyes. Although her breaths calm and her body relaxes, outwardly she shows no signs of the fact that we were only moments away from fucking on this very same table. She's cool, calm, and collected, as if nothing even happened. Like it was all an *act.*

Knuckles whitening into fisted hands, my nostrils flare as my blood begins to boil in rage.

This is why I don't trust people. Liars and users, all of them.

The bell over the entrance peals and two pairs of footsteps stride in our direction.

"Darius?" Griffin calls out, but I refuse to remove my gaze from Lena's. Neither does she as I rise to my feet, leather skimming against leather until I tower over her, leaving not even a finger's breadth between.

"Darius," Griffin repeats, more forcefully than before.

I narrow my eyes on her one last time, then swing my gaze toward the entryway where a confused Griffin and Kace are standing.

"Ajax?" I ask.

"He's all settled," Kace replies in the same moment I feel Lena place a hand on my chest and push, forcing me to take a step back. She glances back at me over her shoulder with an expression void of emotion, before striding away to slip between the two confused males and leaving the room.

Feeling both of their questioning stares, I suck on my teeth before waving them on, unwilling to spend another moment in this room where Lena almost convinced me she was different from everyone else. But of course, she's not. I shouldn't be surprised. I've met very few honest females throughout my life. Why would a woman be any different?

Trailing behind my guards, my gaze wanders to the display case, seeing Aurora on one side with Lena on the other. A dagger, partially wrapped in cloth, lays forgotten between the two as they both lean forward, speaking in hushed voices.

"These are the only metals you work with?" Lena asks.

Aurora nods. "Steel mostly, but I occasionally work with iron or copper."

Lena bends further over the case and whispers so quietly, I have to strain my ears to make out their conversation. "Have you ever plated the metal with anything?"

Aurora shakes her head. "I've seen it done, but I've never done it myself."

"Have you ever seen one plated with anything… unusual?" Lena whispers.

Suspicion rears its head and I pass by Amara, Tristan, Kace, and Griffin where they chat near the front door, positioning myself against the opposite wall where I can see and hear them more clearly.

"Like what?" Aurora asks.

Lena anxiously taps her forefinger against the clear glass,

visibly debating before coming to some sort of decision. She opens her mouth to speak, hesitates, then speaks at normal volume when she notices me out of the corner of her eye. "Have you ever seen a blade plated with a material that was bright white? Similar to the shade of starlight?"

"Starlight?" Aurora asks, her lips turned down into a frown.

Lena nods. "Yes, but unlike starlight, there would have been small flecks of color within it. Purple, blue, pink, a kaleidoscope of colors. Similar to opal, but…not."

"I'm sorry, I've never heard of it," Aurora says with an apologetic smile.

Lena's cheeks puff out and she shuts her eyes, exhaling a slow breath before her lids lift and she forces a smile onto her face. "I didn't think you would."

"Where did you ever hear of such a thing?" Aurora prods, folding the cloth over the dagger.

Lena waves her hand dismissively. "Just from some silly story a friend told me." Her forlorn expression tells anyone who's paying attention how silly she doesn't think it is.

Unclasping a bulging pouch from her belt loop, Lena digs for several silver coins and flattens the coins on the glass, sliding them towards Aurora with a brittle smile. "I was wondering if there was some truth to it."

Lena's head swivels in my direction, and when she meets my gaze, her smile instantly falls. With a grave face, her amethyst eyes reveal a whole slew of emotions. Anxiety, sadness, and possibly guilt. My uneasiness since entering the room intensifies when I feel that link strum with all these emotions, in addition to an overwhelming fear that takes my breath away.

She's terrified.

Her lies, her secrets, the threat she may pose, none of that matters as I feel her crippling terror. All I can think about is snatching her up and whisking her away to a place no one will find her, while I search for the people responsible for eliciting such a response.

I move to do just that when the bond suddenly cuts off, her face hardens, and she nods to me before striding brusquely toward the front door.

A strange feeling encapsulates me, rushing through my blood as she moves towards the door. She knew I was coming to comfort her, knew I wanted to help, and she just… walked away. Not even a glance back. That awful feeling flows into my chest, dozens of needles pricking at the organs beneath. It takes me a moment to recognize the feeling for what it is, to realize the emotion she pulled forth with her dismissiveness.

It's hurt. Not anger, not rage, but hurt.

She's not yours to protect. If she wanted your help, she'd ask.

I stare at her as she reaches for the handle on the entrance door, wishing my rage would return, until she opens the door and raucous sounds blast into the shop.

"What's going on?" Lena asks, hesitating over the threshold.

Aurora and I share a grim look as everyone rushes forward, cramming into the doorway to watch the large crowd gathering outside the shop. Seeing so many wondrous faces, feeling their excitement and the sheer size of the gathering itself, I realize this can only mean one thing.

"Looks like Queenie decided to go for a ride," Kace says, kneeling between mine and Lena's legs.

"What?!" Aurora shouts. Pushing off our shoulders, her wide-eyed face pops into view. "In her carriage?"

"Her horse," Griffin says in his deep voice from his spot behind Amara and Tristan.

Kace, Aurora, and I groan in unison.

Shit.

I glance at Aurora. “She's here for you.”

“You don't know that!” she screams. Her expression twists into rage before her eyes widen once again, features shifting into a desperate hope. “She could be looking for you.”

What a delusional female.

“If she was looking for me, she'd go to the Guard Base.” The way people have surged around Rory’s Swords and Daggers, I'm unable to see my mother above the crowd. But when the crowd begins to converge and thicken in front of Aurora’s shop, I know my prediction is correct. “She's definitely here for you. I told you, you should've gone home last night.”

Her lips slash into an angry line. “I'm a grown ass female, I can sleep wherever I please!” she screeches, loud and piercing enough that half of those gathered turn to stare at the crazy person shouting nonsense. Surprisingly, Amara, Tristan, and Lena barely bat an eye.

Kace rolls his eyes and dusts off his knees as he stands. His emerald jewels flicker with irritation as he steps onto the walkway and turns to face us. “Come on, everyone out. Let's go bow and grovel,” he says dryly. “That's what she's here for anyway.”

Muttering a curse, I slip Aurora's arm through mine and drag her out into the throng.

CHAPTER 10

DARIUS

An electrified excitement crackles the air and murmurs of awe ripple through the gleeful crowd. Rescued from an otherwise monotonous day, Cascadonians revel in the Queen's unscheduled appearance. Exuberant males shout their devotion while ladies jostle their neighbors as they anxiously balance on the tips of their toes. A fae youth scrabbles to the top of a doused street light, his mother screaming threats at the foot of the iron pole. Latecomers warily step out of shops before quickly rushing to join those on the congested street. Storeowners, shoppers, and families alike clamber and claw to the front of the mob in hopes of attracting the attention of the reclusive Queen.

Spying only woolen dresses and work stained trousers, I'm relieved to find not a lord or lady in sight. I would hope that whatever public chastisement Adelphia intends to inflict on me or Aurora could remain outside the court, but after eventually spotting several familiar females dressed in finer fabrics and laden with boxes, I expect it's more likely the nobility's personal shoppers will be squealing to their benefactors within the hour.

Griffin and Kace slip between the boisterous crowd, corralling those aware of the royalty in front, but oblivious to the ones behind. Kace lowers his head to speak into the ear of a mother with an infant on her hip and an older child wrapped around her leg. Her gaze snaps to mine and her eyes widen, snatching the hand of the boy and scrambling backwards. Whispers quickly spread through the raucous gathering of our arrival, and as if contrived beforehand, the revelers part on a wave, clearing a path for the Blacksmith Princess and Bastard Prince.

The scent of vanilla, cinnamon, and cherry precedes Lena's raspy voice as she angles herself towards me. "This is all for the Queen?"

Pivoting towards her, I'm surprised to not only see her walking beside me, but Tristan and Amara following casually behind. She either doesn't realize it or – much more likely – doesn't care that it's not appropriate for her to walk beside royalty.

Aurora and I may not regularly abide by royal protocol, but it's unacceptable in the presence of the Queen. I consider mentioning that to her, but instantly decide against it. She can figure it out for herself.

Striding toward Adelphia, I duck my head towards Lena. "Yes," I reply sharply, glancing past her and trying to avoid being swept up in her disarming beauty and forgetting what she is.

She's a liar. You can't trust her.

"Look at the way they're fawning over her," Lena says to her companions, gesturing to the crowd with a flick of her hand. "Do you think they would lick her toes if she asked?"

"Some would," Amara says with a scowl.

"But most wouldn't be pleased to do so," Tristan adds.

Not even in the slightest, I think. But they also wouldn't fight it, either. These aren't the rich lords and ladies of court, desperate for any scrap of the Queen's attention. Everyone here is either human, or of the middle and lower class. The very same people unhappy and fearful of her rule.

I can already see the novelty of my mother's appearance wearing off for some. Humans, fae, and some immortals garbed in homespun tunics and holey linen trousers watch the Queen with hate-filled glares and slashed lips, but none express their displeasure in any other way. Not if they wish to see the end of the day.

Lena curls her lip, sweeping her gaze back and forth. "It's sickening how your people worship those in power," she says to me. "Does the royalty in this realm think of themselves akin to the gods?"

Realm?

"Mother certainly thinks so," Aurora mumbles.

I tighten my grip around her arm, a warning. "In Cascadonia, she is a goddess and expects to be treated as such," I say to Lena. Do I think my mother is a goddess? Fuck no, but it's best for everyone that Lena realizes her place. Adelphia's tolerance for humans is slim as it is. It's doubtful she'll allow Lena to live if she hears her speaking about her this way.

"Your mother is *no* goddess," Lena says, sneering up at my mother. "And even if she was, I would hope that you wouldn't prostrate yourself at her feet like these fools."

"How else would someone greet a god?" Griffin asks, hovering behind her.

Lena peeks at him over her shoulder, her expression sobering as she glances at him and then Kace, Aurora, and me in turn. "Word of advice to you all," she says in a grave tone. "If you ever find yourself in the presence of a god, run fast and run far. For if not, you're already dead."

Sharing a bewildered look with Griffin, then Kace behind me, I glance back at Lena to ask her what in Azazel's Darkness she's talking about, but she's already turned away, whispering to her companions in that foreign, lilting tongue.

Why does every conversation with her have to be so strange?

Shoving her and any thoughts of her aside, I notice my mother's attention fixated on both me and my sister. I tug on Aurora's arm and lengthen my stride in response to her thinning patience, reaching the edge of the crowd within moments.

Never without a protection detail, Adelphia is surrounded by a slew of males outfitted in all-black leather uniforms trimmed in teal – the same as the Cascadonian guards. Unlike the standard uniform for the Kingdom's guards, these soldiers wear a pin above their left pectoral of the Lesdanas house emblem, distinguishing them as my mother's personal guards.

Hair pinned halfway up in braids intertwined with small teal sapphires, Queen Adelphia sits regally above the masses upon her majestic white mare. Garbed in a flowing white dress made of the finest silks with teal lace and beads sewn within, her neck, wrists, and ears drip with jewels in various shades of the same color.

Visually striking, with her cool expression and imperious poise, her superiority drowns the onlookers as power and authority bleeds from her every pore.

Aerin, a male Air immortal with dark chocolate skin and brown eyes, wears a uniform of all-black leather – the same as I do – while standing silently beside Adelphia's horse. I technically outrank the Air immortal, but seeing as he's the Captain of the Queen's Guard and he's been her protector since before I was born, my mother values his opinion over mine and often rules in his favor.

Arrogant, brash, and cold as he is, we often bash heads over innumerable issues. But being that he's never treated me differently due to the events leading to my conception, as well as his devout loyalty to the Queen, he has my begrudging respect.

Vigilant as ever, Aerin's gaze sweeps the crowd for any threats before he steps forward to address those gathered. Advancing with blue glittering palms, he flicks a wrist and amplifies his voice with a gust of wind.

"All hail Her Royal Majesty!" he thunders. "Queen Adelphia of House Lesdanas, Ruler of Cascadonia! Kneel before your Queen!"

As one, all those who are present lower to one knee, and we bow our heads.

One arm laid across my thigh, I stare unseeing at an orange topaz in the cobbled street, waiting for the Queen's customary order for all to rise. But only silence reigns as the time comes and goes.

"Kneel before your Queen!" Aerin repeats in a booming voice.

After another moment without the traditional "rise", the sounds of ruffling clothing, shuffled movements, and quiet murmurs reach my ears, a pregnant pause engulfing the air.

Confused myself, my gaze wanders about while my head remains bowed, passing over cobblestones and jewels, Aurora's soot covered apron draped over her leg, an apple core that was carelessly tossed away. But when I peek out of the corner of my right eye, my gaze catches on two small, leather-bound feet flattened against the street.

Uneasy at the sight, I rotate my head in their direction and my stomach sinks upon inspection. Hoping I'm wrong but knowing full well that I'm not, I skim my eyes up toned legs clad in burgundy leather trousers, barely pausing at the patch of bare, golden skin, continuing onward past the large bust cinched in the laced leather vest, to where I finally land on the devastatingly beautiful face of Lena. The same Lena who's not kneeling, but standing proudly as she boldly gazes at the Queen.

Fuck!

Hundreds of heads slowly begin to lift, confusion marring their faces until their expressions shift to shock at the sight of the lone human standing brazenly amongst the kneeled.

Adelphia's horse trots sideways as she narrows her eyes at the defiant foreigner.

Snatching Lena's elbow, I ignore the hum from our touch as I tug her towards me. "You're supposed to kneel."

"I can see that." A short errant lock slips past her ear to dangle between us. I itch to sweep it back, even in the face of my anger to her flippant response.

Boots clomp in our direction, rising in volume the nearer they get before a dark shadow casts over Lena. Still standing, Lena tugs her arm free to face the newcomer.

Standing only a few paces away, Aerin scrutinizes Lena from head to toe. "Kneel before the Queen."

She smirks. "No."

"No?" Aerin sputters.

"That's what I said."

Aurora jumps up and bounds forward, but I snatch her arm midstep, dragging her back down beside me. "She's not from here," she says to Aerin."She doesn't know any better!" Turning toward Lena, her expression is earnest as she explains, "Lena, it's customary on our lands to kneel before your Queen."

Lena arches a brow. "This is not my land, and she is not my Queen."

My whole body stiffens, and Aurora's nails dig into my arms as the whole crowd sucks in a collective gasp.

"You insolent human," Aerin snaps, stalking in Lena's direction. "How dare you disrespect the Queen!" My hackles rise at his tone, but I bite back a growl when he stops a few feet away from her, fisting his hands at his sides and gritting his teeth. "Your words are traitorous."

"Not traitorous," Lena calmly states. "The truth."

"Kneel," he hisses, his dark face mottled in rage.

"No." Undaunted, Lena's expression is one of absolute boredom. "I kneel to no one. I will *never* kneel to another." She taps her chin on a feigned thought. "Well, I shouldn't say never. If I manage to find a male who's able to give me multiple orgasms within a single bout, then I'll be more than happy to kneel." Lena sweeps her gaze across the shocked crowd, chuckling. "But I'm sure all the males here can agree that it's rude not to reciprocate."

Is she talking about... She can't be!

"Did she just say what I think she did?" Aurora squeaks my thoughts.

"If you mean, is she talking about sucking dick? Then yes," Griffin says, scrubbing his mouth. "Yes, she did."

"And orgasm. Don't forget orgasm," Kace adds helpfully.

"Oh my gods!" Aurora laughs, slapping a hand to her mouth.

Surveying the crowd, I find a few bowled over in laughter and some visibly stunned, but my heart gallops in my chest when I see more than half with varying shades of outrage directed towards the irreverent human. Eyes darting to Adelphia, my blood runs cold at the look of fury etched on her face, along with her flickering aquamarine and starlight jewels.

"If you won't kneel," Aerin seethes, stalking forward, "then I will force you to."

Lena's eyes hone in on Aerin's reaching hand. "If you so much as lay one finger on me, I'll break every bone in your fucking hand."

Aerin jerks back, eyeing her warily as he unsheathes his dagger and signals to the Queen's guards with a nod of his head.

I move without thought, summoning my flames without a command as I lunge for Aerin with a snarl. But I'm suddenly jerked back, Griffin's arms banded around me to press me into his chest.

"Wait," he whispers in my ear.

Unconcerned with the advancing guards, Lena's eyes remain fixed on the Queen. "Is this how you rule your kingdom, Your Majesty?" she calls out loudly enough for everyone present to hear, but calm, authoritative. "Through fear and forced obedience?" She motions towards the Cascadonians silently watching and publicly challenges the legendary Queen, verbally passing her a noose with which to hang herself. "You arrest or kill anyone who speaks their mind?"

Adelphia's composure implodes. Jewels near blinding and her face reddening into a murderous rage, her green-eyed glare shows every ounce of loathing she feels for the plebeian beneath her.

"Arrest her!" Aerin shouts. The Queen's guards move as one towards Lena.

Neither Lena nor the Queen dare spare a glance at the approaching guards, the shouts of those calling for Lena's death, or from those condemning the Queen. Both of them silently refuse to admit defeat by breaking their gaze from the other.

Removing Griffin's fingers from my vest, I slap both palms to his chest, not even giving him a side-eyed glance as he soars through the air and tumbles across the street. In this moment I see nothing but Lena. Not my mother's rage, not my friends, not even the eventual punishment for my actions. My thoughts, my focus, my entire being is honed on the only thing that matters: Intercepting the guards before they dare to touch *her*.

"Stop!"

I, along with everyone else, freezes mid-motion at the Queen's command. We hold our breath as we wait for her to make her next move.

A faux, charming smile creeps up Adelphia's face, dismissing Lena to address her people. "Of course we don't arrest those who express their thoughts. In fact, I welcome the insight provided by those who are less fortunate." She peers down at Lena, her eyes flashing as her grin shifts to a sickly-sweet grimace. "I thank you for imparting such wisdom."

Lena snickers and it takes everything in me not to strangle her for it.

Adelphia's smile tightens. "Who might you be, little human?"

"Lena."

"Your full name, child?" Adelphia says more sternly, that sickly-sweet smile still plastered to her face.

Lena silently assesses Adelphia. "Dalenna Nectallius."

Adelphia's brows bunch, and she pulls on the reins to halt her restless horse. "I'm not familiar with that surname."

Ignoring the implied question, Lena squints up at her. "My gods… there's so much darkness in you, isn't there? So much pain."

Darkness?

Adelphia's lips pull back and she bares her teeth. "Where are you from?"

Lena shakes herself from her spell and shrugs. "I'm a traveler. You could say I'm from many places."

Abandoning all pretenses, Adelphia's mask dissolves into an expression carved from ice. "Why have you come to Cascadonian?"

"Seeking trade."

"And what is it you trade?"

"Leather."

A surprised chuckle bursts from Adelphia. "In Cascadonia?" she asks incredulously. At Lena's silence, her chuckles flourish into an arrogant laugh, quickly multiplying within the crowd while Lena watches with an apathetic mask of her own.

Adelphia smiles imperiously down at her. "I'm sure you've realized what a fruitless endeavor that will be."

Lena's lips curl into a secret smile that gives the Queen pause. "I have."

Adelphia tugs on the reins, directing her horse forward and

trotting past Lena. Aerin moves to walk alongside her horse, and the Queen's guards encircle them both. Without so much as a glance in Lena's direction, Adelphia tosses over her shoulder, "Well, Lena from nowhere, seeing that you have no real purpose here, I expect you'll soon be on your way." Peering at Lena over her shoulder, her voice hardens to steel. "Sooner, rather than later."

Lena hums noncommittally.

A hate-filled gleam sparks in Adelphia's eyes before she dismisses Lena and trots to where Aurora and I stand at the edge of the crowd. "Aurora, Darius, I expect you both for the evening meal." Not a request, but a demand; her horse clomps away before either of us can respond.

Raucous conversation breaks out as the crowd begins to disperse, hundreds of admiring gazes following Lena as she glides towards us, calmly joining us as if she didn't just publicly defy a queen and barely escape death.

Kace bites his fist and squeals. "You're my hero," he says to Lena. "Insane, but still my hero."

"I can't believe you said that to her." Aurora slaps Lena's arm, shaking her head in disbelief. "She was furious!"

Lena shrugs one tan shoulder. "I wasn't trying to make her angry."

Amara snorts, tossing an arm over her shoulder. "Liar."

Smiling mischievously, Lena wraps an arm around Amara's waist. "I wasn't *trying* to. I just tend to have that effect on people."

Tristan drops his head back and sighs. "Always have to make a statement, don't you?"

Lena shrugs. "I don't kneel."

Tristan grabs both women by the waist with a rueful smile and steers them away from us. "No, you don't."

Watching Lena, Tristan, and Amara merge with the pedestrians now rushing to resume their duties, my mind churns on the enigmatic woman's public spectacle, unsure if I should feel anger towards her or admiration. But one thing I'm certain of is that Dalenna Nectallius is a reckless, impulsive, insane bit of a woman, and absolutely the most magnificent, breathtaking creature I have ever laid eyes upon.

I'm so fucked.

CHAPTER 11

LENA

"I'm sorry, sweet girl," I coo, petting the forehead of my white mare, Layla. "I should have come sooner."

Gleaning feelings of abandonment and intense irritation, I suspect she'd be scowling right about now if she had the facial muscles capable of it. Expressing her displeasure the only way she knows how, she huffs a breath and stares me down with those large brown eyes of hers.

From the day I rescued her, I've been unable to stomach the thought of confining her unless absolutely necessary, and only for short periods of time at that. Since she's incapable of understanding the laws of mortals and accustomed to roaming as she pleases, her current accommodations feel more like a prison than a hostel.

Unlatching the gate, I walk into the stall and brandish a full burlap sack. "I brought treats."

Not appeased in the slightest with my unopened peace offering, she twitches her tail and stomps her hooves on the dirt packed floor. Rolling my eyes, I unlace the bag and present her with the one item that'll exonerate my perceived betrayal. A juicy red apple.

Always quick to forgive once food's involved, she bumps her head to my chest and nuzzles my neck. I laugh when she ignores the single apple in my palm to dive into the bag that contains half a dozen of the fruit along with sugar cubes. Apples clunk together as she burrows for her prize until she suddenly rears back, her ears pinned in alarm. She expels a whinnied breath while shaking her head and almost tramples me to death when she turns her back on me, effectively spurning my bribe.

Peering into the sack, I expect to find a spider or something equally repulsive to her, but I only see apples and sugar cubes.

"Don't you want a treat?" I ask, ducking my head in an effort to attract her gaze. Layla flicks her head and snorts, dismissing me once again.

That's odd.

Frowning, I set the satchel in the corner of the stall farthest away from her and rotate the fruit at eye level. It's ripe, perfectly formed, lacks any pits or blemishes, and is otherwise typical in its appearance. Inhaling through my nostrils, I search for the distinctive taint of poison, but find nothing. Unable to identify anything out of the ordinary, but suspecting Layla's instincts may have perceived something I can't, I shrug internally and take a small bite. Swishing the crumbled fruit within my mouth, I try to find the cause of her rejection, but the only flavors I detect are the sweet tartness native to the fruit. Preparing to swallow, I hesitate before doing so and that's when I taste it.

There it is.

Faint but present, I spit out the foul fruit. Digging for a sugar cube, I inhale an investigatory sniff, but meet with equally empty results. It's only when I lick it that I'm able to detect it, and when I do, I'm instantly accosted. Now familiar with the foul essence, the once faint flavor is overpowering in its toxicity and I notice little else.

Grabbing a brush, I murmur apologies and consoling words to

Layla in an attempt to ease her agitation, sweeping the soft brush through her short hairs. Her ears rest outwards and she nickers her appreciation as I calm her with the brush's soothing strokes. Careful to apply minimal pressure, I gently coast the soft bristles across the numerous silver scars slashed across her sides. The contact doesn't hurt her anymore, but the skin is tight and often aches when overworked. It's unlikely grooming will irritate the old wounds, but I prefer to be cautious nonetheless.

The door to the stables creaks open and a beam of light streaks through, darkening once more when it clatters shut. Layla's ears prick up at the sound and I spread my senses outwards, searching for the source of her discomfort. A cool wave of steadfast calm washes over me and I pat her side reassuringly as light footsteps tread in our direction. Layla's nostrils flare, scenting for the interloper, and once discovering for herself what I've already confirmed, her anxiety settles and she leans in to me, a silent request to resume my ministrations.

The sound of straw crunching beneath boots precedes Tristan's smooth voice. "I thought I'd find you here."

"That wouldn't have been difficult to surmise." Setting the brush down on a wood stool, I turn to face him.

Arms draped over the door to the stall, the mark on Tristan's cheek pulls taut as he smirks. "Not difficult at all, given the events of today."

I internally cringe and drop my eyes, straw whispering beneath my boots as I move towards the corner of the stall where I placed the pail. Dipping my hand in the sheet of glassy water, I retrieve a cloth of sheepskin and ring out the excess liquid. Not necessarily embarrassed, but aware my earlier antics may have made our visit more problematic than necessary, I wipe Layla's face while avoiding Tristan's gaze.

"How's she doing?" he asks, jerking his head towards Layla.

"She hates it here," I reply, grateful for the change of topic. Layla bumps her head with mine and I chuckle, stroking her neck. "She feels trapped and alone. It reminds her of her time before we came along." My eyes dart to her gouged side, recalling the condition we found her in. I wrap my arms around her neck and comb my fingers through her mane, consoling her as much as myself.

Mutilated, broken, and drained of blood, Layla was only a few stilted breaths away from death when we found her unconscious form dumped in the middle of the woods. Imprisoned for weeks – possibly months – her captors dissected and tortured her unto the brink of death. Once her abusers determined her body was no longer of any use to them, they discarded her as if she was nothing more than trash, instead of a living, breathing creature whose only crime was expecting kindness where there was none. It still sickens me the way those religious zealots felt justified in tormenting an animal widely known to possess the purest of souls, stripping her of her very essence, all in a perverted quest for power that was never intended for them.

Fortunately, she was able to recover, though it was long, painful, and arduous. But with time and patience, Layla's wounds sealed, her bones mended, her blood replenished, and her mind slowly but surely healed. She's still loving and gentle as expected of her species, but she's also fierce and strong. A warrior in her own right. It saddens me to see how such an anguished darkness intruded upon a soul it never should have inhabited, but it also gives me a guilty relief knowing she now has the knowledge necessary to protect herself from the atrocities that are sure to come.

Layla's wounds may have healed, but her scars will always remain. Most days she has little difficulty coping with her trauma, but when she has to be cooped up like she is now and is unable to do as she pleases, the memories resurface along with all those dark emotions. Yet, as difficult as these times are, she always finds a way to persevere, but it seems her time in Cascadonia is more trying than usual. More distressing. It's as if she senses something wrong with this place. Something unnatural and wicked in this Kingdom of Jewels.

"That's to be expected," Tristan says. "She's not accustomed to being stabled for so long."

I shake my head. "It's more than that, it's this place. It's cold and sinister. I feel it, too."

Frowning at me, he pops a foot on the door, rattling it as he folds his arms over his chest. "What do you mean?"

"I don't know how to explain it." Frustrated, I toss the cloth into the pail, sloshing water over the sides and onto the hay strewn floor. "It's nothing specific. It's just…" The treats I brought with me catch my eye and I grab the bitten apple, tossing it to Tristan, who catches it one handed. "It's like this apple. I offered it to Layla and she refused to eat it." Rummaging through the sack, I pull out a sugar cube. "This sugar cube? She took one sniff and turned away. Normally, she'd eat a whole wagon of them and beg for more, but she won't touch it. Won't even come near it."

Tristan eyes the apple warily. "Are they poisoned?"

"No, I tasted both myself, but … Just try it. You'll see."

Tristan takes a bite out of the apple, chews thoughtfully, and swallows. "What's wrong with it?" Grabbing the sugar cube from me, he pops it into his mouth and considers it just the same.

"It's sweet and crisp, exactly as it should be, but…" I hesitate, unable to voice my thoughts. "It's like there's a taint to it. A foul bitterness shrouded beneath its natural flavor. It's faint, barely noticeable, but when you do, it's all you can taste." My tongue sticks to the roof of my mouth, my mouth watering as I try to dislodge the insidious flavor. "Its venom still lingers on my tongue, drowning me in its filth and pervading my blood, blackening my veins with its vileness. It feels as if I'll never be rid of its toxins."

Attempting to peer through the wizened wood of the stable wall, I envision the rich kingdom that lays beyond with their beautiful people and jewels. "It's like this place. It screams wealth, prosperity, and beauty, but there's a poison leaching into their realm; a cancerous malevolence burrowed beneath the soil, injecting its filth into the very hearts of their people. It slowly corrupts and defiles their souls until they're nothing but a twisted, warped echo of themselves."

Imagining that oozing blackness thickening my blood and permeating my soul, I wrap my arms around myself, attempting to stave off the invasion. "Can't they see it? If I can, then they must as well. Yet they do nothing." A feeling of defeat surges within me, crushing me beneath its Fate Blessed feet and I hug myself tighter. "How can they be so unwilling to acknowledge the filth within their own land? The rot within their own brethren?" I unwrap my arms and reach for the fresh blanket I brought for Layla, placing it across her back. "Maybe I'm overcomplicating this. Maybe it's simpler than that," I whisper. "Maybe they just don't care."

"Or maybe they aren't aware," Tristan argues gently. Opening the gate for me, he eyes me gravely as I pass through. "The person that you are, the way you were raised and your past ordeals, you're equipped to see what others cannot. Most people have never experienced evil – not evil in its purest form, anyway. They lack the necessary skills to recognize the signs of true darkness." His grave expression contorts, raw anguish lining his face and hoarsening his voice. "Unlike you and me."

My body becomes rigid, breath expelling in a rush when

memories once secured in the deepest part of my mind resurface in a flash.

It's over. Don't think about it. You're safe. You're safe.

I swallow thickly and force my muscles to relax, locking the stable door along with the vault to the memories best left forgotten.

Noticing his trembling fingers when he opens the squeaking stable door, I link my arm through his and rub his arm, urging him to lock away his own nightmares.

I hum to myself as we stroll down the street, watching as the Gods Light lanterns spark to life with the waning sun, listening to the owner of the spice shop closing up for the night, hearing the baker shoo away a bunch of rowdy youths at her doorstep, and trying, yet failing, to ignore the countless stares and fervent whispers.

"You put on quite the spectacle earlier," Tristan notes.

I guess it was naive to think he would simply ignore the incident. Although I doubt anyone could, with all the glares and awed faces tracking our every step.

"It seems being discreet may no longer be an option," he adds with my continued silence. "It may make a difficult situation even more so."

"I suspect you may be right." Peering up at him, I feel a pinch of guilt when I see the lines hardening his face, his tightened lips, and his narrowed gaze as he stares straight ahead. For someone who's most comfortable concealed within shadows, this isn't the ideal situation for him. Not for me either, but at least I've grown accustomed to it.

"You disapprove," I say; a statement, not a question. "You think I should have submitted."

"No, never. I just think you could have been a bit more…" He bobs his head. "*Tactful.*"

I snort. "That's a tall order."

"It is, isn't it?" he says, giving me that disapproving stare that makes me just as defensive as it did when we were children.

"You weren't kneeling, either," I retort. "Neither was Amara."

"Yet no one noticed us." He chuckles dryly. "They never notice us when you're around."

"I'm well aware," I hiss, jerking my arm free and rushing past, irritated he would say something like that when he knows how much I hate the attention.

"I'm sorry. I didn't mea-"

"I haven't heard one kind word about the Queen since we stepped foot in this godsawful city," I say, rounding on him. "The humans despise her. Her people are terrified of her. Even her own children seem to dislike her."

"It does appear that way, doesn't it?"

I roll my eyes at his agreeable response and tilt my chin upward, scrutinizing the massive palace overlooking all Seboia.

The opaque, crystal castle glows with a metallic sheen beneath the sparse light of the two moons. Turrets topped with starlight encrusted gold domes feature stained glass windows depicting Cascadonia's devout representation of the gods embedded within. But all these towers are insignificant in comparison to the colossal domed pillar looming above all the rest. So high, it pierces straight through the clouds as if trying to slice through the veil that separates this realm from the rest.

Beneath the arched dome shrouded in even more extravagant, lush jewels than its neighbors is an open archway that houses the true focal point: a royal blue sapphire the size of a house, hovering magically within an open archway. It's the largest, most lavish, most ethereal jewel I've ever seen. So sublime, it must have been gifted by the gods themselves. For no object of such opulent divinity could have possibly originated from this realm.

It's captivating and enchanting, and after striding beside citizens with dirty, hole-ridden clothing, it's absolutely revolting.

Nauseated at the repugnant sight, I grimace and motion toward the blinding eyesore. "She sits in her beautiful castle, eating the richest foods and wearing the finest gowns, yet she does nothing to better her kingdom."

An older man bumps my shoulder, followed by a mumbled apology as he speeds past with a small boy and girl. Their clothing is patched and worn but fortunately clean, and the man's face is lined in exhaustion as he hurriedly maneuvers his family through the foot traffic. A splash of color catches my eye, and I see three females oohing and ahhing over an extravagant bracelet, garbed in gowns better suited to a ballroom than a leisurely evening stroll. I consider the glaring differences between the gaggle of females and the human family as I watch the wealthy immortals gossip and laugh, while the man – along with his children – appear to be in need of a good meal and a decades-long nap.

"When I saw her looking down her nose at the very same people she's meant to serve and protect, while they worship her as if she was a goddess, as if she is entitled to their reverence all because she wears a crown on her head…" My lips tighten. "I couldn't submit to someone like that. Even if it was only an act."

Tristan blows out an exasperated breath. "Of course you couldn't."

Fisting my hands at my sides, I grit my teeth. "It's not right, Tristan."

"I know," he says with a gentle smile. A street light flares with Gods Light as we pass Rory's Swords and Daggers, casting the swirls on Tristans's cheek in a silverish light. "I know it's unlike you to stand by if you see others being mistreated. Or to remain silent otherwise."

I cringe at his teasing, recalling my slip of the tongue to Darius at Aurora's shop, and of course, the more dire of issues. "I may have made a small mistake," I admit sheepishly.

"A small mistake?" Tristan drawls.

"Very small. Tiny." I pinch my fingers together. "Practically nonexistent."

Tristan eyes me warily. "What is this nonexistent mistake you think you made?"

I glance to my sides, searching for anyone near enough to overhear our discussion, but the number of citizens traveling by foot have depleted dramatically. The remaining walkers are now no longer clumped together, but spread out as their fellow travelers arrive at their nightly destinations, conveniently out of earshot.

I feel Tristan branding me with his gaze and clear my throat, feeling as if a stone has lodged itself there. "I formed a bond with Darius."

Tristan stumbles over his feet. "A bond." Slowly straightening, he blinks. "A bond like the one we share? Like you have with Amara and Zander?"

"No," I reply, and his shoulders slump in relief. "Those are weak. This one's much stronger than ours."

His lips flatten. "Lena, that's not a small mistake. That's a *huge* mistake. One of epic, monstrous proportions. It's probably the worst thing you could've possibly done."

He's going to kill me.

"That's not all," I mumble, chewing on my bottom lip.

He growls, not as rumbling or deep as Darius', but just as terrifying, given the situation. "What did you do?"

"It's not that bad."

"Lena!"

Avoiding his gaze, I stare up ahead at The Early Bird Inn. "Darius caught me in a lie."

"Godsdamnit, Lena." He scrubs his face. "Have you lost your mind?"

"My mind's still intact, thank you!" I snap. The vein in his temple begins to throb and his mark darkens. *Not good, not good at all.* I should probably tone it down a bit. "Before you lose it, the lie just tumbled out by accident. And as for the bond? I have no idea how I did it."

Tristan exhales a long, calming breath. So long, I can see his chest concave with the effort. "How can you not know?"

"I didn't initiate it." I shrug. "It just appeared."

Shoulders beginning to relax at a new puzzle to solve, he continues forward, pivoting towards the inn. "I didn't know that was possible. Has Darius said anything?"

"I don't think he has any idea what it is, and I've seen no evidence of bonds in this realm. He may not even realize they exist."

"He probably thinks he's going insane," he says, ascending the steps to our piteous lodging.

A burst of laughter punches from me at the thought, but I smother it with a cough when Tristan tosses a warning look over his shoulder.

"Are you sure you didn't create it intentionally?" he asks suspiciously.

"Positive. I've thought of nothing else since it happened. I didn't do anything. What do you think this means?"

"I don't know. Let me think on it a bit."

The wood railing on the porch steps snags on my vambraces. I tug it free and look up to see Tristan peering at me with a curious expression.

"Hmm." He hums. "You *do* seem to have a rather extreme reaction to him. I wonder if that could be the cause."

Extreme is too meager a word.

The Captain's ruggedly beautiful face appears before my eyes, causing my body to warm and my heart to race as I imagine his massive form dominating me at this very moment, piercing me with those glacial blue eyes that always seem to burn with a desperate need to consume every inch of me. The same need that has me often fighting against offering myself up as his own personal sacrifice, and in turn losing all sense of self, losing sight of my cause.

Dispelling the thought, I say, "I should probably just focus on avoiding him."

Or try to, at least.

"I don't know. If Darius isn't aware of the bond, this could prove beneficial to us," he says as he steps under the Gods Light on the inn's deck. "That is, if you're able to overcome your... urges."

I grimace. "In other words, suck it up?"

He smiles. "Exactly." He scans the street over his shoulder and purses his lips. "Although, after your spectacle today, any attempted subterfuge with him may be moot. I doubt you can go anywhere in Seboia without eyes tracking you." He peeks at me out of the corner of his eye, a mischievous twinkle to it that the God of Mischief, Saxon himself would be jealous of. "I might just have to lock you up."

"Funny," I say dryly, passing him by.

Reaching for the door handle, I hesitate, my fingers hovering above as I stare down at my fingerless vambraces, wondering what Darius is thinking at this moment. Is he cursing me for my deception? Has he written me off all together? Or is he thinking of me just as I am him? Wondering what it would be like if we were both born to a different life? A life where we could choose to live however we wish? With whomever we wish?

I chuckle humorlessly to myself, curling my fingers around the handle and opening the door. That life isn't in the Stars for me. Never will be, no matter the circumstances. But it could be for him. He could leave this place, travel the world, see these realms. Find a female worthy of him and he of her, settle down and start a family. To build a life filled with laughter and love.

But that's only if I'm strong enough to endure what's to come. Because for him to live in such a world, for him to experience that peaceful existence, blood must be spilled by my hand.

I can only hope it won't be his blood I'm forced to shed.

CHAPTER 12

DARIUS

The wind whistles in my ears, tangling my hair and creaking the branches of the trees inhabiting the Cursed Woods. Griffin stands beside me. His face is pinched in thought as the twin moons peek above the wall, casting a momentary light on Kace as he paces back and forth, before the white beams disappear behind a passing cloud. A precursor for the incoming storm.

"We found them at the end of patrol," the wiry guard says with a tremble to his voice, his eyes downcast and tremors shuddering through his body more violently than the leaves rustling above.

Grunting, I appraise the skittish fae currently staring at my chin, wondering how he managed to become a patrolling guard when he can't even look me in the eye. I may have a rather violent reputation, but one would think the Soulless are much more terrifying creatures than I am.

At my continued silence, sweat begins to bead above his brow and he tugs nervously at the collar of his vest. I curl my lip at the sight and turn away from him, staring up at the white wall encircling Seboia. Or more precisely, the jagged claw marks defacing the once smooth stone.

Shaped like a pyramid, the claw marks start out wide at the base at about five feet off the ground. Then as they rise, it narrows to a triangular point at around twenty feet. The crisscrossed slashes carve a few inches within the stone, appearing to be a victim of an animal mauling. But unlike animals who have a soul, the creatures who did this certainly do not.

"It was a large group, too," the guard explains, finally finding a bit of courage without me looking at him. "We didn't even notice the Soulless until we were almost on top of them."

Sky darkening by the second with the retreating moons, I summon orbs of fire from the palm of my hand. Flicking my wrist, they streak through the air to hover above all present. "How many Soulless were there?"

"I'm not sure. Twenty or so?"

I frown. That explains the number of markings, but not the height. All Soulless were once human, fae, or immortal before they were turned to the undead, and I've never heard of any of those beings reaching that height. Possibly a god, but I doubt gods are clawing at the walls of my city.

"How many guards were injured?" Griffin asks as he begins wading through the fallen leaves and forest growth.

"None. Most of the Soulless ran away."

Surprised, my gaze snaps to his. "Ran away?"

"Yes, sir," he mumbles as his chin drops down to his chest, staring at his feet. "A few stayed and we fought them off, but the rest ran away."

Folding my arms over my chest, I return my attention to the wall, striding closer. The ball of fire floating above my head casts an orange shadow over the wall as I scrutinize the inch-deep indentations carved into the white stone. Squinting, I discover it appears as if someone gouged it with a hook.

"The Soulless aren't subtle creatures," Kace says, tossing the guard a reproachful glare. "It's difficult to believe you didn't hear them before you spotted them."

The guard shuffles his feet, snapping twigs with his anxious movements. "They were silent." The guard's uneasy eyes stray to the stone. "If we hadn't heard the scraping and come to investigate, we never would've known they were here."

Griffin walks toward the wall, crinkling orange and yellow leaves beneath his boots. Raising his arm, he grazes his hand across the markings. "What were they doing when you came across them?"

The guard hesitates, and I wonder how long he's been enlisted if he can barely hold a conversation with a high-ranking officer.

"They were just scratching the wall." He shrugs, seeming unsure.

Griffin's hand stills above the gashes, his brows snapping together. "If they were only scratching, how were they able to scratch *that* high when none of them could've possibly been taller than six feet or so?"

My gaze swings up to the top of the wall as a sickening thought enters my mind, and I shut my eyes at the impossible, but indisputable epiphany.

"I … I… I don't…" the guard stammers.

"A superior officer asked you a question," I snap. "I suggest you answer him."

"They were crawling on top of one another!" the guard bursts out, his words tumbling over themselves. "I know it sounds crazy, but they were. Some were lying on the ground while others were standing on their backs and shoulders. They were digging into the walls!"

"Not digging," I growl, rolling my neck. "Climbing."

Kace gasps. "You think they were trying to climb over?"

I nod and both Griffin and Kace stare back at me, their gazes unblinking. Griffin shakes himself from his stupor and places a hand on the wall. Kace joins him a moment later to scrutinize the slices more closely. But after their thorough inspection, neither one of them can voice an argument.

"But… but…" the guard stutters. "Soulless can't do that! They only hunt and feed. They aren't capable of this!"

"They also don't run away or work harmoniously with one another, but you witnessed both," Griffin says on a long, drawn-out breath, scrubbing his hands over his face.

The guard frantically searches our faces, but upon seeing our grave expressions, he barks a laugh, manic humor overtaking him before he buries his face in his hands with a whimper.

"You're dismissed, Private," I sneer, no longer willing to deal with the sniveling fool.

He sniffles while performing a halfass bow before tripping over his own feet and scampering back within the relative safety of the walls.

Kace chuckles. "He couldn't get away from you fast enough, could he?"

"Reassign him to desk duty," I order, ambling towards the arched east gate.

Did they only try to climb over? Or were they searching for another way to get in?

Sweeping my gaze over the barred gate and the surrounding area, I find deep gouges and crumbled rock in the stone where the black metal is embedded. Eyes passing along the solid slab of iron, I stop when they land on the slit where the two doors mesh, finding several scratches that, fortunately, only scuff the surface.

Palms glittering orange as I return to the wall, I tap into my Air Gifts. Fallen brown, orange, and yellow leaves rise steadily from the ground, coalescing into a spiraling column. The wind sweeps strands of hair across my face, bumps pebbling on my skin as the Fall air cools even more with the gust of wind.

Rotating faster and faster, the cyclone of leaves soars towards the wall on a fluctuating wave, shaping itself to the triangular outline of the claw marks.

The others join me as I command the fire orbs to release their charges, zooming above the outline of the spiraling leaves.

If twenty Soulless can climb this high, how high could forty?

Illuminated in orange light from the roiling orbs of fire, the pyramid of leaves widen and rise to double their size. Calling forth a dozen more orbs, I listen to the crackling flames as they rise above our heads and whoosh towards the point of the triangle, watching as they scale upward one by one, dotting an illuminated path from the tip of the pyramid to the very top of the wall.

“That’s halfway up,” Kace breathes, slumping against a nearby maple tree and resting his head back.

“Darius, if forty Soulless can do that,” Griffin motions toward the wall with a wave of his hand, an urgency to his brown eyes that I feel within myself, “what could sixty do? Or eighty? Or a hundred?”

Kace pushes off the tree, tapping his foot on the forest floor and cupping his mouth, shaking his head. “Soulless don't behave this way.”

“They could,” I reply, sucking on my teeth. “If a Gods Cursed commanded them to.”

The sounds of rustling insects and windswept trees drown out their silence as I drop my head back and lift my gaze, following the trail of flamed orbs to the top of the wall that I once thought seemed so high, but now I fear isn't tall enough. I imagine what would have happened if those demons had made it over. If they managed to sneak into Seboia in the middle of the night while thousands of innocents were sleeping soundly in their beds, believing the walls would keep them safe.

Very few citizens have ever seen a Soulless, let alone fought one. Most haven't even been taught the proper ways to defend themselves against them. Sheltered safely in the city as they are now, there was no need for them to learn. I now see our glaring oversight. Our arrogant naivety in the belief that the walls would always protect, when the truth of the matter is that the walls can also be a trap.

A cage, if the Soulless were ever to breach these walls.

Envisioning these ominous scenarios, my stomach hollows out as the bloody massacre plays out in my mind.

"What does this mean?" Kace asks, he and Griffin coming to stand beside me.

"It means," I reply, grazing my palm across my enemies' scores of intent, "that we now have our evidence."

The Goddess of Life loves all her children, but it is said that immortals and fae are her most favored, her crown jewels. More specifically, Cascadonia and its people, whom she considers her proudest and most beloved creations besides the gods. Some would even argue that she loves Cascadonians more than the gods, but no one would dare to disrespect the gods by speaking that thought so openly.

Yes, Urielle loves the Cascadonians, but after she created them, she realized that although she cherished her new children, she would never be able to forge a true relationship with them. She is a goddess and does not belong within our realm, and we would never belong in hers. Saddened by this, Uriella went in search of a way to establish a bond between herself and the faes and immortals. A way to express her love even if she wasn't present. That was when, while in the gods' realm, Uriella came across the aura crystal – an opaque, white crystal speckled with flecks of shimmering sapphires, dazzling emeralds, glowing rubies, glittering golds, and sparkling tourmaline.

While mesmerized with the glittering, rainbow-like colors from the effervescent stone, an idea popped into Uriella's mind of the most perfect gift. Elated with her newfound discovery, she dismissed her godly Gifts and unearthed these divine crystals with her own two hands, digging and digging and digging until she had more than enough to create this special present. Once finished, she portaled all these crystals to Seboia, melted them into liquid, and began to sculpt. Flowing like water, the liquid crystal created walls and ceilings, formed roofs and beams, framed doors and archways, and molded turrets and pillars to create a grand, opulent palace out of the prismatic stone. Yet, once the Goddess of Light completed her task, she still was not pleased with her offering. She thought the palace was beautiful and lavish, but felt a god's gift should be a bit more splendid, more majestic.

With that thought, Uriella then added liquid gold to the walls and domed rooftops, veining the gold with crushed starlight. But what elevated this gift, what made it a true masterpiece, was the glorious royal blue sapphire that she magicked to hover indefinitely in an open archway of the largest pillar. With the addition of this massive jewel, The Mother of All was now satisfied, knowing all Seboia could bask at the sight of the Gods Touched palace and could now truly appreciate the honor the Goddess of Life bestowed upon them with such a sacred gift. And in doing so, forever sheltering Cascadonians in a home constructed of the very crystal native to the gods' realm, the Goddess of Life forged a spiritual connection that's been felt for thousands of generations.

It's always baffled me how that story has been passed down from one royal to the next, how every royal throughout the ages has sworn they've sensed the Goddess of Life's presence within the divine crystal. Yet when I touch these walls, I only feel cold, hard crystal. No presence of a goddess. No divine, spiritual connection. Only a frozen, unfeeling void. An absence of warmth and life unlike the wooden walls in the homes of Seboia where the wood almost pulsates in an echoed remembrance of the repurposed trees' once beating heart.

No, this palace wasn't a gift from the gods. Only a prismatic frozen tomb that gave plausibility to another tale concocted by the Cascadonian royals.

Climbing the last step to the royal wing, my boots clomp against the marble floor as I stalk past the former quarters of my mother and the late King's. Ignoring the physical hum from the ward placed on the forbidden room, I drift past it and open the door to my mother's private dining area within her chambers.

Dark, earthy colors greet my eyes. Smooth oak wood walls blend seamlessly with segments of molded honeycomb and copper latimer panels. A suitable accompaniment to the Gods Light sputtering from the decorative copper sconces interspersed throughout the dining room. The rollicking flames cast the room in a warm, ambient light, along with the glow of the moons beaming through the floor-to-ceiling arched windows. Fortunately for this room, as well as all the chambers and meeting rooms throughout the palace, they're now composed of only wood. Not a crystal in sight. I can only imagine that before the renovation, it was quite frustrating for my forefathers to be blinded by a rainbow of colors reflecting off their fork while trying to eat. Or to have to squint from the metallic sheen while speaking to a visiting royal.

Fresh rolls, cheese, bottles of wine, and a decanter of spirits are arranged in the center of a long, maple wood table along with a lavish bouquet of peonies, sweet peas, and lilies. Six place settings are laid out on a table that seats twelve, but only one seat is currently occupied.

All but for the messy topknot and a streak of soot on the back of her neck, Aurora is almost unrecognizable, dressed in a fitted red gown and ruby studded heels while she nibbles on a piece of cheese.

"I see that you changed," I say. Dragging the highback chair out, I seat myself beside her.

She eyes me up and down. Seemingly unimpressed, she reaches for a roll. "And I see that you didn't."

"I doubt our attire will make any of this less torturous." Reaching for the decanter of spirits, I pluck the glass top off with a pop, inhale the smooth, oaky scent of the whiskey, and pour myself a generous portion. I'll more than need it within my mother's presence.

Aurora groans and slumps in her chair, cradling a glass of red wine. "Don't crush my dreams! I put on a dress, for god's sake."

"And you look beautiful," I state honestly, swallowing a mouthful of whiskey and relishing the feel of the smooth liquid gliding across my tongue.

"I look ridiculous." She toys with the thin straps of her dress, squirming.

"Only because you missed a few spots," I reply, tickling the back of her neck. She bats my hand away and reaches for a cloth, wiping vigorously at the back of her neck. "You could've tried to comb your hair," I add, spotting the knots and tangles rolled in a ball on the top of her head. "It looks like a bird's nest."

"I'm only willing to do so much," she huffs. Smoothing her hand through her hair, she attempts to tame the untamable before burying her nose into her glass.

Spotting a small patch of smooth hair near her forehead, I smirk. "You couldn't get the brush through your hair, could you?"

"No." She snorts, fogging the glass in which her nose is still buried. "And I couldn't find my lady in waiting."

"Who is your lady in waiting?"

"I have no idea! I haven't used one in so long, I don't even think I have one anymore." She laughs before her face twists into a scowl, and she squirms in her seat once again.

"Stop wiggling. You look like a worm," I chastise.

"But it's so uncomfortable," she whines, her squirming becoming more pronounced. "I can't bind my breasts with this dress, otherwise you'd see them." She slaps her hands to her breasts and bounces them shamelessly. "They're just jiggling away. Free as a bird."

"I really didn't need to know that," I grumble.

"Don't be such a child." She rolls her eyes. "They're just tits, not a disease. With the way you were leering at Lena's today, I know you're quite fond of that particular body part." Tonguing her cheek, she glances down where she palms herself, raising her breasts up and down in a seesaw motion.

Ignoring the Lena comment, I pinch the bridge of my nose. "That doesn't mean I want to hear about your tits. And don't talk like that," I admonish. "You sound like a street rat."

"You *look* like a street rat," she quips pettily.

"I look like someone who went to work today."

"You obviously didn't work all day or you wouldn't have been at my shop," she murmurs snarkily as she lifts her glass. But then her hand stills halfway to her mouth, regarding me as if she just remembered something. "You never did tell me why you came by today. Was it just an excuse to drool over Lena, or was there an actual reason?"

Shit.

After the Lena fiasco, it completely slipped my mind to warn Aurora about the Jareth incident. She wouldn't care either way.

She hates Jareth and his sister just as much as I do, but we both love Theon, and know this'll cause more strife in his life than he deserves.

"Where is he!?"

"That's why." Resigned, I spin my chair to face the door and knock back the rest of my whiskey, waiting for the shitshow from which there's no escape.

Aurora perks up in her seat, her impish eyes sparkling. "This should be entertaining."

I give her a dry look and she giggles shamelessly as she hops her chair around until she faces the door the same as I am. She manages to cross her legs and rearrange her dress over her knees right before my brother's wife slams the door wide open.

Lips puckered and chest heaving, Kiora's feral eyes rapidly scan the room. As soon as they land on me, her face twists into rage. "You son of a bitch!"

"That's not a nice thing to say about your husband's mother." I smirk, knowing full well it'll goad the heartless bitch. "Hello, sister."

With blonde hair smooth as glass in a blunt cut that ends at the chin, porcelain skin, and light brown eyes accented by starlight and emerald jewels, the Nature immortal is considered beautiful to most. But with her waspish personality and her penchant to behave and dress like a whore, to me she'll always be a hideous shrew.

Theon rushes in behind Kiora and tugs on her arm. "Darling," he pleads.

But she pays him no mind as she jerks her arm free, stalking towards me to spit at my feet. "You're no brother of mine!"

"The feeling's mutual."

Aurora leans forward to better look at the glob of spit. Crinkling her nose, she raises her glass of wine to Kiora. "That's attractive."

"Fuck off, Aurora!"

Aurora stills. "Speak to me that way again, and I'll cut your tongue out." Eyeing Kiora over her glass of wine, she takes a slow sip, then lowers the glass, smiling sweetly. "I don't think the males at court will want to play with you anymore if you no longer have a tongue. I can only imagine how difficult it would be to suck them off without one. Although, now that I think about it, they may enjoy you more if you can't speak."

"Aurora!" Theon shouts, as a loud guffaw bursts from me.

This is turning out to be a much more entertaining night than I thought it would be.

"How *dare* you speak to me that way!" Kiora shouts at Aurora, her face pinched in open malice. "I'm a princess."

"Not by blood." Aurora chuckles, bobbing her crossed leg. "Unlike me."

A strangled shriek tears from Kiora and she stalks toward Aurora, raising green, glittering hands. "You dumb cunt!"

Aurora bolts out of her chair, balling inflamed fists at her sides. I gleefully wait for her to knock Kiora on her ass with a searing hit.

A dozen thorns suddenly sprout from Kiora's palms, black liquid oozing from the points as she shoots them towards Aurora with a flick of her hand, only for the thorns to be swept up by a whirling pillar of water that instantly hardens to ice.

A door slams.

"Can someone please enlighten me as to why you're having a shouting match within my chambers?"

At the sound of that cold, authoritative voice, we all turn to face the door that leads to the rest of my mother's rooms, watching in silence as Adelphia ambles towards us, each click of her heels more foreboding than the last. Garbed in the same gown and jewels she wore earlier in the day, her eyes are as arctic as the column of ice she stops beside, fixated on the thorns alone.

Her aquamarine and starlight jewels brighten as she raises a glittering teal hand. The ice melts and returns to her in a stream, vanishing into her palm as the thorns tumble to the ground.

"Poisoned thorns, Kiora?" she asks in a lethal tone with which I'm all too familiar. "You wish to poison my daughter?"

Kiora's jewels illuminate and the dripping thorns disintegrate with a wave of her hand. "Of course not," she says with a brittle smile. "I would never do such a thing to my dear sister."

Aurora snorts and Adelphia gives her a warning look that she quickly heeds, returning quietly to her seat.

"What is the meaning of this?" Adelphia asks, her frigid gaze landing on each of us in turn.

Drawing her shoulders back, Kiora lifts a haughty chin. "Your son," she sneers at me, "has arrested my brother on false charges."

My mother's pale green eyes snap to mine, narrowing minutely before falling to my nose, unable to hold my gaze for long. Fortunately for me, that hateful act lost its sting long ago.

"Darius," Adelphia says, warning laced in her tone.

Kiora's lips twitch into a smug smirk, I'm sure recalling the many instances over the years that Adelphia sided with her family over me. But in her blind arrogance, she failed to realize that in this instance, Jareth performed the one act Adelphia will never condone.

"I have ample evidence that Jareth has assaulted females and women on several different occasions," I say, before adding, "among a litany of other crimes."

Adelphia's back stiffens as her gaze snaps to mine, and my stomach roils at the haunted look in her eyes. "Did he rape any of them?" she asks, a slight quiver to her tone.

I swallow thickly and shake my head. "None that has been

reported, but I wouldn't be surprised if something eventually came to light."

Shutting her eyes, she exhales an audible breath through her nostrils, staying that way for several moments until her eyes suddenly snap open. Her features harden to stone as she slowly pivots to face Kiora.

"You find this behavior to be acceptable? Because he is your brother, he may do as he wishes without consequence?" Adelphia questions sharply. "How would you like it if a male touched you without permission?"

Kiora stares blankly, her lack of empathy towards her brother's victims more than apparent from her bland expression. "I demand he be released at once."

"You demand?" Adelphia laughs, a harsh sound that abruptly cuts off when she hisses, "You will demand *nothing* of me."

But Kiora refuses to back down. "My father -"

"*I* am the Queen!" Adelphia cuts in, stalking towards Kiora, her hand pressed against her chest. "Not your father. Not you. *Me*." Adelphia's face shutters, an apathetic mask slipping into place as she smooths her palms down the front of her gown. Turning her back on Kiora with a regal twirl, she drifts toward the chair at the head of the table and seats herself. "You will remember your place, Kiora. I stand by Darius' sentencing."

Kiora boldly glares at the Queen before whirling on her feet and moving towards the door.

"Did I dismiss you?" Adelphia asks coolly, pouring herself a glass of wine.

Hand pausing above the door handle, Kiora slowly pivots to face Adelphia. "May I *please*," she says through clenched teeth, "be excused?"

Adelphia cocks her head to the side and smiles sweetly. "Of course."

Face mottled in rage, Kiora glares at Adelphia beneath her lashes as she curtsies before rushing from the room.

"Mother," Theon groans, fingers pressed to his temples.

"Don't 'Mother' me!" she snaps, slapping her wine glass onto the table with a loud thunk. "I will not be spoken to in such a way by anyone."

Theon's shoulders slump and he dutifully nods his head.

"And Theon? If she ever speaks to me that way again…" Adelphia waits for his solemn gaze to meet her steeled one. "I'll put her in the dungeons right alongside her brother. Wife or no wife."

Theon purses his lips, but says nothing more as he jerks his head in assent.

A double knock on the door blares within the room and Theon answers it, quietly slipping out the door before several palace servants swoop in with heaping bowls and platters of food.

Well trained, the servants barely rustle, let alone clatter as they serve spit roasted pig, smoked fish, herbed vegetables, and warm bread with freshly churned butter. A fae servant attempts to ladle chilled beet soup into my empty bowl but I wave away her attempts. In silence, she removes the bowl and follows the other servant out of the room, quietly shutting the door behind her.

"How many lashes did he get?" Adelphia asks, taking a delicate bite of fish from her fork.

"Ten," I reply.

She chews thoughtfully. "I would've given him twenty."

I chuckle. "I was tempted to, but decided against it." Reaching for the bread, I tear off a chunk. "Besides, burns last longer than a whipping."

Adelphia and I share a rare smile, but hers drops all too soon when my sister speaks.

"I would've cut off his balls," Aurora says around a mouthful of food.

I grimace, readjusting myself in my seat as I spread butter across the warm bread. "That's a bit extreme," I reply halfheartedly. Jareth may very well deserve it, but there's something inherently wrong for a male to suggest any punishment that involves mutilating a cock.

Aurora scoffs, wiping the pig fat dripping down her chin with the back of her hand. "Lena wouldn't think so."

At the mention of Lena, I shoot a glare at Aurora and she winces, an apologetic smile creeping up her cheeks. Neither one of us has mentioned to the other our involvement with Lena's stunt earlier in the day, or what repercussions would be enacted with so many witnesses. But neither did either of us need to be told that Adelphia wouldn't react well to her children openly defending the foreigner. Of course, I didn't expect Adelphia to forget, but I also didn't expect Aurora to draw attention to it. My gaze veers to our mother, hopeful she misheard Aurora's slip of the tongue. But judging off her puckered lips and sharpened cheeks, it's apparent that the name didn't escape her notice.

"Lena," Adelphia drawls. "Dalenna Nectallius." Swirling her glass of wine, she leans back in her seat. "I see you two have been making new friends."

We say nothing.

"Who is she?"

"I'm not sure," I reply on a swallow, the once palatable bread sticking on its path down my throat. "She only just arrived yesterday."

Adelphia hums, cradling her glass with both hands as she peers out the window. "Her markings are familiar," she mumbles to herself, her brows pinched. "But I can't seem to remember where I've seen them before."

"I thought they were scars." They're perfectly formed, the shape of them precise, unlike scars, but I've never come across any markings like hers. Fae and immortals have jewels. The Gods Cursed's are filled with ruby flecked shadows. Even the gods are marked by jewels, not circular shaped markings dotting their skin. Scars are the only plausible explanation.

"No, they're markings," Adelphia says. "I'm sure of it." Brows smoothing over, she lifts her fork and resumes eating. "I want you to find out everything you can about her." Taking another bite, she narrows her gaze on me, assessing me clinically as she slips the fork from between her lips. "She is unusually beautiful, so that shouldn't be too difficult a task," she says, leaving no room for misinterpretation.

My hand clenches around the knife, the silver bowing beneath my grip as an insidious feeling slithers within my veins. "I'm not a whore," I snarl as I drop the knife on my plate, hardly hearing the silver clink against porcelain as I hold my mother's gaze.

Adelphia rolls her eyes. "Those who serve their kingdom are always whores, one way or another. Whether that's by spreading their legs or by killing foolishly vocal women. No matter how unsavory we might find either act to be."

"Don't lie, Mother," I snap, shoving my uneaten plate of food away. "Like you actually give a fuck whether you kill a human."

"Of course I don't. But I also won't be the one performing the task." Adelphia points her fork at me. "As Captain of the Guard, that will be your responsibility if she causes any more trouble." She lifts the glass towards Aurora and tinks the crystal with her nail, a silent order for Aurora to pour her another glass. "You *will* keep an eye on her, Captain. That's an order."

The very idea of whoring myself to another, even someone as alluring as Lena, has my stomach roiling, acid eating at the lining of my gut. If it was any other time and I didn't currently need my mother's cooperation, I'd tell her to fuck off. But since my loyalty is to my kingdom and my kingdom alone, I ignore Aurora's disapproving glare and reluctantly jerk a nod, knowing that it's even more unlikely for my mother to grant me any favors if I argue with her.

"Mother, there was an incident today," I say. "The patrolling guards found claw marks on the east gate as well as the wall beside it. They appear to be from the Soulless." Adelphia stills, but I continue without pause. "I'd like to send a missive to the other kingdoms and request their reconsideration on the expedition."

"No." Adelphia's jewels illuminate as frost begins to coat the glass clenched within her hand.

"They said they needed more information before sending out-"

"This is not enough information," she interrupts icily.

"It's more than enough," I argue. "They're attempting to breach the city and would in no way have the mental faculties to do such a thing without being commanded by the Gods Cursed. If we could just–"

"No!" my mother commands sharply. Setting the glass down, she waves her glittering teal palm over the glass and the frost disappears, the frozen wine becoming liquid once more. "You will keep an eye on the situation and double patrols, but nothing more."

Fuming, I slouch in my chair, in no way hiding my loathing of her within this moment.

Adelphia cocks her head to the side, considering me thoughtfully. "Have you not thought how coincidental it is that your new friend has arrived just as the Soulless have started acting strangely?"

I rub my temples, wanting nothing more than to walk out the door and escape her condescending tone. "She's not a Gods Cursed."

"That may be so, but that doesn't mean she doesn't serve them in some capacity. It's interesting how on her first night here, she was able to befriend not only the Captain of the Guard, but the

Princess, as well. I find that very suspicious, as I'm sure you do, too." She pushes her plate forward and sets her elbows on the table, placing her clasped hands beneath her chin. "You are to keep an eye on that girl and report anything of note. Who knows? She may very well be the evidence you've been searching for."

CHAPTER 13

LENA

"Where's my foooood?" Amara whines, sprawled out in her chair. "I'm starving."

Feeling the hollowness of my own stomach, I ignore her belly-aching and sweep my gaze across one of Seboia's most popular destinations.

At night, The Quiet Harpy is loud and boisterous, filled to capacity with peasants and nobles alike. But during the day – as it is now – it's eerily vacant, housing no more than a dozen or so patrons. Seated with Amara at one of the many scarred tables crammed into the dining area, my eyes lazily drift to those who have battled the depressing doom and gloom of the popular night spot for a decent mid-day meal. Or for some, like the notorious drunk who's currently sprawled across the bar snoring, to drown themselves in their cups. Several stools down from the passed out fae, two males eat a solitary meal at the bar. Near the entrance, a human couple whispers sweet nothings to one another beneath the bay window. An older fae with bloodshot eyes a few tables down from us grumbles to himself as he downs his ale. Near the cold hearth towards the rear of the pub, a half dozen fae in soiled, tattered clothing play a spirited game of dice. Judging off their rowdiness and the several empty tankards before them, I suspect they've been here several hours already.

Amara releases a hunger filled groan and kicks my foot aside, rudely invading my foot territory beneath the table. I curl my lip at the offending body part and kick her foot back towards her own side.

"Ow!"

"Stop whining," I grit out. "You're always fucking whining."

"I'm not whining," she whines, rubbing her shin.

I grind my teeth. "Yes. You. Are."

She tosses her arms up, dropping them back to her thighs with a loud smack. "I haven't eaten all day!"

Feeling my vexation piqued by my own hunger, I suck on my teeth. "Neither have I, but you don't hear me bitching about it."

"If someone hadn't eaten all the food this morning," she says, eyeing me in open accusation, "then maybe I wouldn't be whining."

"I didn't eat all the food," I lie, watching the drunk roll off the bar and land flat on his face. Surprised but at the same time not, he doesn't crack a single eyelid as he continues snoring.

At my response, Amara's eyes narrow and I watch her fingers curl around the edges of the table, readying to claw my eyes out. "You left me less than a handful of nuts!"

That's because I didn't know there were any more nuts. If I did, I would have eaten those as well.

"I was hungry." I shrug, and she seethes further. "Besides, I needed it more."

She scans me up and down, smirking. "Your fat ass certainly didn't."

I gasp. "My ass is not fat!" My hands twitch to inspect the object of her insult, but unwilling to give her the satisfaction, I still my hands and lift my chin. "It's nicely plump."

She scoffs and rolls her eyes. "That's just a polite way of saying it's fat."

"At least I have an ass."

She frowns, self-consciously staring down at her backside. I do an internal fist pump. "I have an ass," she says. I dismiss her with a snort and she growls. "But if I don't have an ass, it's only because you always eat all our food!"

Folding my arms over my chest, I whip my gaze from hers. "Bitch."

"Whore."

I slowly swivel my head back around, glaring at the cantankerous woman who is currently the bane of my existence. Digging my fingers into my arms, I imagine myself wrapping my hands around her scrawny little neck and choking the life out of her. But I refrain, because when it comes to food, we can both be a bit shrewish.

Only in this instance, I suppose some of our anger may be a bit misplaced, and probably has more to do with our current predicament rather than our hunger.

While Tristan and Zander have been searching the capital for our quarry these last few weeks, Amara and I have been experiencing a much more dire fate. We've been captured. Betrayed. Bound and caged by the very males who claim to care for us.

Subjected to their cruel and unusual punishment, all in their quest to subdue those who refuse to submit to their sexist ideals of how a female should behave. Imprisoned and condemned to suffer a torturous existence all because we females choose to have a voice!

Well... that may be a bit of an exaggeration and not exactly truthful. But it certainly feels that way!

After my disaster with the Queen, I was unable to walk down the street without dozens of eyes trailing my every step. As a result, Amara and I were confined to our room at the Early Bird

Inn, banned by both Zander and Tristan from leaving with the exception of meals or to visit Layla in the stables.

Amara tried arguing that I was the only guilty party and she shouldn't be punished for my transgressions, but her argument fell on deaf ears and was weak at best. She may not have done anything yet, but with her ornery personality, it's only a matter of time. We both admitted their reasoning was sound and grudgingly agreed to their demands, but since we're both unused to remaining stagnant, to say it's been difficult for us would be an understatement.

Frustrated, irritable, and just plain bitchy with the situation at hand, Amara and I have taken every opportunity we could to needle the other, searching for any way to relieve the perpetual boredom. After several heated arguments and a few brawls within the first day, Zander wisely suggested we continue our training within our shared room. We initially balked at the idea. Training in a room that was barely large enough for two people to cohabitate in, let alone spar? It was ridiculous. But after an incident of Amara lighting my hair on fire, her near drowning me while attempting to extinguish said fire, and subsequently, me choking her with a bed sheet, we thought it best for our sanity to at least give it a shot.

Amara suddenly perks up at the sight of Mona passing through the kitchen's swinging doors, heading our way with two steaming bowls. Mona's expression is as emotionless as ever as she plops one bowl of rabbit stew between Amara's hands, then the other between mine.

"Thanks, Mona." I offer the Water fae a smile, with Amara grunting her appreciation through a mouthful of food.

The disk earrings decorating Mona's sharpened ears dangle a chime as she nods her head and walks away, collecting the dirty dishes off an empty table adjacent to ours.

Since arriving in Seboia a few weeks ago, I've been served this dish several times. I already know the rabbit is robust, the root vegetables are hearty, and the savory broth is seasoned perfectly. But I notice none of this as I dig in with gusto.

Anger instantly evaporating with the food's arrival, we enjoy a companionable silence as we dig into our meals. Amara began before me, but she hasn't even eaten half her meal by the time I'm tipping my head back and pouring the remaining broth into my mouth. Lowering my empty bowl, I glare at it as if willing it to replenish itself with my thoughts alone. Unsurprisingly, my efforts are unsuccessful. I'm debating whether I should order another serving now or later when Amara interrupts my musings by shoving her half-eaten bowl beneath my nose. I smile gratefully at her and she laughs, shaking her head. As I'm lifting the wooden spoon to my mouth, I catch sight of the Fire fae a few tables down, staring at me in wide eyed astonishment. Knowing full well it looks like I'm inhaling my food rather than eating it, I choose to ignore him. His reaction to my eating habits may be considered rude to most, but it's actually a quite common occurrence.

Amara breathes out a sated sigh and stretches her legs beneath the table as I swipe the last bits of broth from the bowl, sucking its remnants off my fingers. I stack Amara's empty bowl atop mine and when I'm sliding the dishes aside, two chairs scrape across the oak floors, Zander and a cloaked Tristan seating themselves before us. Knowing they must be starving and feeling like my own hollow stomach is gnawing at itself, I order bowls of stew for each of us with a three fingered wave to Mona. Familiar with my eating habits, she doesn't even bat an eye at the request as she scurries back into the kitchen.

Zander's expression is unusually somber, and Tristan's dark brown eyes are weary where they peek out beneath his hood. We all remain silent until Mona appears with our dishes and ales before she quickly rushes off, leaving us to eat in peace.

Spoons scraping bowls, splashing broth, and slurping of ales are the only sounds uttered as we silently enjoy our meal. After chewing my last bite of stew, I'm finally able to feel the satisfaction of a full stomach and I release a contented sigh, feeling my depleted energy replenish itself.

Sipping my ale, I focus on the two males before me. "What did you find out?"

Zander slurps noisily from his spoon. "Absolutely nothing. These people won't talk. I've tried everything." He swipes a dribble of broth from his chin with the back of his hand, listing all the ways he's attempted to pry information on his fingers. "I've tried befriending them. I've tried drinking with them. I've tried parties, whores, bribery... but nothing." Zander's lips thin. "They don't even pretend to consider the gold I offer."

Tonguing my cheek, I remove Tristan's hood to better see his face. "How about you?"

Pursing his lips, he ruffles his hair. "The only rumor I've heard concerns the claw marks on the wall." Having already finished his meal, he lets the wooden spoon fall to the empty bowl with a clunk, a testament to his frustration for the normally well-mannered man.

A new concern pops into my mind and my brows furrow. "Have you been seen?"

Tristan scoffs, stacking his empty bowl atop mine and shoving it beside the others. "These beings are just as blind as any other. Don't worry, Lena." He winks. "You still have your ghost."

I chuckle, but it quickly trails off. Leaning over the table, I lower my voice. "We know that someone is here. Most likely *multiple* someones. How is it that neither of you has been able to obtain any information?"

Amara leans forward on her elbows, speaking just as quietly. "I don't think it has anything to do with them. I think this person, or people, are very good at covering their tracks."

Biting my lip, I drum my vambraced fingers on the worn table. "You haven't heard anything from Aurora?" I ask Tristan.

Tristan has had several dates with Aurora and even stayed a few nights in the loft above her shop. He hasn't said anything, but it's obvious he's developed more than a casual interest in her. I hate to put him in this position, but just as he's told me many times before, we have to use everything at our disposal.

His shoulders slump minutely as he studies the grooves of the table. "She doesn't know anything."

"She's a princess, for gods' sakes," Amara huffs, curling her short brown hair behind her ear and exposing the singular starlight jewel. "Her mother must have mentioned something to her."

He shakes his head. "They aren't close, and Aurora hates everything to do with court. She distances herself from it as much as possible." Tristan scans the room for any listeners before whispering to me. "I believe your skills are necessary at this point, Lena."

Hating the very idea of Tristan's suggestion, I lean back and avoid his gaze. "Not yet, but soon."

Tristan pats the table in frustration, but nods reluctantly.

"Then what are we going to do?" Zander asks, scratching beneath his jaw. "We have to do *something*."

I blow out a breath. "We keep doing what we're doing and hopefully, we'll stumble upon some answers. In the meantime, I need to see those claw marks. Maybe then I'll have a better understanding of our timetable."

"We'll have to sneak out of the city," Tristan says, removing his cloak and hanging it on the back of his chair. "I tried leaving to see them for myself, but the guards posted at the gate told me I wouldn't be allowed to return once I left."

Amara smirks and bumps her shoulder with mine. "That has the Queen written all over it."

I snort. I'm surprised that's all she did. If anything, I half expected her to kick us out altogether. Although, the more I think about it, it's less surprising if you consider how her whole Queen-to-the-people act would've crumbled to dust if she did. I just assumed she didn't care. It seems I can be wrong on occasion. A very rare occasion.

"There are a few spots left unguarded," Zander says, tossing his thick arm across the back of the empty chair beside him. "We'd have to climb over the wall at night to remain unnoticed, but it shouldn't be an issue."

"We'll need weapons," Tristan adds, cupping his pint between both hands. "We have no hope of remaining unnoticed if we have to fight Soulless without them." He gazes at me with a knot of worry bunched between his brows. I pat his forearm soothingly.

"Don't worry about that," Amara says, a suspicious gleam in her whiskey eyes. "I'll take care of the weapons."

"Don't steal any," I warn.

She rolls her eyes and hooks her ankles around the front of the chair, teetering on its back legs. "I'm not going to steal anything. Just leave it to me. I have an idea." She drops her head back and stares up at the wooden beams of the pub with a shifty expression that has alarm bells tolling in my head.

Zander smiles. "You're definitely going to steal them."

Amara's chair slams down and she swipes at him, but Zander dodges her easily with a laugh. His smiling face drifts towards mine, instantly sobering. The worry lining his face is a punch to the gut. "Do you think we have enough time?"

"I'll know more once I see the marks, but I'm sure we do," I lie, hearing the *tick, tick, tick* of the clock striking that much faster.

"You know there's a much easier way to handle this," Tristan casually tosses out, clasping his hands over his abdomen as he relaxes into his seat. "One where we could just walk out instead of sneaking out."

Tristan eyes me meaningfully and I frown, unable to foresee what he's leading up to.

"You could ask Darius if we could leave and return," he says. I stiffen, instantly furious at the suggestion. "He's probably the only other person besides the Queen who could give us permission."

I narrow my eyes at him but he boldly stares back, unfazed in the slightest in the face of my displeasure. "Not happening."

"That's a fantastic idea," Zander says. Ignoring my glare now directed at him, he lays his forearms on the table and knocks twice on the wood. "That male is a goner for you." He laughs. "He's walked past the inn more times than I can count." Batting his eyes teasingly, he singsongs, "Peeking into windows, staring up at the rooms. Searching for our little seductress."

Irritation wars with humor as I pinch my lips to stifle a laugh at his ridiculous antics.

"He really has come by quite often," Tristan adds. "I've learned his schedule and followed him on occasion." He pauses to swig from his ale. "It's completely out of his way and there's no reason for him to come by unless he was looking for someone. We all know he isn't looking for any of us."

I bow my head and secretly smile to myself. Even though I know it was for the best, I can't say I wasn't disappointed Darius never came by. Well, not disappointed in him, per se, more with myself for pining over someone who hadn't even given me a second thought while he consumed all of mine. Hearing that he's been searching me out in his own way, evidence that I am on his mind, causes an unwelcome flutter to reverberate in my chest.

But that still doesn't change the fact that I don't want to use him in that way. It feels like a betrayal of the worst kind, which is odd in itself since I usually have no qualms with deception. Not if it's necessary, and in this case, it most definitely is. "I still don't think that's a good idea."

"It's a great idea," Tristan argues.

I slap my palm to the table, pointing at him with a warning. "Tristan, don't."

He holds his palms up congenially, but remains firm. "I understand, I really do. But if you can ask it of me with Aurora, then I can ask it of you."

Any excuses I may have had instantly crumble and I jerk a nod. Irrationally furious with him for expecting this of me, even though I require it of him, I veer my gaze from his, following Mona as she strolls towards the couple seated beneath the bay window. That is, until the door opens and three familiar males walk in, followed by one unfamiliar fae.

Darius.

All previous thoughts instantly scatter at the sight of him walking into the tavern. And as if dying of thirst, I greedily drink in every inch of him. The way his wavy, shoulder length, black hair gleams blue beneath the daylight steaming through the window. The way his lush lips shape his words as he speaks quietly to the males who accompany him. His sculpted chest straining at the seams of his black leather vest. Those intense, glacial blue eyes that could swallow me whole with just a look.

He laughs at something the unknown fae says, and a soft smile pulls at my lips at the desirable sound. He inhales a deep breath through his nostrils, then as if a wolf scenting his prey, his head whips around and his eyes snap to mine. Ensnaring me mind, body, and soul, the blue of his eyes burn as brightly as his illuminated gems, searing me all the way to my core. My skin pebbles and a ball of heat forms in my lower belly before that impossible bond strums to life, digging its claws into the organ beneath my chest.

Surprise, desire, hope, lust, anger, longing, wariness, suspicion, affection. All these emotions stream through the bond, colliding and clashing with my own until I have no way of determining which emotion belongs to whom. And although this connection is strange and confusing, now that it's reformed, I notice the void that was once there. A piece of myself that I've been lacking. As if his absence has deprived me of a basic life sustaining element, but now that he's here and the once missing link has clicked into place, the cavity within my soul is now filled. Complete and whole.

Power radiates off him in waves, saturating the air with an almost frantic fervor. Feeling his volatile power blanket the room, the patrons cower into themselves as they yield to their alpha. Several panic and stumble over their feet to rush towards the door while the more courageous lower their gazes and slump in their chair, attempting to become invisible. Not me. I welcome the frenzied savageness of him. Luxuriate in it. Feast on it as the dominant male's eyes lick me with a burning fire, searing a branding trail from throat to pussy. And as my body burns, something in me softens. Weakens. That cage I've built, the one that's pivotal to my survival, rattles violently at the overwhelming emotions.

But I hardly notice the detrimental effect as my heart races, my sex slickens, and I bite back a moan as he strides toward me. No, he doesn't stride. He stalks. He prowls. He hunts for the prey that's escaped his clutches for the past several weeks.

He stops before me and towers above, peering down at me with an intensity that's both savage and wild, and I lose all sense of self as I get lost within those manic blue orbs.

The indomitable pillar lowers himself towards me, flattening both hands on the table, and a ripple of undiluted power knocks my breath from my lungs as he cages me in between his arms. Lowering his head near mine, his lips graze the lobe of my ear. "Where were you?" he asks in his gravelly deep tone.

A buzzing sounds in my ears as I inhale cedar and smoky musk. The scent of him clouds my mind, rattling the cage more viciously. Weakening it at the joints as I subconsciously arch back into his chest, spreading my legs as my juices pool at the juncture between my thighs.

"I've been here," I reply, hearing the lust thickening my voice.

"No you haven't," he accuses harshly. The furious words rumble through his chest into my back, the buzz intensifying as a small fissure forms within the bars.

Darius slides one hand around my waist and splays his large, calloused hand over my abdomen. My skin crackles and my breathing quickens as he buries his nose into the crook of my neck, releasing a muffled groan that vibrates me to my very bones. And that small fissure, that rift, splinters and webs throughout the bars of the cage until it explodes on a thunderous crack that gouges at my chest.

As if a vengeful wave comes to obliterate my mind, an onslaught of emotions crashes into me and I physically rear back into Darius at the unexpected attack. Tristan's furious, Zander's nervous, Kace is wary, and the unknown fae is confused. A fae male across the room is petrified. Mona is amused, but unsurprised. A female two blocks down from here is bored, while the male she's with is peaking in sexual euphoria. Ten clicks from the tavern, a group of humans and fae feel hope and excitement, as well as wrath and bloodlust.

Hate, love, hunger, fear, sadness, weariness, pain, heartbreak, longing. All these emotions and more tumble into me from beings near and far. None of them mine, but they now belong to me just the same.

My breathing becomes laborious, sweat slickens my brow, and my heart pounds a chaotic rhythm as it attempts to break free from my chest. I try to separate the roaring chaos within my mind. To separate myself from all others. But I'm swept up in the whirlwind and swiftly become lost within the deluge.

"Let her go," Tristan commands. "Now."

"No," Darius snarls, pressing me tighter to his chest. The emotions magnify with his touch and I curl into myself, whimpering.

A chair scrapes against the floor, then Tristan bends over the table to crowd us both with a mask carved from fury. "Remove your hands or I will remove them for you," he says with a voice of burning ice. Darius says nothing as a growl rumbles from him into me, riding on a swell of rage and possessiveness.

"Let her go, Darius," Griffin orders. "She's in pain."

Darius snaps his eyes toward him. "She's mine!" he bellows menacingly, a warning to anyone who'd dare defy him. The scent of smoke teases my nostrils and a new wave of rage and possessiveness blasts from Darius, hacking painfully at my mind as it bombards me with a succession of assaults. I throw my head back with an agonized moan.

"Give her to me," Amara says.

Darius hesitates, but eventually curls his fingers into my vest, dragging me into an even more crushing embrace, before suddenly releasing me.

Small, shaking hands cup my cheeks and lift my lolling head, Amara's worried face swimming into view. "You're okay. You're okay," she rushes out, her concerned eyes staring into my amethyst ones. "Control it, sweetie. You can do it. Lock it up," she says in a gentle tone I'm unaccustomed to. "Please," she whispers.

Whimpering, I remain limp, adrift in a churning sea of emotions.

Too much! Too much! Too much!

"Is she okay?"

"What's going on?"

"Is it working?"

Amara's fearful gaze veers from mine and she shakes her head. "I don't know! I don't think so."

"Give her to me," Griffin says quietly over my shoulder.

Amara's gaze snaps to his, her face twisting into a snarl. "Don't touch her."

"I won't hurt her. You have my word," Griffin says in a placating tone. "But I think I know how to help."

Amara holds his gaze for a long moment, then releases me and steps back. My body slackens and I bow my head over my hunched form, whimpering as I try to make sense of the riot of emotions assaulting my person. Though I strain to regain control, I can only cower into myself, submitting to the mental violation.

Griffin crouches before me, carefully avoiding touching my skin as he pushes my sweat-drenched hair back from my face. "Lena," he says softly. "I think I know how to help you, but I need physical contact. May I touch you?"

"Just make it stop!" I beg before crying out. "Please."

"Griffin!" Darius bellows in fury, but hidden beneath his rage is a hint of terror. Wishing I could comfort him, I attempt to do so, but I'm unable to even raise my head.

"Quiet, Darius!" Griffin snaps. His cheeks harden in determination and he reaches for my hand. Uncurling my fingers from my waist, he enfolds my limp hand within both of his.

He jolts, sucking in a shocked breath the moment his skin touches mine. Eyes wide and face slackened, he stares at me with an expression of awe. I groan, my body sagging even more as stars begin to form in the approaching darkness.

"Griffin!" Darius roars.

Griffin catches me before I tumble to the floor and holds me upright. "I have her." Pursing his lips, he tightens his grip around my fingers and I feel a vacuuming sensation pull at me as he absorbs the foreign emotions.

Soothing… Calm… Quiet serenity. A pure, undiluted bliss I've never known envelops me as the chaos within my mind comes to a screeching halt before it withers and dies. A tranquil stillness that has me, for the first time ever, curving my lips into a peaceful smile.

"Griffin?"

The worry in Kace's tone startles me from my peace. Peering down to where my hand clutches another, I trail my gaze along the arm connected to that hand, and my blood runs cold at the sight of Griffin writhing and moaning on the floor.

Bar after bar, I quickly recreate that cage in my mind to be stronger, more resilient than the one prior. Though I suspect the reasoning behind its dissolvement and can fortify a proper defense now that I'm aware, I'll take no further chances.

Gifts properly locked away, I squeeze Griffin's hands between both of mine, press my forehead to our clasped hands, and absorb the emotions from him back into myself just as he did for me. But unlike him, with my hair draped over our hands, my actions are obscured from view.

Griffin's writhing stills and he shuts his eyes with a relieved sigh.

Kace and the unknown male fall to their knees beside him. Zander, Tristan, and Amara hover protectively around me while Darius' feet are planted, his indecisive eyes bouncing between me and Griffin, feeling duty bound to assist his friend, but instinctively needing to care for me.

Griffin sits up with a groan, hanging his head for several minutes while inhaling calming breaths.

Feeling an immense amount of shame and guilt for harming someone because of my inadequacies, for my failures, I swat away Zander's comforting hands and shake my head, tears brimming in my eyes. "I'm so sorry, Griffin," I choke out.

Griffin's eyes crinkle at the corners and he offers a gentle smile. "There's nothing to be sorry about. I'm happy I could help."

Seeing his breathing even out, the color returning to his cheeks, and his once stiffened muscles relax, my guilt lessens at his quick recovery, but only enough to pull back my tears.

"Lena," Darius says in a hushed voice, his regretful eyes searching my own. "I didn't think…" He reaches for me but pulls back and winces, allowing his hands to fall limp at his sides. "I didn't realize I was hurting you." He clenches his fists and the veins in his arms and neck throb as he grinds his teeth, harsh remorse sharpening his gaze.

Staring into those swirling blue orbs, a pinch of guilt nips at me. Shame at what I just did. For what I must do. But I swat it away, realizing how unreasonable I was earlier for rebuffing Tristan's suggestion when the hard truth of the matter is, in the grand scheme of things, neither Darius nor I truly matter. Only my objective.

A vision appears before me of Darius' beautiful eyes glazed over in lifelessness, his cold corpse lying bloody and broken in a kingdom of charred ruins. Any remaining shame or guilt I may have felt evaporates with the image, leaving in its place an impenetrable resolve.

This loss of control is a stark reminder of how he will die, along with countless others, if something like this were to ever happen again. Of what's at stake if I were to lose control again and as a result, alert *them* to my location. They will find me sooner or later; I'm aware of this and I'm preparing for it. But I need it to be much, much later. Because if it's not and I'm found before I am ready, if I have to face them before my plan is in place, we'll lose the war before it even begins.

CHAPTER 14

DARIUS

Our boots thunk against the gray stone floor as Ajax and I walk down the hall of the guards' barracks. A door opens and howling laughter echoes off the jagged slate walls before shutting once again, muffling the sound. Shouting and jeering echo from the common room behind, while chairs scrape and bowls clatter as we pass the dining hall. Several guards walk past, nodding cordially as they do, but most stand at attention, lining the hallway as they avert their eyes in fear or bow their heads in respect. As word spreads of my presence, more males trickle into the hall. Adhering to protocol, they adopt their submissive brethren's stance.

A door opens and a Fire immortal steps out. With disheveled hair and bare chested, the male tosses a tunic and vest over his head and rubs fisted hands to his eyes. He drops his hands with a yawn, his gaze bouncing from one guard to the next until he narrows his eyes once he spots Ajax and me. He pays no homage to my rank as he tracks Ajax's every step. But Ajax holds his head high and stares straight ahead, refusing to acknowledge him.

"Snitch," the male hisses.

I spin on my heels and within two large strides, I grip him by the throat and lift him off his feet, slamming him into the wall. Loose pebbles rain down as he kicks out and scrabbles at my hands, but his efforts are less effective than a gnat's would be. "What did you say?" I snarl.

Doors open and shut as more guards arrive. Their whispers become more animated, rising in volume as a crowd begins to form.

I smile.

Witnesses. Exactly what I was hoping for.

There have been grumblings within my ranks and I've been waiting for one of these fools to challenge my call against Jareth or call out Ajax for his part in it. But fearful of my wrath, no one has dared to do so in my presence.

Until now.

The immortal remains silent, his orange topaz and starlight jewels flaring as he attempts to pry at my fingers. I squeeze tighter, leaving only a breadth of space between his airway.

"What. Did. You. Say?" I repeat, baring my teeth.

Eyes bulging and face reddening, he wheezes, "Snitch."

"I thought that's what I heard."

I release him and he drops to the floor. Coughing and sputtering, he clutches at his throat as I crouch down before him. Reaching for the silver pin attached to his chest, I tear it from his vest and read the inscription.

"Lieutenant Garth," I say, rolling the pin within my palm. "It seems you take issue with my guards performing their duties. It makes me wonder how well you execute yours, if you consider someone who reports sexual assault to be a snitch."

The Fire immortal's eyes narrow to slits. "They were humans, half-breed." He leans forward with a sneer. "*Human.*"

A vicious joy fills me and my palm glitters orange, the pin melting to liquid silver. Garth sits up, eyeing the slithering silver warily.

"Since you're so dissatisfied with my leadership," I say, "then I'm sure you'll be pleased to know I'm no longer in need of your services. But here."

The sizzling silver swims from my palm and dives into his

neck, branding his throat as it reshapes itself into its previous design.

"A memento for your time with us."

Garth screams and claws at his blistered, bleeding neck. I laugh, morbidly pleased that even though one may have Enya, the Goddess of Fire's Gift, they're not immune to anyone else's flames besides their own.

I snatch at his scalded throat and he shrieks as I stand, presenting his dangling form to the watching crowd.

"Would anyone like to add to Garth's comment?" I ask, staring down the crowd.

All remain silent.

"I didn't think so. In that case, return him and his belongings to his family's home."

Dragging the disgraced guard towards me, I peer into his tear-filled gaze.

"He'll be unable to do so himself." My lips curve into a cruel smile and I throw him through the wall, crumbling stone and mortar with the impact.

Surprised gasps and coughs ring out as he disappears within a cloud of debris, only to return moments later beneath a pile of rubble in a broken, bloody tangle.

Task complete, I turn on my feet and stroll towards the door at the end of the hall, Ajax following at my side.

"I didn't need you to defend me," he grumbles, sliding back the iron bolt.

"No, you didn't," I reply, slapping a palm against the door, halting its trajectory. "But he was attacking me just as much as you, and I won't allow a challenge to go unpunished."

Closing the matter, I open the door and level a hand above my brow, shielding my eyes from the blinding sun. Once they're able to assimilate to the newfound light, a dirt packed arena comes into view.

Surrounding most of the outdoor training yard are stone towers and single-story buildings constructed of gray slate, curving into a crescent shape. A sturdy wooden fence completes the enclosure.

The circular arena is separated into a gridded formation, stations where dozens of guards currently perform their daily drills. Two bare chested males swing and jab as they fight in the sparring station.

A fae tosses a fire orb into the air while an immortal with a bow draws back and rapidly fires arrows, the orbs exploding into a shower of orange sparks on impact.

Liquid humanoid creatures summoned from Water magic charge towards an immortal. He dodges their blows, flinging knives as he ducks and rolls, the water creatures bursting into thousands of droplets with each strike.

Near the fence at the back of the training arena, two males and a youth inspect different blades on the weapons rack, the massive trees of the prized Seboia Forest – the only natural reserve found within these walls – serving as a backdrop to their discussion.

Packed dirt and loose pebbles crunch beneath my boots as I watch Griffin lift a dagger and swipe downward, appearing from this distance to be hacking at a tree in the forest that shadows them while speaking to Trip.

Kace rolls his neck and stretches his arms, nodding to Ajax and me when he spots us striding toward them.

At our arrival, Trip turns to us with a beaming smile, while Griffin returns the dagger to the rack and faces me with a neutral expression.

"Trip, have you warmed up yet?" I ask.

"No sir," he answers sheepishly, ducking his head.

"Get going." I jerk my head to the side. "Stretch and run a few laps around the perimeter."

Enjoying laps just as much as an official recruit, Trip's shoulders slump and he drags his feet towards the track.

"Ajax, you'll be sparring with Kace. Griffin will assess," I order. "And no shifting."

Ajax's lips curl in offense.

"Not everyone considers shifting cheating." With a scoff, he moves towards the warded practice ring. The outline of the ring shimmers a frosty blue arc in the dirt where Kace already waits.

I shrug. "That's because they can't win without doing so."

Kace activates the ward with a wave of his hand and a sheer dome of glittering blue shoots from the ground to shape around them.

"You can shift, if you like," Kace taunts, bouncing on the balls of his feet. "I'll win either way."

Ajax snorts, rolling his shoulders and cracking his neck. "Not likely."

"How about a friendly wager then, hmm?" Kace asks with a greedy smile, rubbing his hands together.

"No shifting," I say to the slippery fae with a pointed look.

"You're no fun," Kace pouts, then lunges for Ajax with a fierce battle cry.

Griffin moves casually toward their practice bout and I glare at his retreating back, wishing to knock his head from his shoulders.

"Not you," I say, my tone laced thick with command.

He stiffens. "I thought you wanted me to evaluate Ajax?"

"You can do that while standing beside me," I reply firmly, leaving no room for argument.

Griffin's shoulders expand, and he inhales a deep breath before spinning and striding to my side.

Folding my arms over my chest, I watch Kace swing a balled

fist at Ajax's cheek. Ajax snaps his head to the side, dodging the strike easily as he slaps a palm against Kace's chest, sending him ass over end into the dirt.

"You've been avoiding me," I accuse.

Griffin's nostrils flare, but he doesn't deny it.

Sucking on my teeth, I whirl on him.

"What happened yesterday with Lena? What the fuck was that?"

After dinner with my mother, I silently refused to heed her commands and, instead, decided to avoid Lena altogether. But the longer I went without seeing her, the more difficult it was to stay away.

As the days passed, it began to feel less and less like a desire to be near her, and more a demand.

An imperative need to see her.

To talk to her. To touch her. To be close to her any way I could.

Distracting me from my duties, she burrowed within my mind and planted herself there, refusing to leave until I could think of nothing else but her.

It didn't take long for my willpower to fold to the clawing need and to seek her out. But every time I stood outside the inn, preparing to call on her, my mother's orders played out in my mind and I couldn't do it.

To bed her and use her, then toss her aside as if she meant nothing.

I couldn't do it.

I may have been able to endure it with anyone else, but with her, I already know one taste will never be enough. That's something on which my mind is unwilling to bend. Whether she's my enemy or not is of no consequence.

I won't manipulate her into some twisted relationship, and I sure as fuck won't whore myself out to her. If I ever bed her, it'll be for our own satisfaction, not because my mother commanded it.

But now I wish I hadn't avoided her. Maybe yesterday wouldn't have been so disastrous or so overwhelming if I'd fed myself small drops of her presence instead of withdrawing completely. But I didn't.

I foolishly believed that I would be able to control myself if I saw her again.

That this oppressive need to be with her was all a delusion that could be controlled. But I couldn't have been more wrong. The instant I sensed her intoxicating scent and saw her watching me with a desperation akin to my own, every fiber of my being burned into a possessive rage and I lost my godsdamned mind.

The way I moved, the way I touched her, the way I spoke to her, it was all a manic-induced haze. As if my mind couldn't fully grasp all that I felt and saw. But what I do remember is everything that happened after I released her.

Gods! That'll forever be scorched into my mind.

I've never felt such bone-deep terror watching her scream in agony all because of me. Because of my touch. I don't know what I did or even how I did it, but there's no question that I did something.

And it's been eating me alive ever since not knowing how I caused her so much pain.

The worst part of it all is with Griffin's power of empathy, he can feel my fear. Feel my distress and confusion over this, and he could have helped me understand what happened.

But what did the empathic bastard do?

He ran out of the tavern like his ass was on fire and has been avoiding me ever since.

Griffin stares ahead, pointedly ignoring me.

"Griffin," I warn, having long lost my patience with his evasiveness.

Blowing out a breath, he spins to face me. "She lost control of her Gift."

I rub my brow with my fingertips. "Her Gift?"

He nods. "She's an empath."

I frown. That can't be right. She's human. An extraordinarily beautiful human, but human nonetheless. They aren't granted Gifts by the gods, and even if the divine had chosen to take pity on her race, Lena would've been born with jewels. I've seen no sign of her possessing a single one.

"You're wrong."

Griffin shakes his head. "I'm not. I don't know why or how, but she is an empath."

Brow furrowing, he glances off to the side, appearing deep in thought.

"I remember my father telling me stories when I was younger of humans with Gifts. Gifts that could rival an immortal's. But that's all they were: Stories. I never thought there was any truth to them."

At the mention of his father's findings, my skepticism lessens. Laeon wasn't the Queen's advisor only because of the circumstances of his noble birth. He's a scholar. Nose more often than not buried in ancient scrolls or the newest book, there's not a question to which he can't find the answer.

He's one of the most knowledgeable males in all of Vanyimar. If he told Griffin these stories, even in passing, the likelihood that there's some truth to it is more probable than not.

I scrub my hand along my jaw, pondering Griffin's revelation. This would explain everything about Lena and her companions. How they behave and dress. How naive and secretive they are. The defensive, deadly air they all exude.

Then I think of why they would be so defensive. Why they would feel the need to be so closed off. Of what could have happened to her to create such suspiciousness, and anger burns at the back of my skull.

"The night we met them, you thought they were running from someone. Could this be why? Could someone be hunting Lena for her Gift?"

"Yes." Griffin's lips tighten. "Especially if you consider how powerful she is."

"And how powerful is she?"

"More powerful than any other empath I've come across." Eyes widening, he shakes his head in awe. "She hides it well, but I was able to get a glimpse of it before she suppressed it."

The conversation with my mother pops to the forefront of my mind. Of how she thought it possible Lena could be working with Brecca. "Are Lena's intentions malicious?"

He smiles softly. "Not at all. She's a good soul."

"Are you sure?"

"Auras don't lie," he replies, giving me a droll look.

Having trust in Griffin and his Gifts, I need nothing more to convince me of her intentions. But that won't be good enough for my mother. If she finds out about Lena, she'll kill her.

Or worse, keep her for herself. She won't allow Lena to fall into her enemy's hands.

"We'll tell Kace about this," I say. "But no one else."

Griffin agrees with a grunt. Then he stares at me for a moment, opens his mouth as if to speak, and hesitates.

"I saw something peculiar when I was looking at her aura." His brows snap together. "A connection between the two of you. A bond of some sort."

Dropping my head back, I blow out a breath in relief, a knot unraveling in my chest. "I *can* feel her emotions. I thought I was going crazy, but I truly do feel her." Placing my hands on my hips, my gaze wanders to his. "Have you ever heard of such a thing?"

A shocked guffaw bursts from him.

"Never. But it's real. I can actually see it." He stares down at my chest, looking like he's searching for it. "The bond has an aura all to itself. A mixture of you and her." A soft smile tugs at his lips. "Almost like you're fated for one another."

I scoff. "I don't believe in fate."

"That doesn't mean it doesn't believe in you."

I groan, not in the mood to listen to any of his stories of fate or the Stars. I lost my faith in them long ago. If I were to place it in anyone or anything, it'd be the gods. At least with them, I've seen their presence.

In my Gifts, my jewels, even with the Gods Cursed and their Soulless. But their touch is rare beyond that. Their hate, their love, their involvement with us lesser beings is fickle.

Accustomed to my aversion to speak on his spiritual ideals, Griffin adds nothing more on the subject, but steps forward, an earnestness to his eyes and a somberness lining his face.

"You need to be careful around Lena. She has no ill intentions towards us from what I can see," he reassures. "But your reaction to each other is extreme. For the both of you. Your emotions are heightened and more volatile around each other. I'm afraid that if you don't learn to manage the bond, it may cause you to do something you'll regret."

Manage it? I don't even know what I'm managing.

Turning away from him, I go to join the others near the fence when I stop in my tracks at the new arrivals.

Kace hunches over himself, clutching his ribs as Zander rubs soothing circles on his back. Trip flails his arms around, babbling to Amara and Tristan who both sit on the top rail of the fence. But the only person who holds my attention is Lena.

The cool wind sweeps her rippled, raven hair to the side. Her arms drape casually over the fence. With one leg hitched on the bottom rung, her eyes twinkle in mirth as she tosses her head back, exposing her elegant neck as she laughs.

A laugh that radiates so much joy and happiness, so full of life, I suck in a breath at the sight.

Gods, she truly is stunning.

Tenderness fills me as I study where her jewels should be. The gems that should be illuminated with her heightened emotion. But I only find those circular shaped scars. I saw that joy in her before, but after learning she's an empath, and a human one at that, it's awe inspiring how she can find the strength to love life after experiencing what I'm sure must be a dark past.

With her beauty, her Gifts, and her human weaknesses, there's not a being alive who wouldn't do whatever's necessary to add her to their arsenal. But not as a person. She'd be an object. A weapon. Someone to be owned and used instead of worshipped as she deserves.

I can't imagine what horrors she's experienced, all because she was born with a Gift unbelonging to her race. But I also suspect it's something I'll never want to know.

Protectiveness flares within me, overshadowing the tenderness as I vow right then and there to never allow that to happen to her. I don't know what she's experienced, but I'll die before I allow someone to dim that light in her eyes.

The ferociousness of my resolve has me reeling back as I realize how much I want to be the one to safeguard her from such evil. How even though she's lied and kept secrets, a betrayal all in itself, I want to be the one who protects her from the darkness of the world.

Not Tristan or Zander. Not Kace or Griffin. Sure as fuck not another lover, but me. Only me.

A deep guffaw causes a frown to tug at my lips, and my gaze drifts towards the male with whom she's speaking. As usual when I'm around Lena, I see little besides her, but I now notice who has her smiling and laughing. The one who's causing her such joy.

And it's a kick to the teeth when I see Ajax peering down at her with a besotted expression that I'm all too familiar with.

Blind jealousy rears its head and I frantically search for the bond that was once considered an unwelcome connection, but now a vital one, only to find that she's cut it off once again. Smothered all her emotions so she can make moon eyes at him without my knowledge.

A low growl rumbles menacingly from my chest and I fist my hands at my sides, stalking towards the duplicitous female and the traitorous rookie.

"Annnnd that's the crazy I was talking about." Griffin rushes forward and steps into my path, raising his palms. "This is what I was warning you of. Your emotions are turbulent when it comes to her. You have to control it."

"Move."

"Or not," he grumbles, quickly stepping aside.

I stalk forward and stop before the pair, but neither of them notice me. Smiling up at Ajax, Lena places her palm on his chest and curls her fingers into his vest as he peers down at her.

Possessiveness creeps up my spine and my veins sizzle with rage. "What are you doing?"

Ajax's startled gaze whips towards mine while Lena's brows furrow in confusion.

"We're talking," she says, her hand still resting on Ajax's chest.

I suck on my teeth. "Looks like a lot more than talking."

"Well, that's all we're doing." Her expression hardens. "Not that it's any of your concern."

Hearing her deny my claim in the presence of another, my throat burns with the truth of it. "Like hell it isn't!"

She narrows her eyes.

"I'm confused as to why you think you have any say in who I do or don't speak to, but to soothe your fragile feelings," she says, to which I bristle in response, "I was introducing myself to Ajax here, because you so rudely didn't do so at the tavern yesterday." She smiles up at Ajax. "But then I noticed his beautiful necklace."

I look more closely at the hand I thought she placed on his chest, when in actuality she's holding a silver medallion with a rune stamped in the center, attached to a chain wrapped around his neck.

A common token amongst most humans and some of the lower classed fae. An emblem of the True God.

Her explanation is plausible and seemingly innocent, yet it does nothing to lessen my anger.

"Get back to work," I bark at Ajax. He scurries along, joining Griffin, Kace, and Trip in their practice bout. I round on Lena. "And *you* stop distracting my guards."

She startles and I lean over the fence, whispering in her ear.

"Don't pretend you aren't aware that every male has been gawking at you from the moment you set foot in the training yard. They can hardly train while drooling over you."

She stiffens and digs her nails into the wood railing. "Don't forget to include yourself along with your slobbering guards. You are their leader, of course."

"How can I not, when you show up here wearing that?" I reply, breathing in her alluring scent. Then I grit my teeth and pull back when I notice a hint of Ajax's scent mixed with hers.

"I like what I'm wearing," she says, frowning down at her clothes.

"So do I and every other male of breeding age."

She narrows her eyes, irritation and anger glinting within their depths. I search for the bond again, wondering if I'm feeling her anger in addition to my own, but I only feel my own emotions.

The bond's still present, of course. The lively tether is almost tangible to the touch, but it's static. Suffocated. She's somehow taught herself how to control it to a certain extent. And I'm baffled as to how.

"Why did you do it?" I ask. She cocks her head to the side and stares at me questioningly. "Cut off the link, I mean."

She blinks. "I don't know what you're talking about."

"Yes you do." I press myself against the fence, her knees brushing against my leg as I peer down at her. "Is it so you could flirt with Ajax without me knowing?"

"We were just talking. That's all," she says in a hushed voice, her somber eyes searching my own. "He's not the one I want."

"Who is?"

"I think you know."

I grunt in response. Placing both hands on the top railing, I tower over her, but she remains unmoving, doing nothing as her breasts flatten against me. "Open the bond."

She laughs. "No."

Muttering a curse, I push off the fence and swipe my hands through my hair. "How did you cut it off?"

"You haven't figured it out yet?" When I don't answer, she smirks and pats my chest. "It appears you have some thinking to do."

Biting back a frustrated growl, I unwrap the leather strap around my wrist and tie my hair partially back, unsheathing my sword and pointing to where her companions are shamelessly watching us.

"Go sit over there and try not to distract my guards any more than you already are."

She sighs. "Oh, Darius."

Climbing atop the lower rung, she bends over the fence and my mouth runs dry as she pushes back a stray hair of mine.

"Haven't you learned yet?" She bares her teeth on a smile. "I don't take orders. I give them."

CHAPTER 15

LENA

"He's such an ass," I say.

Amara sighs dreamily. "But what a fine ass it is."

Of course, any male with an ass as nice as Darius' can't be anything other than a prick. It lures you in with its seductive powers, making you forget who it's attached to. Even now it's performing its ungodly magic on me. But I'm determined to keep my wits! Will continue to hold on to that anger even as I watch his ass stretch taut when he parries a sword strike from Trip.

Yet, there's nothing necessarily wrong with me if my anger lessens just a smidge. I am a female, for gods sakes. The wetness slickening my leathers right now is a testament to that. I can only be expected to have so much control while staring at that toned, rock hard, demon magic ass.

Stars save me, it's not fair! Even the shape of it is perfect. There's not an ounce of fat on him anywhere, yet it still miraculously has a roundness to it. Not enough that he could be mistaken for a female, not that anyone ever could, but curved enough for someone to grab on to. I can't help but imagine the feel of it flexing beneath my nails as he pumps into me.

Unable to feed one hunger, I swivel towards Tristan and

reach for the slit in his vest, satisfying the other as I grab hold of a piece of dried venison and take a large bite, barely tasting its smoky, gamey flavor as I recall Darius' jealous accusations.

I snort to myself. That male's insane if he thinks I would go so far as to stifle the bond just so I could flirt with another. The only person I intended on flirting with today was him, which is why I had to smother the link.

Otherwise he would have felt my guilt. He'd know my intentions were dishonorable and there'd be no way he'd give us permission to return to the city after we inspect the claw marks on the wall. If anything, he'd kick us all out.

As for Ajax, I wouldn't have initiated a conversation with him if I hadn't spotted his medallion. I almost choked on my tongue when I saw the True Gods rune. With how much effort the gods put into burying the natural born's existence, it was shocking to find their most devout worshippers passing along the stories.

Although, I guess I shouldn't be too surprised. The immortals and fae of this land benefit greatly from the gods' favor, while the humans on this side of the mountains only seem to suffer for it.

I suspect I'll find many more runes when I make the time to visit the human district.

"A very biteable ass," Zander says. "I'm tempted to nibble on it myself."

"I didn't think you were interested in males," Tristan says, staring at him with a thoughtful look.

"I'm not."

"You're staring pretty hard for someone who's not." Tristan's eyes widen and he snaps his fingers, pointing at Zander. "I knew something happened between you and Kace the other night!"

"Not that there's anything wrong with male-on-male love," Zander replies, "but the reason why we might be a bit more...

friendly with each other is because we shared a room a few times at the brothel."

"That doesn't sound like nothing," Amara chimes in.

"Well, it was," Zander huffs, lifting his chin. "His chambers are quite lovely, and his bed is spacious. More than large enough to share with our chosen females. It was a practical decision on my part."

He raises both palms.

"Now if a finger slipped here or there, it was purely by accident, but there was no penetration." He bobs his head and hums, his face scrunched as he peers upward. "Or I should say, there was no *full* penetration."

I frown.

"How can something not be full penetration? It's either penetrating or it's not."

"It's not if you do a dip." When all we do is stare blankly at him, he explains. "You know? A dip." He raises a pointed finger on one hand and shapes a ring with the other, slowly closing the distance between the two. "When you rim it juuussst past th-"

"I don't want to hear about your exploits," Amara cuts in, wrinkling her nose. "Male *or* female."

"As I was saying…" He gives Amara a reproving look. "I can be appreciative of a male's body regardless of what gender holds my interest."

Leaning against the fence, he places his elbows on the top rung and hangs his hands over the sides.

"And Darius is a very handsome male."

"A delicious one, at that. I doubt he's struggling to find females to fill his bed," Amara says as if wishing to be one of them.

"If you wish to keep your eyes, I suggest you stop ogling his ass before I rip them from your skull," I snap at Amara. Even though I know I'm being ridiculous, I can't seem to help myself when I peer past her and add to Zander, "That goes for both of you."

Amara's eyes sparkle in glee.

"Ooooh, I guess Darius isn't the only one who's jealous."

"I'm not jealous," I retort, tearing off another bite of venison. "I'm irritated."

"Looks like jealousy to me."

"I don't get jealous," I reply around a mouthful of food, watching Trip's arms tremble as he lifts that ridiculously large broadsword. "Gods, look at him! What is Darius thinking?"

"He really shouldn't be working with a broadsword yet," Zander says.

"He'd hurt himself in a real attack," Amara adds.

"Hurt himself?" Tristan scoffs. "He'd be dead before he drew it."

Swallowing, I watch as Trip fumbles around the practice ring and shake my head. He's all wobbly arms and legs. It looks like he's trying to wield a tree trunk.

Hmmm... maybe I'll just -

"Oh, no, you don't." Tristan snaps his fingers in front of my face, disrupting my line of sight. "Don't even think about it."

I smack his hand away. "What?"

"That look." He points at me. "I know that look."

"I don't have a look." *I definitely have a look.*

"Oh, yes you do." He arches a brow. "It's the look you get whenever you're about to do something reckless, something that no matter how hard I try to knock sense into that stubborn head of yours, you're going to do it anyway."

"But he's training him all wrong!" I whine, motioning to Darius with a jerk of my hand.

"I don't care."

"But-"

"No," he cuts me off with a swipe of his hand. "That's not why you're here. You're here because we need to see the claw marks on the wall, and to do that, we need permission from Darius to return to the city after we step outside the gates. That's all. He won't be willing to do anything for you if you criticize him."

"He's right, Lena," Zander says, flicking his hand in a shooing gesture. "Now go use those seductive feminine wiles of yours."

Amara snorts. "Besides her looks, Lena doesn't have any feminine wiles."

I gasp. "I have feminine wiles! I can wile with the best of them. Just the same as the highest paid courtesans, if not better!"

"It's adorable that you actually believe that," Amara replies, patting my head. I grit my teeth at the patronizing motion, barely restraining myself from punching her in the face as she continues. "I told you all before, it's not going to work. No matter how attracted Darius is to her, he's not going to defy a direct order from his mother. We're going to end up sneaking over the wall anyway, so you might as well let her teach him a thing or two."

"You're just bored and looking to stir up trouble," Tristan accuses.

Amara shrugs, not even trying to deny his claim as she climbs over the fence and seats herself on the top rung.

"Maybe I wouldn't be looking to stir up trouble if you hadn't locked me in a room for weeks." She glares at him over her shoulder. "Weeks, Tristan. *Weeks*."

Sputtering, he tosses his arms up, seeming at a loss on what to do.

"Maybe if you two weren't so prone to attracting attention, I wouldn't have had to." We give him a dry look and he looks to Zander for help. "And I'm not the only one who thought it best for you to stay out of sight. Zander did, too."

"Hey! Don't bring me into this." Zander gives us a rueful bow of his head. "You ladies do as you wish. I've learned my lesson."

Amara gives him a solemn nod of her head. "Thank you, Zander."

"You're welcome."

"Coward," Tristan mumbles.

Zander shrugs shamelessly.

"They're biters." Grimacing, he rubs the upper part of his arm and tugs down his tunic, revealing teeth marks that still haven't healed, even with his shifter healing.

"Well, oh wise one," Amara drawls. "Now that we're finally free, how much attention do you think we're going to attract now?"

Tristan groans, pinching his nose. "So this is my punishment? For you two to be even more insufferable than usual?"

"Of course," Amara and I reply in unison.

"You're already giving me a headache."

"That's merely a happy byproduct." Amara beams. "Having said that, Darius' training methods are going to get Trip killed. With a few harsh words to the Captain, Lena can save that boy's life."

Tristan's lips thin, but he remains silent, unable to argue with her logic.

"Plus, dickhead's ego could do with a bit of bruising," Amara says, and I want to hit her less for it. She turns her attention to me. "Go on, Lena. You know you want to." She nudges my shoulder with a goading smile. "You said so yourself. No one gives you orders."

Should I or shouldn't I?

"Lena," Tristan growls.

I absolutely should!

"That weapon is ill suited to him," I call out, hitching my leg on the bottom rung and draping my arms over the top.

Tristan tosses his hands up, pacing. "Here we go."

Darius holds a hand out to Trip, signaling a break, and turns to face me. "Excuse me?"

"It's too heavy for him." Pushing off the fence, I hop over the side and stride purposefully toward the duo. "He needs something lighter."

Darius' lips instantly flatten.

"I did not ask for your advice, nor do I want it. Now I'm allowing you to observe, but if you wish to continue to do so, then you will do so silently," he sneers, turning his back on me. "Without any unsolicited advice, I might add."

"Ha!" Zander barks a laugh behind me.

"He's just asking for it now," Amara adds.

"Is your male ego so fragile that you'll ignore sound advice from a female even if it means it could save lives?" I argue, stopping beside the ward and placing my hands on my hips.

He sighs and turns to face me, irritation lining his face.

"No, but I do ignore advice from women who have no training in battle."

"And how many battles have you been in?"

"More than I can count," he states in all seriousness.

I roll my eyes. "I don't mean challenges with males you've known your whole life. I mean a *real* battle."

He gives me a bland expression. "None have presented themselves, so none." He arches a brow. "Have you?"

"Yes."

"Oh, you have, have you?" He laughs mockingly, glancing back at his friends who've all stopped their bouts to watch us. "And what kind of battle was this?"

A light flashes before my eyes and I suddenly vanish from this world, only to reappear in another. A different time, a different place, a different realm.

Smoke burns my eyes and soot smears my skin. A sky filled with flames and homes incinerated to ash. Fallen swords and thousands of glazed eyes. The scent of blood, sweat, and decaying bodies is so overpowering, I feel like I've never left that blood, muddied battleground.

Feeling an agonizing pain pierce into my abdomen, I slowly drop my chin and press my hands against my stomach, watching as my own life source slips between my fingers.

I squeeze my eyes shut.

I'm no longer there. It's not real. I'm safe. I'm safe.

My eyelids lift, and I find myself once again on the Seboia training grounds. Darius is still watching me with that arrogant smirk.

My anger spikes at the sight and I level him with a cold glare.

"The kind where soldiers burn down your gates and invade your home, slaughtering every living soul in sight. Killing males, females, and children, even babes. One where the streets flow crimson and the wails and cries of the dying slice at your soul. Your ears ring from the screeching of steel on steel, and your nostrils burn from the scent of death and fire. A battle where you selfishly fight for your own life while you watch your loved ones get cut down beside you, along with thousands of others. *That's* the kind of battle I've seen."

Darius, Kace, Ajax, and Trip all look at one another uncertainly while Griffin's gaze bores not into my eyes, but into my chest, seeing something in my aura that causes him to waver on what he believes to be true.

"There's not been a battle like that since the Battle of Brecca." Darius tilts his head, squinting his eyes disbelievingly. "And you weren't alive then, Lena."

A small, calloused hand laces their fingers with mine from behind and squeezes.

"They know nothing of the turmoil outside their own realm," Amara whispers gently in my ear. "You can't expect them to believe without proof. Not on something like this."

Knowing she's right, I inhale a steadying breath and untangle my hand from hers. "Believe what you will, but it doesn't change that your teaching methods aren't appropriate for him."

Darius groans, then sheaths his sword on his back and folds his arms over his chest. "Since you're such an expert, what should I be training him with?"

"A short sword and a dagger," I answer immediately. "He hasn't built up the muscle mass to handle a broadsword yet."

"That's why we start training at an early age," he replies in a tone as if I'm daft. "That way when he's fully mature, he'll have the strength needed to wield it."

Of course he should be trained in all weaponry, but from my understanding, it's the only sword Trip has worked with. He may be bigger than me, everyone seems to be bigger than me, but he'll still be smaller than the average person even once he reaches maturity.

Yet he's fast. Abnormally so. With his small stature and speed, a smaller blade would be more beneficial to him, even as an adult. And Darius hasn't seemed to have addressed that obvious fact.

Unless I'm mistaken.

I frown. "What do you expect him to defend himself with now?'

"Nothing." Brows knitted together, he stares at me in bafflement. "He's too young to join the Guard, and if any battle were to arise, he'll be safe within these walls."

Feeling a headache coming on, I rub my temples, disbelieving how this kingdom can be so blind to everything.

It's as if when they built their walls, they didn't just block out the Soulless, they blocked out all common sense.

"Who's to say the walls won't be breached?" I ask. "Then neither you nor him will have a choice as to when he'll see his first battle, and everything you taught him won't make a lick of difference because you're teaching him to defend himself as an adult, when he's not one."

He growls in frustration, his broad chest straining at his vest with the motion.

"If the walls were to be breached, which I'll add is not possible, the guards would protect him."

I raise a challenging brow. "And are all your guards loyal to you?"

Darius hesitates. Only for a moment, but long enough for me to take notice, before his expression hardens once again. "Of course."

Interesting.

"Oh, really?" I smirk. "So there's no doubt in your mind that one of these 'trusted guards' who are duty bound to protect him, aren't actually working with Brecca? Then you must believe that none of your citizens would be willing to, either. Like a nobleman, or a baker, or perhaps an advisor?"

"Godsdamn it, Lena, you've said too much!" Tristan's voice barks in my mind, only for me to hear.

Darius stiffens. "What are you implying?"

With Tristan's warning, I know I'm straddling a dangerous line, but I press on regardless, needing to know how open-minded Darius can be. How open-minded he can be to *me*.

"There are traitors in every kingdom."

Darius scoffs and I purse my lips.

"Just because your city is full of wealth and jewels does not mean that your people are content. Evil does not show itself willingly, and it comes in many faces. Whether that be a human beggar or a smiling nobleman. Unless you're searching for it, you will not see the rot within their soul until it is already too late."

His lip pulls up into a snarl, but he halts it, breathing heavily as he visibly tries to control himself.

"You were not born here," he says, his tone hard and unyielding, "so you didn't see firsthand the pain and death the Breccans caused. The scars they birthed from their traitorous acts. It is because of this I can forgive you for the insult."

Swiping his hand through the air, the domed ward collapses on itself and he steps closer to me. Placing a palm beneath my chin, he tilts it up, his touch so cold, I feel frost biting at my skin.

"But I will tell you this one time and one time only. No Cascadonian would ever work with Brecca."

I search his eyes, disappointment filling me as I see there will be no swaying him. Not by anything I have to say, at least. He'll need tangible proof before believing a foreigner regarding the loyalty of his people. No matter how wrong he may be.

He'll be no help to us.

"Nonetheless, you and your guards are not invulnerable," I say in a hushed tone. Wrapping my hand around his wrist, I hope I can at least guide him in the right direction even if he won't believe me outright. "You must prepare for all outcomes. It's irresponsible to not give your people the skills they need to protect themselves. Not just for tomorrow, but for today as well."

Darius holds my gaze for a long moment, then his hand falls to his side and he walks away without a backward glance.

Patting my hands on the outside of my thighs, I rock heel to toe, waiting for him to return and continue our discussion, watching as each of his steps takes him closer to the fence and farther away from me.

Confused, I open my mouth, then shut it. Then open it again

and shut it, frowning when I realize, after an embarrassingly long amount of time, that he's not coming back.

Shock at being so rudely dismissed wars with irritation and I finally snap out of my stupor, racing after him. "Where are you going?"

"Away. I'm finished with this discussion." He places his hands on the top rail of the fence and hops over, heading toward the forest.

"Well, I'm not," I say, following him over the fence and matching my pace with his, his strides easily two to my one.

"Why? So you can pinpoint everything I'm doing wrong?"

My lips turn down. "You're not wrong on everything, just the more important matters."

Tossing a dry look over his shoulder, Darius returns his attention to the path ahead and speeds up his pace.

"I'm not interested in anything else you have to say."

Does he actually think that he can beat me in stubbornness? Ha!

"But if you just listen, I –"

"Enough!" he roars, whirling on his feet. "I'll not speak on this matter any longer!"

I blink. Once, twice, three times.

Then he spins away and continues on towards the forest. I make no move to follow. Feet planted to the ground, I'm too shocked at his outburst to do anything else. But the blood sizzling within my veins quickly thaws my frozen feet and I storm after him.

"Don't you walk away from me!"

He ignores me.

"I'm talking to you, asshole!" I shout, but he makes no move to acknowledge me as he stomps past the tree line.

"He's walking away from her," I hear Amara say, along with several pairs of feet following at a distance.

"Oh, no. Bad idea, Darius," Zander warns. "She really doesn't like to be ignored. I wouldn't recom–"

A glittering orange stream suddenly slams into him, lifting him off his feet and flinging him across the grounds with a whoosh, his body smashing through the wooden fence.

"Zander!" I scream.

"I'm fine. I'm fine." Bounding to his feet, he stumbles but catches himself, brushing himself off and giving me a smiling thumbs up. "Just a scratch."

Amara and Tristan howl in laughter, while I feel nothing but rage.

Ever so slowly, I turn my head and glare at Darius, my blood boiling at the sight of his retreating back.

I sprint.

Once reaching him, I quickly crouch down and sweep out his feet, watching him fall flat on his back with a loud *oomph.*

"What the fuck, Lena?!" Darius roars.

Crouching above him, I say in a sinister voice, "Don't *ever* touch one of mine again."

Darius bounds to his feet in a single motion and scowls down at me. "One of yours?"

"Yes, *mine*." I dig my finger into his chest. "Zander. Is. Mine." Giving one last twist of my finger, I slap both palms to his chest, shoving him back.

Jealousy flashes within his gaze and he reaches for me.

I dart to the side. Grabbing his wrist, I twist his arm behind his back and kick out at the back of his legs, slamming him to his knees.

He stills. "Let go of me. "

"No."

Darius grinds his teeth. “I'm warning you, Lena. Let go of me now. I don't want to hurt you.”

I press my lips to his ear, speaking softly. “What makes you think you'll hurt me? Maybe I'll hurt you.”

Darius suddenly spins into the arm lock and whips his free arm out to cuff the back of my neck, dragging my face to his. I can feel the heat of his breath on my lips as he growls, “Lena, I'm not playing.”

I don't know why, but instead of reacting like any sane person would in the face of his wrath, my body fills with excitement, desperate to see how far I can push him.

“Well, maybe I am,” I purr. Slapping his arms away, I shove at his chest and raise my hand, a loud smack ringing in the air when I slap his cheek.

Gasps sound behind me.

“He just got bitch slapped,” Kace says.

“Do you still think locking us up was a good idea?” Amara asks.

“I’m regretting that decision more and more with each moment that passes,” Tristan replies.

Cheek reddening by the second, Darius’ lip curls as he moves to his feet with a growl. “Lena…”

Gods, he’s furious. Maybe I shouldn't have slapped him.

I lunge forward and slap his other cheek.

Or twice. Definitely shouldn't have slapped him twice.

He stills, all but for the muscle ticking in his cheek and the veins throbbing in his neck, and tries to control his rage, but I can see in his eyes the exact moment that thinly-held control snaps.

“Fuck it,” he snarls and jabs at my shoulder.

I swat it away.

He pauses, frowning down at my hand before he jabs at my other shoulder.

I swat that one away as well.

Surprised but undeterred, he lunges for me.

I spin, laughing as he rushes past.

Turning to face me, his anger evaporates. In its place is intrigue, a curious light flashing behind those blue eyes as he evaluates me from head to toe.

Reassessing me.

He swings at my cheek so incredibly slow that I know he's holding back.

Snapping my head to the side, I dodge his blow with a roll of my eyes. "I'm not one of your untrained females, Darius. You don't need to hold back."

"I can't hit you with full force," he replies, his brows knitting together. "You're a woman."

"That won't stop me from hitting you," I reply with a shrug, right before I punch him in the nose.

A collective "Ooooohhhh" echoes within the trees.

Wiping beneath his nose, he studies the blood smeared on his fingertips with a shocked expression.

"Don't worry." I grin. "I won't use my full strength on you, either."

Blood no longer flowing with his immortal healing, he swipes away the last remnants of crimson and bares his teeth on a feral smile "Alright, let's see what you got."

His fist whips out and I barely have time to block it with my forearm.

Shit, that was fast.

He swipes at my stomach and I suck in before leaping back, his fingertips grazing my vest.

He smirks. "Having second thoughts?"

"Are you?" I ask, and throw my elbow into his chin.

"Daaaaaamn!"

He stumbles back, expelling a loud guffaw, before rushing forward, rapid firing a series of jabs.

Blocking strike after strike, I retreat backwards, unnerved that I'm barely able to keep up with him. He swings a surprisingly powerful jab at my face and I crouch down, his arm passing over my head with a whistle of air as I punch him in the stomach.

He grunts and reaches for me, but I spin around to his back and jab him in the kidney. He flinches, barely slowing as he spins to face me, but it's all the time I need. Becoming the aggressor, I throw strike after strike as he blocks and retreats.

"Godsdamn, look at her keeping up with the Captain," Griffin says. "No one can keep up with him."

"Isn't she human?" Kace asks.

"I didn't think humans could move like that," Ajax marvels.

"You'd be surprised what we're capable of," Tristan says dryly, a hint of disapproval hidden within.

Their comments are a warning in themselves, but I ignore them. I'm too high on the adrenaline of having a worthy opponent to care about their words.

I manage to get a few more jabs in on Darius. Clipping his shoulder. Swiping at his ear. A kick to his hip. But the longer we spar, the more my energy wanes. My jabs slow, my movements are less coordinated, and my breathing becomes harsher, while Darius seems to be getting faster and more invigorated.

Empowered.

But he doesn't strike out at me. He watches with calculating blue eyes, tracking my every motion and learning my style.

I swing a fist at his shoulder, but he blocks it. When I jab at his throat, he blocks that, too. Growling in frustration, I aim for his nose once again, but he snaps his head to the side, laughing.

"Come on, Lena. Hit me."

Temper spiking at his taunt, I feign a swipe with my right hand

and drop to a crouch, punching his inner thigh with my left fist. Only a few inches from his groin.

He hisses and cups his balls. "Too close."

I smile. "Not close enough."

Eyes narrowing, Darius strikes out but I dodge it. Grabbing him by the forearm, I step into him and jab him in the armpit. He expels a loud grunt and I move to jump back outside his reach, but before I can he wraps his arms around me, pinning my arms to my sides and flattening me to his chest.

His eyes glitter in amusement as he looks down into my furious ones. "How are you going to get out of this one? Can't throw any cheap shots like this, can you?"

"None of those were cheap shots!" I shout, outraged at his comments as much as my predicament, squirming within his grip.

He chuckles and I still, narrowing my eyes on him, wanting nothing more than to smack that stupid dimpled smile off his face. I'm so focused on wanting to hit him, I miss my opportunity when he quickly unwinds one arm and slaps me on the ass. I shriek, too surprised to act before he re-bands his arm around me once again.

"I guess I'm not above cheap shots myself," he says with an arrogant smirk.

Infuriated at my predicament, I wiggle and squirm, fighting to be released from my bonds, but his arms are like shackles.

"Keep wiggling like that and this'll end much differently than you expected."

I freeze, now noticing the tick of his jaw and his hardened length pressed up against me, lust clouding his gaze. A warmth pools into my belly and I allow a sliver of air to breathe through the bond, feeling his desire trickle down the link.

A devious thought enters my mind and I throttle the bond in an instant. Arching into him, I lick my lips and his gaze drops to my mouth, his arms slackening. When he lowers his head toward mine and I can taste his breath on my tongue, I debate giving into him and allowing him this victory if it means I can finally have his lips upon mine.

But I'm much too competitive for that.

Groaning in regret, I swipe his arms away and push myself up by his shoulders, coiling my legs around his neck. Stumbling back, he grabs ahold of my ass on instinct before righting himself, his blue eyes peering up at me in surprise.

A slow smile tugs at my lips and I wink before squeezing my thighs tighter. Throwing myself back, I flip my legs over my head along with Darius, who lands flat on his back with me sitting on his chest.

“Holy shit!” Trip shouts.

“Ooooh, that hurt,” Kace adds. “That hurt a lot.”

Squeezing his eyes shut, Darius groans in pain.

“Who’s winning now?” I ask, smiling down at him.

He squints one eye open, glaring at me, before they both pop open when he notices my position on his chest. Slapping his hands to my ass, he suddenly bucks his hips and I squeak, sliding downward until my thighs cradle his face once again.

“With your pussy in my face? Me, definitely me.”

Gaze boring into my sex, he digs his fingers into my cheeks and buries his face between my thighs, inhaling deeply.

“Mmmmm, vanilla, cinnamon, and cherry.”

He lifts his eyes to mine and I suck in a breath at the naked desire nestled within those blue globes.

“Is this want you want, pretty Lena? You want me to bury my tongue in that tight cunt?”

Holding my gaze, he lowers his lips to my leather clad pussy and blows out a hot, moist breath.

Feeling the heat of his mouth while imagining his tongue

flicking at my clit, my breath hitches and I tighten my thighs around his head, feeling my sex slicken with need.

But my desire begins to cool as I remember all the other times we've been in a similar position.

"Why bother?" I lower my face to his, the ends of my hair tickling his throat. "We both know you'll choke."

"I don't choke," Darius grinds out, digging his fingers deeper, near bruising. My pussy slickens even more.

I debate leaving it at that, but I can't. This asshole's been giving me whiplash with all his back and forth, and he has more mood swings than a female during her first bleed.

Either fuck me or don't, but stop playing with me.

"You don't, huh? What about the other night? What about yesterday? I was all but screaming for you to fuck me and what did you do? You walked away."

He clenches his jaw and squeezes me tighter. "You hesitated the other night, and you were in no condition to do anything yesterday."

The world suddenly spins as Darius rolls us over until I'm the one laid out and he's pinning me to the forest floor. Placing a large hand over my pussy, he cups me, and I feel the heat of him seeping into me.

"Is this what you want? Is this why you're so angry?"

Applying pressure over my clit, he rubs his finger in a circular motion against my leathers and I suck in a breath, forcing myself to remain still as I imagine that thick digit curling inside me.

"You being a dick is what's made me angry," I state hoarsely.

"No, no, no." He rubs faster, and my chest rises and falls with my panting breaths. "I think you want me to make you cum. *Need* me to."

Yes. Please, please make me cum.

"I can finger my pussy just fine on my own, thank you very

much," I snap, fighting against my traitorous body. "I don't need you for that."

His eyes flash with heat and he releases me.

My body mourns the loss until he brackets my head between his arms and spreads my legs with his knees, cradling himself between my thighs.

"Your fingers can't do this though, can they?" He swivels his hips. "That's it, isn't it? You want me to slide my cock into that tight cunt and fuck you raw?" he says with a hard thrust, skidding me across leaves and hard-packed dirt.

I involuntarily lift my hips to meet his. "I'm not the one with a hard-on right now," I say thickly, hearing the lie in my reluctant words.

Darius flattens his chest against mine and angles his head to the side.

"You know I can smell your arousal, don't you? Can feel the heat of your cunt against my cock?" Prodding deeper, he lowers his cheek to mine and rumbles in my ear, "If I slide my hand beneath your leathers, I bet you're just *soaked*."

With the feel of a large male body laid across mine, the heat of his breath on my ear, and the sensations quickening between my legs, my mind becomes hazy. "Doubtful," I croak.

"Liar." He chuckles. "You're all but begging me to touch you." When he slides his cock right against my clit and I feel that euphoric zing, I curl my fingers into his waistband, mewling. "Look at you whimpering for me."

I squeeze my eyes shut and arch into him, losing myself in a cloud of sensations. That is, until I hear a low, arrogant laugh hovering above me and I open my eyes to the view of his condescending smirk.

Anger merging with lust, I scoff, sliding my hands between us and grabbing his cock through his leathers, squeezing.

"I'm not the one humping you like a bitch in heat."

Darius' smirk falls, expelling a loud puff of breath when I begin stroking him.

"But all this foreplay is pointless." I squeeze tighter and he grunts. "Because when it comes down to it, we both know I'll have to seek my pleasure elsewhere."

"Fuck that!" Jerking his hips, jaw ticking, he slides his length faster against my palm.

"Oh, but I will," I argue. "With a male who will make me scream and moan as I milk his cock dry."

I swipe my tongue against his lips and he releases a pained groan.

Staring into his glacial blue eyes drilling into my amethyst ones, I whisper throatily, "Because you'll choke."

His face suddenly contorts into lust-filled rage and he snarls viciously right before he slams his lips onto mine in a bruising kiss.

The exact moment our lips touch, my mind clears of all rational thought and my body blazes into a roaring inferno.

He slips his wet tongue between the seam of my lips to tangle with mine, and I'm suddenly blasted with the potent taste of his cedar, smoky musk.

All I see, all I feel, all I taste is Darius as I experience the most erotic kiss of my life. Licking, tasting, devouring, I greedily suck on his tongue and beg for more as my instincts rage into an animalistic need to mate. To fuck.

I tear my mouth from his, gasping in a breath. But I've barely taken one before he tangles his hands into my hair, my scalp screaming at the roots as he slams his lips back onto mine.

I burrow beneath his vest and jerk his tunic from his leathers, touching the bare skin beneath.

Sliding my fingers over his flexing abs, past his chiseled pecs, down again to wrap my arms around his back, clawing at his massive shoulders. Shoulders rotating and bulging as he touches me everywhere over my clothes.

My waist, my back, my breasts.

Stroking and caressing as he pumps in a frenzy with his leather-clad cock against my dripping cunt.

Gliding back and forth, his cock slides right against my clit and I toss my head back into the dirt, crying out. His eyes flash savagely, his movements becoming jerkier and uncontrolled as he growls and stakes me to the ground.

Driving harder against me, he reclaims my mouth, syncing his thrusting tongue with the speed of his dick, fucking my mouth as if it was his cock.

Imagining his glistening head slipping between my lips, I drip even more and moan around his tongue, wrapping my legs around his waist, grinding faster against him.

Along with that euphoric friction, that ball of pleasure within me winds tighter and tighter as I chase that delicious snap. And I know to the depths of my soul that even though we're both fully clothed, my climax will be even more powerful than the ones I've found with other males I've allowed inside me.

Reaching for his wrist, I pull his hand up to cup my swollen breasts. He squeezes, kneading them expertly as I arch into his palm with a moan. Darius rips his mouth from mine and peers downward, his gaze fixated on the markings on my breast.

Dipping his head, he slides the wet, rough pad of his tongue along the swells, tracing the dotted lines with a rumbling groan. Lapping, sucking, and nibbling, worshipping my tits. Worshipping me.

Darius tries to slip his other hand beneath my vest, but it's too tight. He moves to untie the laces over my cleavage, but they refuse to uncoil. He suddenly jerks up to sit on his heels.

Cool air whispers across my feverish skin as I look up, my breath hitching in my throat at the look in his glacial blue eyes, blue eyes wild with a manic desperation.

His calloused hands fist the fabric between the laces of my top, preparing to rip my vest at the seams, but hesitates when hissing voices reach our ears.

CHAPTER 16

LENA

"I'm not interrupting *that*," Kace hisses. "One of you do it. Lena's much nicer than Darius."

Tristan snorts. "You need to spend more time with her if you think she's nice."

Please tell me I'm wrong.

Feeling the weight of their knowing stares, I groan, burying my face into the crook of Darius' neck to the sound of his rumbling chuckle, to the comforting feel of him threading his fingers through my hair to scratch at my scalp.

Griffin sighs. "Go tell him, Kace."

"But," Kace sputters, "he'll gut me!"

"Probably," Griffin replies. "But I'm willing to take the chance."

"Oh! That's hurtful," Kace grumbles sourly.

"Stop bitching already," Amara groans. "I'll go."

A sigh of relief choruses within the trees.

"Thank you for your sacrifice!" Kace calls cheerily.

"Cowards," Amara grumbles.

Hearing the crunch of leaves, I turn my head to the side and find a smiling Amara waving at us.

"Hi…uh… sorry to interrupt. It looks like you're both *really* enjoying yourself. But unless you plan on fucking for all to see in broad daylight, you might want to cool it down a bit." Amara fixates her gaze solely on Darius. "And Darius? There's someone named Lennox here to see you."

Gaze wandering past Amara, I find both mine and Darius' friends, along with a new guard standing only a few paces away.

Just Staring. Watching.

Watching, I suspect, for the entire time we've been rolling around on the forest floor, both of us too lost in one another to take notice of anything but ourselves.

Nope, not wrong.

Mortification fills me as the fire from moments ago travels to my cheeks, coloring them scarlet.

Well, this is awkward.

A male clears his throat.

"What is it, Lennox?" Darius asks, his gaze unmoving from mine.

"There's a scheduling issue, Sir."

"You're interrupting me now with a scheduling issue?" Darius snaps.

Darius' frustration flows down the bond into me and I realize I've allowed the connection to reopen.

Lennox's fear lashes out at me and I stiffen, dread filling me as I shut my eyes and spread my senses out. My alarm grows even more when I realize I not only feel Darius' emotions, but all those present.

Slowing my breaths, I attempt to contain my Gift. It's a struggle and it takes much longer than usual, but I do eventually succeed.

But as I try to do the same to the bond between me and Darius, it resists, slinking between my fingers like water.

Darius cocks his head to the side, eyeing me quizzically as I struggle with the unruly bond, and that's when I feel it. A tap. A poke. Then, inquisitive male fingers crawling along the tether to invade my person.

For as far back as I can remember, I've always had the ability to see auras and feel what others do, but I've always been passive in receiving only, never interfering.

Having to safeguard many secrets myself, I know to cross over that barrier, to interact or alter another's emotions is a violation I'm unwilling to take part of.

But here Darius is, expertly maneuvering as if we've had this bond forever. Studying me, mimicking me, dissecting what makes me *me*.

Completely unaware of the intrusiveness of his actions, he digs deeper and deeper and deeper, until he meets my very core to plunge headfirst into my soul.

Squeezing my eyes shut, I try over and over again to stifle that connection. I squeeze, hit, kick, and choke, but I fail at every attempt. I even try to stab the son of a bitch, but nothing. His emotions still flow into me.

Yet, even though I'm anxious and frightened, I remain mostly calm throughout my efforts. But when I try to wrangle the slippery bitch in a last-ditch effort, I feel a strange sensation similar to a caress stroke at my very soul.

I panic.

My eyes instantly snap open and I stare into his glacial blue orbs as I throw myself at that fucker. Digging my nails in, I scrape, claw, and gouge, fighting tooth and nail as I maul it like a feral animal until I eventually manage to strangle the link. Blowing out a relieved sigh, satisfaction fills me as I regain my control.

That is, until I see Darius' lips turn down into a frown and a whisper of male hurt pinches at my chest, and I realize the tether refused to submit. That an almost undetectable, but undeniable breadth of space remains within the flow.

Lennox clears his throat. “Captain, someone’s been altering the guard rotation.”

Darius’ features harden, his nostrils flaring. “I'll be right there.”

Agitation flits down the bond as Darius leans forward, pressing his lips onto mine in a sweet, gentle kiss. Much milder than the lusty kisses he gave me earlier, but infinitely more powerful, more intimate.

“Stay here,” he whispers against my lips, as much a plea as it is a demand.

Tracing a circle with his thumb along my cheek, he stares down at me with so much longing and need that my chest tightens with an unfamiliar emotion. He stares for a moment longer, then lifts off me to stand and strides away without a backwards glance, his guards and Trip following closely behind.

Without his calming presence, all my emotions bite back with a vengeance. My anger, embarrassment, and fear at my loss of control.

My dread at what this could mean. But more prominent is the lust and passion. The intimacy. The combination of all of these emotions is so overwhelming, it affects not just my mind, but my body as well, manifesting into a fizzing sensation that sweeps across my skin and raises the hairs along my arms.

I rub fisted hands against my eyes, trying to quell the sensations, but the results are the same with every action I've taken today.

I fail.

Amara's amused face suddenly appears above mine.

"Wow… Just wow," she says, biting her lip.

"Shut up." Pushing off the ground, I stand and shove her out of my path.

"What?" She rushes to my side, Tristan and Zander trailing behind.

"Just… just don't." Stepping outside the forest's reach, I turn my back on the training grounds, heading towards the city street.

"I wasn't going to say anything bad," Amara replies. "I was just going to -"

I round on her with fisted hands. "Don't, Amara."

I feel a tug on mine and Amara's bond and her amused expression falls as she nods slowly. Then I feel a soft tug from Tristan and a yank from the not-so-subtle Zander.

Standing behind her, their expressions are a mirror image of Amara's. I quickly look away and continue onward, feeling too exposed to discuss any of what just happened.

"Are you alright?" Zander asks, his gaze earnest as he moves to my side.

No, I'm not alright.

"I just want to be alone," I reply, stepping off the grass onto the side street between the palace gates and the Guard's Base.

"I can see that," he says gently. "But I don't think that's a good idea." He glances up ahead, his brows bunching together. "Especially in this part of the city."

"Zander," Amara says, grabbing his arm. "Let her go. She's not a child; she can do as she pleases."

Zander clearly wants to argue, but I know I've won when Tristan squeezes his shoulder and shakes his head.

Unwilling to wait for them to change their mind, I listen to my boots scrape across the jeweled street as I race away. Racing away from them, the forest, and Darius.

Most of all, racing away from myself and all these overwhelming emotions. But when I round the corner and step past the palace gates into the nobility district, I wish I'd heeded Zander's warning.

The entirety of Seboia is rich and luxurious, but in this section of the city where the nobles and upper class reside, their wealth is indescribable. A completely different world.

Roofs drip in gold and walls swirl with embedded jewels; the white stone shops and crystal townhouses are just miniature versions of the grand palace they rest up against.

Gods Luminescence is scripted with brilliant starlight and frosty blue sapphires on a sign hanging above a shop that sells chandeliers, sconces, and various other Gods Light fixtures. Slabs of rubies, pink tourmaline, and yellow garnet the size of my head line a pathway to the entrance of the seamstress's shop, Needles and Thread.

Even the bakery has an entire door made of emerald. A bakery! How can they afford that when all they sell is bread? The only shop that looks even remotely less ostentatious still screams of privilege with a structure made up entirely of black onyx with gold scripted above the door, Fortunes and Truth.

It's all dazzling and extravagant, not to mention blindingly horrific.

But that's not what causes my feet to root to stone or my skin to break out in a nervous sweat. It's the dozens and dozens of immortals and fae casually strolling along, and of the impact of those same beings' emotions blasting into me, rattling the cage of my tenuous control.

When I was younger, I was able to shut out all others. But as I aged and my power grew, I could no longer completely silence them. Conforming to my ever-growing Gifts, I built the walls of my cage, and the bars muffled their feelings.

Not completely, of course, but enough to where I can ignore them if I choose to. Which I often do. For that fact alone, unless I'm with Zander, Tristan, Amara, or anyone else who's aware of my Gift and can calm me if needed, I usually avoid heavily populated areas such as this.

Even when I'm in the right state of mind, the emotions of so many can become loud and abrasive, often testing my control.

For this reason along with thousands of others, the only plausible conclusion as for why I join the bustling shoppers instead of backing into the alley and returning from where I came is a temporary loss of sanity.

Or I can blame Darius. Him and his intoxicating kiss.

Nerves still buzzing from our encounter, I drop my gaze and weave through the masses, hyperaware to avoid skin-to-skin contact with my fellow pedestrians. But it's next to impossible with the street filled as it is.

A female grazes her pinky against my hand. A fae rubs his bare shoulder with mine. A small boy dances beneath my feet and I stumble into a Nature immortal who catches me, placing his hands on my shoulders.

"Are you alright?" he asks, his attraction piercing into me as if a lance.

I flinch and mumble a hurried thank you as I shrug him off and quickly move towards a less populated area.

I shouldn't be here.

No, I shouldn't. Not after we kissed. Gods, that kiss! That wasn't even a kiss. It was a life altering, soul wrenching, ruin-you-for-any-other-male type of kiss. One filled with passion and lust. One you could never replace with another, no matter how hard you try. Even now, just the idea of being intimate with anyone beside Darius is revolting.

I should've stayed away from him. He's dangerous.

That's what Darius is. With his probing eyes and that dimpled smile, he makes me feel wanted. Needed. Special. Not for what I am – for he still doesn't even know what I am – but because of who I am as a person. Who I am in my soul.

Walking at a more sedate pace with more room to maneuver in this pocket of the street, I shake my head and chastise myself. From the first moment I saw him, I knew in my gut he was different. That what I feel for him is different. The hunger, the warmth, the affection. He evokes too many emotions within me. Too many *forbidden* emotions. Ones that test my control when it's imperative that I remain in control. There's no other option. When I don't, people die. But I'm afraid this may be something I can't control. That the intensity of our bond is too strong for me to ignore.

What would happen if I didn't ignore it?

Passing a casual glance over the magicked crystal fountain that shoots crystalline jets of glittering teal water from its ports, I chuckle humorlessly.

I don't know. Maybe I'll run into the middle of the city with dozens of emotional beings while my control is flimsy, at best.

Turning to the side, I avoid stepping on a female's gods-awful balloon dress, frowning. Maybe my loss of control isn't because we gave in, but because I've been spending so much energy trying not to.

I sigh. That may explain the less-than-ideal choices I've made, but it doesn't explain the bond or the magnitude of our desire. That need isn’t common. Very rare, actually. The only relationship I've ever encountered that's even remotely similar in its intensity is my mother and father’s. But that can’t possibly be happening here. The depth of their relationship is preordained while my destiny lies elsewhere.

A flash of yellow catches my eyes, interrupting my musings, and I look up to see a family heading in my direction. The female holding the babe is garbed in a saffron dress, her hair pinned up with crystal flowers, while the male is wearing a silver tunic beneath a royal blue surcoat. Both are Air immortals, marked by their sapphire and starlight jewels near the outer corner of each eye, and they appear to be born and bred within the upper class. Besides that, there's nothing unusual about them that would've caught my attention. They seem completely ordinary as they stroll down the street hand-in-hand. But when I peer closer and really *see* them, I discover what has captured my attention. Something I never would’ve noticed before, but laid bare as I am now, I can't help but to.

He wraps his arm around her waist, tugging her to his side while she nuzzles her babe’s cheek. Leaning down, he smiles and whispers in her ear. She laughs, genuine and free, and snuggles closer while he stares down at his wife and child with a look of complete adoration.

Jealousy nips at my heels for the second time today as their emotions trickle between the bars of the cage when I feel their happiness and devotion. Their love.

I’ve never allowed myself to wish for another life. To do so would cause unjust pain I can do without. Before now, it wasn't difficult. I've never loved or truly cared for someone outside my family and friends, so any hope for a romantic relationship was fleeting and easily suppressed. But with Darius, everything is *more*. So much to feel. So much to absorb. So much so, that my soul aches as I wish for what will never be.

For a babe. For a family.

For love.

Tears brim in my eyes and I shut them, trying to rein in my desolation. *This* is why I've been trying to avoid Darius. *This* is what I was afraid of. That his presence in my life would make me wish for impossible things when the most I can ever wish for is to find hope within others. To give hope to others. For hope belongs to those who can truly be free, and I never will be. Can never have that life. Not when I'm enslaved as I am, my life belonging to everyone but myself. There will be no family in my future. No loving husband or adoring babe. Just an empty existence alone. Forever alone.

Dropping my gaze, I rush past, refusing to torture myself any longer. I attempt to rein in my emotions again, but I can't. Not with Darius dragging all these long-suppressed desires to the surface, kicking and screaming the whole way. The lust, the fire, the bond; it's all too much. I know that future isn't intended for someone like me, but its power over me is staggering. Its strength, overwhelming. So much so, I fear the damage he has caused may be irreparable.

Strong fingers wrap around my bicep, dragging me against a male's broad chest.

"Are you lost, my lady?" a Water immortal says, peering down at me with a greasy smile. "This is no place for a human unescorted. Allow me to offer my services."

His lust slinks between the bars and my stomach lurches onto itself, his touch burning as if prodding me with a hot poker. Wrenching my arm free, I slip between the crowd before he can insist on 'escorting' me anywhere.

Yet even though I manage to escape him, I can't escape the

cacophony of emotions bombarding me. No longer muzzled, dozens of beings shout their feelings. Anger, happiness, irritation, love; they all rattle the cage with my dangerously teetering control. My heart races, my breaths quicken, and I slap my hands to my ears, desperately trying to shut out the noise clawing and screeching at the bars. But their shouts persist while the burn from the Water immortal's touch spreads and intensifies, acid radiating down my arms and legs as it eats away at my flesh.

Breathe... You have to breathe. Take back your control. You have to. There's no other choice.

With great effort, I slow my breaths and my heart thuds at a more leisurely pace as I carefully place a frail muzzle on the sounds. When I feel like I've managed dominance over my unruly Gift, I allow my hands to fall to my sides, and I inhale a deep, rejuvenating breath. But then I sense it... Much darker emotions. An oily, sinister cloud of corruption and perversion that slithers quietly through the cracks of the cage until it blankets me, suffocating me.

Scanning the street, I search for the masters of the darkened souls. It takes several moments for my gaze to finally land on the dozen or so males laughing and joking only a few paces away. But when it does, my stomach sours even more, my breaths hitching in my throat as I stare at them. The instant they look up and catch sight of me at a standstill in the middle of the street, I have to press the back of my vambraced hand to my mouth and swallow back bile as their inky, black souls blast their depraved intentions to me with a wave of all too familiar perversions. My mouth waters and my throat clogs with tears as I break their gaze and bolt down a side alley.

Boots slapping against stone and splashing in puddles, I race between buildings with single-minded purpose. I cup a hand to my mouth and breathe through my nostrils to stop the vomit that strives for release, but find no relief the farther away I race from them. My skin continues to crawl from their vileness and the bars of the cage bend, molding towards me, entombing me within their depravity.

The alley dead ends and I slap my palms to Seboia's own cage of a wall, hunching over and vomiting all the contents of my stomach. Once my gut hollows out, I hack and spit, swiping the back of my vambraced hand against my lips, and place my cheek against the cool stone wall.

I don't know if it was their inky souls, the stone biting into my palms, the desolation within me, or all of that combined, but when I close my eyes, a memory flashes before me. A dark shed. Alternating waves of hunger and cold. Chained wrists to an unmoving beam. Paralyzing terror and the tearing pain as sweat slicked skin slides against my own. Their cruel laughter as I flick my hands over and over again, desperately trying to release power that refuses to be unbound. Bound for my safety, but now as much of a chain as the iron around my wrists.

Stone crumbles beneath my nails as I claw at the wall, wishing to purge my mind as much as my stomach, but it's a fruitless wish. For I already know I'll never be able to scour my mind of those twisted memories.

A lingering taste of acid lingers within my mouth and I hang my head, gagging around my finger as I try to rid myself of the evil coating my tongue, attempting to ease my turbulent stomach and the darkness that refuses to recede. Yet, if anything, it seems to be magnifying, heightening. Then it suddenly slams into me on a torrential current.

"That's a good girl," a lecherous voice coos. My head instantly snaps up, leveling with the wall. "Look at you already bending over for me."

My breath halts in my lungs, the bones in my legs lock, and my heart stutters as that same paralyzing terror from my memory smothers me.

The sound of his footsteps echo deafeningly within the alley as he moves towards me. Then he stops, hovering behind me, and I feel the heat of him pressed up against my back. "You just can't wait for me to stick my cock in that cunt of yours, can you?" Leaning away, he groans, then returns, his breath moistening my ear as he whispers, "Damn, look at that ass. Maybe I'll fuck you there, too."

Several males cackle as I remain frozen, staring at the gouges on the white wall beneath my hands.

Move. You have to move.

I tell myself over and over again to move. Just a finger. A toe. Fucking blink, for gods sakes, but do something! Anything! Don't just stand there and wait for them to do *that* to you.

Not again. Never again.

I'm not that girl anymore. Magically chained, I was unable to protect myself, but I'm no longer bound, will never be completely bound again. I have more power in my fingernail than all these males combined. They can't do anything to me that I don't want them to.

So fucking move!

But I can't. My muscles refuse to unlock. No matter what I do, no matter what I tell myself, I can't lift so much as a finger since, as it would seem, I can bind myself just as well as any magic can.

"I hate it when they don't fight back," the male behind me mock pouts, sighing in regret. "But she is a beauty. I guess I'll have to make an exception." A chorus of jeers rings out in the alley and my trembling becomes violent.

Willing to do anything to escape this, even if that means releasing more of my Gifts, I try to break free of my cage. But to my horror, with every strike to the bars, the door welded by my terror refuses to budge. My power rages against its prison and slams into the bars as if it's a feral animal, clawing at the metal with a grating shriek, only to gradually slow into a frenzied panic once it realizes the metal's indestructibility. Having no more supremacy than I do over my self-inflicted bonds, its fear and desperation echoes my own on a howl that drones within my ears.

The male flattens his palm against the middle of my back. When his fingers begin to crawl down my spine, a lone tear tracks down my cheek.

Please move. Please, please, move...

Unable to break free of my own cage, I try to prepare myself for the inevitable and burrow within that pocket in my mind to which only I have access. But I don't know how to make myself *not* feel. Don't know how to separate myself and not experience every excruciating second. Not even with my years of experience erecting mental walls.

He prods his hardness against me and squeezes my ass cheeks. Groaning, he digs harder as he slowly hooks his thumb into my leathers, preparing to lower them. But as I feel the cool breeze slip between my trousers and his thumbs, I hear a low, vicious growl bounce off the walls in the darkened alley.

He's suddenly torn away from me with a scream, and I whimper in relief. At the delicious sound of his terror, my mind releases its hold. Trembles easing and muscles unlocking, my fear morphs into a blistering rage at the ones who dared to accost me. Intending to enact my own justice, I turn to face the vile males, but stop when I find my revenge stolen from me.

Having not seen his face, I can only assume the immortal crumbled beneath the cracked wall of the building is the same one from whom I was freed. Lifting my gaze, I watch as nine others stare with horrified gazes at the furious Fire immortal blocking the only exit.

Chest heaving, his hands and jewels illuminated, merciless, glacial blue eyes burn with white fire on a face contorted in murderous rage. Darius releases a snarl so primally animalistic, it shakes the very ground upon which I stand.

The male closest to him raises his palms and takes a cautious step towards him. "Captain, we weren't going to do anything." He laughs nervously as he takes another step. "We were just play–"

Darius' arm streaks out so fast and snaps the male's neck, I would've missed it if I had blinked. He doesn't even look at the dead immortal when he hurls him toward the mouth of the alley as if he weighs no more than a feather. Instead, he glares at the remaining eight males with eyes half-crazed in blood lust.

"The Gods Wrath," an Air immortal whispers, backing away in horror as if he's seen Desdemona, the Goddess of Death herself.

You can see the exact moment they realize they won't be leaving this alley alive. There will be no interrogations or imprisonment. No trial or a chance for them to bribe their way out. No... Their only means of escape will be through the release of death.

Seeing their demise reflected within those manic eyes, every one of their auras darken so black, the inky tar swallows any remaining light. With jewels illuminated, a single soul releases a terror-filled battle cry that the others quickly echo before raising their shimmering hands high and charging Darius as one.

The first one to reach Darius summons a spear of water and thrusts at his chest. Turning to the side, Darius easily catches it, freezing it within orange, glittering palms before snatching the blade away to stab his attacker in the throat. Blood gushing from his neck, the male crumples to the ground while another rushes Darius from behind. Darius swivels his torso and stabs downward into the immortal's groin, slicing upward until he retrieves the frozen blade from his chest.

One of the fae screams, holding a dagger over his head as he races forward, but he's abruptly thrown back by the frozen spear jutting out of his chest, streaking through the air until he's impaled into the white wall beside me. A Nature immortal calls forth dozens of thorns and shoots them at Darius, but Darius sweeps them up within a whirlwind and returns them back to its sender, riddling him through the eyes.

Listening to the Cascadonians speak fantastical tales of Darius, of his viciousness as the *Gods Wrath*, I just couldn't believe it. Darius is powerful and can be a complete ass, but I couldn't reconcile the monster so many claim him to be with the bright soul I know Darius to have. But looking at him now as he strikes each attacker down with such skill, precision, and power, it's baffling that I could ever doubt it. Watching Darius bash one male's head against the side of the building, caving in his skull, I realize that when the gossips spoke of the infamous *Gods Wrath*, they forgot to mention one crucial detail.

Of how breathtakingly beautiful Darius is when he exacts his vengeance.

A beautiful monster.

I can feel his primal need to kill these males with his bare hands. He doesn't even twitch toward the sword strapped to his back as a Water immortal slices downward with his own. Stepping to the side, Darius evades the strike before slamming his fist through the male's chest and ripping out his heart.

The leader of these twisted souls, the one who was seconds away from raping me, slowly regains consciousness. Horrified gaze bouncing from one body to the next, he trembles in fear when he sees a god-like Darius standing amongst the dead with a still beating heart clenched within his fist.

Darius' eyes narrow on the alert male and he throws the heart at him, smacking him in the face. The male yelps before scrambling backwards until his back hits the wall. Darius stalks forward to crouch before him.

He cowers and refuses to meet Darius' gaze until the Gods Wrath fists his hands into the male's hair and jerks his head back, forcing him to.

"You. Touched. Her," Darius snarls.

The male sputters and pleads as Darius' power electrifies the air, nipping along my skin with crackling bites.

Cocking his head to the side, the Fire immortal's lips curl into a cruel smile. "I saved something for you," he says forebodingly. And for the first time ever, I watch true joy light up Darius' face as he presses a single, orange, glittering finger to the terror-frozen male's lips.

Dozens of flamed threads slither into his mouth and he coughs and sputters, clawing at his throat. But when nothing more occurs, he peers up at Darius, his brows pinched in confusion. Several moments pass as Darius stares wordlessly down at him, and I find myself confused as well. Until the male suddenly slams his head against the wall with a resounding crack and the veins within his face ignite in glittering flames. His mouth gaping on a silent scream, the male convulses as flamed serpents burn through his blood vessels, blackening the skin of his cheeks as the glowing snakes slither down into his neck, spreading outward into the dozens of jagged veins throughout his body, mapping his bloodstream in fire as he burns to ash.

Crouched before him, Darius watches every second of the fire eating away at the male's body as if he doesn't want to miss a single moment. Even after he has long passed and the body is nothing but smoking bones and ash atop scorched stone, Darius watches. He seems to find some sort of cruel pleasure in the male's torturous end.

Blue eyes suddenly snap to mine and Darius stands from his

crouch. His steps are measured, calculated, the sound of his boots meeting stone thundering within the alley at a much slower rate than the heart that beats against my chest as he walks slowly toward me. He stops in front of me where I've plastered myself against the wall. Peering down, his blue orbs bore into my amethyst ones with the same savageness he had while slaughtering the males who lie dead around me.

Flattening a hand on the wall above my head, he raises the other to my cheek and strokes it gently with a single, crimson painted finger, igniting a fiery spark along its path.

He stole from you.

At the thought, my blood chills and all reverence over his brutal performance is instantly wiped clean. Fury bubbling to the surface, I snatch at his throat, hooking my leg around his knee and spinning us both as I slam his back to the wall.

"Don't touch me," I hiss, tightening my hand around his throat in warning.

His face softens, and he slowly raises his palms above his head. "I won't," he promises in a soothing tone. "Not without your permission."

"You killed them," I accuse.

Darius nods. "I did."

"That was not your punishment to give. It was mine!" I seethe.

Cocking his head to the side, his brows furrow. "This is my kingdom. Those males were my citizens." His throat bobs on a swallow, pushing against my hand. "And you are mine to protect. Their punishment belonged to me."

"You had no right!" My gums burn and I instantly clamp my lips together. Clenching the column of his throat once more, I shove off him and stride towards the opening to the alley with fisted hands.

Calloused fingers wrap around my wrist as Darius whirls me around to face him.

"I had every right!" he roars, his eyes burning in fury.

Growling, I flick his hand away and smack mine against his chest, shoving him back.

Blowing out a calming breath, he raises his palms. "I have every right when it comes to you," he says softly. "I'll kill anyone who touches you."

He doesn't understand. He was just trying to protect me.

My anger cools at the thought, dousing the indignant flames. In its place, a colossal wave of despair slams into me. Treading water, I struggle to take a breath.

Feeling the burn within my gums recede to an ache, I unclench my lips. "It's not your fault, it's mine."

It's true. I should've listened to Zander. He tried to warn me but I ignored him. All because I can't handle the emotions coursing through me, the emotions Darius awakened.

His eyes flash in anger and he stalks towards me. "This is *not* your fault. No female ... or woman," he adds, " should have to worry about being assaulted while walking the streets."

"Not with this face," I retort, smiling grimly as I point at my face. "I'm beautiful. Distracting. You said so yourself." Laughing bitterly, I add, "Males just can't seem to help themselves, can they?"

"We can and we do." He grits his teeth. "Some just choose not to."

"But why do they always have to choose me?" I whisper, my bottom lip quivering. "What is it about me that says they can take what does not belong to them?"

His expression morphs, contorting into one of torment; the same torment that etches his face flows down the bond and into me, clashing with mine. And I can take no more. No more pain, no more fear, just …no more.

“Is it my clothes? You said they showed too much.”

The waves crash over my head, dousing me in despair as they sweep me up within their depths. Sinking, sinking, sinking. The water swallows me whole, drowning me in agony. Fumbling with the laces of my vest, my fingers tremble as I desperately try to tear them apart.

“Stop,” Darius pleads as he places his hands atop mine, enfolding them within his.

“Maybe that’s it,” I say, tears blurring my vision. “Or my face? Or all of it. Just take it, then. Take it all! I don't want it. Never have. Give me one of those ridiculous dresses and burn the skin on my face until only scars remain.” I unclasp my hands from his and raise his stiffened hand to my cheek. “I can't go through something like that again, Darius. I won't survive it. Help me. *Please*.”

Jaw clenched, Darius searches my eyes for several moments before his face softens and his stiffened hand relaxes, molding to my cheek. “How could I burn such perfection?”

“Because it's a curse,” I choke out.

He shakes his head. “No, Lena. It's a blessing.”

My vision blurs even more as the tears brimming my eyes spill over, trailing down my cheek. “It's not just them, Darius. It's everyone. The actions of the cruel and corrupt may be more sinister than most, but everyone wants something from me. Wants to use me one way or another, no matter how honorable they may be.” My fingers travel toward his forearm and wrap around his wrist. “Can’t they see I can do no more? That I'm already doing everything I can, and if they continue to take, take, take, they'll deplete me to an empty shell with nothing left to give? Why can't they see, Darius? Why won't they just stay away and leave me be?”

He stares at me for a long moment, his arctic blue eyes a reflection of my own pain. I know he wishes he could save me from my agony but he can't. Not from something that has already come to pass. Not from what has already come to be.

Stepping closer, he presses his chest against mine. Lifting his other palm to my other cheek, he cradles my face so gently, so carefully, it's as if he believes I could break with just a touch. "I don't know why there's evil in the world. I don't know why some males are cruel. If you're a good person, I don't think it's something you can ever truly understand. But I do know if they're willing to harm you, they're willing to harm anyone." His eyes flash in conviction as he swipes away my tears. "That has nothing to do with you."

His features soften as he strokes a light caress along my cheek with his thumb. "As for why people can't stay away from you, it's not because of your face or your beauty. It's everything about you. It's because of who you are in here." He presses a palm over my rapidly beating heart. "You're kind and caring. You're whip smart and funny." He chuckles. "Gods, you're funny! No one makes me laugh like you do." His smile slips, and his expression becomes serious once more. "You're fiery and strong. Protective of those you love. You have this way about you where you can make everyone around you feel special. Doesn't matter if they're a prince or a beggar, you make them feel needed and cared for. When you walk into a room, all eyes fall on you, not because of your beautiful face, but because of the beauty of your soul. So bright and pure, it's like a bright star in a blackened sky. People feel if they could just share one word with you, one touch, one kiss, your light could swallow the darkness within them. The question isn't why they won't stay away, Lena. It's how can they?"

Affection lurches from him, hurtling down the bond into me, along with something else. Something so much more than affection or attraction or tenderness. It's powerful, potent, and could be absolutely devastating. An emotion I'm too terrified to acknowledge.

Placing my hands atop his, I give him a watery smile. "Thank you."

"No reason to thank me. Every word was the truth."

"I know."

His chest expands, regret lining his face as his hands fall to his sides and he steps back. Sniffling, I swipe beneath my nose and scan all the lifeless bodies scattered around me.

It's a good thing he got here so quickly. If he'd arrived even a minute later...

A thought pops into my mind and I frown. "Darius, how did you find me?"

His face shutters, and his lips tighten. "I felt you."

Humming, I nod to myself.

He opens his mouth, hesitates, then says, "Lena, that pain..." He shakes his head in bafflement. "It was indescribable."

"Yes, it is," I reply quietly, walking to the adjacent wall and resting my head back with a sigh.

"Why are you here, Lena?" No answer forthcoming, he prowls towards me. "It's not for trading leather. I haven't seen you approach a single vendor since you arrived."

I know what he's doing. Can feel his calculation through the bond. I'm cracked raw, vulnerable. He knows this and is using it to his advantage. I've evaded every personal question he's thrown at me, but it seems his patience is long gone. And laid bare as I am, I'm simply too tired to fight him on it, so I neither agree nor disagree.

"Are you in trouble?" Silence. "Are you running from someone?" Nothing. Lifting an arm, his movements are aggravated as he swipes a hand through his hair. "Let me help you."

I meet his eyes. “If anyone could help, it would be you, but you can't. No one can. This journey is for me and me alone.”

He steps into my space, his blue eyes searching my own. “It doesn't have to be that way.”

Placing both hands on his chest, I rise up to my toes and press a soft kiss to his bristled cheek. “I wish that was true,” I whisper in his ear. Then, I slip between him and the wall, heart aching in loneliness as I stride down the alley without a backwards glance.

CHAPTER 17

LENA

Knees bent and back relaxed, my boots absorb the impact as I land on the balls of my feet outside the Seboia wall. Hardly a moment passes before two pairs of feet touch down beside my own; Amara and Tristan's landing is muffled by the grassy terrain.

"Oh, shit!" a male voice whisper-shouts before Zander's large body streaks through the air, hurtling past us to collide with the ground. His less than graceful fall and the ensuing oomph rings through the night as if a toll to a bell.

"Be quiet!" Tristan shushes. Peering down the narrow stretch of grass, he crouches down, searching through the trees of the Cursed Woods.

Zander pushes up to all fours and hangs his head. His winded breaths fill the silence for several moments until he groans, rolling onto his backside and eyeing Tristan with a withering look. "Oh, I'm sorry! How inconsiderate of me to not think of you while suffering through the pain of my face breaking my fall."

"Very selfish," Tristan replies, oblivious to Zander's sarcasm as he cocks his head to the side, listening for any signs of the guards. "Do try to be more cautious in the future."

Zander's lips thin. "I'll do my best."

Lowering the hood of my cloak, I scan the forest. "There doesn't seem to be anyone around to hear you so that's something, at least."

Bounding to his feet, Zander is no worse for wear as he rolls his shoulders and joins Tristan to walk the treeless stretch of land between the wall and the Cursed Woods. Amara and I follow closely behind.

"There wouldn't have been anything to hear if *someone* had actually controlled my fall like they were supposed to do," Zander says, tossing an accusing glare over his shoulder.

Amara and I laugh.

"Don't waste your breath on those two," Tristan says, shaking his head. "They just can't help themselves."

Eyes straying to the top of the wall, Zander's expression falls with a mournful sigh. "I wish I could fly over," he murmurs, his somber words traveling to me on a whisper of wind.

My own smile slips at the sight and I stride towards him and wrap my arms around his waist. "So do I," I say, pinching his side with a teasing smirk, wishing to rid him of his dour mood.

His lips quirk and he tosses an arm over my shoulder as we trail behind the others.

"I wish we didn't have to go over at all," Tristan says quietly.

"Maybe we wouldn't have had to if Lena wasn't so busy sticking her tongue down Darius' throat." Zander laughs at my answering scowl and with eyes sparkling in mischief, he drags me against his chest, licking a hot, moist trail from my chin to my forehead.

"Ugh!" Shoving him off, I swipe away his disgusting slobber while Zander's quiet laugh morphs into a howl.

"Quiet! Someone might hear us," Tristan hisses over his shoulder.

Zander tosses his arms out, gesturing around us. "Who's going to hear us? There's no one out here."

"You don't know that."

Amara rolls her eyes and points at me. "She does."

"We're alone," I confirm. Peering into the woods, I watch the beams of moonlight flit playfully through the leaves of the swaying trees before being devoured by the all-consuming shadows. Spreading my senses out further, I feel no souls of any kind. Frowning at the peculiarity of the lack of life, I focus on my more common senses. Straining my ears, I expect to hear buzzing insects or scurrying rodents, typical sounds of a forest brimming with life, but I find nothing.

It's quiet. Too quiet.

"Aren't there supposed to be guards out patrolling?" I ask, feeling needle-like pricks crawling along my skin. A sensation easily dismissed, if I hadn't already been well acquainted with the ominous manifestation.

"Yes." Tristan's gaze sweeps through the trees with a hardened jaw, just as wary as I am with the eerie silence. "Usually this is a heavily guarded area, but someone has been altering the patrol schedule. There's been several occasions in the last few days where only two or three guards are on duty. Or in some cases, none at all."

"That can't be safe," Amara adds, her lips turned down into a frown.

"It's not," Tristan agrees, stepping over a windswept branch. "It usually takes two to three immortals to defeat one Soulless. If a guard has to fight any more than that, they would most likely be killed."

"Do they have any idea who's doing it?" I ask.

"Not yet, but I heard Darius is furious. He assigned Lennox to lead a special team to sniff out the culprit."

Whether this is a person who simply enjoys sending people to their death or this is a small step in a more sinister plot has yet to be decided. I would need more information to determine that, but one thing is for certain. Whoever's doing this, their intentions are anything but benign.

"The second they find him, I want to know," I order. They all nod in acknowledgement.

Amara unsheathes a dagger and flips it into the air, catching it by the hilt. "At least we can say one good thing came out of this."

"I can't believe you broke into their armory," Tristan seethes, the marking on his cheek twisting with his displeasure. "Lena told you not to steal any weapons."

"It's not stealing if they're already ours," Amara quips, her single starlight jewel twinkling beneath the light of the two moons. "The way I see it, they stole from us." She shrugs. "I was simply reclaiming what's already mine."

Humming to myself, I secretly agree with Amara as I, too, have felt naked without the weight of my blades. Stroking the hilt of one of the obsidian and starlight daggers strapped to my hip, the warmth of it spreads a comforting heat to my palms.

Rounding on Amara, Tristan folds his arms over his chest. "And what happens when they realize they're missing? Who do you think their first suspects will be?"

"Us," Amara replies with a droll look, twirling the dagger. No doubt just to irk Tristan even more.

Tristan's answering smile is all teeth. "Exactly. Which will attract even more attention to ourselves than we already have."

Zander huffs, unstrapping the leather strap from his wrist and tying his glossy, blonde hair back, giving Tristan a reproachful glare. "Stop your bitching. What's more important to you?" Placing his hands on his hips, he jerks his head towards me and Amara. "Calling attention to ourselves, or keeping them safe?"

Uneasy with Zander's comments, I watch them share a silent conversation for several moments until Tristan concedes defeat with a nod of his head. My uneasiness grows with the gesture and I beg the Stars for the thousandth time that my friends, my family, would never again speak of such things. Or at the very least not within my presence. But I already know my fate is already painted by the Stars and I'll forever endure listening to how important it is for them to keep us safe. Of how they would do anything for it to remain that way. Like my life is more valuable than theirs, when in truth it's not. Everything I do is for them. For those I love. If I didn't have them, I wouldn't have the strength to continue. Nor would I be willing to do so.

"Here we are."

Tristan's voice tears me from my thoughts and I glance up, finding myself standing before the same white wall alongside which we've been walking parallel. But unlike the rest of the stone cage, this section has large slashes and gouges blemishing the pristine white.

Out of precaution, I stretch my senses once more and confirm no other signs of life. "Zander, I need more light."

Zander's copper and starlight jewels flare and glittering gold crawls up the veins of his forearms, up to his chest and neck all the way into his lower jaw, illuminating his once green, but now glowing gold eyes. Raising shimmering gold palms, he summons a massive funnel of gilded, twisting fire. With a monstrous roar, the flames barrel toward the claw marks, shaping themselves to them.

Amara reaches toward the fire, but jerks back when a wayward flame attempts to lick at her skin. Swinging her gaze to Zander, a devious smile quirks her lips, seeming more sinister with the flickering flames reflecting off her whiskey eyes. "I would love for these arrogant Fire immortals to see what *true* fire power is. They're all but a spark compared to this beast."

The flames flare to near blinding, howling in agreement. "Born in fire, I rise from the ashes," Zander whispers, brushing his fingers through the gilded flames of his creation before reverting his attention to Amara with a menacing grin. "They may be able to wield the flames, but I *am* the flame."

Chuckling at the hypocrisy of his own arrogance, I, along with everyone else, study the crisscrossed slashes in silence. Tristan grazes his fingers across the markings and dips his finger into a gouge, the wall swallowing his finger down to the second knuckle.

"So the Soulless were climbing atop one another?" Biting my lip, I cock my head to the side. "Trying to breach the walls?"

Tristan rubs his fingers together, dusting off the residual powdered stone as he steps back, his brown, almost black eyes bouncing over the scores. "Appears that way."

"So the Breccans ordered them to breach the walls?" Amara asks. Tristan jerks his head in a nod, a grim slash to his lips.

This timeline is too close. Too coincidental. There's no way this isn't the beginning.

Tick, tick, tick. The time is near.

"Tristan, how far into the palace have you infiltrated?" I ask, fiddling with my lip while pacing through the grass, my mind bouncing from one thought to the next.

"I've mapped it out almost in its entirety."

Raising my hand, I count off on my fingers. "So the royal wing, throne room, and meeting rooms?" I ask and Tristan nods. "Did you have any trouble with the Queen's wards?"

He scoffs. "No ward can keep me out." As if oil filling a well, ruby speckled blackness spreads and fills the swirled marking on his cheek. Flicking his wrist, wisps of shadows spotted with rubies drift from his flattened hand, tendrils dancing along his palm before his hand snaps shut into a fist, the shadows dispersing like smoke in the wind along with the darkness of his markings.

"Stupid question," I say, waving the thought away. "Have you found anything of note?"

"I've found a few secret passageways. But at this point, none of them seem to be of much use."

"That's not much help," Amara says, tapping her fingers on her hips. "Might as well walk through the front door."

Bobbing my head, I say in all seriousness, "At the rate we're going, we just might."

A laugh bursts from Amara. "It'd definitely make a statement."

"What else?" I ask Tristan, hoping he can give me more than the nothing he's given me thus far.

"Nothing." Staring up at the moons, he scans our surroundings once again. "But I haven't had the opportunity or time to investigate the royals' private chambers just yet."

"Make time," I snap, much harsher than I intended. "We're running out of time as it is," I add in a softer tone, though it is no less commanding.

My boots swish through the grass as I return to the wall, halting my steps when I feel the waves of heat blast into me from the funnel of flames. Dropping my head back, I stare up at the Breccans' assault once more, my eyes rapid firing from one claw mark to the next with the same chaos jarring my mind.

This is important. I know it is. Every instinct tells me I have all the information I need. I have all the pieces to the puzzle, but they're all jumbled and each time I attempt to slip them into place, they refuse to mesh.

Narrowing my eyes, I step forward into the pyramid of flames and am instantly devoured by the roaring beast. Feeling nothing but a warm caress, I trace my fingers across a claw mark several spans wide as I imagine that very same mark inflicted on an immortal. On how that injury would be instantly fatal to the powerful beings. Regardless of my task, that's something I can't allow. I refuse to. Even if it's before I find who I've been tasked to seek.

Where are you, you son of a bitch?

The flames release their embrace as I stalk towards my companions. "Have any of you acquired any information that could possibly lead to who is working with Brecca?" I ask, and they all shake their heads in answer. Jaw locked, I meet each individual gaze, my amethyst eyes stressing the urgency of our situation. "We have to find him. Him, her, them." I flick a hand. "Whoever the fuck it is, I don't care. I just want them found. *Now*."

"It has to be a royal or a noble," Amara says as she sits down on the grass, crossing her legs.

"I'm leaning more towards a royal," Zander adds, rubbing his chin. "Nobles may appear to be held in high esteem, but they don't have access to the guards, and none are on Adelphia's council."

My interest piques with this information. "Who is on her council?"

"Only the Captain of the Queen's Guard and her children."

"What about Theon's wife?" I scrunch up my face, trying to remember the female's name. "Kiora?"

"That's her," Zander says. "But she's not on the council."

Interesting. If I was a princess destined to be Queen, I don't think I'd be too pleased with the idea of not being part of the current one's inner council.

"Could she be the one working with the Breccans?" Amara voices my own thoughts, plucking at the grass.

"Unlikely," Tristan replies with a sneer. "She prefers to spend her time drinking and fucking her way through court."

Amara snorts. "Sounds like a happy marriage."

"From my understanding, the heir is oblivious to her promiscuous activities," Tristan says, peering over his shoulder with an anxious tap of his boot.

"Could it be the heir?" I ask.

Tristan's tapping ceases. "No. from everything I've learned about him, he's an honorable male."

"It could be Darius or Aurora," Amara proposes.

"No," Tristan and I answer in unison.

Zander and Amara share a look before Zander speaks in a gentler tone. "I know it may be difficult to believe such a thing about someone you care about," he says, his gaze darting between me and Tristan. "But it could be either of them."

Pursing his lips, Tristan balls his fists in fury, ruby flecked darkness pouring into the swirled marking on his cheek as he lunges for Zander.

I snatch at his forearm and drag him behind me, feeling unnerved at the role reversal when I give him a warning look. "I've searched both Aurora's and Darius' auras," I say, returning my attention to Zander once I'm sure Tristan has calmed. "It's not them."

"You're sure?" Zander asks, his expression dubious at best.

Eyes narrowing, I bite out, "It's not something one can fabricate."

Zander looks to Amara who shrugs her shoulders. I roll my eyes at their lack of faith.

"Alright, then," Zander says. "What about the Queen?"

"She's capable of it," I reply. "She has a darkness to her, but it's not her."

"It might be," Amara argues.

I shake my head. "No it can't."

I think back to when I first saw Adelphia in front of Aurora's shop. Arrogant, vain, selfish, and drowning in darkness. But that darkness was not inherently cruel or evil. It was created from grief and pain, something I know firsthand how difficult it can be to resurface from.

"The darkness within her was caused by the Breccans. As such, she would never work with them. In her eyes, she lost everything to them." I try to tuck my hair back into my cloak, but the rippled, wavy strands continue to pull loose. "I doubt she'll act against them unless she has no other choice." I gather my hair to one side and wave the ends at Zander. He chuckles, walking past my line of sight to stand behind me.

"If she lost so much to Brecca, why wouldn't she act against them?" Zander asks as he weaves his nimble fingers within my hair, plaiting the locks with a speed and skill I've always been envious of.

"Because she's terrified of them," I reply, recalling the thick terror coating her entire aura. It's the same terror that has engulfed me, but unlike her, I've never allowed it to define my actions or determine how to treat others undeserving of blame.

She suffers, but that doesn't excuse her need to make everyone else suffer along with her. I doubt she even sees the effect it has on those around her. She's too narcissistic to take notice.

Zander tickles my cheeks with the end of my plaited hair and I giggle, snatching it from him and tucking it back into my cloak. He wraps his arms around my neck from behind in a familial embrace and I clasp my hands around his forearms. I wish for a different male's arms wrapped around me, but I'm comforted by my friend's affection nonetheless.

Amara stands and swipes grass off her backside as she peers over her shoulder. "Okay, so none of us think it's any of the royals." She turns to face us and slaps her hands to her sides with a frustrated huff. "Which brings us back to having no leads."

Tapping Zander's arms, he releases me and I step forward. "Tristan, search the royal chambers as well as Aurora's loft above the shop." He nods and my gaze ventures to Amara's. "Since you've already managed to get into the armory, I'm assuming you've mapped out the Guard's base?"

"Of course."

"Did you find any blades made from anything besides steel?" I doubt she did, otherwise she would've already mentioned it, but I must ask.

Wincing, Amara stares a hole through her shuffling feet. "No, but I wasn't really looking for it, either."

"Of course you weren't." Tristan rolls his eyes and she smacks his arm.

"I was just trying to get in and out," she spews through clenched teeth.

"You should have searched for it anyway," he scolds, smacking her back.

"You can look for it now," I say, ignoring their bickering. "And search Darius' office while you're at it. I know he's not the one we're looking for, but you may find something that can be of use." Turning, I meet Zander's blue gaze. "I want you to find out who's changing the guards' schedule. I have a few questions for him, and I suspect this person will lead us straight to the source." Debating for a moment, I add, "And I don't want Darius discovering who it is first."

Zander hisses in a breath and rubs the back of his neck. "I don't know if that's possible. They've already been searching much longer than I have. They may already know who it is."

My lips purse. "Then keep Darius in the dark as long as possible, but I need to speak with the perpetrator first."

Zander gives me an uncertain look, but nods his assent.

"We need to leave," Tristan says, peering over the side. "Guards will be patrolling this area anytime now."

Amara snorts. "If they were scheduled, you mean."

Zander brushes past me and we all follow behind.

Hearing a crackle and a pop, I whisper Zander's name.

Zander glances at me over his shoulder, his gaze traveling up when he catches sight of the inflamed wall. Jewels illuminated, his gold, shimmering hands call forth the twisting flames. The flames uncoil from the marks, and with spitting sparks, a wave of fire barrels towards Zander, heedless of Amara, Tristan, or me blocking its path.

Amara and Tristan cry out and dive to the side as I shut my eyes, allowing the fire to blast into me, consuming me. Tendrils of golden, sputtering flames tease my skin as they play with my hair and lift my cloak. With a soft whoosh, they release me from their embrace and vanish into Zander's palms.

"Dick," Tristan grumbles, returning to his feet along with Amara.

Zander shrugs and walks away, the rest of us following behind.

"You can't use your Gifts here," Tristan chides Zander, falling behind to walk beside me. "Your fire is too different from theirs."

"Oh, I've noticed," Zander replies in a huff. "It's awful not being able to use them. It's like I'm missing a part of myself."

"You get used to it," Amara says bitterly, walking at his side.

He squirms as if his skin's stretched taut. "But my animal is getting anxious. It wants out."

"Zander," I warn, boring a hole into his broad back.

"I know, I know." Glancing at me over his shoulder, he rolls his eyes. "Don't worry. I won't let him out, but we're going to have to leave soon. I can't suppress him much longer, and you need a release, too." Rolling his shoulders, Zander expels a frustrated groan as he rubs the back of his neck.

Amara, unable to stomach this gloomy side of him anymore than I can, distracts him with a yank on his bun. He yowls and bats at her hands, which Amara quickly reciprocates. Zander narrows his eyes on her and she instantly mirrors his look. A split second later, they reach for each other in unison and begin slapping at each other's hands.

They look like two little girls fighting over a doll.

"I'm just waiting for them to start pulling each other's hair," Tristan says and we both laugh.

Ignoring their slapping sounds, Tristan peeks at me out of the corner of his eye. "I've been watching you, you know?"

I do know, but I was hoping if I pretended I wasn't aware, he'd skip whatever lecture he's no doubt about to issue.

"Stalker," I tease, nudging my shoulder with his in a last-ditch effort to avoid the inevitable.

Tristan rolls his eyes. "As I was saying, I've been watching you. You're having difficulties containing your power, aren't you?"

I stiffen. "I wouldn't say that."

Disbelieving, he quirks a brow. "You wouldn't, huh? Then why are you freezing when you're attacked, or losing control in an empty tavern?" Unable to come up with a suitable explanation, I remain silent. "If you can't explain that, then why are you eating triple what you normally would? Why are you half dead from exhaustion before the sun descends?" He shakes his head. "You may not want to admit it, but I will. You're expending an inordinate amount of energy trying to control your Gift, and you're still unable to manage it. Why is that?"

No answer forthcoming, he hesitates before releasing a long-winded sigh. Regret lines his face as he says in a gentle, yet hard tone, "You lost control before and the aftermath was catastrophic. We can't allow that to happen again."

"I know that," I snap, feeling anger and a pinch of hurt that he would make the comparison.

He scrubs agitated hands through his hair. "Then tell me what's wrong. Maybe I can help."

"I…" Hesitating for a moment longer, I puff out my cheeks and blow out a raspberry. “I think it has to do with Darius. How I…” I bite my tongue, hating to admit this but knowing I must. “How I feel for him.”

“And how he feels for you,” he replies, unsurprised.

“Yes,” I mumble, staring down at my feet.

Cocking his head to the side, Tristan’s brows furrow. “Is this surprising to you?”

I huff a bitter laugh. “It’s not to you?”

“Your emotions are tied to your Gifts, so no, this isn't surprising.”

“So what do you think I should do?” I ask, brushing my hand over a leaf on a passing branch. “I can't keep going on like this. It’s dangerous.”

He smiles and wraps an arm around my shoulders, pulling me into his side. “Maybe you should stop fighting it.”

“What?!” I squawk, jerking back, but he grips me tighter to him, holding me hostage. “You can’t be serious.” I would expect this kind of advice from Zander. Maybe Amara. But never would I imagine Tristan would propose such a thing.

“Shocking, I know.” Rubbing my arm, he smiles down at me. “Just try and listen for a moment.”

“Alright,” I reply warily.

Releasing me from his hold, he stops walking and steps back to face me. “I love you. You, Amara, and Zander are my family and you mean everything to me. I trust your judgment implicitly and I would follow you through the ends of the realms, no questions asked. That being said, there are some instances, only on occasion, when you can be just a tad bit… stupid.”

Scowling at him, I mumble, “You really need to work on your people skills.” Rubbing my head with my fingertips, I can't decide whether to be angry at him or be upset over the ding to my confidence.

He winces. “I know.” He holds his palms up in a placating gesture. “Let me explain.”

“That might be best,” I reply with a tight smile.

Tristan steeples his fingers, pressing the point to his lips. “You think there's only one path that exists for you; one that requires you to form no relationships.” He twists his mouth to the side, then adds, “Besides Amara, of course.”

“Because it does.”

Ignoring me, he continues, “You also thought you couldn't have friends, but here we are.” He gestures to Amara and Zander up ahead.

“Wellll…” I scrunch my face. “I didn't really invite any of you along. You all followed me around like a pack of stray dogs.”

“And we always will,” he replies. “This journey you're on, it's not just one set path. There's a thousand other paths you can take and still reach your destination.”

“You don't know that,” I argue, irritated with him for insinuating anything differently.

“I do. I can feel it in my bones.” He slaps a palm to his chest. “Fate is fluid and ever changing. Even yours.”

“But some things are set in stone,” I remind him with a glare.

“Yes,” he agrees. “But I believe one of those things may be Darius.”

Stunned is the only way I can describe myself in this moment. Tristan is the steady rock of our group. The calm one. The one who wrangles all our craziness. He doesn't act on emotions, he's never quick to make a decision, and he never *ever* wavers from our mission. If something needs to be done, he'll do it no matter how unsavory the task may be. That's what makes him such a good spy. He deals in logic and facts. So to hear from him – someone who knows what trials lay ahead for me, someone who already knows how impossible it is for me to form any type of romantic attachment – try to convince me otherwise is a jagged blade to the chest.

My lips thin. "I know you think you're being helpful, but you're not. This is cruel, Tristan." Shaking my head, I turn away from him, striding ahead to where Amara and Zander wait.

"I wouldn't say it if I didn't believe it," he says, rushing to my side. "This could very well be in the Stars' plan."

Uncaring of any other souls about, I lengthen my stride and shout, "But it can't be! Not with me."

"See?!" he says, tossing his arms up. "This is where your stupid comes in. Why can't it be you?"

I bark a humorless laugh. "Because I'm too different from him."

Too different from everyone.

He scoffs. "You're special, I'll give you that, but you're as much Uriella and Azazel's child as the rest of us."

Anger rising with every word that drips from his lips, I whirl on him. "Tristan, I am a slave to the will of others. Forever bound and gagged, I'm destined to live a broken existence filled with darkness. There is nothing in my future besides death and pain. You know this!" I shout, completely flabbergasted he would suggest such a thing. "Anyone who stands beside me will suffer the same fate I do. How can you possibly ask me to bring another person into this life?"

Placing his palms on my shoulders, his brown eyes drill into my own. "Coming from a man who has already suffered alongside you, I'll tell you that every godsdamned second was worth it if it means I can remain by your side."

"I can't do that to him," I whisper. Wrapping my fingers around his wrists, my eyes beg him to stop pressing the issue. "It's selfish."

"I think it's selfish to take the choice away from him."

"I…" My words trail off as I attempt to argue, but I hesitate at the accusation.

From my very first breath, I've never had any say on what path my life would take. Every moment of my life has revolved around the shifting demands of others. Yet all I've ever wanted is to be free to make my own choices. Good or bad, I want to live my life how I choose to. But if what Tristan says is true, then I'm doing the very same thing to Darius: taking away his choices. My intentions are noble and meant to protect him, but I'm still taking away his choices without considering his desires. And that is something I cannot do. But how can I ask someone to give up everything he knows and loves? His home, his family, possibly his very life? Or what's even more terrifying to consider, what will I do if he finds me unworthy of such a sacrifice?

"I can't tell him the truth," I say, my mind a whirlwind of possibilities, though none I can commit to in this moment.

A slow smile creeps up Tristan's cheeks as he places a hand on my back, rubbing circles between my shoulder blades. "No, you can't. Not yet, at least. But give him the opportunity to prove himself to you." Ducking his head, he levels his eyes with mine as he whispers, "Give him a chance to show you he is strong enough to stand beside you."

Shaking my head, I can't help but chuckle at his hopeful smile. "It's so weird talking to you about this."

"I know," he breathes on a sigh, straightening as he drops his hand.

"That was so mushy," I tease, stabbing my finger into his chest. "I think Aurora's turning you into a romantic."

"Stop it," he says, turning away from me and striding forward.

"Aww, don't be like that," I call out, rushing to his side. "It's adorable."

"Just…stop talking." Glowering at me out of the corner of his eyes, he shoves me to the side and I laugh.

Stumbling over my feet, my laughter cuts off when the needle-like pricks intensify. Morphing into stinging pecks, it snaps along my arms and legs, gouging at my skin and drawing blood. Shutting my eyes, I stretch out my senses and sparks of life flit into view. One… two… two souls, bright and whole racing through the woods, consumed by fear. Ignoring Amara and Zander's approach, I stretch my senses even further, my heart rate increasing when I discover a cluster of death nipping at the heels of the two terror-ridden souls.

The Soulless.

Snapping my eyes open, I look to my three companions standing before me. "The Soulless are hunting two people in the woods. Probably guards."

"How many?" Zander asks, unsheathing his sword from its scabbard.

"Too many," I reply, palming my twin daggers.

Amara slices through the air with her short sword before stabbing an invisible opponent with a stiletto. "It seems tonight just got a lot more interesting. Do you still think I shouldn't have stolen back our weapons?" she asks Tristan.

"No," he replies in a dry tone, checking the sharpness of his longsword with a swipe of his finger.

"I love it when you're wrong." Amara laughs, following the two males as we cross over the Cascadonian border into the woods.

"Weapons only and no magic," I instruct. "We're taking a big enough risk as it is by showing ourselves to the creatures."

"Then don't show yourself," Tristan replies, glancing between me and Amara as he ducks under a low hanging branch. "We'll take care of it."

Amara and I share an affronted look.

"So we can do what? Stand by and watch like good little ladies?" I scoff. "Not happening."

Amara smacks the back of his head. "These sexist Cascadonians are rubbing off on him."

"Just thought I'd ask," Tristan mumbles, rubbing his head.

"It's annoying that you felt the need to." Sensing the Soulless gaining on the guards, I hurry Amara along with a palm to her back. "I don't need protecting."

Tristan comes to an abrupt halt, Amara slamming into his back as I crash into hers. Ignoring our muttered curses, he peers over his shoulder to meet my gaze. "You're wrong. You're the only person in all the realms worth protecting."

Groaning, I reach around Amara and shove him in the back. "Just go! You're going to make me cry with all the sappy shit you've said tonight."

"Gods forbid," he drawls, rolling his eyes.

"What about me?" Amara asks.

Tristan's gaze veers to her. "What about you?"

"Aren't I worth protecting?" she asks with a pout.

"Of course not!" Tristan says, staring at her as if she's gone mad. "You're nothing more than fodder."

Features twisting into rage, Amara kicks him in the shin. "Tell the Stars that, you ass! Gods! I don't know how Aurora puts up with you."

"Focus." Snapping my fingers between the two, I draw their attention to me. "We don't have time for this. Remember, no Gifts, no shifting," I order, pointing at Zander, who sticks out his tongue. "And get back over the wall before anyone suspects we left."

Acknowledging my command with a nod of their heads, we all lift the hoods of our cloaks and slink between the trees, disappearing into the Cursed Woods.

CHAPTER 18

SILAS

Sweat drips down my nape and my breath saws from my lungs as I dart between the trees of the Cursed Woods. Branches scratch my cheeks and tear at my clothes, but I ignore the stinging pain. For the trees' talons are wisps compared to the claws of the creatures stalking us.

A fallen maple appears, blocking my path, and I spring over the trunk, my feet already moving before they touch the other side.

"Shit!" a male shouts, followed by a loud oomph.

Glancing over my shoulder, my irritation spikes when I discover Calder sprawled at the base of the log. Cursing internally, I race back to the idiot guard. "Get up," I order, my eyes searching the shadows for the Soulless.

"I can't!" he cries, rubbing his ankle. "I think I broke it."

"You're fae," I hiss. "You'll be healed within minutes."

Tears trailing down his cheeks, he pushes off the ground, only to crumble in an instant. "I can't! My ankle won't hold my weight."

Curling my lip at the pitiful excuse of a guard, I grip his arm and jerk him up to his feet. "Do you want to die?" I ask, shaking him. “Because if you don't get up, that's what’s going to happen.”

“We shouldn't even be here,” he moans, leaning all his weight on me. “Not with only two guards.”

“It doesn't matter what *should* be. We are here, and right now there’s a pack of Soulless hunting us.” Hearing the sound of pounding feet closing in on us, I shout, “Run, dammit!”

He pulls his arm from my grasp and hops once… twice… three times, then falls like a sack of potatoes.

Watching the fully grown Nature fae wail and sob while snot drips down his nose, I can't help but to consider leaving him here. In normal circumstances, I would never do such a thing, but he isn't really a male at all.

His appearance is mediocre, his power weak, he’s useless at absolutely everything, and he makes this odd donkey sound whenever he laughs. I can only imagine how awful his future children will be. No, this fool should not be encouraged to procreate.

No one will ever know. I'll say he ran off half-cocked into the woods.

I'd be performing a service to Cascadonia! Saving whatever poor female he's destined to pair with from a life of annoying laughter and dimwitted chatter. All I have to do is walk away and allow the Soulless to drink him dry.

Having already spoken my Guards Oath and knowing a male is only as good as his word, I dismiss the idea with a groan and crouch before Calder.

“I’ll shift, and you can ride on my back.”

His wailing cuts off and he meets my gaze. “But shifters don’t allow riders.”

I grit my teeth. “I'm aware of that.”

Sniffling, he wipes beneath his nose. “You’ll let me ride you like a horse?”

"Not like a horse," I snap, then pause to inhale a deep, calming breath. "I'm a tiger."

"But I've never ridden a tiger before; only a horse." His lips turn down into a frown. "How will I hold on if I don't have any reins?"

Regretting my offer more and more with each passing second, I reply, "You'll figure it out."

Red, puffy nose scrunching, he gives me a wary look. "You won't eat me, will you?"

I'm leaving him here. That's just too much stupid to exist in the world.

"I'm not going to eat you, but the Soulless will."

Grunts and growls echo through the trees, raising the hairs on the back of my neck.

"But don't tigers-"

"No more questions!" I shout, cutting him off with a swipe of my hand. "You can stay here and die, or you can ride on my back. Make your choice."

"Okay, okay," he says, pushing up to his knees. "You don't have to yell at me."

Unstrapping my scabbard and the sheathed sword from my back, I pass it to him. "Hold on to this."

"Thank the gods!" He blows out a relieved sigh. "I lost mine."

Of course you did.

Growling, I shut my eyes and summon my Gift. Copper jewels spear through the darkness with a flash of light as a wave of glittering amber washes over me. My pointed ears extend, my teeth sharpen and grow, orange and black fur sprouts along my skin, and my bones break and reform into a half-ton beast, double the size of a domestic tiger.

Standing on all fours, I position myself next to Calder.

"You're huge!" Calder states wide eyed, ignoring my invitation to climb on. "Are you sure you don't want to eat me?"

Having lost all patience, I hiss and bump him with my hip.

"I'm going, I'm going," he mumbles. Stumbling upright, he pulls himself onto my back. The moment he seats himself, I spring forward, racing towards the wall.

Paws pounding against the forest floor, my movements are more swift and agile in this form than my two legged one. My sense of smell is heightened as well, and the scent of death is much closer than I initially thought.

As I weave between the trees, Calder cries out and grabs a fistful of fur. But I pay no mind to his cries as I urge my powerful muscles to get us within the safety of the city.

A Soulless jumps out and I slip between twin trees, barely dodging its reach. Popping out on the other side, I swerve as another one reaches for me, its claws slicing through air.

"There's more over there!" Calder shouts, pointing to the three Soulless blocking our path. Attempting to slow, my claws dig into the dirt as I veer to the right, racing away from the safety of the wall and deeper into the woods.

Scraping against trees and tearing through thickets, my paws are shredded within minutes. Shadows swallow up all light, the forest darkening by the second; all I can see is inky blackness as I gallop between trees.

Even with my sharpened feline vision, I can't make out the Soulless until they're right beside me. And they're everywhere! They lie in wait behind trees and bushes, carefully corralling me into a trap.

A claw slashes out at me and I stumble over my paws. Calder flattens against my back and tightens his arms around my neck, strangling me as I right myself. But not even a moment after doing so, another demon streaks towards me and I barely dodge its cursed arms.

Swiping at its throat, I tear its head from its shoulders and spring over its body, only to be met with two more. Calder tears at my fur and screams as I race forward, pouncing on top of them and crushing their skulls beneath my thunderous paws.

Slinging their tainted blood from my paws, I sprint towards a tight cluster of trees when the scent of rot overpowers me and over a dozen Soulless slip from the shadows. Skidding across wet leaves and moss, I tumble and fling Calder from my back.

I bolt upright to all fours and swing around, searching for an escape, but my fear grows at the sight of more Soulless separating from the shadows, surrounding us.

Grunting and snarling, enshrouded in black shadows speckled with ruby flecks, the decaying creatures stare us down with glowing red eyes, ravenous for our deaths.

Gods, I've never seen more than two Soulless at a time and there's what? Over two dozen? Three dozen? Three dozen Soulless! This is impossible!

We've been told they are nothing more than mindless demons consumed with bloodlust. They don't ally with one another and once they catch the scent of their prey, they don't stop until they've captured their food. Because that's what we are to them: Food.

They feed off our blood and gift our souls to their masters. They have no recollection of the life they once lived, can't recall that they were once one of us. Cursed by darkness, they only serve their masters and hunt the very same beings they once called kin.

"Oh, gods! We're going to die!" Calder cries out, scrambling to my side. His trembling fingers fist into my fur and he buries his face into my side. Curling my lip, I shake him off and lift my fallen sword with my teeth, dropping it into his lap.

Petrified, Calder looks down at the sword but doesn't retrieve it. I decide right then and there that if I make it out alive, I'll be having a word with the Captain about higher standards for screening recruits. Paralyzed as he is, this male can't even protect himself, let alone a kingdom.

I'm not ashamed to admit that I'm terrified as well. I'd be a fool not to be. But unlike him, there's no way in Azazel's Darkness I'm allowing these motherfuckers to take me down without a fight.

Hissing at the pathetic fae, I return my attention to the Soulless surrounding us, my hackles rising at the sight of their red glowing eyes and unnatural shadows. One jerks forward, his bones creaking as it tosses its splayed hands out and unsheathes its claws.

My muscles tense in response and a growl rumbles through my chest, preparing to do whatever is necessary to survive.

Its maw elongates, exposing the demon's dagger-like teeth with a snarl. As if the sound is a call to arms, three dozen clacking-limbed Soulless charge toward us.

Dropping my muzzle, I nudge the sword toward the idiot one last time, hoping he can shake himself out of his stupor. By the time I lift my head again, they're already upon us.

Two Soulless reach for me and I swipe my claw through one's neck before slicing through the other's arm. The severed limb falls to the ground and I stab my claws into its chest. Another reaches for me and I pounce on its torso.

Biting down on its neck, putrid black blood fills my mouth as I rip out its throat. Another creature rushes me from the side and wraps its arms around my torso. Dragging my paw across its spine, I tear the creature off my back and slam my paw on its head, crushing its skull.

"Help!" Calder screams.

At Calder's call, I quickly slice through one demon's neck with my claws, its head rolling from its shoulders as I swivel my gaze to him, only to find him still not using the sword sheathed on the forest floor, but showering two Soulless with flowers summoned from his shimmering green hands.

Useless.

Growling, I spring on top of Calder's assailants and claw at their chests, piercing their hearts. A Soulless jumps on my back and I buck it off. Another reaches for my muzzle and I bat it away.

A piercing pain stabs near my hip and I yowl, whipping my head around to find a Soulless' claws embedded there. Kicking out my hind legs, the Soulless' claws carve a chunk from my side as it careens through the air.

The metallic scent of my blood seeps into the air and the Soulless' movements become more desperate, frenzied. Clamoring to get to me, they're too busy fighting with one another to notice they've given me the window I've been searching for.

Bounding to Calder's side – who miraculously doesn't have a scratch on him – I crouch beside him.

He places his hand on my hip to lift himself up, but pulls back at the sight of my blood coating his hand. Terror-filled eyes then look to the Soulless, watching them for several moments before his gaze clears and he smiles up at me. "Go on now," he says without an ounce of fear. "I'll be fine."

Hesitating, I bump him with my muzzle and present my back to him once again.

"You can't carry me injured as you are, and someone has to live to tell the Captain about this." He shoves my side. "Go!"

I may have thought I was willing to leave him behind, but that's all they were: thoughts. Thoughts comprised of fear and irritation at the situation at hand. Calder was right. We shouldn't have gone on patrol without a suitable team. But even if we did have the appropriate number of guards, we still would have been ill equipped to deal with a band of Soulless this size.

It's not something anyone could have predicted. Yet, this isn't merely unusual behavior. This is a sign that something is wrong, *very* wrong. A change of behavior could be a precursor to much darker times, and that's something we must relay to the Captain. Our vow as a guard demands it.

But what Calder fails to realize is that the Guards' vow is to protect Cascadonia and all its citizens. The last time I checked, Calder was a born and bred Cascadonian.

Turning my back on Calder, I stand before him, a fae shield between him and the Soulless.

"What are you doing?" He shoves at my shoulder. "Go! Save yourself!"

Ignoring him, I face forward, waiting to meet the mob of undead rushing toward us.

"Fine, you stubborn ass," he grumbles. Unsheathing the sword – *Finally!* – he steps forward and positions himself beside me, holding his stance as the Soulless slam into us as a roiling, jostling swarm.

Growling and snarling, monster meets beast in a tangle of claws and fangs. Torn fur, gouged throats, severed heads. The red blood of the living and the putrid blood of the dead swirl and coalesce, painting the Cursed Woods in tainted crimson as life and death battle for the right to exist.

Uncertain where I begin and the Soulless ends, I kick, paw, claw, and bite, striking at anything and everything that moves. When Calder cries out and collapses beneath a horde, I don't hesitate before charging forward, batting them away.

Something slams into my side, flipping me onto my back, and three Soulless pounce onto my chest. I slice my claws through one Soulless' neck and move to swipe at the other, but before I can, another stabs its claws into my gut.

Dazed by the pain, yet another monster drops down onto my

chest, stabbing its claws into my shoulders and pinning me to the ground.

The most intense, excruciating pain I've ever felt pierces into me, dousing me in glacial fire as icy flames travel from my wounds to burn through my extremities. My heart slows, blood spurts from my wounds, and when I attempt to lift my paws, they refuse to answer my call.

My emerald gaze meets those unnatural, glowing ruby eyes and I realize in that moment that this is where I will die. This monster will feed off me, inject me with its venom, and rob me of my soul, turning me into one of the Gods Cursed's demons and forever barring me from the gates of Elysium.

It answers my roar of fury with a rumbling growl. It then elongates its maw, exposing daggered fangs, before the frothing creature strikes down on my neck, burying its fangs into my throat.

Another set of fangs pierce my hind leg, its claws scrabbling at my abdomen and shredding my gut. No longer paralyzed, my body convulses from the venom beneath the creatures feasting on me. The glacial fire intensifies, incinerating me.

The Soulless feeding off my leg is suddenly ripped away, its claws and fangs tearing at my skin and fur before the one sitting on my chest is thrown back as well. I search for my savior and I'm shocked to find a bloody Calder standing above me. Panting for breath, he meets my gaze for only a moment before he swipes his sword clean through a Soulless' neck, then skewers another through the heart.

There are two types of males in the world. Those who roll over and allow death to have its day, and those who are willing to survive no matter the cost. You can't really look at someone and know which person they are until you throw them into a life-or-death situation such as this. But I'm ashamed to admit I assumed Calder would be the former.

Yet, he's not. He's a survivor.

Cutting down Soulless after Soulless, the guard I once saw literally stab himself in the foot because he thought a rat had scurried across his boot, is now wielding the sword as if he was born to do so. Skilled and precise, he uses every technique the Guard has taught him better than more experienced veterans I've seen. But all veterans will tell you that no matter how strong your will is to survive, there are some things you just can't overcome.

I was afraid in the moments before the Soulless began feeding on me. Its daggered fangs and glowing eyes were terrifying to watch as it slunk closer and closer until it bit me. But when a Soulless pounces on Calder's back, terrifying isn't an adequate word to describe the all-consuming guilt and horror coursing through me as I watch the demon extend its jaw, tear its daggered teeth into Calder's throat, and feed off the brethren I'm charged to protect.

Arcs of crimson blood gush from where the creature savagely chews on Calder's throat, clashing with the black blood splashed across his skin. Another Soulless grasps Calder's face with its claws, jerking his chin up to strike down on the other side of his throat, all three tumbling to the ground. As I watch the creatures feed off Calder's venom-induced twitching, jerking body, all I can do is wait for the remaining Soulless to converge on me.

But they suddenly stop. Stop feeding, stop growling, stop hunting; they cock their heads to the side and sniff. Discarding their meal in the face of this new prey, they toss Calder aside and search by scent.

"You really are some nasty little creatures, aren't you?" a female's voice says.

"Vile," a male voice agrees.

Weakened by my injuries and blood loss, I can only move my eyes as I search for the source of the voices, but I'm unable to spot them. That is, until a flash of movement within the darkness catches my eye. Concealed within shadows just as much as the Soulless, four cloaked beings with blades in hand and hoods shielding their faces slip from the darkness into the clearing.

The Soulless pause, staring at the intruders in silence before they all toss their heads back and release an earsplitting screech into the night. The high-pitched noise reverberates within my ears and echoes throughout the forest, until they all issue a series of disconcerting clicking sounds from their throats. Another sound I've never heard from the creatures before. Almost as if they're communicating with one another, or calling for someone.

A female points a sword at the Soulless, tsking. "No need for that. You'll not capture anyone today."

Confused by her comment, I watch the Soulless growl and snarl at their group as if, unlike me, they understood her perfectly.

That's not right. Soulless don't communicate with anyone but Breccans. How could they possibly understand her? Unless they are Breccans...

"Stop toying with them," a male voice orders. "We have to get back."

The tsking female sighs, peering at the speaker over her shoulder. "You can't ever enjoy yourself, can you?" Turning to face the Soulless, she raises a palm and beckons them forward. "Come, now. Like he said, we don't have all night."

The Soulless snarl in a blood-lusted craze and converge on them in a crushing throng, but the Soulless don't get anywhere near them. They claw, slice, growl, and snap their teeth, barely coming within reach of the newcomers before one member of their party is slicing off their head or stabbing them in the heart. Moving at a speed I can barely keep track of, they hold no fear as they laugh and taunt one another before slicing and dicing with a skill far exceeding any I've ever known. They are the very embodiment of death as they slaughter dozens of Soulless within minutes.

"That was a bit underwhelming," the tsking female pouts, standing with her companions in the middle of a massive grave.

A tall, broad-shouldered male almost as large as the Captain steps forward and pats the female on the back. "Don't be like that. Maybe it wasn't as much of a fight as we were hoping for, but it was nice to stretch the muscles."

"How can the Cascadonians be so terrified of these things?" She nudges a prone body with her boot, lifting it off the other bodies it's piled atop of. "They're nothing more than annoying gnats."

"Silence," a different female orders, rushing towards me to kneel at my side.

With her hood still up, I can't search her cheek for the swirling mark that distinguishes her as a Cursed, but how can she not be with the way she and her companions move? The way the Soulless reacted to them? There's no way she's fae or immortal. She's Gods Cursed. They all are.

"Let's take a look at these wounds," she mumbles, weeding through my blood matted fur to inspect my wounds.

Now that the Soulless no longer have their fangs and claws in me, I've regained some movement, but I'm still in no condition to fight. Not that I believe I could hold myself against them even if I was at my best, but I still raise my head and growl, unwilling to lay here and do nothing as this creature places her tainted hands on me.

She swivels her hooded face towards mine and whacks me on the muzzle. "Don't you growl at me," she scolds, wagging her finger. "I'm trying to help you."

Did she just slap me on the muzzle? As if I'm no more than an unruly cub?

Shocked, I stare at her in silence as she returns her attention to my wounds.

"Alright." She nods to herself, then looks up at me. "I need you to shift."

I chuff the tiger equivalent of a scoff in response. Even if I did trust her, which I certainly don't, I don't have the energy to shift, wounded as I am.

"Listen to me." Grabbing one of my paws, she pays no mind to my claws as she places it on her palm and begins stroking the fur. "I need to see you in your natural form to properly assess your wounds."

The more I watch her and her companions move, the way they speak and interact with each other, the more I sense they aren't Cursed at all. But whether they're Cursed or not is inconsequential. I still have the Soulless' venom coursing through me, and there's no way this female can help with that.

"I can help you shift, but I can't do it on my own," she says in a strange, lilting accent. "Can you at least try?"

Feeling her stroke the fur on my paw, I think about how she can't possibly heal me, but if I could manage to shift, I could at least send her to the Captain with a message and warn him of what happened here tonight. Maybe, even though Calder and I will die, at least we can use our last breaths to protect Seboia.

But how can she help me shift? That's not a known Gift. Maybe she is *Gods Cursed.*

Unsure if she's Cursed or Seboia's savior, I chuff in agreement.

I still can't see her expression within the darkness of her hood, but I hear the smile in her voice when she says, "Perfect! Now I'm going to count to three. When I say three, I want you to shift." She places both palms on my sternum. "Ready?"

Ah, fuck it. What more do I have to lose?

I chuff in response, and she curls her fingers into my matted fur.

"One…two… *three*!" she shouts, and I try to shift. But as I wait for a wave of glittering copper to wash over me, nothing happens.

Inhaling a deep breath, I try once again to summon my Gift, but I can't call forth even a trickle of power. Feeling foolish for even entertaining the thought, my muscles loosen and I scour my mind for a way to pass a message along to her. But suddenly, my mind blanks when a bright light of undiluted power explodes from the female's hands, searing my eyes and slamming into my chest, remolding me into my two-legged form in the blink of an eye.

What the fuck what the fuck what the fuck what the fuck!?

Eyes still burning from the flash, I squint and gape at the woman poking and prodding the wounds on my now naked body. "What *are* you?" I ask. She laughs and continues to inspect my gut.

"A pain in my ass is what she is," a male voice growls.

"Shush it."

"I will *not* shush." He stalks forward and crouches beside her. "You can't do this. It's too risky."

"I don't take orders from you."

"No, you don't," he replies. "But you must be reasonable."

She whips her head towards him, and even though I can't see her face, I can feel the glare directed at him. "What should I do, then? Leave him here to die?" She redirects her attention back to me, prodding the wound on my thigh. "Why is his life less deserving than others?"

"One soul will never carry more weight than all the souls of the realm."

Frowning at the strange conversation, I watch the female's fingers freeze, hovering above my wound. "Except for mine, of course," she replies, her voice filled with contempt. "The realms could perish as long as I still breathe."

"The Stars demand it."

"Well," she says, crawling up toward my head. "I've had

enough of the Stars making demands of me." Cupping my cheeks, she lifts my chin up and to the side, speaking as if her mouth has been filled with wool. "This might hurt," she says before I see a flash of glowing eyes and fangs, and she strikes down on my throat with a hiss.

I sink into darkness.

CHAPTER 19

DARIUS

"What do you mean, she's indisposed?" I ask, glaring at the Air immortal guarding the door.

"What I mean is," Aerin drawls, "the Queen is not accepting visitors at this time."

Upon hearing of the Soulless attack, I, along with my commanders rushed to the infirmary to speak to the survivors. I have to admit, I assumed the reporting guard had embellished events. It was more likely the guards were the victims of an animal mauling or something else more believable. Even when I saw Silas and Calder's wounds, those now fully healed, seemingly years-old, pink scars shaped as a Soulless bite would be, I was still skeptical. But only until I saw for myself that massive ring of unanimated dead in the middle of The Cursed Woods. At that point, there was no denying the truth of the events.

Uriella's Light!

We've known for years that there is no cure to be found for the Soulless. For they were reanimated by the power of the gods, and a gods' power can only be defeated by another god's. And although Silas and Calder themselves admit that their memory of events is hazy at times, there are two things on which they both agree. They were both healed by the bite of a mysterious cloaked female, and she was anything but a goddess. I'd have to agree with them on that fact. For I doubt any goddess would be hiding away in the middle of the forest, lying in wait to save distressed guards.

After leaving the woods, we went directly to the palace to report the attack to my mother. The Kings Council required more evidence before actively investigating the Breccans, and I was eager to present my findings. Even if they don't believe Silas and Calder's account that they were healed by the bite of an unknown female, the other rulers can no longer ignore the threat the Gods Cursed pose when their creatures are attacking us in droves.

But once we reached my mother's private chamber and requested an audience, we were denied entrance by the son of a bitch currently blocking my path.

"It's urgent," I bite out.

"Unless there is an imminent threat to the Queen's life, it will have to wait."

Feeling my ire begin to rise, I suck on my teeth and fist my hands at my side. "Step aside, Aerin."

"No."

I walk towards Aerin with slow, calculated steps, my boots thunking against the wooden floors, the sound booming within the hallway and echoing off the crystal walls. "I outrank you and I'm ordering you to move."

Lifting his chin, he meets my gaze with an almost bland expression. "No one outranks me when it comes to the Queen."

Grinding my teeth so hard it feels as if the molars are beginning to crack, I eye the male who's been my mother's personal guard since before I was born.

Aerin and I have never been close. I'm not overly affectionate and neither is he, but since he's never far from my mother's side, he's been a constant presence throughout my life. That in itself forged a somewhat tenuous relationship. Not a perfect one, for we've had our fair share of rows. Mostly because he's an arrogant dick, and being the Queen's closest confidant, he rarely disagrees with her while I often do, but I've never once doubted his loyalty to the Queen, and by extension, her family. Including me, the unwanted bastard. Which is surprising to say the least, considering Aerin was the first person to find my mother after King Rainer's assault.

I don't know the exact details of that day, but from what has been told, once Aerin found his beloved Queen broken in mind, body, and spirit, he lost all sense of self and fell into the throes of bloodlust. Consumed by a crazed, trancelike rage, Aerin killed King Rainier before carving his body into over a thousand pieces. They say that many tried and failed to pull him back from the brink of madness, but he was only able to regain his sanity once he realized how close to death my mother truly was.

It's difficult for me to grasp that Aerin was capable of such violence when I've only ever known the Air immortal as a calm, apathetic individual. But in moments like this, when he's determined to uphold my mother's bidding and his eyes are hardened to steel slits, I can see the madness glinting beneath.

A growl rumbles within my chest as I press forward, forcing him to step back. "I could move you myself."

"You could, but you're on thin ice with the Queen as it is." He glances at the three commanders standing at my back and lowers his voice to a whisper. "If you disobey her again, she'll not think twice to follow through on her threats. I don't want to see you on the streets, Darius." With a sincere expression, he adds, "Neither would Theon or Aurora."

At the mention of my siblings, I roll my neck, easing the tightened muscles as I attempt to calm myself. My mother's threat to strip me of my rank and banish me from the palace may be a new one, but it isn't surprising. What *is* surprising is that she thinks I actually give a shit about my rank. I don't. I'm the most powerful and skilled warrior alive to date. Her stripping me of my command won't change that, and I couldn't care less about gold or status. What I *do* care about is the Gods Cursed knocking on our door and the Kings Council refusing to acknowledge it.

The little control I have over the situation would be lost if I was stripped of my command, and I can't trust whoever my successor would be to take the necessary actions to protect our Kingdom. Griffin would, but it's not guaranteed that as my second he would assume my role. Which is why instead of blasting Aerin out of my way and storming through the door, I take a reluctant step back from him and blow out a calming breath.

"There's been another Soulless attack."

Aerin pinches his eyes shut. "Was anyone injured?"

"Two guards," I reply. Wanting to keep this information quiet as long as possible, I sweep my gaze across the hall, searching for any possible loiterers before lowering my voice. "They said they were attacked by over three dozen Soulless."

"Three dozen?" Eyes widened in shock, his head jerks back. "That's not possible."

"I thought so too, but it's true," I reply with a bitter laugh, rubbing the back of my head. "We can't continue to field these attacks blind, Aerin. We need to act." Placing my hand on his shoulder, I implore him to comprehend the severity of the situation. "I need to speak with my mother."

Aerin groans, his shoulders slumping. "I can't disobey a direct command, Darius. I'm sorry."

Anger spiking, I curl my finger into his shoulder, digging all the way to the bone. "If I was Theon or Aurora, would you allow me through?"

The ensuing silence is answer enough.

Frustrated and livid, I shove him into the door and storm away, my commanders falling silently into formation behind me.

"Your mother spoke to me after you made your proposal to the Kings Council!" Aerin calls out. I slow to a halt, glancing at him over my shoulder. "For what it's worth, I agree with you."

"Did you tell her that?"

"I did." He nods, his lips flattening to an irritable line. "But she was not interested in my thoughts on the matter."

All I can do is grunt in response, imagining how infuriated my mother must have been when her most loyal servant spoke out against her to back an idea presented by me.

"Your mother is a *complicated* female," he states delicately. "But when it comes to Brecca, she's incapable of thinking rationally." Aerin glances over his shoulder, seeming afraid that Adelphia could be listening on the other side of the door before he returns his gaze to me. "Usually I wouldn't involve myself in such matters, but I'll try to speak with her again. With the Soulless activity and the disappearances in Raetia, there's a possibility she may reconsider her decision."

Stiffening, I slowly turn to face him. "What disappearances?"

"The missing Raetians?" he asks, his brows bunching in confusion at my blank stare. "There have been several disappearances over the last few months. King Luthais hasn't acknowledged them, but my sources believe them to be suspicious."

"Why am I just now hearing of this?"

"I assumed you knew."

"I did not," I growl, furious I'm just now hearing this from him when it should have come directly from my mother.

He watches me for several moments before lifting his chin, his features hardening in resolve. "I'll speak to her."

Good luck with that.

Nodding stiffly, I spin on my heel and storm down the hall, my commanders trailing behind as I force myself to retreat before I race back and break down that fucking door.

Passing my chambers, then Theon's, Kiora's, and Aurora's, we descend the staircase before leaving the royal wing altogether. Rage bleeds from my pores and seeps into the air, casting a palpable menace around myself that all can sense. Palace staff scurry past or duck within alcoves, lords bow with trembling limbs, and I have to restrain myself from barking at the bumbling guard when he struggles to open the arched doors to the palace.

"She's really not going to do anything?" Ajax asks, moving swiftly across the palace grounds.

"No." I nod to the guards before stepping through the golden gates, feeling the hum of the ward vibrate along my skin before entering the courtyard of the nobility district. Attempting to calm my mind and the fury singing in my veins, I watch the lords and ladies of the nobility casually stroll along.

Completely unaware of the threats lurking outside our walls, they bask in the sunshine of another beautiful day. Shopping, socializing, gossiping. Laughing children weave between legs and hide beneath skirts while others linger near the magicked water fountain, dipping their hands into the water before praying to the gods with a toss of a golden coin. They all seem so happy and free, without a care in the world. I fear if we continue to do nothing, they won't remain that way for long.

"That's horseshit!"

Kace barks a humorless laugh. "Welcome to the selfish minds of royalty."

Selfish, vain, and cruel. Adelphia is all these things and more. But my mother wasn't always that way. She was once a kind and compassionate Queen. Loved by all her people, including humans. But after the death of her husband and King Rainier's assault, something inside her broke, twisting her into a fearful creature so full of hate and pain, I sometimes wonder if that other version of herself ever truly existed.

I can't deny that I've seen that loving version on occasion. When she smiles at Aurora and laughs with Theon. I even think I may have seen it once or twice directed at me when I was a child. Regardless, all these moments are fleeting, swept away with the wind in a blink of an eye before she burrows back into herself, returning to the cold Queen of Cascadonia. But as I watch the Seboians laugh, play, and live, feeling ignorantly secure in the knowledge their Queen will keep them safe, I realize that even though my mother's trauma was no fault of her own, her refusal to acknowledge it is. That is what has made her unfit to rule. As a result, she is no longer a queen I can blindly follow.

The moment the thought enters my mind, my anger instantly cools within my veins. My muscles ease and the turbulence within my mind slows to a pinpoint focus, determined to protect Seboia regardless of the consequences. Adelphia may not be willing to face the truth, out of fear or indifference, I can only guess, but I can use her detachment to my advantage.

"Kace, activate your network."

Kace rears back in surprise. "All of them?"

"All of them." I nod. "Post them in the capitals of each Kingdom, focusing more so on Raetia, as well as the outlying villages." I suspect these disappearances are coming from there. The people there either won't be missed or their families can't cause too much of a stir when they are. Searching for them won't be a priority for Luthais, even if he is not directly at fault.

Kace's lips spread into a wide smile. "I'll get on that."

"Start recruiting a team," I say to Griffin. "One that requires all its members to be loyal to Cascadonia, but not necessarily to the crown."

"What are you thinking?"

"I'm thinking it's about time we see for ourselves what Brecca's planning."

"If you do this, you'll lose everything, Darius," Griffin warns, eyeing my aura with a frown.

Shaking my head, I meet his grave gaze with one of my own. "It has to be done. We can't wait around for my mother to act. If we do, I won't be the only one to lose everything."

"I know a few males we can ask," Ajax interjects, watching me with an eager expression. "They're well trained and know how to keep quiet."

"Work with Griffin on it." Folding my arms over my chest, I glance up at the golden gates to the palace, feeling lighter now that we have a plan in place.

"Fuck yeah!" Kace shouts, pumping his fist in the air. "I've always wanted to be part of a rebellion."

I groan, rubbing my temples. "It's not a rebellion."

Fuck! I hope it's not a rebellion.

"Try telling your mother that." Kace laughs at my answering scowl, patting me on the back. "I can't wait to see her face when she finds out what you've been up to. She's going to lose her godsdamned –"

Something suddenly rams into my back, tossing me into the air and skidding me across the jeweled street. Pain shoots through me as I slam down on my shoulder but I ignore it, rolling with the movement before springing to a crouch.

Screams, shouts, and cries. A cacophony of panic-laced sounds blare into existence as the nobles race away from a lone guard standing across the courtyard with orange glittering hands, watching me from eyes gleaming with hatred.

"Fuck!" Kace groans, rising to his feet along with Ajax and Griffin.

I don't even glance in their direction, refusing to remove my gaze from the attacking fae as I assess the situation. If it was just me and him in an unpopulated area, I wouldn't hesitate to blast him, but I can't without harming a bystander.

I'm debating the best way to subdue the fae when I see him whip his palms up with a snarl. Unable to find a way to strike at him without risking someone else being injured, I toss up a wall of water, shielding us in the same moment the fae flings an orb of fire. But as the orb streaks towards me, a flash of power suddenly wrenches through the air, blasting into our realm with a thunderous crack as a ward made of glittering diamonds appears. The fiery orb slams into the ward with a boom, bursting outward in an explosion of flames.

But then the ward captures the blast. Encapsulates it. Appearing as if it's liquid diamonds flowing around the billowing flames, the ward ripples and expands with the flares before devouring the flames and collapsing in on itself with a blinding flash, winking out as quickly as it appeared.

Frozen from head to toe, all I can do is stare in shock at the space where that unimaginable white power blinked out of existence.

That power was… baffling. Inconceivable. Immense. An infinite, raw magic that can only be described as divine. I can barely comprehend the magnitude of it. Could never imagine such power existed if I hadn't experienced it for myself. It swept through me as nothing has before, electrifying the air and singeing my cheeks, pebbling the skin along my arms. I can still hear the crackling sound sizzling in my ears as it fizzled out. It was breathtaking, glorious, terrifying, and it was fucking *white*.

"Holy shit," I breathe.

"Was that white?" Griffin asks, his mouth gaping in shock. "Which god's power manifests white?"

Ajax shakes his head, his eyes rounded. "No one's. No power manifests white."

A groan breaks through my thoughts and my gaze flits to the Fire fae, who was launched onto his back by the initial blast. As I watch him struggle to his knees, my shock recedes and fury takes over.

Charging towards the fae, I flick a glittering palm and four chains made of fire spear towards him, coiling around his wrists and ankles before drilling into the ground, rooting themselves there. Snapping out my hand, I clutch his throat and drag him towards me. He cries out, his limbs overextending as he arches against his restraints. Rumbles vibrate from my chest and my lips contort into a snarl.

"How dare you attack me!" I roar, enraged at the coward for attacking me while my back was turned. Fury swelling within my chest, I clench him tighter and pinch around the column of his throat. "Do you know who I am?"

The Fire fae begins to chuckle, quiet and low, before it slowly rises into a maniacal cackle. "Oh, yes! I know who you are. *The Gods Wrath.* A prince. A bastard. An immortal. You think you're a god amongst man and fae, but you are no god, Darius Lesdanas," he spits. "You are vermin. A plague. A disease in need of eradication."

Blinking slowly, my anger begins to recede as I attempt to follow the fae's incoherent babble. Loosening my grip around his throat, I scan him from head to toe. He wears an ill-fitting uniform that's soiled and torn; oily, matted hair; sunken cheeks and pale skin; and what I initially thought to be hatred gleaming within his eyes, I now realize is insanity.

"He's crazy." Scratching the back of my head, I watch males and females warily step out of shops and alleys, moving towards us to see the show. I have to suppress a groan at the nobility's insatiable need for gossip. "Take him to the dungeon. We'll keep him restrained, but we'll see if the healer can help him," I say to my commanders. Kace and Ajax nod, but Griffin jerks his head in refusal, scowling at the guard's aura. Confused, I'm just about to ask for an explanation when the Fire fae begins hissing in laughter, an eerie sound that raises the hairs on the back of my neck.

"You believe me mad? Oh no, Captain, I'm not mad! I'm blessed. Enlightened. For he has shown me the truth. Has shown me *her*."

"Who is her?" I ask, unsure if I should be encouraging his madness.

The man's eyes flash with hysteria. "She is blood and pain. Terror and darkness. She is who lives in the shadows. The Goddess of Death."

Desdemona.

Scrubbing my hands across my face, I blow out a breath and crouch down, motioning the others toward me. "Let's get him down to the dungeons." Flattening an orange palm above him, I'm about to release his binds when a voice halts my hand.

"Does he have a tattoo?"

Searching for the owner of that seductive, raspy voice, I find Lena standing between us and the crowd, only a few paces away.

Drumming her fingers on her hips, she jerks her head toward the fae. "Search him."

Frowning, I tear my gaze away from Lena to face the others, seeing that Ajax, Kace, and Griffin all appear to be just as confused as I am. Shrugging, I lift the sleeve of his tunic and search his arm, while the others check him as well. I'm starting to think I'm just as crazy as he is for even entertaining Lena's odd request, but as I lift his vest and look beneath his tunic, I find a black swirl tattooed on the side of his ribs.

He's Cursed!

"You're Cursed!" Ajax shouts my thoughts, rearing back and falling on his ass.

Griffin quickly tosses up a blue shimmering palm, flinging the Cursed flat on his back with a whoosh of air in the same moment a dozen more chains of fire shoot from my palms. They twine around the fae's torso, staking him to the ground as Kace raises a glittering green hand and thick branches sprout from the ground. The serpentine wood crumbles stone and cracks jewels before curving around the fae's limbs, shackling his arms and legs.

Heart galloping in my chest, I study the bindings on the Cursed fae, searching my memories for any clue as to how to immobilize these creatures. But I already know the answer to that.

"I am their servant," he claims boldly.

I feel a momentary relief that he's not one of the indestructible Gods Cursed. For if he was, these bonds would not hold him for long. But that relief is brief and short lived. As the feeling wanes, fury surges.

"A fucking Breccan in my Guard," I growl in the same instant that understanding dawns on me. "*You're* the one who's been altering the patrol. You're the traitor."

"Me, him, her, them. We are everyone and no one, Captain," he rambles. "We live to do his bidding, and he wishes for your end."

Raising the heat on the chains, I watch his clothes melt away to reveal his chest beneath and revel in the sight and scent of his blistering skin. Yet he remains silent. Cheeks spread in a deranged smile, he's unconcerned with his blackening skin. The crowd gasps in horror, unaccustomed to witnessing the vengeance of the Gods Wrath firsthand, but I pay them no mind. For this male is a traitor, and there will be no mercy for my enemies.

Boots scrape across stone and jewels and Lena appears at my side. "How many of you are in Seboia?"

The traitor swivels his head in her direction. When he sees her, his mouth slackens. "My gods! You are a beauty."

"So I've been told," Lena replies dryly, her lips flattened into a tight line.

He licks his lips and trails his lust-filled gaze across her every curve. "Silky hair, lush tits. I bet your cunt tastes divine. A worthy gift for my Master."

Watching him leer at her, every protective instinct in me claws to the surface and I grip his chin, jerking his gaze to mine. "You don't *talk* to her, you don't *look* at her, you don't *breathe* near her!" I hiss, feeling his skin bubble beneath my glittering fingers.

"It's you!" he says to Lena, peeking at her out of the corner of his eye. He suddenly jerks up, tendons bulging as he struggles against his restraints, his skin sizzling against the flamed chains. "I should've known from the first moment you spoke. Those markings, your beauty, your eyes. But of course it's you!"

He knows her.

The guard returns his feverish gaze to mine and once he sees my confused frown, he cackles. "You don't know, do you? She's right under your nose and you have no idea. He's been searching for you a long time, darling," he taunts Lena.

Lena's expression is hardened to stone as she watches him, seeming unfazed by what he may reveal about her. Only her trembling, vambraced fists betray her fear.

My instinct to protect Lena wars with my need to know who she is as I debate whether to end him now or search for more answers about her. But when I remember asking her time and time again about herself and her refusing me at every turn, my need to know her truth wins out.

"Who's searching for her?"

"The King, of course."

"Brecca has no king," I snarl. "All their royals died during the Battle of Brecca."

"Yet, you live," he says with a sinister smirk, and I grind my teeth at the reminder of who my sire is. “Word of advice, Captain: you should enjoy her while you still can. Because when he comes for her – and he *will* come for her – she'll be chained to his bed for all eternity.”

Without thinking, my arm snaps out, slamming into his face and crunching bones beneath my fist. “He won't touch her!” I roar, spittle flying into his face.

He bares his teeth with a bloody smile. “So naive to think you can win against the Goddess of Death’s most favored.”

“What does he want with her?” I snarl, feeling a knot of foreboding burrowing into me as I watch Lena toy with the straps of her vambraces before dropping her hands to her sides with an expression of reluctant acceptance.

His eyes widen, frenzied with excitement, and he appears even more deranged with the flames reflecting off the glassy sheen. “She is the key to him ruling all of Vanyimar. And when he finds out you’ve been keeping her from him, you and your mother and your siblings and your whole fucking kingdom will *burn*.”

“Who is she?”

He lifts his head off the ground and whispers, “Your damnation.”

At the thought of this so-called king forcing Lena into his bed to be raped and abused, a slave to his perversions, a blinding, white-hot rage consumes me, slicing into me with a blistering heat along with a wild, instinctual need to protect Lena above all else.

I slam both palms down onto the traitor’s chest, relishing in the sounds of his screams and cries as I release a torrent of fire that sweeps over him, melting his skin and bones until he's nothing but ash.

“You shouldn't have done that,” Griffin chides.

"I know." Standing from my crouch, I follow Lena's every step as she slips through the crowd.

"We could've interrogated him."

"Yes."

"We can't get anything from him now, can we?" Ajax says, waving away smoke as he moves to stand on the other side of Kace. "Do you think what he said was true? About Lena?"

"He sounded mad," Griffin adds from beside me.

"He did," I reply, watching Lena jerk a nod to Amara and Zander as she passes them by, ascending the porch steps to the seer's shop, Fortunes and Truths.

"But he still may be right about her," Kace says, rubbing his jaw. "Do you want me to bring her in?"

"She won't talk," Griffin answers for me, watching Lena as closely as I am.

"Do you want her followed?"

I shake my head. "She'll notice, then she'll shut me out completely. I need her to tell me what she knows willingly."

"She won't." Griffin folds his arms over his chest. "She doesn't trust us."

Lena places her hand on the iron handle of the shop's door and pauses. Turning her head to the side, she meets my gaze across the courtyard. Her amethyst eyes are unflinching as mine drill into hers, meeting my challenge with one of her own until she opens the door and vanishes inside.

"Then I'll have to find a way for her to trust me."

CHAPTER 20

LENA

I roll the amethyst cluster in my hand, its jagged peaks digging into my palm and pricking my fingertips before I set it beside its jewel companions on the curved oak hutch, one of many skirting the circular room. A Gods Light lantern flares, drawing my gaze to the light reflecting off jeweled baubles and crystal figurines, and I follow its path up to the black tapestry hanging above. My eyes flit along the dark cloth as I admire the countless starlight jewels woven within, sparkling beneath the sparse light. The combination of the moody tapestry, the starlight jewels, and the drawn drapes gives the shop the illusion of a starry night. A stark contrast to the brightened sky outside Fortunes and Truths.

The shuffle of slippered feet sounds behind me and I turn to find a female gingerly placing a tray of tea on a circular table in the center of the room.

"It sounded like quite a commotion out there," she says, seating herself at the table.

"When the Captain executes a traitor in the middle of the nobility district, it's bound to cause a stir," I reply, walking towards the table and seating myself in the chair opposite hers.

She bobs her head. "Yes, I believe it would, wouldn't it? And what did this traitor do to anger the Captain so?"

"Oh, you know," I say with an absent flick of my hand. "A few threats to his mother's rule, crazy rants about the Goddess of Death, something about fire and kingdoms burning. Nothing too concerning."

"I doubt that's why he made such a spectacle with his execution." She pours me a cup of tea. The floral aroma rises with the steam as she adds two spoonfuls of sugar, then she pours herself a cup as well.

"He may have mentioned a few other things," I mumble reluctantly, my gaze drifting over her head.

"About you?"

I give her a dry look. "Do I really need to tell you that, Seer?"

Her silence is answer enough, not that I need one. She already knows what happened, already knows how difficult it was for me to stand by and do nothing as that traitorous guard prepared to spill all my secrets.

My palms itched to end him then and there, but even though he was an admitted traitor, he was clearly a born Cascadonian. Darius wouldn't have reacted well to me murdering one of his citizens in broad daylight, and neither would the dozens of witnesses.

So instead of forever silencing him with a slit of his throat, I had to stand by in agony, waiting for Darius to discover the truth.

Knowing how important trust and honesty is to him, I knew he wouldn't have reacted well.

The Captain's view of the world is a bit skewed and narrow minded. Everything to him is right and wrong, good or bad, black and white.

There is no gray in between. No excuse to not make the decision he believes to be the correct one. He doesn't understand that sometimes, for people like me, we never had a choice. Never will have a choice.

With everything that traitor would have revealed about me,

Darius would've seen the truth as a betrayal, branding me an enemy without allowing me a single word in defense. But I won't rehash all that to her just to ease her boredom.

"No, but it brings comfort to others to believe I'm not all-knowing. My Gifts can be unnerving to some, even if they seek me out for those very same Gifts."

"We both know I don't think that way." I sip the tea, but instantly set it down with a wrinkle of my nose, revolted by the bitter taste even with the added sugar.

"No, you've never been one to shy away from the truth." Eyes softening, her lips pull up into a fond smile. "Hello, little one."

"Hello, Auntie."

It's been too long since the last time we've seen each other. A few years, in fact. I'm thankful to find her aura shining just as brightly as before our separation. It's a comfort to know nothing terrible has happened in my absence.

If it had, the colors would be much duller than they are now.

But even though her aura hasn't changed, I'd have to be blind not to notice the other differences. With long, curly, black hair, light brown eyes, and tan skin, she's a very beautiful female. Some would say gorgeous.

Time and distance could never change that. Yet, her hair is too wild, her lips too narrow, eyes too dull, skin too dark, and that is most certainly not the face she was born with.

"I like this glamour," I say, drawing a circle in the air around her face. "Who are you this time?"

Lifting her chin, she places a delicate hand to her chest, speaking in an airy voice. "I am Zenith, the Gods Blessed Water immortal. Seboia's very own seer."

"Ooh, I like that one," I tease. "Very mysterious."

She laughs and shakes her head.

"Your father doesn't think so. He thought these Cascadonians would think me a bumbling fool." She nudges my tea towards me before adding, "He doesn't understand that I choose who sees which mask."

At the mention of my father, a whole litany of emotions tumble into me. Longing, pain, sadness, regret, but most of all, guilt. Avoiding Zenith's gaze, I toss back the entire cup of tea and try not to gag at the taste, giving myself a moment's reprieve before meeting her gaze with a pasted-on smile.

But that's never worked on her before, and it appears it won't now, either.

Placing her cup onto the round table between us, she folds her arms on the table and leans forward. "I visited them not too long ago."

"How are they?"

She chuckles, resting her chin on her hand. "Your mother is still crazy, and your father is still crazy about her. Your brothers are still wild heathens and your sisters are either aiding them in their mischief, or plotting ways to kill them."

A loud guffaw escapes me when I recall all the teasing and pranks my siblings and I pulled on each other. One epic dare pops to the forefront of my mind of the time my brother Jathro and I shaved our father's head while he slept after a night of one too many pints.

I was so sure he was finally going to set my ass on fire, but even after the fact, I was still my father's little princess and thankfully weaseled out of punishment. Jathro, unfortunately, cannot say the same.

"Gods!" I shake my head. "I'm surprised Mother didn't drown us all at birth."

"She's regretting it now, I assure you." Zenith cocks her head to the side, watching me with a solemn expression. "They miss you."

"I miss them, too," I reply with a sigh, toying with the hem of the black tablecloth. "But I can't visit too often. It's not safe for them."

She reaches for my hand and clasps it. "They're not safe anywhere, little one. I understand why you're scared, Lena. After everything that happened to your brother…"

I instantly stiffen and try to jerk my hand free, but she holds tight.

"I know you're trying to protect them, but you can't. Everything you're doing, everything that has already happened, all of it will be, whether or not you include them in your plans. You can't do this alone, no matter how much you believe you can. They are *necessary* to your success." She finally releases me to arch a single stern brow. "You will report to them after you leave Seboia," she orders, leaving no room for argument.

Nodding in reluctant assent, I pass my gaze over the room, taking note of all the baubles and knick-knacks scattered throughout. Items that seem to have accumulated over several years as opposed to a few months. I assumed she arrived here when I did, intending to watch over me as she has done many times before, but after seeing all this, it seems I may have been mistaken.

"When I was younger and you went on your travels, you refused to tell me where you were going. Were you coming here? To Seboia?"

She nods, her gaze drifting absently over the shop. "I opened Fortunes and Truth not too long after you were born."

My heart drums in excitement at this admission. As a child, it drove me crazy that she wouldn't tell me where she went when she left home several months out of the year. I imagined she went on these epic, exciting adventures, and I knew if I could manage to convince her to tell me what she was doing, I was sure I could weasel my way into tagging along. Knowing what I know now about Seboia, I'd have to say that child me would have been severely disappointed.

"You've been here the entire time I have, haven't you? Why didn't you show yourself?"

"You needed to discover some things for yourself before I could reveal myself," she says in that blasé tone all Seers speak.

"And have I?"

Humming, she bobs her head. "More or less."

"Feels a lot like less," I grumble to myself, feeling a pinch of hurt knowing she's been here the entire time I have without even so much as a hello. But that pinch of hurt is instantly forgotten when I make a startling connection.

Practically vibrating in my chair, I lean over the table with an eager smile. "So if you're here and I'm here, that means I'm meant to be in Seboia. It means I'm on the right track?"

She smirks. "Perhaps."

Slouching in my chair, I drop my head back and groan. "Gods!"

"Hmm… fitting."

"It's like pulling teeth with you!" I shout, tossing my hands up. "I'm so sick of being handed these tiny breadcrumbs whenever you deem it necessary. Just tell me what I need to know."

"I have told you what you need to know. If I tell you any more, it may change the future," she says, unconcerned by my mini tantrum. "You need to trust yourself."

She makes it sound so obvious, like it should be easy to believe in myself just as ardently as she does. But it's not that simple. Not when I've been the cause of so much death and pain. Why my family is forever torn apart because of my actions.

"Trust in myself," I say bitterly. "How can I trust myself after everything I've done?"

Sighing, Zenith reaches for my hands again. "That was not your fault. There was nothing you could've done to change the outcome. These events in your life, although horrible and tragic, had to come to pass for you to be where you are today."

Staring into those brown eyes boring into my own, I can see a glimmer of the power hidden beneath, that vast knowledge she wields without recourse. There's never a moment that Zenith doesn't know where I am, what I'm doing, or where I should be, occasionally maneuvering me as if I'm a chess piece on a board in this game of war. It can be frustrating, but I'm not bitter towards her for it. It must be done and it's through no fault of her own. It's simply the lot we've both been handed in life. But occasionally, I do wonder…

Did she maneuver me there? Did she in some ultimate, cosmic plan allow those males to take me? Did she know that I would one day lose control and destroy my family and home all in the same instant?

I've always been too afraid to ask. Too afraid to know that my aunt, whom I love so dearly, would willingly break me so thoroughly, just so she could remold me into this Stars-chosen shield. But as I peer into those all-seeing eyes that I used to believe could prevent anything, could see anything, I finally feel a spark of courage.

"Did you know?" I ask quietly, my voice void of emotion. "Did you know those males were waiting for me that day?"

Clutching my fingers to near breaking, she squeezes her eyes shut and shakes her head. "No, it's one of the few times the Stars did not allow me to see. I suspect they knew I would not have sat idly by and allowed that to happen."

A flash of lifeless, golden eyes appears before me and I ask in a guttural voice, "What about Faygar?"

Releasing my hands, she sighs, weary and sad as she sips her tea. “What happened with your brother was … different. I did not foresee that happening, and I don't think the Stars did, either. Fate changed that day. It realigned to something I never could have predicted.”

“To what?”

Her saddened gaze clears, brightening with an eager hope. “A much clearer path.”

Unsure how I feel about Faygar’s death creating such optimism, I clear my throat and veer the discussion to a more bearable topic.

“And has Queen Adelphia met this dappy Zenith?”

She smiles, her eyes glinting with mischief. “She’s seen this face, but not the mask. I require a much different one when handling her.”

“You say handling. I say *meddling,*” I reply in a teasing tone, even though we both know I'm not. Slinging my feet up on the table, I clasp my hands over my stomach. “Then you’ve met Darius.”

Frowning at my dirty boots soiling her black tablecloth, she flicks an onyx and gold glittering finger and a stream of power pierces my shins, flinging my legs back onto the floor. “Many times, as have you.”

Muttering a curse, I rub away the needlelike pricks piercing my shins as I consider pressing her about mine and Darius’ strange bond. It’s intense and volatile, almost carnal in its desperate need to break down all my barriers. So unlike any of the other bonds I’ve formed. It's confusing and unnerving that it exists at all. I never thought I could form a connection with another being such as the one we have, and I sure as fuck never thought one could be created without either of us initiating it. I have so many questions and not a clue how to find the answers. Which is unusual for me. I'm much more knowledgeable than most, thanks in large part to the female sitting across from me, and I usually handle situations such as this easily enough. This should be a nonissue for me. But ever since arriving in Seboia, I realize how little I actually know, and how much more I need to learn.

With the way Zenith watches me, her eyes full of mischief and a smug smirk, it's clear she knows what I'm thinking. It's almost like she's daring me to ask. But I never know with her. On one hand, Seers are mysterious and evasive by nature. If she doesn't want to answer, she won't. On the other hand, her insight could prove invaluable, given the situation. And this is a situation with which I desperately need help.

"Darius and I have formed a bond," I say, feeling anxious she won't give me answers, and just as anxious that she will. "But neither one of us created it. Tristan seems to think it may be preordained."

Zenith nods sagely. "Tristan is a wise soul. You know he wouldn't have said such a thing without careful consideration." Placing my teacup and saucer on the tray, she slides it to the side, then focuses her inscrutable gaze on me. "Why don't you ask me what you really want to know?"

I hesitate, rifling through the dozens of questions tumbling within my mind. My aunt is giving me a rare opportunity. I know if I don't ask the right question the correct way, she won't answer. It's like a game where she's the only one who knows the rules. And anyone who plays, must abide by the rules.

"Do Darius and I have a bond like my mother and father?"

Her smile widens, telling me I've asked the correct one, and a surge of excitement bubbles within my chest.

"It is similar, but no, it is not the same. Neither is it similar to any of the other bonds you have formed. This one is ....special," she says delicately. She pauses for a moment, then her uncanny eyes sharpen. "I need you to listen to me very carefully, Lena, and remember this, because there will be a time in the near future that you'll wish not to, but you must. Gods, man, immortal, fae, we all make mistakes, but the Stars do not. Accept the bond." I open my mouth to speak, but it snaps shut when she purses her lips and shakes her head. "Don't question me any further on this, but do know that this bond is meant to be. As for Darius..."

Her eyes glaze over and the blackness of her pupils churn, whirling outward to swallow up all the white as if a storm sweeping up all light. It suddenly stills, revealing the ancient fragments of starlight hidden beneath. She blinks, and when she lifts her lids once again, the whites of her eyes have reappeared and the starlight has disappeared.

Smiling warmly, she says, "I have known Darius since the day he was born. I opened this shop so I could watch over him."

"What?" I rear back in surprise. "Why?"

"Darius will be vital in the war to come. I had to keep him safe until that time neared."

Panic trembles my limbs, quaking through my chest and lungs, rattling my voice. "What will his role in the war be?"

Lips thinning, she shakes her head. "I cannot tell you any more than that. This is one of those things that you must discover for yourself, but I will give you one last breadcrumb, as you like to call them."

Those familiar, yet unfamiliar brown eyes pass over my face, touching on the markings beneath my brow, on my eyelids, coiling around my arms, then dropping to my vambraced hands. The sight of the leather hide does something to her, and an anger I'm unaccustomed to seeing from her hardens her features. Sharpening her cheekbones. Hollowing out her cheeks. Illuminating her eyes. Making her appear ethereal, yet eerie, unnatural.

"Darius must be protected at all costs," she says in a booming voice, a thousand ancient voices lacing her own. "If he does not live to see the war, if he does not survive the battle, blood will spill and the realms will fall, washing away all that you hold dear."

CHAPTER 21

LENA

Rounding my lips, I blow out a breath on the parchment. A cloud of charcoal dust plumes above, speckling the air before falling to fuse with the film already coating the wooden tables. Lifting the parchment, ignore Lottie eyeballing me from behind the counter and instead scrutinize the sketch.

It's a basic design of a short sword and dagger. Not even a very good one. It's clumsily drawn across vellum and appears to be sketched by a child. But I'm not concerned with that. I've never claimed to be an artist, and I'm not really designing it, per se. I'll leave those stylistic decisions up to Aurora. This was just the only way I could think of that would guarantee there was no miscommunication on my part as to where I need the gems to be placed. I doubt many people request a blacksmith to embed jewels along the center of a steel blade.

A leather pouch drops on the table, round cut emeralds and sapphires tumbling out as Amara seats herself beside me.

"Zander blessed these, but he still needs to do the others." Reaching for my mug, she tosses back the last remnants of coffee, then sighs contentedly. "How can Lottie make such terrible food, but amazing coffee? It's baffling."

"I've never seen her eat the food she serves, but she does drink the coffee." Stacking the drawing on top of the others, I pass the stack to Amara. "I suspect her standards for what she ingests are higher than what she serves."

“I bet you're right,” she mumbles, flipping through the pages. “There’s what, five here? One for Kace, Griffin, Aurora …You’re commissioning weapons for all of them?”

I nod. “I can’t guarantee we won't have to pick up and leave without a moment's notice. If that’s the case, I can't leave Darius unprotected. Not after speaking with…Zenith.” I stumble over my words, almost forgetting I can’t use my aunt’s real name. “If I'm going to order one for him, I might as well for all of them.”

“I still can’t believe she's been coming here all these years.” Amara laughs and shakes her head. “That old bat’s such a sneaky bitch.”

Hearing someone noisily clear their throat, I look up to find Lottie standing at the edge of the table, staring us down with a disapproving frown. “You should not speak of the Seer that way. She’s a well-loved member of our society and highly respected.” She sneers. “Unlike *some* people.”

Snorting, Amara ducks her head towards mine, whispering, “That female doesn't have a respectable bone in her body.” She chuckles, then whips her gaze toward Lottie. “Shut it, you nosy cow!”

Not as easily startled as she once was, Lottie takes a frightened hop back, but quickly recovers to meet Amara’s glare with a scowl of her own. They eyeball each other for another moment, but no matter how familiar Lottie has become with us, she can’t hold that menacing stare for long. Lifting her nose with an indignant huff, she marches away, passing through the swinging doors to the kitchen.

Chuckling at Amara’s smug smirk, I gesture toward the sketches. “Do you think they’ll like them?”

“Who wouldn't?” Amara replies, picking up the drawing of a broadsword I made for Griffin. “But these blades are still useless against the Breccans.”

"I know, but at least it will help against the Soulless." Frowning, I fold my arms on top of the table, drumming my fingers against my forearms. "Did you find anything in the armory?"

"No," she says with a grim slash to her lips, tossing the stack onto the table. "Every blade was made from steel or iron."

I shrug. "Then this is the best I can do at the moment."

Scrubbing her face with a weary sigh, she glances at the sketch of a short sword and dagger. "Do you think Darius will train Trip with these? Or will he continue with the broadsword?"

"He'll train with them," I reply confidently. Darius is as stubborn as a mule, but he knows I'm right. Once he gets over his wounded pride from being corrected by a human woman, he'll see that.

"I still don't understand why he didn't in the first place. Or why he trains his guards the way he does," Amara says, lounging in her chair with a baffled expression. "Their methods are outdated."

"Because it's how it's always been done," I answer simply. "Besides the Battle of Brecca, this realm hasn't experienced a war in centuries. They haven't been tested in battle for so long, they don't realize how ill-equipped they truly are."

"They will soon though, won't they?" Amara says with a tight smile.

Groaning, I brush my fingers through my hair, sweeping through the wavy locks and trailing downward to clasp my hands on the back of my nape. Fear and guilt are a solid presence within my mind as I debate which step to take. I could either continue on my path to search for my quarries throughout Vanyimar and leave Darius, Aurora, and all my friends to battle the unknown alone, or I could help them first, losing valuable time in the process, and possibly condemning them all to an even worse fate.

Either way seems cruel, but until I find who I've been searching for, there's not much else I can do. I'm stuck between a bad choice and an even worse one. But even as I say this to myself, I know it's not true. There is another way, one where I can guarantee the safety of every Seboian citizen. But it's risky, dangerous. If I were to do it and I was captured or killed, which is more probable than not, it could destroy everything I spent my whole life preparing for. Everything I've sacrificed for.

Shaking my head, I shove the thought aside, unwilling to entertain such a perilous venture. I know what I need to do. I should pretend I never met any of them and focus on my own search. Zenith said I had to protect Darius, but I'm sure I could figure out a way to get him to leave with me. No matter how gruff he may appear, he's a good soul. All I would have to do is threaten Aurora or his brother, and he'll do whatever I asked. He would hate me for it, but I suspect he already will when he learns the truth.

Mind made up, I attempt to form a plan, debating which kingdom to target next and the best route to take. But even as I do, knowing this is the only logical path to take, I also know that in truth, I could never abandon these people I've come to care about, even in the face of my quest.

"We can't abandon Seboia," I whisper to myself. But Amara answers all the same.

"Of course we're not," she replies, grabbing a charcoal stick and adding her own contributions to the sketch for Trip's blade.

Feeling as if a weight has lifted off my shoulders, I fold one leg over the other, repositioning myself to face Amara. "What I mean is, we're going to do whatever we can to help them."

Pausing with the charcoal stick hovering above the parchment, she eyes me with a puzzled expression. "I know."

That was easier than I thought it would be.

Shrugging internally at her odd behavior, I slouch in my chair while fiddling with my lip. "Alright, then. I need to figure out a way to tell Tristan and Zander. Zander shouldn't be an issue, but Tristan won't be pleased."

"They already know."

Focusing on the best way to present this deviation to Tristan, it takes a moment to realize what she said. "How can they? I just figured it out for myself."

"You're kidding, right?" Seeing my blank stare, she shakes her head with a soft smile. "From the moment we stepped foot on Seboian land, we knew you wouldn't be able to leave without preparing them."

"But," I sputter, "it's not part of our plan."

"When have we ever followed the plan? Hmm?"

"Well, I'm glad we're all on the same page," I huff, irritated that I'm just now realizing what they've known all along. "But it would've been nice to be included in the plan."

"I can't believe you're just now figuring this out." She tilts the sketch back and forth, appraising her work until her eyes widen with an epiphany and she slaps it to the table "Wait! Is *that* why you've had your face scrunched up like that? You've been debating whether we should stay or not?"

I grit my teeth. "Yes."

"Huh. I just assumed you ate Lottie's food and were starting to get the shits."

"No!" I shout, appalled she would think such a thing. "That was my thinking face."

"And your 'I have the shits' face."

"How would you know what I look like when I need to shit?" I snap, irrationally angry at her for pointing that out to me.

She shrugs. "I'm observant."

"You're disturbing, is what you are," I grumble in embarrassment, wondering how many other people have interpreted my expression that way.

"You know I'm thrilled you've finally decided to stay," she says dryly as she lifts the coffee mug to her lips, before peering into it with a frown when she remembers it's empty, "but I have to say I wouldn't mind sacrificing a few of these Seboians to Brecca."

I chuckle. "Me too."

Amara scowls at the swinging doors. "Like Lottie, for starters."

"Definitely Lottie."

"Those asshole guards we met on the way in."

"Every last one of them," I reply, making a mental note to ask Darius what the pervert's punishment was. Hopefully it was painful and bloody. If not, I wouldn't mind extracting my own form of vengeance.

"The handsy drunk at The Quiet Harpy."

"We don't even need to wait for Brecca to get rid of him. We'll take care of him ourselves."

"Griffin."

"And Griffin." I nod before rearing back. "Wait! What? Why would you sacrifice Griffin?"

"He's an asshole," she replies, her expression darkening even more at the mention of his name.

"He rarely talks!"

"He's always looking at me funny," she huffs, folding her arms over her chest.

A shocked laugh escapes me. "He's an empath. He's not looking at you funny; he's reading your aura."

"No he's not! He's always watching me with this pissed off expression."

Squeezing my eyes shut, I rub my temples, unable to comprehend why she would want the sweet Air immortal dead. "Maybe he likes you."

She gives me a dry look. “Nobody likes me.”

“What I mean is,” I roll my eyes, “maybe he's attracted to you.”

Oh!” she shouts in surprise, obviously having not considered the thought. “Yes, that's possible, but no. I left with a male the other night and when I came back to the tavern afterward, he was furious. He lectured me about how reckless it was for me to leave with someone I don't know.” A flash of anger sparks in her eyes. “He treated me like a child!” Shaking her head, she dismisses the thought altogether. “If he was attracted to me, he wouldn't have treated me that way.”

Biting my lip to stifle a laugh, I state slowly, “That's exactly how a male treats a female he's attracted to.”

“Lena, Lena, Lena,” she sighs, patting my hand. “I know you're accustomed to every male you meet fawning over you, but for us simple folk, the ways of love and sex are a bit more complicated.”

“You must be right,” I reply, unable to keep the laughter out of my voice.

The bell tolls over the entrance, drawing my attention towards the door as it opens, casting a stream of light onto the dust motes swirling within the dingy inn as Aurora and Tristan walk in.

Tucked beneath Tristan’s arm, Aurora speaks quietly to him as they walk towards us. He smiles down at her, utterly absorbed with what she's saying, watching her with brown eyes full of affection. Aurora tosses her arms up, waving her hands animatedly as she recounts her story, and then he laughs. Eyes crinkled and smile wide, a loud guffaw punches out of him, deep and boisterous. A genuine laugh that I've never heard from him in all the years I've known him.

Tristan is a somber person, almost grim in his countenance. Preferring to deal with logic and fact over emotion, some consider him to be cold and unfeeling. Yet, he's never been this way with me. Maybe it's because we've shared so much together, but he's never shied away from giving affection or receiving mine. But even if we are close, share a bond even, I can now see how reserved he has been, because Tristan has never been as relaxed around me as he is with Aurora. The overly observant man hasn't even noticed we're here yet; his sole focus is on Aurora as she steers him toward us. It puts a smile on my face to see him so happy, even as I feel a tightening within my chest with the knowledge this won't end well.

Finally taking notice of us once reaching our table, his smile stutters and a nervous energy slips from him. My control is unwavering today, Gifts safely tucked within their cage. So for me to be able to feel nervousness from the usually unflappable man, there must be something horribly wrong.

Aurora claps her hands together, smiling down at us. "You're already up. Perfect! Are you ladies ready to go?"

Frowning, I share a look with Amara and see the same confusion marring her face. "Ready to go where?"

"To the market," she says, bouncing on the balls of her feet. "Tristan did tell you we were going today, didn't he?"

"No, he did not," Amara says with a smirk, her whiskey eyes dancing with laughter.

"It must have slipped my mind," Tristan replies with a wince, scratching the back of his head.

Aurora looks up at him with a stern look, and I press my lips together to stifle a laugh when I see his sheepish smile

Rolling her eyes, Aurora swats his chest. "Now you know. Are you both ready?"

"Aurora, I really don't think this is a good idea," Tristan says, his gaze darting nervously between me and Amara.

"Why not? It's just a bit of shopping. You already told me they haven't been yet."

"I do need to stock up on a few things, but…" Amara hesitates, her brows pinched as she watches me. "I don't think it's – ow!" she yelps.

I jerk my hand back from where I pinched her thigh. "We'd love to!"' I say with a winning smile, truly meaning it. Not the shopping part, of course. That sounds awful. But for being able to spend hours watching this new side of Tristan as putty in Aurora's dainty little hands. I'll have teasing material for centuries. "I wouldn't miss this for the world."

"See?" Aurora smirks. "I told you they'd love to. Come on." She walks toward the door, no doubt in her mind that we'll follow. "We'll grab Zander from the brothel on the way there."

Tristan tosses us a worried look and I chuckle when he groans, racing after Aurora.

No, no, no, I wouldn't miss this for all the realms.

"You said this was a bad idea," Aurora says, her eyes rounded in horror.

"I did," Tristan replies, his lips pressed in a tight line.

"Numerous times."

"Uh huh."

"But…" she says, seeming at a loss for what to do. "I didn't believe you. I thought you were being silly."

Tristan gives her a dubious look out of the corner of his eye. "When have I ever been silly?"

She rounds on him. "I don't know! It just sounded ridiculous that you couldn't bring two women out in public!"

"Does it seem ridiculous now?"

Whimpering, she buries her face into his chest. "No. If anything, you under-exaggerated." Tristan rubs soothing circles on her back and she pops one eye open, watching Amara argue with the leathersmith. "What do we do?"

"Watch it play out." He shrugs. "Make sure there aren't any sharp objects nearby, and hope for the best."

Aurora winces.

Feeling an immense amount of joy that I'm not the one on the other end of Tristan's disapproving stare, I tear my gaze from the couple, sweeping over wood beams and a burgundy leather canvas, passing by an arguing Amara and a blustering fae male, before continuing past the wooden displays of leather trousers and vests, to finally share a smile with an amused looking Zander.

Cheeks stretched in a wide smile, I raise a single finger. "I'd like to point out that I'm doing very well today."

Zander snickers before his expression morphs into a mock serious one. "You are." His lips twitch. "I'm proud of you."

"Thank you."

Tristan snorts, and my hackles rise at the sound. "What was that for?"

"What? I didn't do anything."

Ducking around Aurora, my hair slips past my shoulders, falling into a rippled sheet. "You snorted."

"So?" He shrugs, feigning innocence. "I snort all the time."

Eyes narrowing to mere slits, I open my mouth to tell the irritating man exactly what I think of him when strong arms wrap around my waist, tugging me against a broad chest.

"Hello, Beautiful," a deep male voice whispers in my ear.

Chuckling, I pat his forearm. "Hi, Kace."

"And where has my violet-eyed goddess been today? I swear I've been searching everywhere for you!"

"I doubt the brothel counts as everywhere."

"It's a large establishment." He rests his chin on my shoulder. "Lots of rooms to check. Alcoves, secret passageways."

"Lots of orifices to check, you mean."

"Ahh, you know me so well," he says, pride in his voice. "See? A perfect match."

"Let her go, Kace," a deep, rumbling voice growls.

Snapping my head toward the sound, I suck in a sharp breath when I find the furious Fire immortal standing a few paces away. Hands fisted, lip curled, and his chest expanding with each angry breath, Darius' glacial orbs flash with white fire, fixated on the arm currently wrapped around my waist.

"Oh, no! Someone's getting jealous," Kace taunts, tugging me tighter to his chest.

"And angry." Raging is more like it. Most would be trembling in fear at the lethal air wafting from Darius, but I can only assume the Stars forgot a few crucial ingredients when creating me, because instead of removing Kace's arms, I drop my head back instead, resting it along his collarbone as I watch the fire surge within Darius' gaze, enlivening my nerves with a dangerous thrill.

"You know you love that possessive growl," Kace says with laughter in his voice, flaunting his lack of natural instincts.

"It does cause a tingle here and there."

"Kace," Darius warns. Clenching his teeth, he flexes his fingers before curling them into a fist. I can see the blood rushing through the throbbing veins of his neck.

Kace presses his lips to my ear and lowers his voice to a whisper only I can hear. "Do you want to see how much more we can rile him up?"

Nope, Kace has no sense of self-preservation. Or else he's as crazy as the rest of us. I'd have to bet on the latter when I peek out of the corner of my eyes and spot a mischievous sparkle in his that

I've seen all too often in Zander's. One I'm sure has manifested many times in my own.

Raising my thumb and forefinger, I press them together until there's only a breadth of space between. "Maybe just a smidge."

Kayce snickers, then smothers it, raising his voice. "Last night was amazing, my little fruitcake." He groans, nuzzling my cheek. "The things you did with your tong– I'm kidding, I'm kidding! Ahhh!" Kace's arms are suddenly torn from me, his body thrown through the canvas opening by a furious Darius.

"I was just joking, asshole!" Kace shouts from his spot on the cobbled pathway between stalls, but Darius pays him no mind as he stalks toward me.

And then he's there. All of him. Too much of him. So massive and imposing, he blocks out all sight, scent, and sound, banishing all else besides him and me as his intense gaze lashes into me, slicing straight to the core of my soul.

The bond flares, strumming along the tether until he rushes into me. His thoughts, his emotions, all of what makes Darius *Darius* crashes into me in a colossal wave, battering my senses and drowning me in an onslaught

But just as I submerge within its depths, choking on the sudden invasion, the waters calm and level out, transforming from a violent torrent into a gentle stream that's more natural and smooth as it flows alongside me, intertwining with me. I suck in a breath, shocked that his presence alone could invoke such a euphoric tranquility. But as the shock subsides and logic prevails, I realize as much as I crave this feeling, as much as I'm desperate for it, until I choose to reveal all, this bond is still unwelcome, even if I'm beginning to realize it's no longer unwanted.

Shutting my eyes, I smother the link and I feel Darius' presence return to him with a whoosh, leaving me alone with myself once again. He frowns, clearly unhappy I've cut off the connection, before his eyes narrow and the tether vibrates. Darius tries and fails to reopen the bond.

I should be happy about this, thrilled even. I've managed to cast him out completely, where not even a shadow of him remains. Yet, even though I can no longer feel his emotions, which is exactly what I intended, I can't escape mine. Nor the hollow feeling within me that forms with his retreat.

Seeing his displeasure and feeling my own, I make an impulsively foolish decision, quite possibly a dangerous one, and loosen the clamp on the tether, allowing a trickle of the bond to seep through. I sigh in relief as he fills the void within me.

Kace slaps at the flaps of the leather canvas, jarring me back into the moment as he walks through the opening to the stall, rubbing the side of his scraped cheek. "You didn't have to throw me so hard."

Darius snaps his arm out, pointing in Zander's direction without removing his gaze from mine. "Stand over there," he barks.

Kace tosses him an accusing glare while dragging his feet towards Zander, mumbling profanities all the while.

"Hi," I breathe, but Darius says nothing. He just stares back with those glacial blue orbs. So wild and intense, it's like he's fucking me with his eyes. I've heard the saying before, but that's all I thought it was. A saying. With the desire curling within my belly and the sensations pulsating between my legs, I can no longer be sure.

Can you orgasm from just a look? Hopefully not, otherwise this situation may become quite embarrassing.

Attempting to regain some of my mental faculties, I clear my throat. "What are you doing here?"

"Aurora told me you'd be here today," he says in his low, gravelly voice, speaking directly to me for the first time today. "I thought I'd join you."

I feel a smile stretch across my cheeks. "Is that so?"

He glances towards my lips. Seeing the joy there, his mouth creeps up into a smile of his own. The dimple one I've become so fond of. "It is." He swallows, his throat bobbing with the motion. "How are –" he begins to say, but his words cut off at the sound of a feminine growl, dragging both our gazes towards the source. "What's going on?" Darius folds his arms over his sculpted chest, brushing his arm on my shoulder. A physical hum spreads with the contact.

"Amara's causing trouble," I reply, watching her get angrier by the moment while the gangly male she's arguing with seems to be getting more flustered.

Peeking at me out of the corner of his eye, Darius' lips curl into a teasing smirk. "You're not aiding her?"

"I don't *always* cause trouble," I retort in the same moment I hear a snort.

That snort!

"Stop it," I snap, ducking around Darius to glare at Tristan.

He raises his hands innocently. "It was just a snort."

"No," I hiss. "It's that condescending snort you do that makes me want to punch you in the face."

"Fine. I'll admit it was." Tristan arches an unrepentant brow. "If you admit that the only reason why you're not letting your psycho loose right alongside Amara is because you're not in need of new trousers."

Folding my arms over my chest, I snap my gaze from his. "I'll admit nothing."

Darius barks a laugh and I elbow him in the ribs as I return my attention forward, watching Amara's movements become more aggravated the longer she speaks with the poor vendor.

"She's getting really angry," Griffin notes from his spot beside Darius. His voice startles me a bit since I hadn't even realized he was there.

"And she'll be even angrier by the time we leave," Tristan says.

"Shouldn't one of you do something?" Griffin asks, waving a hand towards Amara.

Zander and I share a look before we both bellow a laugh, Tristan joining in with his own quiet chuckle as everyone watches on in various states of confusion. Except for a snickering Kace, of course. Since crazy always recognizes crazy, Kace doesn't need to be told how foolish Griffin's question is.

Zander wipes tears from his eyes and leans against Kace. "Now Griffin, if I were to intervene, Amara would not only get angrier, but she would then direct that anger at me."

"We try very hard to avoid being the object of Amara's rage," Tristan adds, Zander and I nodding in agreement.

Griffin huffs a laugh and gives each of us a disbelieving look. "It can't be *that* bad."

"Oh," Zander says, smirking at me. "He's adorable."

I cock my head to the side. "Isn't he?"

Griffin is right, though. Amara is getting angrier. Much angrier. Her muscles are tense and her chin tilts downward, her hair curtaining forward to partially conceal the glare beneath. But don't forget that smile. That terrifying, deranged smile that no sane person is capable of producing is directed at a male even more foolish than Griffin. A male who should be backing away from that smile, but is instead, visibly irritated by it.

"Just," Amara says slowly, "make me a pair of trousers."

"I told you," he replies with a droll look, leaning against the partition that separates the two. “The dressmaker's shop is across the street.”

“And I told you, I don’t wear dresses,” she growls, fisting her hands at her sides. “I wear trousers.”

“A lady should not wear trousers.”

“Do I look like a fucking lady to you?’

“Sure don't sound like one,” he mumbles to himself, rubbing his eyes.

Amara expels a long breath, her cheeks stretching into what I’m sure she believes is a charming smile, but in actuality, is even more horrifying than the first. “It's really not that difficult. Just measure me.” She raises her arms out and spreads her legs, expecting him to take her measurement just as he would for any other customer.

“I would have to touch you.” The fae cringes, pointing at her pussy. “There.”

“I'm aware,” Amara states dryly.

He sucks in a shocked breath. “That's not appropriate.”

“It doesn't bite,” she snaps, but he shakes his head, refusing. “Fine, you big prude.” She turns to face me, her arms out and legs spread once again. “Lena, come cup me.”

“As much as I'd love to play with your lady bits…”

“Godsdamnit, Lena,"' Darius groans. “You can't say shit like that!”

I arch a brow toward Darius and then at Amara. “I don't know how to measure a pussy.”

Kace stabs his hand into the air. “I'll measure your lady bits.”

Amara nods and turns to face him, but Griffin intercepts the overly enthusiastic Kace with a palm to his chest, shoving him back. “Don’t even think about it.”

Giving a now visibly sour Kace a parting glare, Griffin moves to stand by Amara. “Can’t you just do what you normally would for a male," he says to the leathersmith, steepling his fingers into an upside-down V, cringing, "but shape the groin area like this?"

The leathersmith shakes his head. "I'm sorry, Commander. I don't make trousers for females or women." He lifts a finger over their heads, pointing to the stall across the street. "She should go buy a dress."

"I can't fight in a dress," Amara spews through gritted teeth.

"You shouldn't be fighting at all," the male replies, shaking his head disdainfully. "You should be at home taking care of your babies and husband like a proper woman, not playing warrior." The leathersmith must have a death wish, because instead of leaving it at that, he leans across the partition and pats Amara's shoulder. "You're not a male, sweetheart."

That'll do it.

Amara's eyes widen and an odd, strangled sound tears from her throat.

The leathersmith foolishly turns his back on her, I'm sure believing that will be the end of it. That is, until Amara's eyes narrow to slits, her face mottles red, features contorting into fury, and she sucks in an audible breath and screams. Not one of those feminine shrieking screams, either, but a feral, rage-filled, realm shattering, never-ending scream that has everyone who's not familiar with the sound jolting away from the psycho. Including the leathersmith, who I suspect is now thinking, judging off how his eyebrows now mesh with his hairline, that maybe he should've just made her the godsdamn trousers. Or at least been more mindful of his words. Especially if you consider the look of horror on his face when Amara's features twist into a murderous snarl and she catapults herself over the partition.

Fortunately for him, the instant her feet touch down on the other side, Griffin snatches her by the waist and drags her back over. "Oh, no, you don't."

"I'll kill you, you sexist son of a bitch!" she seethes, death in her gaze and spittle flying from her lips. "I'll carve your skin from your bones! Cut off your cock and shove it up your ass! Gut you like a stuck pig and bathe in your blood!"

"That was very descriptive," Darius murmurs, watching the show with an almost morbid fascination.

"She's quite poetic when she's enraged," I agree.

"Amara, calm down."

A collective groan fills the tent at Griffin's foolish choice of words. The males in disbelief and the females in outrage, but all present wait with bated breath for Amara's fury to divert to him. Of course, Amara is never one to disappoint.

She stills, her feet hovering above the ground where she dangles from Griffin's grip. "Put me down, Griffin."

"If I do," he replies, his gaze drilling into the side of her cheek, "do you promise not to kill him?"

"Fuck no!"

"Then I can't put you down." He shrugs, lifting Amara with the motion.

"He deserves it!"

"It doesn't matter. You can't go around killing people who annoy you."

"Watch me," she hisses.

Griffin shakes his head, unafraid in the least, and begins walking toward the canvas opening.

"I'm warning you, Griffin. Put. Me. Down."

Lowering his lips to her ear, he enunciates slowly. "No."

Stupid, stupid male.

Amara stiffens for a long moment, her toes pointed and arms locked, before she suddenly explodes into a flurry of movement. Arms flailing and legs kicking, she spits and hisses like a feral animal as she tries to dislodge his grip, but Griffin's arms remain strong as he watches her with a placid expression.

"Alright," Griffin says, tossing the wiggling creature over his shoulder and moving towards the canvas opening. "Let's find somewhere for you to cool down. Some place far away from here."

Unused to being so easily thwarted, Amara's movements become more frantic and desperate, and she actually manages to get a knee to his chin. Swiping at the blood that trickles out of the corner of his mouth, Griffin tightens his arm around her thighs and bounces her farther over his shoulder to hang over his back. "Stop that," he chastises. Then, to everyone's surprise, he raises his left palm and spanks her ass.

A shocked Amara squeaks, a very feminine sound that I'll no doubt tease her about later, before she roars a very unfeminine battle cry, digs her claws into his leather-clad ass, and bites down with all her might.

Griffin yowls and leaps into the air, dropping Amara headfirst onto the ground. Unconcerned for the moaning Amara laid out on the cobbled street, Griffin rubs his cheeks with a grimace. "Let's try this again," he grumbles, lifting and then draping a dazed Amara back over his shoulder. "If you're good this time, maybe I'll take you to Aurora's shop and we can test out some of her new pieces."

Amara suddenly swings upright, peering down at him with wide eyes. "Really?"

He smiles softly up at her. "Really."

Cheeks spreading into a beaming smile, she drops down and shimmies down his chest until she can wrap her legs around his waist and her arms around his neck, clutching him chest to chest. "Why didn't you say so!"

Griffin freezes. Mouth agape and his arms hovering near her back, he doesn't seem to know what to do with this change of position. Until he slowly coils one arm around her waist and splays the other palm on the spine of her back, walking out into the pedestrian traffic of the market.

"Annnnd that's why we try not to make her angry," Zander says, to which everyone nods in understanding.

Leaning to the side, Kace watches their retreat. "She's a rather frightening human. Thank the gods she wasn't born a fae or immortal. I doubt the world would survive her wrath if she had any powers."

Biting my lip to stifle a laugh, I ask Aurora, "Where to next?"

"The dress shop!" she squeals, her orange topaz and starlight jewels flickering with her excitement.

Amara isn't the only one with an aversion to dresses, but since Aurora seems so excited, I attempt to control my grimace and instead offer an answering smile. "Sounds like fun."

My feelings must be obvious despite my best efforts, because Aurora chuckles at my expression before her gaze bounces between me and Darius, her lip curling into a sly smirk. "Or *we* can go to the dress shop while Darius takes *you* to the Gods Garden."

"The Gods Garden sounds wonderful!" Zander says. "Let's all – *umph*." A loud thwack pierces the air as Kace cuts off Zander's words with a slap to his cheek.

"Shush," Kace says, waving a chastising finger.

At Aurora's suggestion, a surge of excitement spears down the bond, rushing into me to blend with my own elation. Darius and I could be alone. Not truly alone, of course. I'm sure there will be people nearby, but it won't be any of our friends or family, and we haven't really had that. Not under the right circumstances, at least. I'm not sure if that's intentional on my part or his, possibly even both. We've both known we want something from the other, but neither of us has decided what that *something* is. Maybe this time alone can help in determining it for the both of us.

Ignoring the others, Darius watches me, saying nothing as he waits for me to respond. Not pushing or retreating, he's allowing me to decide without his input. His willingness to give up his control, to allow me to decide his fate, and his calm acceptance regardless of the choice I make is what finally sways my decision.

"I'd like that."

CHAPTER 22

DARIUS

No one can deny that Seboia is a marvel of a city. From our magicked water fountains to the crystal palace, even the jeweled street is meant to impress you with its opulent grandeur. But there are many, me includ ed, who believe this beauty is excessive, pretentious even, and merely another calculated act for the Cascadonian royals to lord their superiority over the other kingdoms. But whereas Seboia itself could be considered to have vapid, brittle allure, the Gods Garden could never be misinterpreted as such.

Encircled within towering hedges, the Gods Garden is filled with thousands of flowers. Purple irises, yellow lilies, white hydrangeas, orange marigolds, pink hollyhocks. Their spicy and sweet floral scents perfume the air, mingling with that of freshly churned dirt. Honeysuckle climbs up the walls of secluded stone grottos. Delphinium and foxglove form pocketed plots with hand carved benches hidden within. Pale pink sweet peas and bushels of red roses line the cobblestone walkways, leading up to the dozen or so crystal statues of the gods.

No, the Gods Garden's beauty could never be misconstrued as a hollow one. You can feel the love and care put forth from those who created this sanctuary. See their devotion to the gods in the way each flower was carefully chosen and placed. It is elegant and magical, enchanting to the senses, not to mention the most romantic spot in the city.

"Your sister isn't subtle, is she?" Lena asks with a chuckle, her shrewd gaze sweeping across the garden.

As subtle as a battering ram.

"Aurora has many redeeming qualities," I sigh, glancing towards my feet at the crushed starlight jewels embedded in the stone pathway. "But subtlety isn't one of them."

"Neither does that couple over there," she says, pointing toward a male towing a giggling female into the darkness of the grotto.

A smirk twitches at my lips as I recall the many, many times I enjoyed a quick romp within that very same grotto. "The Gods Garden is a favorite amongst new lovers."

"I can see that." She tosses me a playful look. "Maybe we'll just avoid that area for the time being. Oh!" She startles, her words trailing off as we watch the couple pop back into view. "Or not." She winces. "I think he's already finished."

Shaking my head in sympathy, I recall a similar humiliating moment in my youth. One I wouldn't mind suppressing until the end of my time. "Poor male. He must be so ashamed."

"I don't know." Lena cocks her head to the side, squinting at the very pleased looking fae. "He doesn't look too upset about it. The female, on the other hand…" She presses her fingers to her mouth, pinching her lips together on a laugh as we watch the irritated female smooth her rumpled dress and stalk off into the distance. "I doubt they'll be lovers much longer."

Lena and I share another smile before she turns away, continuing on the walkway as I follow behind, watching her. Watching the way her wavy locks flitter in the breeze. Watching the way her cheeks stretch into a smile. The way she crouches before a patch of star jasmine, cradling the flower within her palm as she breathes in its rich, sweet scent. Completely entranced with the way she moves. The swing of her arms, the sway of her hips, the proud lilt to her chin as she ignores each female's sneer and each male's leer.

Each motion is languid and graceful, confident and sure, but with the same lethal grace of a predator on the prowl.

But this danger she exudes, this indestructible veneer she wears as if she's a goddess amongst mortals, is only a facade. An illusion to disguise what she truly is. A human. And no matter how hard she trains, no matter how prepared she may be, no matter what she and Amara may believe, as a human, Lena is and always will be prey.

I grind my teeth as a flash of heat flares within my veins. Clenching my hands into fists, I attempt to control the flames sparking at my fingertips from the memory of her terror that day in the alley. Of the broken devastation on her face when she alluded to her tortured past. In that moment, I have never wished for anything more than to find the males who stole her innocence and slaughter every last one of them. I can't even comprehend how cruel and evil someone must be to attack someone like her. Someone so beautiful and pure, so full of life. She's a human empath, for godssakes! There hasn't been a single instance in recorded history of a human being blessed by the gods. She should be revered and worshiped, coveted for the rare jewel that she is. Instead, they used her soft, weak, human body to fulfill their own perversions. Rape isn't just a crime to the body, but an assault to the soul. I could see that pain writhing within her amethyst eyes, could feel the jagged scars created from such a vile act.

"His jewels are so dark," Lena says, jerking me back into the moment. Hands on her hips with her head tilted back, she peers up at the face of the fifteen-span tall crystal statue of Rhaegal, the Shifter God.

Since gods bestow our Gifts along with our jewels, it's not surprising that theirs would manifest quite differently than ours. Rhaegal, for instance, doesn't have any starlight jewels. What he does have are blackish, copper jewels dotting his top eyelid and feathering outward until reaching his hairline. He's also not limited to four or five Gifts like fae and immortals, but rather he's Gifted in all. Lust, empath, death, nature, fire, and so on. The one similarity you can find between immortals and the gods is that our colored jewels are a direct reflection of our dominant gift, or for a god, what power they hold dominion over.

"I imagine it's difficult to find jewels the exact shade as the gods'," I say, knowing Rhaegal's jewels are dark, but doubting they're *that* dark.

"I bet. Soooo, these are your gods." A crease forms between her brow as she hums to herself, glancing from one statue to the next, scrutinizing them as if learning of them for the first time.

"Do you not know of them?" I ask. She's spoken of the gods before. Not favorably, of course, but I assumed she knew of them. Although that may have just been a vague mention of them. Maybe she's never received a proper education of the divine beings. Every other being throughout Vanyimar has been taught since birth, but I wouldn't be surprised if she was the exception. More often than not, Lena's knowledge of the world seems to be lacking.

"Oh, I know all about them." She chuckles bitterly. "I just don't worship them."

I don't actively worship them either, but I do believe in them. How could I not? I wouldn't be where I am today without the Gifts they bestowed on me, and for that I'll be forever grateful. One would think as a human with a god's Gift, she would be, too. Then again, from what I've surmised about her, her Gifts seem to be more of a hardship than a blessing.

"Who do you worship?"

"Myself." She laughs, a playful glint to her eyes. "I'm kidding. I don't worship anyone. Why would I?"

"To receive their blessings."

Her expressions shutters, hardening to steel as she stops before

Desdemona's statue and says in a voice so sinisterly quiet, I'm taken aback by the venom brimming within. "I could strap myself to an altar, offering my very life for their favor and they still wouldn't bless me. No." She shakes her head, her features relaxing as she turns her back on the Goddess of Death. "I'll make better use of my time."

Enjoying a companionable silence, neither of us says anything as we stroll past statue after statue. Keyara, the Goddess of Vengeance. Saxon, the God of Mischief. Alura, the Goddess of Lust and Love. Enya, the Goddess of Fire. The ground at their feet overflows with trinkets, presents, and sometimes even food and wine. Occasionally she stops to appraise one more closely than the others, but more often than not, Lena gives them a passing glance and continues on.

"Do you think they look like this?" I ask.

"They don't," she replies, sounding sure of herself. She caresses her fingers along the arm of Calix's statue, smiling softly as she saunters past The God of Protection and Compassion. The very same god who blessed her with his empathic Gifts.

"No gifts for Faith," she says, her lips turning down into a frown as she stops before the Goddess of Fate. Not a single offering lays at her feet.

"They say she's the cruelest of them all, spinning our fate as she sees fit." Moving to her side, I brush my finger along hers. My skin hums with the contact as I look up at the face of the Goddess. Her alternating onyx and gold jewels glare against the otherwise opaque crystal.

Lena rolls her eyes. "She decides nothing. She can see and act, but more often than not, she remains neutral. At least she feels, unlike most of the other gods."

I've heard this before. Some believe the gods to be cold and unfeeling, void of a soul. But they're usually only spoken of by humans and some fae, followers of the True God.

"What about Uriella?" Flicking my wrist, I gesture towards the statue with the most presents. Piling one atop the other, her offerings burst over the path, spilling onto the grass to circle around her.

"Oh, she's the worst of them all," Lena says, strolling towards her. "Whereas most of the gods are incapable of truly feeling, she chooses not to." Lines bracketing her lips, Lena glares up at the statue. "Goddess of Light, Mother of All. She is a mother of *nothing*."

"They say she birthed a son from her very loins, the True God."

Lena snaps her gaze to mine and says in a tone so surprisingly bitter, a knot forms between my brows. "Yet she abandoned him. Spurned him from her body as if an unwanted seed. That doesn't make her a mother. It makes her a broodmare."

"You really shouldn't say things like that." Grimacing, I peer up at the cloudless sky, waiting for the goddess to smite me. Or her lover Azazel, the God of Darkness, the Father of Creation. "I imagine Uriella would take offense."

"I've called her much worse things than that and nothing has ever happened to me. I doubt that'll change now." Cocking her head to the side, Lena bites her lips on a laugh. "Are you afraid she'll portal her golden ass down here and strike you down?"

"I'm sure she can do that just fine from her throne in the Gods Realm," I reply dryly.

Lena tosses her head back and laughs, uninhibited and throaty, her eyes sparkling in glee. "Don't worry. You have nothing to fear from her while I'm near. I'll protect you." Eyes crinkling, she shows all her teeth in a blinding smile as a spark of joy hurtles through the bond.

Gods, she really is beautiful. So much so, it physically hurts to look at her. Her smooth skin, her curvaceous body, her blood red, heart-shaped lips. And those eyes. Those brilliant amethyst eyes that seem so ancient, yet so young at the same time. They're like a drug, ensnaring me with just a look, dragging me down into their depths with whispered promises of pleasure and warmth. I've tried to fight their beguilement. To resist her allure, but I don't think I have the strength to do it anymore. Truth be told, I'm not sure I even want to.

I shouldn't be watching her like this. What I should be doing is questioning her about the guard. What the traitor said about her and this so-called Gods Cursed King is concerning, and I have no doubt in my mind that she has information that could prove useful to me. She may even know what that strange diamond power was. But Griffin is right. She doesn't trust me. Not yet, at least, and she won't give up that information easily.

Before I met her, I would've considered her secrecy a betrayal, but after meeting her and learning of her Gifts, as well as the snippets about her abuse, I can no longer fault her over such a thing. I'd do the same if our roles were reversed.

Yet, even though she wants to keep her secrets and has good reason to, I can't leave it at that. I have to press her on it, even if she resists. I came to the market today intending to do exactly that. I even alluded to the others that I planned on forcing her or manipulating her into doing so. But I could never do that to her. She's already had others force her to their will. I'll not become another one. I doubt the others thought I would anyway. If they did, I suspect they would've tried to stop me somehow. I'm not the only one who has become attached to her. Not to mention the attachments they've begun to form with the others.

Griffin and Amara's weird hate-friendship. Kace and Tristan could be twins, for how similar they are. Even Aurora is in a romantic relationship with Tristan.

Nevertheless, regardless of what friendships or relationships we've begun to build with one another, I still need to discover what Lena knows. Her life, my family's life, this whole kingdom may depend on what secrets she holds, and that I cannot allow.

With a rope wrapped around his hand, a human man, along with his wife and son tow a goat to the foot of Uriella's statue. Lena steps back to give them more space and bumps into me, aligning her body with mine. I instinctively wrap my arm around her waist and splay my hand on her stomach. At the feel of her bare skin, my heart instantly speeds up. A crackling sensation speeds through me as I drag my thumb in a slow circle, tracing more of those circular scars. So soft, yet firm. Warm. I bury my nose into her silky hair, and the moment I inhale her cinnamon, vanilla, and cherry scent, the warmth within me hurtles into a blistering heat. Cock hardening in an instant, I wrap my other arm around her waist and tug her tighter to my chest.

I'm so lost in the feel of her that it takes a moment to realize that not only is she unresponsive, but her whole body has stiffened and she's staring straight ahead as if trying to ignore my presence. Ice douses the lust within my veins and my cock deflates as I step to her side, searching her face along with the bond. Lena cut it off earlier, but a sliver of her still seeps through. I blow out a relieved breath when I only feel her confusion and concern, and nothing to signify my touch was unwelcome.

"What are they doing?" she asks, her brows bunched in confusion as she watches the father usher the goat forward and crouch before it.

Seeing the humans' sunken cheeks and rail-thin bodies garbed in tattered linens, I reply, "They're making a sacrifice to the goddess."

"The goat?" she asks, her eyes rounded. "They look like they haven't eaten in weeks!"

I purse my lips and breathe in a long breath through my nostrils, wishing we had come at a later time so she didn't have to witness such suffering. “Which is probably why they're sacrificing it. By offering their most prized possession, they’re hoping Uriella will be more likely to grant them her favor.”

“That’s insane!” Lena hisses, her features twisted in outrage.

The goat struggles, kicking and bleating as the human clutches it to his chest. The man then lifts its chin and bares its throat as he retrieves a dagger from his waistband. Watching this, Lena is all but shaking in aggravation, pacing back and forth as she chews a hole through her bottom lip. Until the man raises the dagger above his head and Lena suddenly lunges forward, grabbing his wrist and halting the blade's descent.

“Please don't,” Lena pleads.

He sneers at her. “This is no business of yours.” He weakly shoves her back and I reach for her, preparing to drag her away. Until she snaps her hard gaze to mine, warning me not to intervene.

“No, it's not, but…” Lena snatches the knife from his hand and crouches before him, shoving the goat closer into his chest “The gods won’t help you. Take him home and *eat*.”

The man curls into himself, his features slipping into one of hopelessness. “Don’t you think I want to? I have no other choice. We have no food, no coin, I can't find work, and my family is slowly dying. Uriella is our only hope.”

“Any god that requires your last meal while starving doesn't deserve your loyalty.” Lena flicks the wooden medallion on his bracelet. “Put your trust in someone worthy of it.” She unclasps a bulging pouch from her waist, her gaze drilling into his as she places it on his open palm and curls his fingers around it. “Take your goat, your family, and go home.”

The man pulls from her grasp, eyeing the pouch warily as he

begins slowly unlacing it. Curious as to what its contents are, I take a few steps closer, listening to the sounds of clinking metal as I watch him widen the opening of the pouch. I suck in a breath when he reveals the solid gold coins nestled within.

"I'll be robbed for sure!" he gasps.

"You won't." Smiling softly, she re-laces the pouch within his trembling palm. "Go home and feed your family. After you've had a nice, hot meal, you and your son head down to the bakery in the nobility district. Tell Vasha you're in need of work. She'll help you."

The man hesitates, watching her with rounded eyes as if he can't believe she just handed a stranger a full bag of gold. As if this is a cruel trick and he's preparing himself for her to snatch it away. But then she smiles at him. Eyes softening and cheeks widening, she flashes him that brilliant smile that always manages, without fail, to charm even the surliest of persons. And this human is no exception.

"Thank you." Eyes brimming with tears, he returns her smile with one of his own. Rising with the pouch clutched tight to his chest, he hands the goat's roped leash to the boy. Kissing his son's forehead, he wraps one arm around his scrawny shoulders and the other around his wife and walks away.

Moving to her side, I peer down at her and offer my hand. "That was kind of you."

Lena shrugs, clasping her hand with mine as she rises from her crouch. "It's what anyone would have done."

"Lena," I enunciate slowly. "No one would have done that."

She frowns. "Then maybe they should," she says.

As if it's so simple. As if kindness is a common expectation and not the rarity it is.

Searching her face, I try to puzzle out this woman. This compassionate yet ruthless, funny yet solemn, broken yet whole,

Gods Blessed woman. Completely flummoxed on how she came to be this flawless creature.

Unaware of the thoughts whirling in my mind, Lena watches the human family slip beneath a stone arch with a frown on her face.

“Is that …” she squints her eyes, “the human district?”

“Yes,” I reply reluctantly, wishing I had been paying more attention to where we were going than to her. “There's not much else left to see here. Let's head on back.” Clasping her hand with mine, I tug her towards me, but she rips free from my grasp and storms towards the arch.

Muttering a curse, I follow behind, my view of the human district sharpening with each step I take, along with my sense of dread.

CHAPTER 23

DARIUS

If someone was to venture into the human district after visiting the rest of Seboia, they would think they had left the capital altogether and entered a completely different kingdom. In a sense, they'd be correct. Neither are even remotely similar. The human district's smell alone would have some finding the Cursed Woods more favorable. My stomach's already roiling from the scent of human waste and despair, and I've yet to leave the Gods Garden.

Sectioned off to the eastern side of the city, the human district is a small, narrow stretch of land that extends from the edge of the market district all the way down to the eastern gate. There's no bakery or healer. No seamstress or tavern. No butcher or apothecary. The only business that can be found is the brothel, crammed between hundreds of homes lining the pitted dirt road. If one could call them homes. They're more like hovels; small structures with dirt-packed floors, mud hardened walls, and straw thatched roofs, sheltering only a single room for an entire family to eat, sleep, and wash in. Sometimes two or three families, for the most unfortunate. The more well-to-do humans have windows with wood shutters or a flimsy door, but most only have a tattered cloth to block out the elements. Or in some cases, nothing at all. And that's it. That's all there is. Nothing else besides desolate stares and an overwhelming air of hopelessness.

"How inviting," Lena says dryly, leaning against the Gods Garden stone entrance as she looks out over the human district. She scans her gaze across Seboia's slums, seeing the true depth of our darkness for the first time.

Blowing out a breath through my nostrils, I face Lena and press my back against the archway. The stone bites into my back and foliage tickles my neck as I ignore all else but her reaction to Seboia's shame.

"It's baffling," she says. "I could carve out one of the jewels in that garish street of yours and it would provide enough coin for these people to live comfortably for decades." She flicks her hand. "Yet they live like this."

Lena turns away from me, not even looking in my direction, but I know by the anger trembling through our bond that she expects a response. But there's nothing I can say. She's not wrong and I knew she would react this way, which is why I never intended on bringing her here. At first it was because I didn't trust her not to use it against me. Lena insinuated before that Cascadonia had a darkness to it. I vehemently denied it, of course, unwilling to admit our faults to someone I considered at the time to be an outsider. But seeing her lip curl in disgust as she listens to the cries and screams from the ramshackle brothel, I feel like I should have at least prepared her.

Folding her arms over her chest, she turns only her head to meet my gaze. "If you hadn't been the son of a queen, would you have grown up here?"

I scowl down at her, a last-ditch effort in avoiding this topic, but Lena's gaze is unwavering, refusing to submit.

"Yes," I hiss through gritted teeth.

"Doesn't that bother you?"

"Of course, it does," I reply, feeling my ire rise beneath her righteous stare. "But there's nothing I can do about it."

She tosses her head back and scoffs, "That's horseshit. You're the Captain of the Guards, for godssakes. You could've done *something*."

"I've tried." Several times, in fact, but my mother put a stop to all my efforts before any of them came to fruition.

"Not hard enough," she bites back, jabbing her finger towards me. "That could've been *you* offering up your last goat. *You* watching your wife and son wither away to nothing." She pushes off the wall and stalks towards me with a palm above her breast. "If you could feel what they feel, could feel their suffering and pain, you would have done more."

"You mean if I were an empath like you?" *Fuck it! If she can push, I can, too.* I haven't prodded her about her Gift. I've tried to be respectful of the pain she's experienced from revealing such secrets, but with the way she's practically admitting to it and her assumptions that I voluntarily stand by and do nothing while something like this happens within my own kingdom, I no longer give a shit.

"You don't need my Gifts to see their misery," Lena says without pause, not even attempting to deny her power. "Nor to see how scorned humans are. Gods," she breathes, squeezing her eyes shut. "The looks your people give me. So much hate and disgust. I can hardly walk down the street without choking on it." She clutches her neck, swallowing thickly. "There's a poison within your lands, Darius, infecting every crevice of this stone cage."

"And what do you expect me to do about it?"

Features hardening, she says in a voice so cold, I can feel its icy tendrils pierce my very bones, "How do you rid someone of toxins? You make them *bleed*."

The hairs on the back of my nape rise with her statement, uneasy with the similarities between her words and that of the traitor guard. But I immediately dismiss the eerie feeling with a shake of my head. Lena can occasionally seem cold and ruthless, but she could never be like that traitor. "Not everyone hates humans."

"Only the ones who have the power to change all this. Like your mother," she sneers. "She could change all this with a snap of her dainty little fingers."

"She has good reason to hate humans," I argue, feeling an odd protectiveness for my mother. She never asked to endure what she did, to be raped by her husband's murderer and become pregnant with his child. I doubt others would feel much differently than her if they experienced what she had. She may not be a perfect queen to humans, but one of their own broke her. Her behavior isn't surprising, nor unexpected.

"Because of the Battle of Brecca," Lena says, a statement, not a question, but I answer all the same.

"Yes."

"Are these Breccan sympathizers?"

"Possibly some." Frustrated, I suck on my teeth. "But not all."

"Yet they are punished for something in which they took no part." She arches a chastising brow. "Do you not see how ignorant it is to vilify an entire race by the actions of a few?"

"I do, but…" I suck in a long breath, my chest expanding as I try to control my anger. "It hasn't always been this way."

She laughs, a harsh, mirthless sound, and gestures towards the human district with a jerk of her hand. "Look around you. Do you honestly believe this neglect and abuse only began thirty years ago?" She shakes her head and purses her lips. "This has been going on for generations. The Battle of Brecca was simply the spark immortals needed to justify the humans' complete subjugation."

A niggling of guilt rears its head but I instantly smother it, refusing to allow her twisted perception to take hold. "That's the natural order of life. The more powerful will always suppress the weak."

"And humans are weak because they don't have your Gifts?"

Lena retorts with a curl of her lip, leaving no quarter to her verbal lashing.

"Do you think humans are the only ones suffering?" I snap, furious she can look at me with such scorn for something I have no control over. "Because they're not. It's just more apparent with them because they haven't figured out what the rest of us already know."

"Which is?"

Stepping forward, I brush my chest against hers, ignoring the feeling of her breasts pressed up against my stomach as I glare down at her. "That the ways of fae and immortals are harsh and brutal. Cruel, even. And to survive this archaic way of life, you must fight cruelty with cruelty."

Tilting her head back, she peers upward, unflinching from my gaze. "Just as you do."

"Just as I do," I agree. "If you wish to survive in this world, there is no room for weakness."

"What if you wish for more than survival?" she asks quietly, her expression slipping into a more somber one. "What if you simply wish to live?"

Confused, my brows furrow together. "Isn't that what surviving is? To live?"

"No," she replies with a slow shake of her head "Surviving is to endure. To tread through life in a perpetual state of struggle. With fear, pain, loss. To live is to find hope, happiness, and love. To live is to be *free*."

A short laugh bursts from my chest. "That's not the world we live in, sweetheart."

"What if you could?" she asks, her voice barely audible as she searches my gaze. "Would you wish for it?"

"I'll not hope for something that will never come to be."

Her expression falls and her shoulders slump as she breathes out a weary sigh. "Then I pity you."

"Pity me? Why?" I ask, offended at the very thought.

"Because you'll only ever be destined for survival." Her eyes brighten, glowing with a feverish intensity as she places a palm upon my chest. Her warmth seeps into me and rids me of my anger, banishing all else but me and her. "Because there are those who hope. Those who fight for all beings throughout the realms. Humans, fae, immortals. For *you*. To live in a world where happiness and freedom isn't a privilege, but a Stars-given right."

Lifting my hand, I thread her fingers with mine, soaking in the feel of her bare skin. "I don't have the luxury of believing in such fantasies," I reply quietly. I feel as if I'm disappointing her somehow, but I can't pretend to believe in a fairy tale. Not even for her sake.

"In that case," she smiles softly, squeezing my hand, "I'll just have to hope enough for the both of us."

You really are extraordinary, aren't you? So bright and pure. Such a light in this darkened world. The only light within mine.

Staring into those amethyst orbs and seeing that sweet, tender smile of hers directed at me, words slip past my lips without conscious thought. "Go to dinner with me."

"What?" She rears back, just as surprised as I am by my words. Flexing her fingers, she tries to pull from my grasp, but I clutch tighter and place my other hand atop hers, swallowing it within both of mine.

"Go to dinner with me," I repeat myself, not regretting my statement in the least. This is right, her and I. I can feel it to the depths of my soul. She can, too. We've both just been too stubborn to accept it, but I don't want to fight it anymore. I *can't* fight it anymore. And I won't allow her to, either.

Cocking her head to the side, Lena scrunches her face. “Are you asking me or telling me?”

“Telling you.” I nod. “Definitely telling you.”

“Most males ask.”

“I'm not most males.”

“No, you're not, are you?” She shakes her head with a rueful smile. “I should say no on principle alone.”

“Probably,” I agree, and she laughs. “But you won't.”

“So sure of yourself,” she teases, then narrows her eyes. “Why should I?”

“Because you want me.”

Her eyes widen and she releases a startled laugh. “I don't remember ever mentioning that.”

“You didn't have to.” Lowering my head, my voice is a deep rumble within her ear. “I can see it when you look at me. Can feel it when we kiss.” I bury my face in the crook of her neck and inhale a deep breath, returning to the lobe of her ear with a flick of my tongue. “The scent of your desire for me is so strong, I can taste it on my tongue.”

“You only asked for dinner,” she says with a more pronounced rasp, a shiver wracking her body. “Even if I am attracted to you, you must have hit your head one too many times if you believe that guarantees I'll end up in your bed.”

“Because that's where you belong. In my bed, on my tongue, on my cock.” Her hand falls limp against my chest as I drop mine to her sides, feeling her every curve as I rock into her with my hardened cock, tangible proof that this desire is mutual.

But then she suddenly pulls from my grasp and steps back. One step, two steps, three steps. Dragging all her warmth with her, she leaves me with arms still raised, holding nothing but air.

“Is that all you want from me?” she asks quietly, a raw timbre to her tone. “Sex?”

No, I want all of you. Your mind. Your body. Your very soul.

But instead of speaking my thoughts, I remain silent. A cold chill sweeps through me, tightening my chest.

She flinches – she physically flinches at my continued silence as if I'd backhanded her across the face, before she quickly composes herself. "While your offer is tempting, I think I'll pass." Her lips spread into a brittle smile, causing that tightening in my chest to twist painfully before she turns and walks away.

Stunned. Cold. Alone. I stare silently at her retreating back, scrambling for anything to say without me having to admit more than I wish to.

"I wouldn't have asked you to dinner if that's all I wanted!" I call out, hoping I said just enough without revealing the extent of my feelings for her. But when she peers over her shoulder at me and I see the look in her breathtaking eyes, I know it's not enough. I'll have to offer her more if I want her to stay, but I don't know if I can.

Her lips lift into a small, sad smile. Then she returns her gaze forward, continuing on the stone walkway and leaving me behind.

A whoosh drones in my ear as I watch her walk away, imagining what my life would be like if I were to let her go, never to see her again. How I would feel if I were never able to speak to her. Never able to see that sassy smirk or hear her throaty laugh, never see the fire flash within her eyes when I piss her off, and never feel the warmth that fills me when she looks at me with that small smile I know is meant for me and me alone. I don't even think about how I'd never be able to hold her in my arms again or how I would never know what it felt like to be inside her. All I can think about is how bleak and dark my life will be if she was just not there. As if she had died and I was destined to walk the world alone, forever grieving. And in this moment, I realize, as much as I don't want to admit how much I've come to care for her, as much as I don't want to expose myself to another, that's not a life I'm willing to live.

"I don't laugh, Lena!" I shout.

She stops and turns to face me, her brows knitting together in confusion. "What?"

Heart galloping in my chest, I stalk towards her until the tips of my boots touch hers. "I don't laugh." I cup the back of her neck and tilt her head upward, forcing her to meet my heated gaze. "I don't smile, I don't play, I don't have fun. I don't *feel,* Lena. Not until I met you. You're the only person who can make me blind with fury in one instant, then roaring in laughter the next. Or so jealous that I'll rip out any male's eyes who would dare to look upon you. Or how I would burn the world to the ground if it meant it would put a smile on your face. For all but my anger, I was numb before I met you. I don't want that life again."

That single errant hair that I've been itching to touch slips free to dangle near the corner of her eye. Reaching up, I brush the silky strands back, curling them back around her ear. My thumb caresses her jaw on my path to reclaim her nape.

"You said you wanted me to stop surviving and to live. Then help me live, Lena. Come to dinner with me."

She watches me, saying nothing as her eyes bore into mine. The ensuing silence thickens with each moment that passes until it's all but smothering me. I was confident she felt the same way. So much so, I would've bet my very life on it. But the longer she remains silent, the more unsure I become. Maybe I was wrong. Maybe I wanted her so desperately, wanted *us* so desperately, I imagined it all. Maybe I wished for something that was never truly there.

Fear suddenly lashes out at me, wrapping around my throat and robbing me of my breath, clutching tighter and tighter as I wait for her rejection. As I imagine her removing my hands from her person, and the look of pity she'll offer before she walks away, taking a piece of me with her.

But then she slowly raises her hands and wraps her fingers tightly around my wrist, clutching me as if I'm her anchor to this world. "Okay."

"Okay?" I repeat stupidly, sucking in a breath and hoping I didn't imagine her words.

"Okay." She leans into me, plastering herself against me as she nods her head. "I'd love to."

I blow out a long breath, not giving a shit in the least how obvious my relief is. She laughs, throaty and sensual, and I'm mesmerized by the sound. Mesmerized by the sight of her teeth dragging along her bottom lip as she attempts to stifle it. And as I look down upon her, on the most beautiful face on an even more exquisite woman, I can't help but lower my head until I share my breath with hers, pressing a soft kiss to her lips.

Swift and sweet, the kiss was only supposed to be a taste. A small sign of gratitude, but nothing more than that. Yet, when I brush her lips with mine and feel her tongue sweep along the seam of my lips, I know I must have more. More of her taste, more of her scent, more of *her*.

Parting my lips, her tongue strokes against mine, slow and languid as I twine mine with hers. The taste of her cinnamon, cherry, and vanilla scent blasts into me, overwhelming me in its potency and fogging my mind as I drag her into my chest. Her breast pillows beneath my chin as her soft body molds against mine. She places her palms on my chest, sliding upward to wrap her arms around my neck, and I tangle my hand in her hair, tilting her head to delve deeper within her, to consume every part of her until there's no longer me and her.

There is only *us*.

So soft and warm, this kiss is so different from the single kiss we shared before. That one was filled with urgency and heat, animalistic in our need for one another. There's plenty of lust with this kiss, too; I can hardly be around her without hardening to half-mast, but whereas that kiss was more carnal, this one is tender in its passion. More affectionate. Debilitating in its need to share more than just our bodies. A kiss similar to what I would imagine a couple in love would share.

I try to shake the thought from my mind, unwilling to acknowledge anything as deep as that. But as she puffs a soft moan into my mouth, I feel a warmth travel down the bond from her to me. A raw emotion I won't put a name to that rattles me to my very core. A life altering emotion that has me clutching her tighter, refusing to ever let her go.

"Captain," a male voice says.

Lena's lips part from mine. But I follow, sucking on her bottom lip as she moans, her body becoming pliant once again.

The male clears his throat. "Captain, it's an urgent matter."

Lena tears her lips from mine and pulls away, holding me back with a palm to my chest when I attempt to follow again.

With swollen lips and panting breaths, she meets my gaze with eyes glazed over in lust, looking at me like she wants nothing more than for me to fuck her right here for all to see in the Gods Garden. Instead of doing that, she loosens my grip and slides down my chest, taking a measured step back.

The moment she's outside my reach, my palms flare with glittering flames and I snarl, whipping around to face the male with a death wish, intent on ripping out his throat. But that snarl abruptly cuts off when I see the expression on his face.

"Sir, there's been a Gods Cursed attack."

CHAPTER 24

DARIUS

Bounding up the staircase, my gaze remains fixed on the depiction of Urielle on the floor-to-ceiling, stained glass window. Bronze skin, golden tresses flowing within a mystical breeze, gold jewels dotting her eyelids that feather outward to meet her hairline, and a tranquil smile tugs at her lips as she raises her arms, her palms sparking with glittering, gold magic. The Goddess of Light's entire being swirls with power as she bestows her love and Gifts upon her immortal and fae children.

I thought Lena's rejection of the goddess was simply bitterness on her part, her perception distorted from her own past experiences. But now that the wool has been torn from my eyes, I can see what she does, what the rest of the world has chosen to ignore.

The Mother of All abandoned us long ago. If she ever gave a damn in the first place.

Reaching the top of the staircase, I turn my back on her likeness as much as the goddess herself and continue on, rounding the corner to the royal wing. My strides are long and purposeful, filled with fury as I storm down the hall. The sound of my boots webs through the wood of the floor, vibrating beneath my feet.

I pass Theon's chambers, mine, then Aurora's. When I near the next royal suite, the sounds within stop me in my tracks. Hearing female moans, male grunts, and a muffled banging

Naked and bare, Kiora's mouth is rounded in an O as she bends over the edge of her bed, her breasts swaying with each thrust from the male fucking her from behind. A male who is *not* her husband.

Gripping her by the waist, the male's face is contorted in rapture. Grunting and groaning, he continues ramming into her, oblivious of my presence despite my loud entrance. Unlike Kiora.

Locking sparkling brown eyes with mine, Kiora's lips slowly lift into a brazen smile. "Harder," she moans. "Fuck me harder."

He picks up his pace and the wet sounds of his balls slapping against her cunt along with the scent of sex dripping in the air cause my lip to curl. I bound toward him, reaching him in two large strides to grab him by the throat and hurl him at the window. His body shatters through the glass, his startled cries deafening as he soars out into the air. Until the sound abruptly cuts off when he collides with the palace grounds far below.

Kiora sighs. "Is he dead?"

Folding my arms, I turn to face her. "Probably."

"That's unfortunate." From her bent over position, Kiora rolls onto her back and stretches her arms above her head. "He was a fantastic fuck." Her head suddenly pops up. "Was that your plan all along, Darius? You assumed that I'd be more willing to take you to bed if I was on the verge of release?" She props herself onto her forearms, chuckling. "I'd rather fuck myself than bear the touch of a half-breed."

She flattens her feet on the bed and spreads her legs, baring her pussy. Her smile darkens as she trails her fingers down her body to dip her fingers into her cunt. Her need drips down her hand as she slides her fingers in and out, faster and faster, until she tosses her head back and screams her release.

Disgusted, my cock doesn't even twitch at the sight of one of the most beautiful females in Vanyimar orgasming mere steps from where I stand. I only feel abject loathing towards my brother's wife. “You've gone too far this time, Kiora.”

Ignoring me, she releases a sated sigh and slithers off the bed, sauntering towards me. “I may not let an abomination such as yourself touch me, but I am benevolent enough to allow you a small taste.” She raises two fingers, slickened from her release, to hover above my lips. “A taste of what you’ll never have.”

The food lining my stomach revolts at her sour scent. As she lowers her fingers to my lips, my arm snaps out, snatching her wrist and flinging her across the room. Her body soars through the air with a shriek as she tumbles across the bed.

She retreats, scurrying towards the headboard as I barrel towards her with a snarl, slapping my hand on the wall above her hunched over form. “If you ever put those foul fingers near me again, I'll bite them off.”

Fearful but not quelled, she glares at me beneath thick lashes. “How do you think Theon will react to his brother dismembering his wife?”

Growling, I lower my head closer to hers. “I don’t think he’ll give a shit after I tell him I caught his whore of a wife with another male. *Again.*” Shoving off the wall, I move towards the door, attempting to keep hold of my fraying control, but the sound of Kiora’s laughter halts me in the doorway.

“Who do you think Theon will believe? You? The bastard brother who’s always hated me?” The sound of silk sliding against skin precedes Kiora’s slippered footfalls. Her muffled steps rise in volume until she stops beside me to whisper in my ear. “Or me? His loving wife who rides his cock every night until the break of dawn?”

Gritting my teeth at the brutal truth of her statement, I claw at the door frame, wood shredding beneath my grip.

"We both know he'll always choose me," she says with a laugh, pressing her back against the doorframe.

"I don't have time for this," I say, whipping my gaze toward hers. "I need to speak to my mother."

Now clothed in a silk dressing robe, Kiora's mouth turns down into a mocking frown as she places a palm over her heart. "I doubt your mother will appreciate you interrupting her meeting with King Luthais and Queen Celene."

"Luthais and Celene are here?"

"They are." She nods. "But of course, you're already aware of that, aren't you? As the Captain of the Guard, your presence is required at all royal gatherings." Cocking her head to the side, her lips stretch into a wide smile. "Yet… you're not." Brown eyes sparkling in glee, she pats my chest over my stampeding heart "I wouldn't be too concerned about it. The Queen would *never* intentionally exclude you."

Shrugging her off, I push off the doorframe and race out the door, Kiora's laughter ringing in my ears as I storm towards my mother's chambers.

Kiora is wrong. My mother may not be fond of me, but she would never so brazenly undermine my position. Behind closed doors, of course, and often, but she wouldn't do it in public. Especially in front of the other royals. They'd see the strain between her and her private council as a sign of instability, and my mother would never allow that.

Yet, when I find Aerin guarding the door to my mother's private meeting room and see his eyes widen in panic once he sees me storming toward him, I realize Kiora was right.

"Darius," Aerin says, his palms raised. "You can't disturb her."

"Move," I growl. My strides become longer, faster. My anger inflames to volcanic proportions with each step I take.

He shakes his head in apology, but remains unmoving. “I can't allow you through.”

There are traitors in my Guard, the Gods Cursed are attacking, the Soulless are amassing, and my people are dying. Yet here my mother is, safe and sound inside her crystal palace. She’s spurned my repeated warnings, refused to see the threat breathing down our neck, and now she’s removing me from my most basic duties because I won’t allow fear or Court horseshit to blind me as it does her. Well, fuck her. Fuck Aerin, fuck the Kings Council, and fuck anyone else who gets in my way.

My control releases with a snap and I give in to my rage, bathing in the fiery fury as I charge towards my mother’s faithful servant.

“Darius, don’t,” Aerin warns.

But I don't miss a step as I continue forward, flames slicing through the air from my orange, glittering palms.

His sapphire and starlight jewels suddenly illuminate and he tosses up a barrier of air with shimmering blue hands.

My lips tip into a vicious smirk at his weak display of power. Allowing my flames to sputter out, I summon air to my palms, forming two solid spheres as dense as granite. When I'm only a few paces away, I flick my hands and the orbs spear towards Aerin, blasting holes through his barrier and punching him in the chest, flinging him off his feet to crash through the door.

Queen Celene and King Luthais bolt out of their chairs, staring wide-eyed at the unconscious male sprawled out on the floor mere steps away. Only my mother remains seated as I step through the hole where the door once stood.

An ice-cold blizzard brews within Queen Adelphia’s gaze. Her fingers whiten as she clutches the armrests of the massive crystal throne raised up on the dais, several steps above the solid slab of stone centered within the room.

Carved from the Mandala Mountains, the ancient stone table is all jagged peaks and pitted divots, veined with serpentine threads of crushed starlight and royal blue sapphires, glinting beneath the shimmering crystal walls and the Gods Light sconces arrayed throughout the room. The jewels' luster is only slightly diminished by the half a dozen royal blue tapestries decorating the walls of the Queen's private meeting room, a smaller version of the throne room located stories below.

"Darius, what is the meaning of this?" Adelphia demands.

Once seeing me, Queen Celene seats herself beside an already seated King Luthais as I round the table.

Unperturbed by my mother's wrath, I speak directly to her. "There's been a Gods Cursed attack."

Adelphia's face pales. "Where?"

"Outside the wall," I reply. "During patrol."

"Urielle's Light," Celene breathes. Cupping her mouth, she shakes her head, the tail of her bound, black hair swaying with the movement.

"How many died?" Adelphia asks.

"Eight," I hiss through clenched teeth, sorrow and guilt rearing its head to blend with my anger, heightening it.

Adelphia squeezes her eyes shut and drops her head back against her throne, her chest expanding with quickened breaths.

"You can't possibly believe this," Luthais says, his incredulous gaze darting between Adelphia and Celene. "It was a Soulless attack, nothing more. What's more likely, as I've mentioned before, is that this is a security issue on your part, Adelphia."

My mother's eyes snap open, her queenly mask hardening her features as she slowly swivels her head in Luthais' direction. "Nothing breached our walls, therefore there is no security issue."

Luthais says nothing. Lounging in his chair, he shakes his head and offers a condescending smirk.

"It wasn't a Soulless attack. It was the Gods Cursed, just as I warned you it would be," I retort bitterly, eyes bouncing from one royal to the next, meeting each of their gazes with my accusing one.

"Darius," Luthais sighs dramatically, "I humored you before. You may be a bastard, but you are the Queen's bastard, which affords you some respect." He rolls his eyes, his lack of respect obvious despite his words. "But this is absurd."

"I have a witness."

"If it was a Cursed attack, there would be no witnesses." Clasping his hands over his abdomen, the King of Raetia chuckles. "I doubt your people are even dead. I imagine if you searched the whorehouse, you'd find these so-called dead males buried headfirst between a pretty female's thighs."

Adelphia and Celene relax into their seats, both visibly relieved by Luthais' distorted interpretation of the attack, disregarding me just as they did during the last Kings Council meeting.

Frustrated and feeling that I'm losing ground on this front, I decide to attack on another. "And where are *your* people, Luthais?"

Dropping his gaze from mine, Luthais smooths a palm across his golden stitched vest. "I'm not sure what you speak of."

"Lies." Flattening my hands on the table, the jagged stone bites into my palms. "Your people are missing, yet you refuse to acknowledge them." Cocking my head to the side, I ask, "Why is that?"

"There are no missing people in my kingdom," he replies stoically, his cultured voice devoid of any emotion.

"I've heard differently," I argue. "The Gods Cursed could be the cause of the disappearances, although that's doubtful. You wouldn't dismiss me so easily if that were the case. What's *more likely,*" I sneer, using his own words against him, "is that *you're* the reason your people are missing."

"Darius, hold your tongue!" Adelphia orders, but I ignore her. My gaze remains locked on Luthais as I wait for his response.

Arching an unrepentant brow, he watches me for a long moment. "I've never hid my particular taste in punishment. I've killed many people and I will continue to do so. Why would I hide this?"

"That's the question, isn't it?"

Adjusting himself in his high-backed chair, Luthais flicks his fingers absently in my direction. "I do not have to explain myself to you. I am a king."

"And *I* am the most powerful male in all of Vanyimar." Flames flare from my palms, spreading outwards, gyrating along the top of the stone table to emphasize the fullness of my claim. "You will answer me."

Celene arches away from the fire, but Luthais remains unmoving, scrutinizing me. "You still haven't learned the most basic of principles in your thirty-three years of life, have you? In our world, true power comes not from your Gifts, but by your station in life."

"I have royal blood," I remind him.

"Yet you are not a legitimate royal, are you?" He grins, one full of mocking pity. "You are not a king, a prince, an heir, or even a noble. This belief that you have some sort of power over me is nothing more than a delusion." Leaning over the table, the flames set off an orange cast to his blonde hair, his eyes darkening with a cruel gleam. "You, Darius, are nothing more than the bastard seed of a rapist. A human one, at that."

Baring my teeth, I lean farther over the table, the flames enfolding me in their dark embrace. "I could kill you right now and no one could stop me."

"And in killing a king, you would have all of Vanyimar hunting you down," he retorts. "Including your mother."

Clenching my hands into fists, my knuckles scrape across stone as the fire blazes upward with an earsplitting roar, blasting all those who are present with its sweltering heat.

"There's that infamous fury of the *Gods Wrath*." Luthais laughs with a slow clap. "Quite frightening, actually. Yet we both know you won't act on it." He smirks, his entire demeanor brimming with arrogance. "And now you've learned a valuable lesson. I hold all the power, while you have none."

Rage claws at me, shredding my insides as if a wild animal begging to be released. With a snarl, I give in to its seductive call. Summoning my flames, I gather them to the center of the table and condense the fire into a ring of frolicking tendrils.

Luthais leers, but that leer turns to a frown, then abject fear when the flames begin crawling towards him, slithering up his armrests to engulf the top of his chair. "Darius," he warns, a tremble to his tone.

He cries out, tucking into himself as the flames reach for him, curious licks lapping at his skin. They crawl toward his neck, his face, then his tunic, branding him before retreating once again.

"Darius, stop!"

Inhaling a euphoric breath, I relish in his screams and cries. The sight of his panicked movements. The scent of terror from the one who thought he could challenge *me*.

"You'll be executed for this!" he screams, slapping at the flames singeing the ends of his blonde hair.

Bestowing the same arrogant smirk he offered me only moments ago, I say, "Anyone who tries will suffer the same fate as you."

"That's enough!" Celene bolts out of her chair and races to my side, but stutters to a stop only a step away, rearing back from my inflamed hands. "If you kill him, the Kings Council will have no choice but to declare war on Cascadonia."

I still. The flames freeze mid-motion as I consider her threat. The lives that would be lost if we had to battle on two fronts. Not only a war with the Gods Cursed, but another one with the entirety of Vanyimar. A war of which I would be the catalyst.

Swiveling only my head, I look up to my mother raised above all. Frigid and cold, she glares down at me, her entire being appearing carved from the very same crystal she sits upon. My purpose in coming here was to convince her to see reason, to demand her to open her eyes to the inevitable war to come. But seeing her wrath, her barely leashed anger, I realize my lapse in control may have set my goals farther out of reach.

Sensing my hesitancy, Celene takes a wary step closer and wraps tan fingers around my forearm, her copper painted nails digging into my skin. "You are the most powerful male in Vanyimar; there is no denying it." She levels a glare at a panting Luthais. "I pity anyone foolish enough to challenge that." Her gaze veers back to me. "But you are still only a single person. If war comes, you cannot protect an entire kingdom." She strokes my arm in a soothing gesture, speaking softly. "Rein in your Gifts."

Inhaling a fortifying breath, I call forth my flames. The fire vanishes into the palms of my shimmering hands before my power dims.

"That's better." Patting my chest, Celene returns her attention to my mother. "Was there anything else we needed to discuss?"

"Nothing comes to my mind," my mother states coldly, her arctic, pale green eyes fixated on me.

"In that case..." Celene smiles, behaving as if I hadn't almost murdered a king and incited a war between five kingdoms. "Luthais, I believe I am in need of a handsome escort."

Luthais stands with a proud tilt of his chin, appearing every bit the arrogant King he is, even with scorched patches blackening him from head to toe. He silently offers Celene an arm and ushers her through the broken door. As he steps across the threshold, he doesn't so much as look at my mother when he tosses a warning over his shoulder.

"Learn to control your dog, Adelphia."

CHAPTER 25

DARIUS

A loud groan echoes within the room.

"Leave us," Adelphia orders.

Rolling on to one bended knee, Aerin pushes off the floor with one hand, appearing dazed as he stumbles to his feet. "Your Majesty," he croaks with a bow, sending me a parting scowl as he maneuvers himself sideways through the hole that was once a door. Frowning, he peers into the room before placing a glittering blue hand on the doorframe. Spiral branches sprout from the misshapen wood, twisting and braiding with each other to create a gnarled, knotted wall.

Trapping me and Adelphia inside.

The silence is suffocating. Oppressive. Stretching endlessly as my mother and I say nothing while glaring at one another. Not even the shimmering blues and purples reflecting off the crystal walls from the setting sun can breach the darkness encompassing us.

Fully aware my mother can stew indefinitely and knowing I'll have to be the first one to speak if I want to have this conversation within the next century, I say, "Mother–"

"Get me a drink," she orders, unmoving from her throne.

"Do you really need a fucking drink right now?" I snap, having no patience for her petty displays of power.

"Around you?" She raises a blonde brow. "Always."

Ignoring the sting, I skirt the table to the trolley loaded with spirits. Adelphia and I rarely see eye to eye, but our preference for whiskey is one of the few qualities we share. Popping the top off the decanter, I pour her a generous glass.

Then, I turn to face her and hold her gaze as I toss my head back, guzzling from the decanter itself. A satisfying tick forms near her eye as I swallow deeply, allowing the warmth of the spirits to burn away the cold from her frosty stare.

Slamming down the decanter, I wipe my mouth with the back of my hand and stride towards her, passing her the glass.

"Do you know what you have done?" she asks quietly, sipping from her drink. "You've made me look weak. *Again.*"

"I made you look powerful."

"You showed them I can't control my own son." She stands, descending the dais to pace beside the table. "If I can't control my own children, how can they expect me to control a kingdom?"

Always so worried about how she appears. Gods forbid anyone ever believe her to be less than perfect. "It doesn't matter."

"Of course it matters!" she hisses, stalking towards me. "It will always matter."

Stopping a few steps away, she shuts her eyes and leans a hip against the table.

"You may have permanently strained relations with Raetia. Possibly even Arcadia. I doubt Luthais will continue negotiations with me after this."

"What negotiations?" I ask, a pit forming in my stomach at the thought of forming any agreement between Raetia and Cascadonia, let alone one that she went to such great lengths to keep hidden from me.

"If I wanted you to know that, I would have requested your presence during the meeting." Swirling the whiskey, she sighs, staring a hole in the bottom of her glass. "It appears there's no harm in telling you now, is there?" she mumbles, lifting her gaze to mine. "We were negotiating a marriage contract."

She couldn't possibly be negotiating on her behalf. The Kings Council would never permit a union between two ruling monarchs. Neither would it be for Theon, who is already wed. It's laughable to even offer me as a suitor.

Being a half human bastard, I'm not a suitable match for a common immortal, let alone royalty. So the only other person she could be negotiating for is…

"For who?" I ask hoarsely, dread slinking through my veins.

"Aurora."

This female must have lost her godsdamned mind! That's the only plausible explanation I can come up with as to why she would offer her only daughter to that fucking sadist.

I should've killed him when I had the chance.

"You really are a cruel cunt, aren't you?" Scrubbing my eyes, I try to calm the panic engulfing me, fogging my mind along with the spirits.

Adelphia shrugs. She fucking *shrugs* at her confession. "Better that she be married to a king than that disfigured human she thinks I don't know about." She shakes her head and utters a mirthless laugh. "Stupid child."

"You hate humans so deeply that you'd rather marry her off to that son of a bitch than allow her to be with someone who truly cares for her?"

"I don't hate humans. I just don't like them." She gives me a loaded look. "Not all of them, at least."

I snort at her bullshit answer. Her pretty lies can't deceive me.

Just as Lena said, my mother could've changed their lives with a snap of her fingers. Yet, she's done nothing.

Narrowing her eyes at my snort, Adelphia speaks with the authority of the Queen she is. "I will not allow human blood to weaken my line again. She will marry someone befitting her station."

"And that person is Luthais?" Fisting my hands at my sides, I bare my teeth with a snarl. "You've heard the same stories I have. The revolving women he beds. The same women he beats, mutilates, *rapes.*" She flinches, and it's the first time in my life I can say that the reaction to her past is satisfying. "He'll kill her, if Aurora doesn't kill him first."

Lifting her head, she levels me with an unapologetic gaze, saying nothing.

She doesn't deny my accusation, nor show a hint of concern that her only daughter will suffer the same fate as her. In this moment, I finally see her for who she truly is. Something I've ignored for too long.

The Battle of Brecca didn't just break her. It destroyed her; slowly eating away at her until she was nothing but a cold shell of a female. One who would forsake the daughter she claims to love, all in her insatiable quest to gain more power. There is nothing redeemable about her. Nothing even remotely immortal about her. She might as well be one of the Gods Cursed she fears so much.

Pursing her lips, she blows out an audible breath through her nostrils. "Which is why I have no intention of marrying my daughter to him."

Confused, I stare blankly at her as she passes by me toward the trolley and pours herself another drink.

"Luthais sent me a missive a few weeks ago," she says. "He's in need of a queen to produce an heir and requested Aurora's hand. Today, we were discussing his proposal."

I frown, confused even more. Luthais has often made his distaste for marriage quite clear. For a power-hungry male like him who sees females as nothing more than pretty toys to be broken and discarded, I can see how unappealing it would be to share his power with one. Which is why it's shocking to hear this.

Even more so that he specifically requested Aurora's hand when he has females within his own kingdom who would be more than willing to be his Queen, despite his depraved inclinations.

If it was a matter of needing an heir, he has bastards aplenty. It's not common, but it's also not unheard of for a King to legitimize them. Either way, he doesn't need a princess from another kingdom to do any of that.

"Why would he ask this of us? Our kingdoms' dislike for one another is no secret."

Tapping the side of her glass with her forefinger, Adelphia strolls toward the table, tracing the finger on her opposing hand along a river of sapphires. "His reasoning was to ally our kingdoms through marriage. To strengthen our bonds. But we're already allied, aren't we? That's the sole purpose of the Kings Council." She shakes her head, staring out the arched window. "He's lying. He wants something from me. Something that makes him believe if he has Aurora, he can force my compliance. That's why I went along with this ruse of a negotiation, to try to find out what that snake is up to."

Adelphia's palms flare glittering teal as water pours from her fingertips onto the table, streaming down jeweled rivers and crashing against jagged stone, then suddenly freezing, coating the table in frost.

"But your tantrum destroyed all that, didn't it?"

She can blame me for this as much as she likes, but I wouldn't have destroyed anything if she had simply included me in her machinations. This may not be something I needed to know as Captain of the Guard, but there's no denying that as a member of the Royal Council, I should have been made aware. In addition to the other many issues she's been hiding from me lately.

"Do you have any idea what his agenda is?" I ask, choosing to ignore my irritation. At least for the moment.

"No, I don't. But I believe it may be connected to the disappearances within his kingdom."

At the mention of Raetia's disappearances and Luthais' absurd accusation that the males who died today were only *misplaced*, I recall the whole purpose of me coming here. Raetia isn't the only danger we're facing. Not even the most pressing one.

Seeing as I've already pissed her off more than enough today, I walk towards her in a slow, calm manner, placing both hands on the back of the highback chair beside her. "Mother, we need to discuss the Cursed attack."

The temperature in the room plummets. Ice spreads from the table to the floor and races up the walls, stiffening curtains and frosting the windows.

"There's nothing to discuss. It was a tragic Soulless attack," she says, emphasizing the word 'Soulless'.

"It wasn't," I reply, my lungs constricting with the cold, my breaths pluming in front of me. "The surviving guard –"

"Was mistaken," she replies harshly. Raising the drink to her lips, the glass vibrates within her trembling hands.

I groan, rubbing two fingers above my brow. "Mother, you have to address this. More of our people will die if we continue to do nothing. The Gods Curs–"

Adelphia suddenly slaps her palm to the table, the glass shattering beneath her hand and puncturing her skin. “Don’t! Don’t even speak it.” Eyes widened in terror, she swipes her hands through the air, splattering blood across my chest. “The Gods Cursed have not returned!”

“Mother,” I breathe, reaching for her. But when she flinches away, I pull back, fisting my hands at my side. Attempting to ignore the barb that she still fears me when I've never so much as laid a finger on her, when she herself can't say the same, I inhale a frustrated breath. “I understand how terrified you must feel –”

“You understand *nothing*,” she interrupts. Slowly raising her bloody hand, Adelphia rotates her wrist back and forth as she stares at the large chunk of glass piercing the center of her palm. “You didn't see that creature come onto our lands and slaughter hundreds. Killing humans, fae, immortals. Anyone who possessed a soul. But I did.” Eyes glazed over, she doesn’t even flinch as she grips the shard of glass between her fingers and plucks it out, watching the flow of blood quicken and stream down her arm to rain droplets onto the frozen floor. “I watched it feed off babies, Darius. *Babies*. That abomination drank them dry and stole their very souls, damning them for all eternity.” Gaze clearing, she swallows thickly. “Don’t tell me you understand terror. You don't understand the meaning of the word.”

“You’re right.” I sigh, loosening my fists. “I've never experienced anything of the sort. But that doesn’t mean I'm wrong.” Taking a wary step closer, I speak in an as soothing a tone as I can manage. “Let me send a small scouting party up the Mandala Mountains to investigate further. I'll send my best guards. They’ll be silent, stealthy. Brecca will be none the wiser.” Her pale, green eyes dart to mine, and the vulnerability within hoarsens my voice. “If we don’t, I fear history will repeat itself." Holding her gaze, I plead with her to see reason. “Trust me.”

"Trust you?" she scoffs, twisting to face me. "Like how you're already forming a scouting party behind my back?" She laughs at the shocked look on my face. "You think I don't know about that?"

"You've been spying on me?" I spew through gritted teeth.

"I spy on all my children," she says without remorse. "There's nothing you have done that I'm not aware of." Raising a blonde brow, she gives me a knowing look. "Like how you're shacking up with that foreign human."

"You told me to seduce her," I say, feeling no need to mention that Lena and I aren't actually fucking. Not yet, at least.

"But I did not give you permission to form a relationship with her, did I?" she retorts, her features hardening once again. "You expect me to trust your judgment when you deceive me at every turn?"

A laugh bursts from my chest, though it doesn't contain an ounce of humor. "That's a convenient excuse, but that's not why you don't trust me. You never have."

"How could I?" she sneers, eyeing me from head to toe. "You who came from *him*."

It always comes back to this, doesn't it? Anything I do, everything I say, she sees me as nothing more than the Savage King's child. It hurts, but it's understandable. Which is why I've never attempted to gain her affection, knowing how fruitless that would be. Yet, although I've accepted a life without a mother's love, a love that she bestows so generously upon my siblings, I still haven't managed to accept her hate. I can often ignore it or pretend I don't see the fear and derision. But no matter how hard I try, that need to be if not loved, but accepted, is still there.

That small voice in the back of my mind whispers to me that if I'm loyal enough, if I train harder, be smarter, be better, maybe one day she'll manage to see not how much I look like him, but finally see how much of herself is within me, too. But she refuses to. She's unwilling to see me as anything more than her rapist's son, preferring to blame and torture me for all the pain he caused because he's not here for her to exact vengeance on.

I've never questioned her on this. I didn't think knowing why she refused to see the real me would make any difference. But in this moment, with my emotions heightened as they are, seeing her arctic green eyes filled with so much scorn, something in me snaps.

Tossing the chair aside, it slams into the trolley, splitting wood and shattering glass as I step forward, towering over her. "If you can't trust me, if you hate me so much, why am I still here?" I snarl. Ignoring her flinch, I swipe my hand through the air. "Send me away. Banish me. Or better yet," I lower my head towards hers and she retreats, arching back over the table with frightened, wide eyes, her curled fingers whitening over the edge of stone, "why not just kill me and be done with it?"

Eyes rounded and limbs trembling, she watches me for a long moment. Until her fear dissolves and her features contort into a blistering rage. "I *tried*."

Shocked, I stumble back. "What?"

She slowly straightens, hate-filled eyes boring into mine. "I tried to kill you."

A sharp pain pierces my chest and twists painfully, tearing at my heart. My boots thunk against the wood floor as I walk backwards, rounding the table in retreat. Retreating from her hate, from her words, from the truth of my own mother wishing me dead.

Yet she follows, stalking every step with that cruel sneer. "The moment I realized that traitor's seed had taken root, I knew I couldn't bear to birth his child. So every morning and every night I drank the tea, praying the gods would expel you from my womb.

But as my belly continued to grow, I realized I had to take more drastic measures to ensure your death." She stops, her lips spreading into a smile devoid of any warmth. "I planned to drown you at birth."

Each hateful word slashes at me as if a whip, shredding my skin and gouging at my very soul. I've never felt her hate as strongly as I do now. So visceral and debilitating. A poison that weeps from her pores, dousing me in darkness.

Clawing for a scrap of hope that she doesn't despise me so much that she would murder me before I even took my first breath, I say, "But you didn't."

"No, I didn't." She purses her lips, appearing irritated that she did not succeed. "Did you know that Zenith is a trained midwife? Absurd, isn't it?" She chuckles, shaking her head. "A powerful seer as a midwife." She turns her back on me and rounds the table. "She's the one who helped birth you, and while I was in labor, she had a vision." She reaches the other side of the table and lifts her gaze to mine. "A vision about you."

Frowning, I search my memories for any mention of prophecies at the time of my birth. Although I'm not sure why I bother. Seers are rare to begin with, and prophecies even more so. If there was a prophecy, I would have known. Everyone would have. Unless it was something terrible. Something so devastating, so horrific, it must be kept hidden.

"What did she see?" I ask, still raw and bleeding from her verbal assault but unable to curb my curiosity.

Adelphia lifts the shard of bloody glass and scrutinizes it as she twirls it above her head, the light of the setting sun spearing through the clear spots not mottled in scarlet. "She said that one day in the near future, war will touch down on Vanyimar. Blood will spill and fire will reign, burning everyone and everything to ash." She pauses, cupping the sharp crystal within her palm. "But the Stars offered an alternative path. Or I should say, they offered us someone who could alter our fate. Someone who could save us all." Lowering her arm with the glass still in hand, she locks pitiless eyes with mine. "The Stars chose *you* as our savior, Darius."

Disbelief smacks into me and I shake my head in denial.

"Yes." She nods. "Our entire world, every soul within, is dependent on you." Squeezing her eyes shut, her face contorts into such heartbreaking grief, it robs me of breath. "But the only way to ensure your creation was for the Stars to orchestrate, to *manipulate* the events that led up to your conception."

Sweat dots my brow, my heart thunders, and my stomach churns as my body physically revolts at her insinuation. "Are you saying I am the cause of the Battle of Brecca?"

"You are," she hisses, all but spitting venom. "The reason why all those people died, why I lost my husband, why I was raped and tortured. The very reason why the Goddess of Death cursed Brecca and gave them the power to create the Soulless."

I jolt back. My world sways on its axis as I reach outwards for anything to ground me to this reality, but all I manage to do is knock over a chair before grabbing hold of the table. Hanging my head, I stare blankly at the rivers of crushed starlight and sapphire embedded in the stone.

Thousands dead. So many souls forsaken. So much terror and pain… all because of me. Because the Stars chose *me*. It makes no sense. I'm powerful, yes, but otherwise, as Luthais so bluntly mentioned, I don't hold true power. Not the type of power that makes a lick of difference in this world. Not enough to be this Stars-damned savior.

Shaking my head, I let out a loud guffaw. My mother is mistaken. It's not possible. The Stars would not damn so many to conceive a half-breed human bastard. An abomination to all, even the gods. Yet… as much as I want to deny this claim, as much as I want to tell my mother to fuck off and keep her crazy rants to herself, I can't deny all the unanswered questions that are clarified with this revelation. All the missing puzzle pieces now clicking into place.

How the humans were able to orchestrate an attack without our knowledge. How they were able to overcome us when they were incapable of such power. Not without divine intervention, at least. Intervention from gods who despise their weak blood even more than immortals do. And what's even more damning, what solidifies my mother's every word, is how the battle ended the moment she was impregnated with me.

Adelphia cocks her head to the side and mumbles to herself, "How can you be our savior when you are the sole cause of so much death?"

Feet planted to the floor and my eyes locked on hers, I say nothing. I'm unable to speak or move with the chaos warring within my mind.

Shaking her head, she skirts the table. A loud screech grates my ears as she scrapes the glass against the stone. "Of course after she told me this, I was even more determined to end your life. But Zenith had a vision of this too, and warned me if I were to continue on that path, if I chose not to accept you into my family or treat you as one of my own, my other children would pay with their lives."

Standing before me, she tilts her head back, unflinching from my frozen gaze. "So I allowed you to live. I clothed you, fed you, housed you. Placed you as an integral member of my Council and gave you the position of Captain of the Guard. I kept you safe until you were able to do so yourself. I did everything the Stars required of me to keep my son and daughter safe. But no more than that. For even the Stars do not have the power to control who I do or don't love. And I could *never* love that monster's spawn." She raises my hand and flattens my palm. "And neither will that girl."

She places the shard of glass on my palm and curls my fingers around it. Enclosing both her hands around mine, she squeezes until the glass punctures my skin and rivulets of my blood seep between our clasped hands.

"For monsters are not destined for love. Only blood and death."

CHAPTER 26

LENA

The two moons hang high in the starlit sky. Heavy and bloated, their bright light beams across the jewel-encrusted street, sparkling beneath dozens of nighttime revelers' feet.

A Gods Light flares, illuminating the stack of parchment clenched within Aurora's hands. Green eyes bounce from one end of the vellum to the next, her expression morphing from assessing to thoughtful, then finally excitement before she repeats the process all over again when she flips to the next page.

"This is amazing, Lena," Aurora says, raising a single parchment above her head and tilting it to the side to examine it more closely. "I never would've thought to put jewels in the blade. In the hilt, of course, but never the blade." Stacking the drawing atop the others, she looks at me with an enthusiastic smile stretching her cheeks. "I love it."

Relief fills me and I share a smile with Amara, who peers at me from where she walks on the other side of Aurora. I wasn't sure Aurora would be able to make the weapons. This may be common practice within my realm, but I haven't seen any with that style in this one. Although, that's not surprising. The steel here isn't as strong as ours; it seems too pliant to contain a single jewel, let alone several. Not to mention there are no beings in this realm who possess the power needed to bless jewels like Zander can. But after seeing Aurora's work firsthand, I thought if anyone could do it, it would be her.

Reaching across Aurora, Amara taps the parchment. "I especially like Griffin's. His sword is in need of replacing, anyway."

"Oh, gods!" Aurora slaps the stack of sketches to her side. "I've pleaded with him time and time again to let me make him a new one, but he refuses every time."

Huffing, she shakes her head.

"He says there's no need, it does exactly what he needs it to do."

"Unless it snaps in half in the middle of a fight," Amara adds with a scowl. "The stubborn ass is just cheap."

"Or he's pragmatic," I argue, turning sideways to allow a group of drunk humans to stumble by. "I've had my sword my entire life and I've never replaced it."

"Yours," Amara drawls, "is in impeccable condition." Scrunching her nose, she extends her arm, flopping it from side to side. "His wobbles. It looks like the blade is about to fall off."

"It really does," Aurora agrees, appearing pained at the very thought.

"Then it's a good thing he'll be getting a new one," I say, feeling confident Griffin will accept the gift despite his protests.

In the small chance he doesn't, I can always *persuade* him to do so. In normal circumstances, I would never do such a thing. But in this instance, when someone's preference puts their safety at risk, I'll decide for them.

Aurora flips to the parchment with the design I drew for her. It's similar to Darius' with round, orange topaz jewels studding the center of the blade from hilt to point, but a bit shorter in length and narrower.

"Is it weird for me to ask you to make your own present?" I ask, questioning myself once again whether it's rude to even ask. "Maybe I should find another blacksmith to create yours."

I reach for the drawing, but Aurora jerks it above her head, outside of my reach.

"Don't you dare! I'm a blacksmith. I can't use someone else's creation." Lowering her arms, she peers down at the parchment, stroking the sketch in a loving manner. "This is perfect. You've given me two presents. Not only do I get to create it, but I get to keep it."

Pulling me into a tight hug, wisps of her blond hair tickle my cheek.

"Thank you, Lena."

"You're welcome," I reply, wondering if she would react the same way if she knew the true purpose of the sword.

Amara eyes Aurora with a dubious look, her short brown hair partially shielding her face. "Do you even know how to wield a sword?"

"I *am* a blacksmith," she states dryly, releasing me.

"It's a valid question," I say, shrugging when Aurora whips her narrowed gaze to me. "Cascadonians seem to have an aversion to females doing anything besides wiping snotty noses and rubbing their husband's feet."

Aurora rolls her eyes.

"Point taken. Yes, I know how to wield a sword." Peeking over her shoulder, she searches for anyone nearby, then lowers her voice. "My mother's guard Aerin has been training me since I was a child."

"I would think your mother wouldn't approve," Amara says.

"She wouldn't." Aurora smirks. "If she knew."

"Isn't Aerin the same guard who wanted to arrest me?" I ask, recalling the sneer of the dark-skinned Air immortal.

Aurora winces. "That's him."

"He seemed loyal to your mother," I reply. "It's surprising that he would disobey her."

"He's loyal to a fault, but he's also the one who found her after the Battle of Brecca." Her expression morphs, sobering in a blink. "He said he couldn't bear the thought of something like that happening to me as well, so when I told him I wanted to learn, he was more than happy to help."

"Smart male," Tristan says. Coming up from behind us, he wraps his arms around Aurora's waist and tugs her against his chest, nuzzling her neck.

"What are you ladies up to?" Kace asks, strolling up beside me. Zander squeezes between us to place a wet smack of a kiss to my cheek.

Cringing, I wipe off his slobber and he laughs. So I punch him in the gut.

"They're not ladies," Zander grunts, bent over at the waist and clutching his stomach. "They're savage brutes."

"Except for Aurora," Amara adds.

"I'm not a lady!"

Amara snorts. "You think because you slapped on a pair of britches you're not a lady? You are a born and bred lady no matter what you wear."

She slaps a palm to Tristan's face and shoves him back, his body slamming against the cobbled street.

"What is wrong with you?!" he bellows.

Ignoring him, Amara tosses her arm across Aurora's shoulder, winking. "But you're the kind of lady I actually like."

"That's a high compliment coming from her," Zander says, ducking around me to speak to Aurora. "Amara doesn't like anyone."

"I certainly don't like you."

"That's just mean," Zander pouts, and I bite my lip to stifle a laugh. She really is terrible to him.

Kace jogs ahead and turns to face us, walking backwards. “So where are we going? The brothel?” Squeezing his eyes shut, he drops his head back and peers up at the stars. “Please, *please* say the brothel.”

“No,” I say with a fond smile, shaking my head at his theatrics. “The Quiet Harpy.”

Bobbing his head to the side, Kace hums in thought as a chilled breeze swoops by, revealing his emerald jewels and the tips of sharpened ears beneath his brown hair. “That's good, too.”

“In the mood for some dancing tonight, my lovely Lena?” Zander bumps his hips with mine with a goofy smirk.

“I don't think the people here would appreciate our style of dancing,” I reply, recalling the few times the tavern's patrons took to the dance floor.

They were all stiff arms and raised chins. So formal. Boring. Even the commoners danced in the same style. Nothing like how my people dance. Free and languid, we move however we wish by the emotions the music invokes.

Whether that's sultry, passionate, or even silly. None of these predetermined steps and awkward spins.

“Pish! These stodgy fools can kiss my ass.” Zander grabs my limp hands between his and separates me from the others, twirling me in the middle of the street.

Several nearby lords and ladies in fancy gowns and surcoats give us the evil eye, but Zander pays them no mind as we dance away under the starlit sky like we have a thousand times before.

I chuckle to myself, imagining the scandalous looks we’ll receive tonight. “Alright, just one.”

“If there's to be dancing,” Aurora says, waving the stack of parchment, “I should drop these off at my shop.”

“Do you want me to walk you back?” Tristan asks.

"I'll be fine." Placing a hand on his chest, she kisses his cheek. "I'll meet you at the pub," she tosses over her shoulder, walking away.

Hearing giggling, I shift my gaze from Aurora's retreating back, only to grimace at the sight of Zander and Kace with their arms above their heads, gyrating their hips in a dance move I've never seen before and hope to never see again.

Zander does a strange twitch with his hips, then glances at me over his shoulder. I motion up ahead with a jerk of my head.

Zander nods, tugging Kace to his side. "Come on, then. I'll not wait around for these slow folks. They can meet us there."

Zander speeds their pace, while Amara, Tristan, and I slow ours.

Once they're out of earshot, I ask, "How many died?"

"Eight," Tristan replies.

"Fuck!" Amara barks.

"They're here," Tristan says, his tone somber as he stares straight ahead. "Some of them are, at least, and more will follow. "

"I know," I sigh, glancing at all the shops lining the street. The baker, the seamstress, the apothecary. So beautiful with their white stone structures and curving dark woods.

Magical with the greenery crawling up the walls and the jeweled pathways leading up to their wizened oak doors.

The question is, will they still be here when war ravages this city? Or will they fall to charred ruins when the Gods Cursed and their army of Soulless descend on this kingdom like a plague, infecting every soul within with the Goddess of Death's filth?

The former is more likely. These people aren't prepared. Don't even have the proper means to defend themselves. Not yet, anyway. But with one simple conversation, I can change all that. If Darius is willing to listen.

"What do you want to do?" Tristan asks, dragging me back to the present.

"I'll talk to Darius tonight," I reply, nervous at the thought, yet anxious to get it over with.

"I don't know how receptive he'll be," Tristan warns, slowing as we near The Quiet Harpy. "Aurora saw him after he spoke to his mother today. He wasn't in the best mindset."

That's an understatement.

I'm not sure what all Darius spoke to his mother about, but it couldn't have been only about the Gods Cursed attack.

When the guard told him of the attack in the Gods Garden, I felt mostly anger from Darius. Yet when he was with his mother, I felt a whole slew of emotions.

Rage, guilt, worry, shock, and the worst one of all, a deep, emotional pain that tore away at him.

I wanted to go to him, to help or comfort him somehow, but I wasn't sure he would welcome my company. Instead, I sent my concern for him through the bond, but instantly severed our link at his responding anger.

"I don't have much of a choice," I say. "If I wait any longer…" My words trail off and Tristan and Amara both nod in understanding. Nothing more needs to be said.

"Are you going to tell him the truth?" Amara asks.

"No." I stop a few spans from the pub. "Just enough to get a read on how he'll react. He's just now beginning to trust me. If I tell him what Brecca is planning, he'll want to know everything else, and you know I can't reveal that."

"Not yet, at least," Amara replies, no judgment in her tone.

I smile at my wonderful friend. Always there. Always supportive. The first constant in my life. The first to choose me instead of feeling obligated to, like others have. Although, that's not fair to say.

My family loves me and would sacrifice their lives for me, but they were forced into this life. Not like Amara, or even Tristan and Zander. They chose to stand by my side of their own free will. Even when I did everything in my power to push them away, they stayed.

I'll never forget that, and I'll never take their friendships for granted. And there's nothing, absolutely *nothing* in this world or the next that I wouldn't sacrifice for them.

I'll watch the realms burn, dancing on its ashes with a smile on my face if it means I can keep them safe.

"Did you find anything of note in the royals' chambers?" Amara asks Tristan.

"Nothing," he replies, his lips slashed in a frustrated line. "But I wasn't as thorough as I would've liked. Kiora and one of her many lovers came back earlier than I expected."

"Ugh! The heir needs to rid himself of that viper," Amara says, her single starlight jewel glowing with her rising anger. Amara dislikes just about everyone and everything, but the one thing she hates most of all is disloyalty. "Do they have divorce in these lands?"

I shake my head. "No, they're only released upon dea–"

Pain suddenly lashes at the bar of my cage, the snap as sharp as a whip, rattling the bars in its terror. Familiar terror.

"Trip," I whisper and bolt, my boots slapping against stone and splashing in puddles as I race down the darkened alley beside the tavern.

Another spike of pain pierces me just as I near the end of the alley, where I find Trip pushed up against the wall of the tavern by a male with an aura as black as tar. The attacker kicks him in the gut and Trip cries out, falling to the ground.

I widen the bars of the cage, allowing more of myself to seep through. My legs move quicker, faster, my feet barely touching the ground as I speed towards them.

The male swings back a leg, ready to deliver another blow just as I reach his side. I grab him by the back of the throat and fling him through the air to smack against the wall of the opposing shop.

Crouching before a curled over Trip, I stroke his back. "Are you alright?"

"Lena?" Trip winces, clutching his ribs. "You can't be here. He'll hurt you."

A shuffling noise echoes off the stone wall and I give Trip a reassuring smile, turning away from him to stand before a wiry male with slicked back, blonde hair and what appears to be a blackened handprint on his throat.

"You stupid cunt! Do you –" The Air immortal's words abruptly cut off and his eyes widen in awe. "Gorgeous."

I crinkle my nose. I don't think I'll ever get used to people reacting that way to me.

Shaking himself out of his stupor, the Air immortal strides towards me, his face twisting into a cruel leer as his eyes run along my body with vicious intent.

"I planned on killing you slowly, but now that I've seen you, I'm sure I can find much more enjoyable ways to punish you."

I'll bite your dick off before you ever touch me with it.

"Not interested."

"Even better." He groans and squeezes the bulge of his trousers. "I do love when you females scream."

Pausing mid-step, he narrows his eyes, scrutinizing me more closely.

"You're not a female though, are you?" He startles. "You're a human!"

I roll my eyes. These beings are so naive to believe humans

can't cause them harm just because they don't have magic. It's kind of embarrassing.

"How dare you put your hands on me!" he shouts. "Do you know who I am?"

I shrug. "A rapist."

He sputters in fury and lunges for me. I kick him in the balls, dropping him like a sack of potatoes.

See? You don't need magic to defeat a male. All you need is a good swift kick to the balls.

Or if it's a female, to the cunt. It may not be as painful for a female as it is for a male, but from someone who has received many cheap shots to the pussy, mostly from a pissed off Amara, I know firsthand how effective it is. It fucking hurts!

"Do you want me to kill him, or just break a few bones?" I ask Trip, gesturing to the Air immortal rolling around on the dirty street.

"Lena, don't," Trip says. Now standing, he presses his back against the pub's wall, attempting to become one with it as his frightened eyes dart between me and his attacker. "He's Princess Kiora's brother."

"How lovely," I say on a smile that's all teeth, my amethyst eyes honing in on the Air immortal. "Is there anyone in your family who isn't an asshole?"

"I'm a powerful male," the would-be rapist squeaks, clutching his balls. "You don't want to make me your enemy."

"I believe I already have."

"Lena," Trip grasps my vambraced wrist and tugs me towards him. "Please let him go. He…" He shakes his head, speaking with a tremble in his voice as he watches the Air immortal struggle to his knees. "You'll just make it worse for me."

Feeling Trip's terror, seeing it etched on his face – a face that is the exact replica of the male sprawled at my feet – I open the door to my cage and allow the darkness to slip through.

Those cold, obsidian shadows I was born with surge through my veins, injecting my heart with bloodlust, swiping away any mercy for the Air immortal kneeling before me.

Removing Trip's hand from me, I push him behind me and crouch down before the male.

"Tell me..." I ask, my voice low and cold, sinister. "Why would I allow someone who beats his own child to live?"

The monster's gaze instantly snaps to mine, filled with a darkness that could rival my own. "You shouldn't have said that."

"Lena," Trip breathes. "Run!"

The Air immortal's sapphire and starlight jewels suddenly flare and he whips two glittering palms up.

I reach for him, grabbing him by the forearm and snapping it in half all in a single motion, quickly doing the same to the other arm before he can release a bloodcurdling scream.

"It's interesting," I note, watching him scream and sob, his eyes rounded in horror at the sight of broken bones piercing through his skin. "You fae and immortal love to tell your silly stories of how the gods love you so much that they blessed you with their divine Gifts. But if your almighty gods truly favored you, one would think they wouldn't limit your ability to summon your Gifts through only your palms."

Leaning forward, I smack his flopping, useless hands and he shrieks.

"So much magic right at your fingertips, but all I had to do was break your arms. Now look at you. No better than a dirty human."

Snatching him up by the throat, I drag him towards me.

"You believe yourself so powerful, but you're not. You're a coward. You prey on those you deem weaker than you, because in your twisted, cruel mind, you feel it makes you superior to them, but you're wrong. Too blind to see that some of us only *appear* weak."

Grabbing one of his broken arms, I twist. More fragments of bone spear through his skin with a sickening crunch. A choked cry rips from his throat as blood spills from his wounds, blanketing us in its coppery warmth.

"Some of us," I hiss, "are wolves tethered within sheepskin, salivating for an excuse to bathe in your blood and wipe you and your filth from the face of the realms. Is that what you see when you look at me?" I ask, cocking my head to the side. "A sheep? Someone meant to be used and abused at your will? No." I shake my head. "You won't make that mistake again with me. But you will with another, won't you?"

My gaze snaps down to the blood soaking my vambraced hand, and I lift my fingers to my lips, groaning at the rich, iron taste of his lifesource soaking into me, coating my tongue and enlivening my nerves.

"Well, I cannot allow that, can I?" Digging my thumb into the skin beneath his chin, I jerk his head back and lick up the column of his throat, the salty taste of sweat and fear mixing with his blood.

"Lena!"

A sharp command pierces through the haze and my gaze snaps to Tristan where he stands guard at the mouth of the alley with Amara.

"Not here," he says, jerking his head towards Trip.

Squeezing my eyes shut, I try to control the bloodlust flowing through my veins, the throbbing in my gums and the darkness within me starving for another taste. But it's been too long. I'm weak and tired. So very tired.

It's too difficult to pull back. Even now as I grit my teeth and hold my breath, using every ounce of willpower to control myself, every fiber in my being screams at me to just give in. To allow those obsidian shadows free rein. But then I recall who I am, what I am, and how I choose to be. Remembering that even though I was born of darkness, I've also chosen to follow the light.

Slamming the lucky son of a bitch to the ground, I use his trousers to wipe his blood from my arms and lips, grateful it didn't soak too far into my vambraces.

"Let's go," I say to Trip. He grabs his satchel off the ground, collects the spilled items, then rushes to my side.

"You'll pay for this, bitch," the Air immortal croaks.

"No, I won't," I say without a backward glance, striding out of the alley. "But you will."

Slender fingers grab hold of my arm, tugging. "You shouldn't have done that," Trip says, glancing nervously down the alley. "Jareth is dangerous."

"Don't you worry about that. I can take care of myself." Stroking his arm, I give him a reassuring smile. "How do you feel?"

"I'm fine." He shrugs and stares down at his feet. "Nothing's broken, just a few bruises."

"Good." I nod, clearing my throat. "Head on inside."

Trip shuffles awkwardly, then suddenly lurches for me, wrapping gangly arms around my neck in a tight hug. "Thank you, Lena," he whispers. "And please don't tell anyone he's my father."

Emotion clogging my throat, I wrap my arms around him, fisting the back of his homespun tunic. "I won't."

Trip pulls back, offers me a small smile, and turns to walk up the porch steps of The Quiet Harpy, disappearing through the door.

"Find out where Jareth lives," I order.

"On it," Amara replies, striding away from us without even glancing in Aurora's direction as she passes her by.

"Where is she going?" Aurora asks with a furrowed brow,

thumb gesturing over her shoulder. “And what are you all still doing out here? Wait…” She pauses, squinting her eyes to peer down the alley. “Is that screaming I hear?”

Tristan and I share a look, and I shrug. “Yes.”

“Oh my gods!” Aurora gasps, placing a palm to her chest. “Are they alright?”

I laugh. “Nope.”

Tristan cringes and scratches the back of his head. “Uh… Aurora… You see –”

“I broke Jareth’s arms,” I cut in, then add after a moment's thought, “and maybe his balls.”

Aurora blinks slowly, ponders my claim for a moment, then shrugs and offers a *meh* sound. “Alright, then.” Passing by us, she climbs up the porch steps and peers at me over her shoulder once reaching the top. “Can you really break someone's balls, or is it more like a pop?”

“I can't be sure,” I reply, following behind. “I didn't feel anything burst when I kicked him, but I don't think I would with my boots on.”

Tristan climbs up the steps, bounding ahead of us and placing a hand on the door handle. “Please stop talking about breaking balls.” Pulling open the door, he cringes. “Or popping them.” He steps within the doorway, but instantly steps back, snapping it shut and pivoting to face me. “Actually, I don’t think I’m in the mood for tavern food. Why don't we head down to the bakery instead?”

Aurora and I share a frown.

“The bakery is closed,” I say, waving over my shoulder at all the darkened shops behind me. “Everything is closed.”

“Then why don’t we head to Aurora’s shop and I'll cook us something?” Tristan grabs me by the shoulders and spins me around, guiding me toward the porch steps.

Rolling my eyes, I twist from his grip and move towards the

door. “Do what you like, but I'm starving. I'm not going to wait around for you to cook when we're already here.” Wrapping a hand around the iron handle, I pull open the door, but Tristan slaps a hand on the wood, slamming it shut.

“Please don't go in there, Lena,” he says quietly, his hands flattened on the door, barring me from entering.

I stare at his somber face, the plea within his brown eyes. Brow furrowing, I open up my senses and travel down our bond, feeling anger, worry, and protectiveness. All on my behalf.

What does he not want me to see?

Never one to avoid the truth, I smack his hand away and swing open the door.

Shrieking laughter and boisterous jeering instantly accosts me. The scent of roasted meat and ale tickles my nostrils, and the smoky air makes my eyes water. But the bombardment to my senses is not what causes me to freeze only a step within the doorway. It's the male sitting at the bar between a pissed off Kace and a concerned looking Zander.

It’s Darius.

Oh, and a beautiful blonde female draped across his lap.

Feeling as if I’ve been punched in the gut, my breaths stall in my lungs. Surprise and hurt course through me as my entire being wishes to look away, but I can't. I’m held captive by the sight of Darius holding another female in his arms. The very same arms that were wrapped around me just a few hours ago.

Confused, I release the tether on our bond and feel down the link, then nearly crumble to the floor when his emotions blast into me. So many emotions. Too many. Pain, hate, grief, anger, fear, confusion. I feel everything and nothing all in a debilitating swirl of chaos, fire and ice burning me from the inside out.

Darius' hardened gaze snaps to mine and his anger swells,

rushing into me in a crushing wave. I instantly sever the link, unable to bear it any longer.

Aurora moves into my line of sight, cutting off my view of Darius. "I know what you're thinking," she says, her expression earnest, almost desperate. "But it's not what it looks like."

"I think it's exactly what it looks like," I reply quietly with a thick swallow.

"You don't understand," she growls, her orange topaz and starlight jewels flickering with her frustration. "He had an argument with my mother today, and is always a piss to be around afterwards. That's all this is." Eyes softening, she clutches my fingers. "He's crazy about you."

"And now he's crazy about her," I state coldly, feeling my own ire begin to bloom.

It's no secret that he beds women casually, as do I males, but after today … the things he said … I thought he wanted more. But evidenced by the blonde plastered to him, it was all a lie.

"Danya?" Aurora scrunches her petite nose and glances over her shoulder. "He hates Danya."

"Clearly." His sister opens her mouth to speak, but I cut her off with a raised palm. "Darius owes me nothing, Aurora. He can do as he wishes."

She bites her lip, seeming like she wants to press, but nods when I give her a hard look.

"Okay." She places a kiss on my cheek and stalks off to Kace, whispering fervently with him while glaring at Darius.

"Maybe we should leave," Tristan says, sounding unsure.

"No," I reply. "I need to speak with him. Tonight. There's not much time left."

Tristan peers down at me in the same moment I feel a tug on our bond, his expression morphing to that of desolation once he feels my pain.

I cut it off and give him a brittle smile. "It's better this way, anyway. No more muddled feelings. No more distractions. We just do what we came here to do."

"If that's what you want," he says quietly.

"What I want?" I laugh bitterly. "No, but it's what I have to do." Then I walk towards the only person I've ever developed romantic feelings for while he holds another female in his arms.

CHAPTER 27

DARIUS

She's staring at me. I can feel it. Those amethyst eyes sear me like hot iron, inflaming my hair to scorch through the back of my skull, branding me with her anger.

Tossing back my whiskey, I slap the glass onto the bar rail. "More."

Trip eyes me from behind the counter, his green eyes accusing as he slowly reaches for my private stash of whiskey beneath the counter and pours me another glass.

I ignore him. I ignore Aurora and Kace's angry whispers, ignore Zander's concerned looks, ignore Griffin's confusion as he enters the tavern and strides towards us, and I ignore the burn of Lena's stare. Swigging my whiskey, I let the spirits wash away all the pain and grief of the day, leaving behind nothing but fury.

Our bond flares. Only for a moment, but long enough for me to feel Lena's anger. The strength of it matches my own.

Good. That's all I want to feel from her. None of the worry she sent hurtling down the bond after I left my mother. Or her sadness. And I sure as fuck don't want the pity she tried to hide, but I felt it all the same. She can keep that shit to herself. I don't need anyone's pity, let alone hers.

Red nails scrape across my chest and Danya lowers her lips to my ear. “Are you ready to get out of here?”

My lip curls at her husky tone. A failed attempt to be more enticing, but instead she sounds like a grunting male. Nothing like Lena’s natural, throaty tone. She could tell me to eat shit and die and my cock would still twitch at the sound. But that’s why Danya’s still sprawled across my lap when all I want to do is throw her ass onto the tavern floor.

Since Lena and her companions rarely separate from one another, I knew when Zander walked in with Kace that Lena wasn't far behind. Needing to send a strong, undeniable message, I glanced to where Danya had been loitering ever since I arrived. All it took was a jerk of my head to have her crawling on top of me. Lena doesn't need to get any ideas about us. Today was a mistake. I shouldn't have said any of that to her. I lost sight of what to expect out of my life. Of what's important. My friends, Theon and Aurora, my kingdom. Not her. Not someone who refuses to confide in me. Not someone who plans to leave me.

“Get her off your lap,” Aurora hisses in my other ear. Squeezing between the stools, she glares up at Danya like she wants nothing more than to slam her pint in her face. “Lena’s coming this way.”

Not exactly what I was hoping for, but maybe that'll make this easier. She can see firsthand how little I care for her. She’ll take one look at me with Danya in my arms and walk right on past. Hopefully right out of the city and out of my life forever.

Grinding my teeth at the thought, I clench my hand around the glass, watching as a crack webs through.

Uncaring of the shards of crystal drifting in the amber liquid, I toss my head back and drain every last drop before passing the broken tumbler to Trip. Then, I swivel on my stool just as Lena appears before me.

Gods, she really is beautiful.

Even when she's angry like she is – and she's livid, judging off the scarlet rage mottling her golden cheeks – she's still the most stunning creature I've ever seen. Or ever will.

She's not meant for you. She never was.

Clenching my jaw, I drag Danya higher onto my lap, pressing her tighter to my chest.

Lena follows the movement, her narrowed eyes flitting from my fingers wrapped around Dayna's waist to the crimson nails scratching at my chest, before she lifts her gaze to mine and a mask falls into place, her expression slipping into one of indifference.

"I need to speak with you," she says, not a request but an order.

Betraying none of the turmoil within, I say nothing in response, meeting her apathetic gaze with one of my own.

"It's urgent, Darius," she tries again, but when I remain silent, her mask slips and she rolls her bottom lip between her teeth, chewing on it. Something she does when she's trying to conceal her emotions. Or apparently, as she is now, when she's deep in thought.

Ignoring the odious female sitting on my lap, she steps closer, her brow furrowing as if in pain. "Please."

A loud cackle draws Lena's gaze up.

Danya wraps a possessive arm around my neck and sneers, "Darling, why would he speak with you while *I'm* here?"

"Because unlike you, I don't still carry the scent of three different males." She inhales deeply, then crinkles her nose. "You fucked them what? No more than an hour ago?" Lena cocks her head to the side. "Did they at least pay you well enough?"

A strangled sound bursts from Danya and I try my damnedest not to laugh.

"Careful, Lena," I say, smothering a smirk. "You're beginning to sound a bit desperate."

Lena's hard gaze snaps to mine. "I wasn't the one begging in the Gods Garden today, now, was I?"

My smirk falls.

"Watch your tone, human," Danya snaps, appearing only a hair's breadth away from lunging for Lena. "You're in the company of your betters."

"Is that what you believe?" Lena asks me, ignoring Danya. "That you're better than me?"

"I *am* an immortal," I reply, tightening my arms around Danya.

"*Half* immortal, Darius." Lena grins wickedly. "Half."

"I still have royal blood," I snap, her words reminding me too much of my argument with Luthais today. "What are you? A nobody. A scarred human hiding away in a decrepit inn."

Even with the warring noises in the pub, I can hear the creak of her leather vambraces as she clenches her fists at her sides. "You're such an asshole."

"I never pretended otherwise."

"No you didn't, did you?" she says quietly, searching my face for something. Something I'm sure she won't find.

"Alright, alright," Zander says, moving towards Lena. "Let's cool it a bit before Lena makes Darius a eunuch." Coming up from behind her, Zander wraps both arms around her upper chest. I bite back a growl when Lena clutches his fore-arms. "How about that dance you promised me?" Zander asks Lena.

"Yes! Dancing." Aurora hops down from her stool. "We'll meet you out there."

Lena doesn't say anything, but she allows Zander to steer her away, holding my gaze until they reach the cleared off space before the cold hearth.

"That's better," Aurora sighs, drawing my gaze to her. Wiping her mouth with the back of her hand, she turns to face me with a sickly-sweet smile and slams her tankard into the side of my head.

"Godsdammit, Aurora!" Cupping my ringing ear, I feel warm blood slither between my fingers. "Why do you always have to go for my ear?!"

Her smile widens, but she says nothing more as she saunters off to join Zander and Lena, dragging a pleased looking Tristan behind her.

"Oh, my prince!" Danya gasps, reaching for my ear. But I jerk my head back and snatch her up by the wrist, dragging her off my lap with a startled yelp.

"Fuck off, Danya."

"But… I thought…" she says with a slight tremble to her lip. I might've thought she was sincere if I hadn't seen that same manipulative pout a thousand times before.

"Leave."

Her lip stills and she narrows her eyes on me. With a huff, she spins away and stalks out of the tavern, rattling the door when she slams it shut.

Spinning on my stool, I find Griffin staring wordlessly at me.

"Don't even start," I warn. "I don't want to hear it."

"I didn't say anything."

"No lecture?"

Griffin arches a brow. "Would it make a difference if I did?"

"No."

Glancing at my chest, Griffin's brows pinch, the same look he gives when scrutinizing someone's aura. "Didn't think so." He inhales a deep breath through his nostrils, then turns and walks away, following the same path as Danya.

Grateful I can now drink in peace, I wave Trip down, but the little shit turns his back on me, ignoring me. Sucking on my teeth, I bend over the bar and grab the bottle of whiskey hidden beneath.

"You're a damn fool."

"For fuck's sake." Plopping down on the stool, I scrub a hand over my face and throw a glare Kace's way. "Not you too."

"Yes, me." Anger I've rarely seen from the fae reddens the sharp points of his ears and cheeks. "You were unnecessarily cruel to someone who has become a friend of mine. A friend to all of us."

"Lena's no friend of mine," I grumble, swigging directly from the bottle.

"She is, you're just too blind to see it." Brown eyes probing into me, he licks his lips, visibly calming himself before lowering his head and huddling beside me. "I know your mother said something to fuck with your head, but you need to snap out of it. If you don't," he shakes his head, "you're going to ruin the best thing that ever happened to you."

"Piss off." Dismissing him, I palm the neck of the bottle and swivel on my stool, seeing Lena has corralled a minstrel with a vielle to the floor with her dancing.

An arm snaps out into my line of sight. Kace rips the bottle away from me and takes a drink, slamming it back on the rail with a glare. "Immortality is a long time to live with regrets, brother." Wiping his mouth with the back of his hand, he turns his back on me and strides off to join the others. My gaze trails behind him until it darts to Lena once he reaches her side.

Dropping her head back, Lena shuts her eyes and raises her arms above her head, swinging her hips to the strum of the vielle. So lost in the music, she takes no notice of anything happening around her. For instance, when a male with a lewd smile comes up behind her.

I rise from my stool on instinct, ready to tear off the hand reaching for her. But then Tristan grabs him by the back of the tunic and tosses him away. Another sidles up beside her. Zander slaps a hand to his chest and shoves him into the hearth. Even Kace and Aurora join in. Warding off male after male, they encircle her, orbiting around her in a ring of protection.

I don't know what it is about her that calls forth such loyalty. It doesn't matter that they don't know anything about her. Not where she's from or who she is. There's just something about her that demands blind devotion from every person she comes across.

I sweep my gaze over the tavern, seeing slackened jaws and feverish eyes. Males, females, women, men. Race and gender are inconsequential. They all stare at her as if she's a goddess amongst mortals.

Fuck, I can't see her like this, smiling and laughing while all her admirers watch on. Not when I can't be with her. Not when it takes everything in me not to drag her off the dance floor and sequester her away from the numerous probing eyes. Yet, as much as I want to rip all their eyes from their sockets, I'm no better than them. I can't seem to tear my gaze from the gracefully divine creature no matter how hard I try.

You don't deserve her.

I knock back the rest of the bottle, not even savoring it on its fiery path down. Kace may think Adelphia fucked with my head, but he's only partially right, because everything she said is the truth. Alura's tits! I just can't wrap my mind around it. A savior. A savior of what? Of darkness? That would be a more apt title. Everything I touch turns to ash. It's in my blood, my Gifts. More often than not, it's in my thoughts. Fuck, it's ingrained in the shadows marking the entirety of my back.

No, the Stars made a mistake when they chose me. I'm no savior. If anything, I'm an executioner.

Tristan strides in my direction, saying nothing as he slips into the spot beside me. Staring straight ahead, I ignore him, seeing only Lena. But I can still feel his eyes drilling a hole into the side of my face.

"They look ridiculous, don't they? A bunch of puppies begging for any scrap of her attention." He chuckles, drawing my gaze to his. "This happens everywhere she goes. Males, young and old, human and immortal, all fall at her feet. She rarely takes notice, of course, and on the rare occasion that she does, they don't hold her attention for long." Nursing his pint, he eyes me quizzically. "Except with you. I thought that was a good thing, but now I'm not so sure."

His expression sobers, and his cheeks sharpen into an expression carved from ice. "I don't know what game you're playing with her." Lips thinning, he jabs a finger in Lena's direction. "But that female has lived through more horrors than you could ever dream of, and her life will continue to be difficult as long as she takes breath. She doesn't need anyone or anything adding to her struggles."

Guilt nips at me, regret even more so, but I'm careful to keep my expression neutral. "You called her female."

He shrugs. "Female, woman, makes no difference what she is, only *who* she is." His gaze drifts towards Lena, a small smile tugging at his lips as he watches her and Zander walk out of the tavern, arm-in-arm. "She's the most loving, compassionate soul I know, and she deserves so much more than the shit life she's been given." Smile slipping, he lifts his tankard, hesitating halfway towards his mouth as he turns to give me the same solemn, almost piteous look Kace gave me moments ago. "If you can't be that something more, if you truly hold no regard for her, then leave her be. The world would benefit from your sacrifice."

He finishes off his pint and sets it down, jerking a nod to Aurora across the tavern as he tosses a few coppers on the counter. "They looked good together, didn't they?" Peeking at me out of the corner of his eye, his lips quirk. "Her and Zander?"

Any neutrality that may have remained instantly falls. "She said nothing's ever happened between the two of them."

"And she was telling the truth. But they both looked quite cozy." Paying no mind to the rage no doubt etched into every line on my face, he retrieves his cloak from the stool beside me and slips it over his shoulders. "If I were you, Darius, I'd figure out what I want real quick. You can't fix what's broken if someone else already has."

CHAPTER 28

LENA

"Do you want me to ask Lottie to set you up a bath?"

Stilling my hand within the trunk, I peek past the lid to give Zander a dry look. "You want to wake her up in the middle of the night to bring me up a bath?" I snort. "She'll fill the tub with piss."

"At least it'd be warm." Sprawled across my bed, Zander sweeps his arms through the air as if conducting a symphony, commanding the glittering gold flames floating above in a dance with complex flicks of his wrists.

Crinkling my nose, I continue rummaging through my trunk, tossing aside clothes, maps, weapons, and a waterskin until I reach the sheer white slip buried beneath. Uncaring of Zander's presence, I toe off my boots and unlace my vest and leggings, and slide the slip over my head.

Zander's head suddenly pops up and he gives an approving nod. "Good choice. He'll like that one."

"Who?" I ask, genuinely confused.

The floating flames suddenly hurtle towards his chest, soaking into him to meld with the gold blood illuminating his veins. "Darius."

The floating flames suddenly hurtle towards his chest, soaking into him to meld with the gold blood illuminating his veins. "Darius."

I slam the lid shut with a loud bang, clamping the lock in place with an angry jerk of my hand. "I'd fuck Jareth before I ever allowed Darius to see me in this."

He'll be lucky to see me ever again after the shit he pulled today.

Zander barks a laugh. "I wouldn't bet coin on that." Rolling to the side, he raises to one elbow, resting his head in his hand. "Are you that angry with him?"

"Yes," I reply, but when Zander yanks on our bond and arches a knowing brow, I sigh. "No. I'm more hurt than angry." Hiking the slip above my knees, I crawl onto the bed and curl up next to him.

"Oh, my lovely Lena." Sweeping his arm beneath my neck, he gathers me to his chest. "People say stupid things when they're upset, and Darius was clearly upset."

"Oh, yes," I say dryly, peering up at him. "Darius looked so upset with the beautiful female practically fucking him in the middle of the pub."

Her red claws scraping across his chest, her toned leg wrapped around his thigh, she watched him with a hunger I know too much about. My whole body itched with the need to snap her perfect little neck. Not just for how she had her hands all over Darius, but for the way she looked at me. Like I was nothing more than the scum beneath her fancy heeled shoes. I don't understand how Darius could allow such a vile creature to touch him. But I guess it doesn't matter what type of person you are as long as you have a willing cunt.

"He was simply trying to make you jealous."

"Well," I snuggle closer, "it didn't work."

Zander smirks. "Or it worked all too well."

Narrowing my eyes, I pinch his side and he yelps, shoving me away to roll off the side of the bed.

"Why are the females in my life so violent?" he asks, rubbing his side with a grimace.

I shrug. "At least I didn't bite you this time."

"There is that." Patting his side, he strides towards the door. "And now I must be off. I heard from a little birdie that Tabby is itch free." He waggles his brows and opens the door. "I have lots of plans for her tonight."

The bed creaks as I sit up, leaning on the back of my hands with a smirk. "I wouldn't think an itch would deter you so easily?"

"Usually no, but one can't be too careful with these courtesans. You never know; they could pass me some sickness that'll make my dick fall off." He shivers, his face twisting in horror.

"That would be tragic," I reply in mock seriousness.

"It would," he agrees. "What else would I do with my free time? I'd have to take up knitting or something equally as boring." He starts to walk out the door, but stops, glancing back at me with furrowed brows. "Are you going to be alright by yourself? I can stay if you like."

"I'll be fine. I don't need you mothering me." Placing my bare feet on the creaky wood floors, I flinch at the shock of cold. Wiggling my toes to regain my lost warmth, I walk around the bed to the side table where my hairbrush is.

"Are you sure? I don't mind," he asks, seeming unsure.

Rolling my eyes, I shoo him away with the brush. "Yes. Go on now. Remember, you have a full night with an itch-free Tabby."

Zander's eyes light up. "That I do." He moves forward, yet stops once again, dropping his head back with a groan. "I almost forgot."

All I can do is stare as he charges toward me, grabs me by the shoulders, and places a big, wet kiss on my lips. I shove him back, wiping my mouth with the back of my hand. “Stop kissing me!” I know he's not doing it for his enjoyment, and he’s definitely not doing it for mine. It’s for some sort of roguish plot, I’m sure, but I'm too tired to figure it out at the moment.

“I couldn't help myself,” he says alongside a mischievous smirk.

Narrowing my eyes, I swipe at him but he dodges it, loud guffaws bursting from him as he rushes out into the hall, shutting the door behind him.

Chuckling, I run a brush through my long, wavy, black hair. The repetitive motion and the bristles scratching at my scalp soothe me even more than Zander’s theatrics. Loose strands slither down my chest, marring the pristine white of the slip beneath. I swipe the hairs away to pluck at the sheer fabric, rolling the silky fibers between my fingers.

Darius would love this, wouldn't he?

It's feminine and flowy, sensual. Not something one would expect to find in my wardrobe. The strange, scarred woman who curses and drinks, preferring a sword to a dress. Danya probably has dozens of these. She’s probably wearing one of them for Darius right now. Or nothing at all.

I slap the brush onto the bedside table, the sound of wood colliding with wood rending the air in the eerily silent room. Inhaling an audible breath, I shut my eyes and drop my head back, running my hands through my hair to massage my scalp.

I shouldn't let Darius get to me like this. Neither one of us made any promises to the other. He may have insinuated as much, heavily so, but that’s not the same as staking a claim. I have no say over who he fucks. Even if it is with a beautiful blonde whom I would love nothing more than to rip her perky tits off.

The sound of boot steps reach me from the staircase down the hall. Muffled at first, then they rise in volume to a thunderous staccato, stomping in my direction. Glancing at my trunk, I debate grabbing my daggers, but I barely have time to complete the thought before my door is blown off its hinges.

"Where. Is. He?" Darius growls, low and rumbling from where his massive frame looms menacingly within the doorway.

"What in Azazel's name are you doing?!" I shout, completely confused who he's asking about or why he's even here in the first place.

Ignoring my question, he moves fully into the room, his gaze darting from one end of the space to the next, searching every crevice. "Where. Is. He?"

I toss my arms up, huffing. "Care to share who this 'he' is?"

"Zander!" he roars, snapping his maddened gaze to mine.

"Zander? You charged in here like a raging psychopath because you're looking for Zander?" I scratch my head, even more confused now than when he initially barged in here. "Why?"

Darius answers with a grunt, then turns away from me to whip back the privacy screen, shredding it even more when he tosses it across the room. Grabbing the lone chair, he lifts it up. When he doesn't find anyone cowering beneath, he tosses it, too.

Seeing as Darius has lost his godsdamned mind and all speech capabilities are limited to grunts and growls, I sit on the edge of Amara's bed and clasp my hands over my lap, calmly watching him tear apart the room. But when he lifts up the bed and lets out a frustrated growl, I can't contain a burst of laughter.

"He's nearly as large as you. He can't fit under there," I say between laughs. "*I* can't fit under there!"

Holding the bed aloft, Darius' gaze snaps to mine, but he says nothing. He simply stares at me with eyes filled with a possessive rage. Something I've only seen from him a few times before. Once, the day we met when he found out about the guards touching me. Later that night when someone squeezed my ass. Whenever a male's gaze lingers on me too long. The one commonality between each event is that not only was Darius angry, but he was *jealous.*

You selfish, greedy son of a bitch!

"How dare you?" I hiss, hearing the soft thuds from the padding of my feet striking against wood as I stalk towards him. "Get out."

Who does he think he is? He had a female draped all over him not even an hour ago, and here he is, charging into my room, destroying everything within sight, because he's jealous. In all my life, I have never met anyone more egotistical, more controlling, more manipulative than this asshole!

He tosses the bed aside, flipping it end over end until it slams into the cool hearth with a resounding crack. "Did you fuck him?"

"What? No!"

Lifting his chin, he inhales a deep, long breath, then stiffens. His face contorts into a blistering rage as he suddenly lunges for me, slamming my back into the wall and knocking the breath from my lungs.

"Liar," he accuses. "I can smell him on you." Slipping his knee between the crevice of my thighs and pinning me to the wall with his hips, he buries his head into the crook of my neck, grazing his nose along the column of my throat. His ragged breaths tickle my skin as he follows the path up, slowly tracing along my jawbone, then he snarls, smashing his lips onto mine in a violent kiss.

Shocked by the brutality, I don't even have time to respond before he jerks his lips from mine and smacks his hands on the wall beside my head, caging me in between his arms.

"I can taste him on you," he says, his face so close to mine, I can see every flicker of the rage-fueled flames within those glacial blue eyes.

Recalling the mischievous glint in Zander's eyes, I now realize he had no intention of screwing with me, but with Darius.

I'm going to bite the shit out of him after this... No, two bites. On the nipple!

"It was just a kiss." Slapping my palms to Darius' chest, I try to shove him back, but he barely budges. "I didn't even initiate it."

"You. Let. Him. Touch. You?"

"I didn't *let* him do anything. Zander does what Zander wants." Shaking off the ridiculous feeling that I need to explain myself to anybody, let alone him, I ignore the warning in his eyes and add, "And if I did choose to kiss him, that's no concern of yours. You have no say over who I do or don't bed."

"Fuck if I don't!" He slams his lips onto mine in a kiss just as brutal as before and jerks away just as fast, yet I feel an unwanted warmth begin to bloom within my lower belly. "You're *mine*." Digging his hips even harder against mine, he wraps a large callused hand around my throat, overlapping his fingers to tilt my chin up.

"Mind." Slapping my head against the wall, he presses a rough kiss to my forehead.

"Body." Lowering his head, he bites down on my shoulder. The sting causes a shiver to wrack through my body, that warmth within me coiling even tighter, lower, as he closes his mouth around his mark.

"And Soul." He slides the thin strap of my slip down to dangle over my arm. When he runs the rough, wet pad of his tongue along the top of my breast, my juices begin to drip down the inside of my thigh.

Rising above me once again, his eyes flash with a renewed heat and he tightens his fingers around my throat, partially cutting off my airway. "And nobody touches what's mine."

"I'm not yours," I wheeze out, vaguely wondering how he hasn't noticed the need glistening his leathers. I knock his hand from my throat and slip my fingers beneath his vest, dragging him toward me to slam my lips against his. But I've barely tasted him when I'm bombarded with the overpowering, toxic scent of powdered roses. Danya's scent.

Rage instantly surging through me, I bite down on his bottom lip until I pierce through the skin. Darius tries to jerk away but I dig my blunt teeth in deeper, moaning when the iron taste of him fills my mouth.

Hands suddenly re-clamp around my throat, and my teeth tear the wound wider as Darius rips himself free from me.

"Lena," he warns through panting breaths, blood smearing his lips.

"I'm not yours!" Licking my lips, I sneer, "You made that crystal clear with that show you and Danya put on at the pub tonight."

Squeezing my throat tighter, he slams his lips onto mine in a swift, hard kiss. "You are mine." A firm kiss. "You're mine today." A longer kiss. "Tomorrow." A softening kiss. "A week from now." His hand loosens, and he presses lingering, molding lips to mine. "Just as you were yesterday and the day before that." He strokes my throat, kissing beneath my jaw. "You were mine twenty years ago and you'll be mine for a thousand more." Ducking his head, he strokes his tongue along the markings on the swell of my breast and I moan as he places an openmouthed kiss there. "You were mine before I took my first breath, and you'll still be mine long after our flesh and bones burn to ash and our souls ascend to Elysium."

He lifts his head, tenderness mixed with lust blazing within his eyes as he places his lips upon mine and slips his tongue between to graze against mine. He pulls back, blowing out a shaky breath as he shuts his eyes and presses our foreheads together. "Lena, you always have and always will belong to me," he whispers, his thumb stroking my cheek. "Just as I will forever belong to you."

My chest rises and falls in sync with his, the organ beneath swelling to near bursting beneath his penetrating stare. All my thoughts, all my plans, all my reservations flit away with each reverently spoken word, leaving behind nothing but a single, irrepressible, viscerally choking demand.

I pounce.

Smacking into his chest, I wrap my arms around his neck, my legs around his waist, and I give into this want. This desire, this need, this anger and hurt and jealousy, giving him and I what we've both been so desperate for when I slam my lips down onto his...

Us.

DARIUS

Deprived.
Starved.
Ravenous.

Those are the only words I can think of that are even remotely comparable to the feeling of having Lena in my arms. As if, for my entire life, I've been nothing but a desiccated husk, and now that she's within reach, I can't control this desperate hunger for her. A gluttonous need drives me to take everything she has to offer, and demands that she gives me everything she hasn't.

Lena tightens her legs around my waist but rips free from our kiss, gasping for breath. But I can't have that. I can't be separated from her any longer. Not after my foolish display with Danya. Not after the rage and turmoil I felt when I thought I'd find Zander in her bed.

Grabbing the back of her neck, I jerk her towards me, colliding our lips in a violent clash of teeth and tongues. Lena bites down on my lip again and I feel a sudden sharp pain. Blood fills my mouth and my lip begins to throb, but the pain vanishes when she begins sucking on the wound. A flash of light suddenly explodes behind my eyes, shocking my nerves into an animalistic frenzy from a euphoric sensation that feels like she's not only drawing my life's essence through my lip, but that she's sucking it straight from my cock.

Without breaking our kiss, I spin her in my arms and lay her across the bed. Molding my lips with hers, I sweep my tongue against hers one last time, then pull free from her to unstrap my sheathed sword from my back and shuck off my boots. Her eyes darken when I slip my vest over my head, revealing the sculpted, broad chest beneath and the black shadows curling around my shoulders and the base of my throat from the mark covering my back. But when my cock bobs free from my leathers, she fists her hands into the sheets and exhales a quiet moan. And I swear to all the Stars and gods above that her amethyst eyes flash with a glowing light.

Placing my knee on the bed, I lift her arm to my chest and begin unbuckling her vambraces.

"No." Lena jerks her hand from mine, clutching her wrist protectively to her chest. "They stay on."

Wanting no barriers of any kind between us, I open my mouth to tell her just that, but the only sound I can utter is a strangled grunt when she sits up and I watch her pale slip slither down her chest to pool at her waist, baring full, round breasts just large enough to fill my hand.

Mouth watering at the sight, I lower my head and cup my hand beneath her breast, pebbling her nipple with a flick of my tongue. She gasps, arching against me, and I increase my efforts, enclosing my mouth around her breast and rolling the nub with my tongue. She moans, a long, drawn-out sound that has my dick twitching between us. I switch to the other side, giving it equal attention.

More. I need more.

Releasing her breast on a pop, I lower to my knees and begin licking a trail down her abdomen, tracing more of those circular shaped scars that I now realize aren't scars at all, but some other type of marking I can't name. The way they dot her skin with various designs, they almost appear to be ruins. But I've only ever seen ruins in books. Not on a woman's thighs, her hips, or in between her breasts. Nor have I seen any crawling up the side of a woman's ribs.

A shiver wracks through her body when I lick beneath the silk draped around her waist. Unable to wait any longer, I fist the fabric in my hand and rip it from her, and I almost choke on my tongue when I catch sight of the most perfect pussy hidden beneath.

It's bare, with not a single hair. Just smooth, golden skin, her lips glistening in need.

Slapping my hands against her ass, I drag her to the edge of the bed and bury my nose into her cunt, breathing in cherry, vanilla, and cinnamon mixed with that of musky desire with a pain filled groan, bathing her godly scent into my every pore.

I glance up to find her watching me, her mouth partially open and panting for breath. "Gorgeous," I breathe, and I watch her every move as I flatten my tongue at the bottom of her slit, slowly licking up to stroke at her clit.

She snaps her head back and cries out, bucking against my face. At the sight of her, her scent, and the taste of her ambrosia coating my tongue, I snap.

I shove at her chest, flattening her against the bed. Digging my fingers into her ass, I lift her pussy to my face and descend with a snarl. Flicking, licking, lapping, sucking, I gorge on her like the starved creature I am. She cries and moans. Twitching and bucking, squirming beneath my ministrations. Peeling back her lips, I roll her clit between my fingers and spear my tongue into her pussy. She groans and squeezes her thighs tighter around my head, ripping my hair out at the roots. With a snap of her hips, she bucks harder against my face, chasing her own release. I move faster, fucking her with my tongue and rubbing her clit with my entire hand. And when her moans become louder, longer, when I feel her tighten around my tongue and her cream begins to drip down my chin, she stiffens and cries out, mewling her climax.

Her legs drop to the sides, sated and languid, but I'm not finished with her yet. Lapping up the last droplets of cream, I crawl on top of her to cover her body with my own, wet my cock between her lips, and surge inside of her.

We shout in unison.

"Fuck!" I groan, burying my face into the crook of her neck. She's so tight, strangling my cock. I can still feel the walls of her cunt fluttering from her orgasm. She squirms against me and I still her with a hand to her hip, trying to hold back the orgasm throbbing at the base of my cock.

Just a minute. Just one godsdamn minute and maybe I won't embarrass myself.

But in typical Lena fashion, she seems determined to push me to my breaking point.

Wrapping one arm around my neck, Lena presses her cheek to mine and whispers in a voice hoarsened with lust, "Please, Darius… fuck me."

I lose my fucking mind.

Gripping her by the hips, I pull out and slam back in, pistoning my hips in a manic rhythm, losing myself in the feel of her slick cunt and the sounds of our grunts and groans as our bodies slap against each other.

She wraps her arms around my shoulders and claws at my back. Lifting her hips, she matches each thrust of mine with one of her own. I lift her leg and drive deeper, grinding in circles against her clit. She groans, pressing those gorgeous tits against my chest. Ducking my head, I drag my teeth over her nipple and she clutches my head to her chest, holding me to her like she never wants to let me go. Like she would die if I ever stopped.

Fury pours from me and I grip her to near bruising, driving into her faster. Harder. Punishing her for keeping this from me for too long. For not giving in to us sooner. For denying me what's mine.

Shackling her wrists in my hands, I pin her arms above her head. "Say it," I growl without breaking my stride.

"Wh… What?" she asks between whimpers. "Say what?"

"Say you're mine." Pulling all the way out, I slam into her with a single violent thrust, skidding her across the bed.

"Oh, gods," she moans, eyes rolling into the back of her head.

"Say…" Thrust. "You're…" Thrust. "Mine…" Thrust. Reclasping her wrists within one of my hands, I raise the other and slap her clit.

A shocked cry escapes her that quickly shifts into a moan when I soothe away the sting with a roll of my thumb.

"Darius." Shutting her eyes, she squirms beneath me. "I … I can't."

Rage like no other blinds me and I raise my hand, slapping her harder, knowing she'll feel more pain than pleasure.

"Say it!" I bellow.

"I'm yours!" she shouts with a broken cry. "I'm yours!"

And that's it. I'm gone. All rational thought ceases to exist, replaced by a manic, instinctual need to give into my body's demands and make her mine.

I slam into her with a snarl, ramming into her with wild abandon. More beast than male. Brutal and raw, I take it all. Her screams, her cries, her moans and groans. She mewls and cries, tears streaming down her cheeks in rapture, but she can do nothing more as I power into her over and over again. Dominating her. Forcing her to submit.

A burn starts to build, tightening my balls and thickening my cock. And when I inhale our scents mixed with that of sex, hear the wet sounds of my balls slapping against her cunt, see the droplets of sweat dripping on her bouncing tits, and feel her pussy clamp down on my cock, sucking me in as she screams her release, I follow with a roar, pumping into her until every last drop of my seed spills into her. Filling her. Marking her. Claiming her. Taking what's mine.

We lay there for some time. Lena on her back, me lying atop her, cradled within her thighs. Content to say nothing.

"I think we broke Amara's bed," Lena says between waning pants.

Just now realizing that the bed is angled at a slant, I reluctantly lift my head from the crook of her neck and pass my gaze over the room, wincing at the destruction. "That's not all I broke."

"No, but I hoped we could've at least spared her bed," she says, playing with the ends of my hair. "She's going to be pissed."

"At me or at you?"

She grins. "Definitely you." Raising her head, she peers around me. "We'll have to use your chambers next time." She pulls me down for a kiss, giggling against my lips. "I can't wait to see the look on your mother's face when she sees the wreckage you cause from a good fuck."

A laugh bursts from me and I press my lips to hers. "Next time, then," I say, both of us laughing between kisses. "Next time."

Smiling from ear to ear, I rest my chin between her breasts, holding her gaze as she watches me with a warm smile, running her fingers along the scruff of my jaw.

"Say it," I demand in a guttural voice, needing to hear the words again, desperate to know it wasn't spoken only in the throes of lust.

Her smile falls and my heart thuds against my chest in dread, anticipation, and hope, vibrating against her as she searches my gaze. Lifting her hands, she cups my cheeks between her palms and pulls me down into a fleeting, yet heartbreakingly tender kiss.

"Yours," she whispers, pressing her forehead against mine. "Only yours."

Something in me breaks in that moment. That casing around my heart as strong as stone, as impenetrable as a ward, crumbles into rubble and tumbles into the abyss, revealing the person I've sequestered beneath. The child who always hoped for a mother's affection. The adult who wished for a companion. The male who desired a lover. The person who needed someone to stand by him and him alone, to accept him as he is, vowing to forever be loyal, honest, and loving only to him. And the way Lena is looking at me now, so warm and affectionate, like I'm the single most important person to her in this cruel, fucked-up world, she makes me believe she could be that person for me.

Emotions clogging my throat, I raise a trembling hand to caress her cheek and lower my head to place a soft kiss on her lips. She wraps her legs around my waist and her arms around my neck, hugging me tightly to her chest. Cock hardening once again, I slowly rock into her. Not rough or aggressive, but affectionate. Loving the way we share more than just our bodies, melding our very souls.

I rotate my hips, angling myself to hit deeper in the way I've learned she likes. Lips parting, she moans, sharing her breath with mine as I sweep my hands over her, touching everywhere. Her throat, her thighs, her breasts, loving every inch of golden, silky skin. Our breathing becomes more labored, our chests rising and falling in sync with one another, but neither of us breaks our kiss. Not even when she moans and I groan do we separate. Not until her pussy slickens even more as she contracts around me and we shout in unison. Both our climaxes rumble through us as I crash into the most powerful orgasm I've ever felt, blinding me in its intensity and forever altering me.

Arms trembling and breaths heaving, I stare down at this stunning creature, mesmerized by the way her rippled raven locks are splayed out beneath her. The dewy sweat coating her skin. Her kiss-swollen lips slightly parted, and her amethyst eyes glazed over in contentment. Awed by not only her beauty, but by the extraordinary soul within. I'll never be able to be with another after this. It's doubtful I'll be able to look at another woman or female, let alone touch them. Not after experiencing what it feels like to be inside her, finally feeling that sense of completion that I long ago convinced myself I would never find. In one explosive, life changing act, Lena has damned us both, shackling me to her for eternity with irrevocable binds. A sentence I'm just now realizing I'll gladly endure.

Lena smiles up at me and places a palm to my cheek. I open my mouth to speak the three words I vowed never to say to another, but then she suddenly stiffens and cries out, clutching her head.

"Lena?" I ask, confusion marring my brow.

She bolts upright, forcing me to scramble off her. Squeezing her eyes shut, she shakes her head, moaning in the same instant her agony streams down the bond. Fear tightens my chest and I grip the tops of her arms.

"Lena… what is it?" I shake her. "Lena!"

The agony cuts off and her eyes suddenly snap open. "They're here, Darius. The Soulless are here."

CHAPTER 29

DARIUS

Sword... Sword... Sword.

"Where's my sword?"

Lena snaps her vest over her head and tugs her hair free, pointing at the floor. "Over there."

Ripping back the rumpled sheets, I snatch up my scabbard and strap it to my back. "Stay here." Stalking towards the door, I open it. "I'll come get you when it's safe."

"Wait!" she calls out, shimmying into her fighting leathers. "Let me just find..." She trails off, peering beneath the bed to pull out her boots.

As I step over the threshold, I glance at Lena over my shoulder, something making me hesitate. An instinctive feeling nags at me that this isn't how women send their males off to battle. I don't expect her to sob and beg me not to go. That's not the type of person she is. But I would think she would show her concern in some way. Or at the very least, send me off with a goodbye kiss. Yet, she does none of that. She's calm and focused, preparing.

"What am I waiting for?" I ask, already knowing the answer,

Sitting on a trunk, she pauses slipping on her boots, her black brows pinched. "I'm coming with you."

Like hell you are.

"You're not going anywhere."

She huffs a laugh. "I'm certainly not staying here."

Gritting my teeth, I crush the door handle within my grip. "Lena."

"Darius," she mocks.

"I can't focus out there if I'm worried about you."

"I don't need you worrying about me."

She peers down at her chest as she threads the laces of her vest. "I can take care of myself just fine."

I groan, rubbing my fingertips on my forehead. "Lena, be reasonable."

"I am being reasonable," she replies, standing. "I heard your concerns and I'm *reasonably* ignoring them."

Fuck me. Does she have to have an answer for everything?

I don't have time for this shit. My people are dying out there and here I am, wasting time arguing with her because she wants to play warrior.

It was cute before. Sexy, even. But now I see how dangerous it is to allow her to believe such a thing.

We are who we are, and Lena is not an immortal. Not even fae. She's human. A gifted one, yes, but still slow and weak, breakable.

She wouldn't last a minute with a Soulless.

The traitor guard flashes into my mind. My stomach roils in remembrance of his warning that the King of Brecca has been searching for Lena, then of his plans for her when he finds her.

If he ever gets his hands on her…

I slam the door shut. "The Soulless have never breached these walls."

"They have today," she snorts, rummaging through her trunk and tossing clothing over her shoulder.

"Have you considered the possibility that it might not be a coincidence that the Soulless managed to breach them while you're here?" Bracing for her reaction, I add, "When the Breccans have been searching for you?"

Her back stiffens and she stands, slowly turning to face me. "Are you implying this is my fault?"

"Alura's tits, Lena!" I say, scrubbing my face. "Of course not."

Biting her lip, she watches me for a long moment. She seems to be debating something, but then she shakes her head and turns her back on me before crouching before her trunk. "They aren't here for me."

Guilt suddenly flashes down the bond, but Lena quickly smothers it.

She knows something. Something pivotal.

The traitor guard admitted as much, but I foolishly assumed that if it was a direct threat to Cascadonia, Lena would share that information.

But as I watch her evade my gaze, feel her guilt, and see the way her hand trembles as she tosses a pair of leggings aside, I'm no longer sure.

With two large strides I reach her side, grabbing her by the arm and jerking her to her feet. "How do you know?"

"I just do."

Snatching her arm from mine, she steps back, but I follow, stalking her, forcing her to retreat until her back presses up against the wall. "How?"

She says nothing, dropping her gaze to her feet.

Done playing games with her, I grab hold of her chin and jerk up, ducking my head toward hers until we're nose to nose, hissing, "How?"

"Because they don't know I'm here!" she shouts, then gasps, slapping a hand to her mouth.

A surge of excitement shoots through my veins at finally discovering something, anything about her, but it just as quickly sputters out. "So they *could* be searching for you?"

"I didn't say that."

"But you didn't deny it, either."

Her lips tighten, shutting me out. Even after everything, she still doesn't trust me.

Frustration, worry, and anger, but above all hurt slam into me and I slap my hand to the wall above her head with a growl. Lena jolts as her startled eyes fly to mine.

"You're staying here and that's final," I growl, pushing off the wall and heading towards the door.

"I'm not."

"If you go out there, you'll die!" I roar, spinning on my heels and charging back towards her. "You'll get yourself killed or get me killed trying to protect you."

Lena's hurt rushes down the bond and my shoulders slump, all my rage seeping out of me in a blink.

Lifting my hands, I cradle her face tenderly between my palms, emotion clogging my throat. "I can't lose you."

She softens against me, her gaze roaming my face. "Darius," she pleads.

I press my lips against hers in a soft tender kiss, filled with the words I'm unable to say, before I pull back. "You'll stay here where I know you're safe."

"Darius, I…" She wraps her hands around my wrists and offers an apologetic smile. "I can't stay here." Her features harden. "I won't."

She means it. I see it in her eyes.

Despite my fears, despite the truth that she won't survive, she won't stay here. She'll either follow right behind me or she'll just wait until I'm gone.

Even if I lock the door, she'll find some way to sneak out and join the fray. She's too stubborn to know her limits.

If I wasn't Captain, I'd stay here and personally ensure her safety. But I can't. An idea pops into my mind, bile rising with the thought. But I swallow it back.

Slipping my trembling hands into her hair at the base of her skull, I squeeze my eyes shut, savoring the feel of her arms wrapping around my waist, the feel of her body softening against mine as I press a firm kiss to her forehead, praying to the gods this won't be the last time I'm able to do so.

With my body crying out for hers, I release her and step back, slicing an orange, glittering palm through the air.

Branches and vines spear through the floors, cracking and splintering wood as they coil around her wrist and ankles.

Lena's eyes round in horror as the nature-made shackles whip her arms above her head and root to the ceiling, her feet widening as the vines and branches plant her to the floor.

She struggles against her binds, panicked eyes darting from her arms to her wrists, down to her legs and ankles. "Darius wh… wh…wh…" she stutters. "What are you *doing*?"

"Keeping you alive." I turn my back on her and walk towards the door.

"Darius, wait!"

I keep walking.

"Wait… Just wait!"

I open the door.

"Waaait!"

Hand placed on the iron handle, I grit my teeth and turn my head to the side.

"Don't do this," she pleads. Her gaze is desperate, beseeching;

torment lines her face as her raw anguish slams into me. “I can't be…” she whimpers, tears trickling down her cheeks. “I can't be chained. Not again. Please.”

“I'm sorry, love,” I choke out and walk out the door.

Lifting a shimmering hand, slate shoots through the floor, clunking together as it molds to the door and seals it in stone.

“DAAARRRRIIIIUUUUS!”

Another wave of agony slices down the bond into me, robbing me of breath as the sound of her screams and broken sobs carve into my soul, but I wasn’t lying.

I can't lose her. I won’t survive it.

So I ignore her and continue walking down the hall. Even if it means she'll forever hate me for it.

As long as she lives.

“Lottie!” I shout as I descend the staircase. Just as I step off the last step into the main room, a bedraggled Lottie walks through the kitchen’s swinging doors.

“Captain?” She rubs her eyes. “What’s wrong?”

“Seboia’s under attack.”

“Uriella’s light!” she gasps, cupping her mouth.

“Lock the door behind me,” I say, moving towards the door. “And make sure Lena doesn't leave.”

“The human?” I hear the sneer in her voice when she adds, “Good riddance.”

Grinding my teeth, I spin on my heels and lunge towards her.

She squeaks as I snatch her up by the throat, lifting her off her feet and dragging her towards me.

“If Lena so much as steps one foot out of her room,” I hiss, “I'll kill you. I'll kill your sister. I'll kill that half human nephew you think no one knows about. I'll kill every single person you know and love. Every person you've ever spoken with, and I’ll make you watch. Then, I'll burn this inn down with you inside it.”

“Please,” she begs between sobs, dangling within my grip.

“Lena doesn't leave her room.”

She nods her head and I release her and race out the door, not sparing a backward glance as she falls to the floor.

The night is quiet and peaceful. All the shops are closed and darkened for the night. Their owners are tucked safely within their beds.

One could almost assume it's another ordinary night. But I can feel the underlying darkness. Can feel Desdemona's filth invading my lands.

I shut the inn’s door just as a shirtless Zander and a rumpled Kace rush out of the brothel, the madame and staff shutting all the doors and windows as they meet me in the middle of the street.

“Where is she?” Zander demands.

“Inside!” I shout, not missing a step as I barrel down the street. “Keep her there.”

He doesn't reply as he rushes past, climbing the porch steps and darting into the inn.

“What's going on?” Kace asks, running up beside me, straightening his vest. “Zander said we’re being attacked.”

“The Soulless are here.”

Frowning, Kace glances over his shoulder, seeing the quiet streets that surround us. “Are you su-”

A shrill scream suddenly pierces the air and we slow to a stop, right before the roof is blown off the Early Bird Inn.

“Lena,” I whisper, shock rooting me to the ground as I watch wood planks and debris float down into what was once the second floor of the inn, but now is just a blackened, smoldering hole.

The same floor on which I chained and entombed a pleading Lena.

But the shock barely surfaces before a voice suddenly booms

within my mind. A raspy, seductive voice I'm beginning to know better than my own.

"The East gate has been breached. The Soulless have invaded your city. Gather your weapons and protect your home."

"Did you hear that?" Kace gasps. "That was -"

"Lena," I growl, relief warring with irritation at the discovery that she has another Gift. A human with two Gifts.

More fucking secrets.

"The human district," Kace whispers.

Then there are no more words as we bolt down the street. Not when Griffin rushes to join us. Nor when Calder, Silas, and Ajax appear.

Not when bleary-eyed immortals, solemn fae guards, and terrified humans rush from their shops and homes, brandishing knives and swords to run beside us.

No sounds can be heard besides our breaths sawing from our lungs and our feet pounding against stone.

Not until we race through the market district do we begin to hear the screams, which grow louder and more tortuous as we round the hedges of the Gods Garden and enter pure chaos.

Hundreds of humans fill the street. Their shrill cries meld with that of the creatures' frenzied shrieks. Screaming women drag sobbing children.

Terrified men frantically board up windows. Families huddle atop homes. But there's no escape from the snarling Soulless crawling into windows and ramming through doors.

An undead scurries to the top of a hut and claws at the thatched roof, diving headfirst into the home.

A woman's scream quickly follows, but it instantly cuts off. A man rushes a Soulless with a pitchfork, stabbing it in the abdomen. It takes no notice.

Pouncing on the man, it buries its fangs into his throat and then discards him, adding his bloodless corpse to the dozens of twitching bodies littering the pitted road.

It's a massacre.

Ruby flecked shadows trail behind the Soulless, blackening the night even more and obscuring my vision.

I squint my eyes, trying to see past to the East gate, needing to know how the Soulless breached our defenses. My stomach hollows out when I see the East gate undamaged and spread wide open.

"Someone let them in," I breathe.

Traitors... traitors everywhere.

"Fuck!" Kace shouts, running his hands through his hair.

A Soulless catches sight of us and snarls, racing towards us.

Reaching over my shoulder, I unsheathe my sword and meet his snarl with a growl of my own, slicing cleanly through its neck.

Turning my back on it before its body crumples to the ground, I look to where Silas and Calder hover nearby.

"Search for any survivors and take them to the brothel," I order, assessing the ramshackle building.

It's not secure in the least, with its thin windows and flimsy door, but the Soulless haven't reached it yet. That's more than I can say for the humans' homes.

"Check everyone for bite marks before they enter."

They both nod and unsheathe their swords, jogging away to the closest hut.

"Ajax, gather as many males as possible and form a barricade." Leveling my sword, I draw a line through the air where the human district ends and the Gods Garden and market begins. "Don't allow anyone or anything past."

Ajax hesitates, frowning. "What about the survivors? Shouldn't we be helping them escape?"

Glancing down at the street, I watch as humans who were dead only moments ago rise to their feet, now enshrouded in shadows with glowing red eyes and wickedly sharp fangs.

"No one leaves." Knowing Ajax won't dare question me further, I pivot away. "For the rest of you," I shout, readjusting my grip on my sword as I stalk forward, Griffin and Kace beside me, "kill every last one of them."

Battle cries sound behind me just as I reach a Soulless crouched over a man, feeding off his twitching body.

Its head snaps up with a snarl and I swing my sword, cutting off its head before stabbing the man in the heart.

"Kill anyone who's been bitten!" I call out, stabbing a woman in her eye as it begins to fill with glowing crimson. That's all we need right now. Soulless breeding more Soulless. Adding *my* people to their ranks.

A claw swipes at me and I duck. Swinging my sword upward, I slice through the creature's wrist and swing again, severing its head.

Another charges toward me, frothing red spittle and I kick out, connecting with its chest as I grab my dagger from its sheath and stab up beneath its ribs.

I jerk my dagger free and as its body falls, I hear a pain-filled shout. Lifting my gaze, I see Griffin struggling against three Soulless while clutching his abdomen.

I throw my dagger, hitting one of his assailants directly in the heart. Griffin stabs another just as I reach him, and I skewer the third Soulless through the back.

Gripping Griffin's arm, I drag him up to his feet. "Are you alright?"

He winces. "I'm fine." Peeling his hand back, he peers down at the blooming red spot. "It got me with its claws."

A shriek sounds behind him and I shove Griffin out of the way, raising my sword. But when I move to swing, another blade suddenly spears through its chest.

"I hate these things," Kace says, kicking the dead off his sword before spinning to swipe at another.

A Soulless lunges at my side and I dodge it, slicing above its knee. It topples to the ground and I stomp on its head, crushing its skull.

A loud, concussive boom rumbles beneath my feet and I look up, finding a fae with orange, glittering hands shooting fire orbs at the Soulless surrounding him.

They instantly catch fire but continue forward, burning torches who pounce on the fae with a screech.

Dumbass.

I can't even feel pity for the fool as I watch the demons feed off him. He knows just as well as I or any other Cascadonian that the Soulless can't be killed by magic. Before, we only had to concern ourselves with fangs and claws.

Now, he'll burn Seboia to ash in his stupidity.

Just as the thought enters my mind, a flaming Soulless runs into a hut.

Screams and shouts sound inside before the thatched roof catches fire, blazing into a wildfire that quickly spreads to the hut next to it, then the ones beside that one.

Until all the homes on that side of the street are inflamed in billowing, orange flames that rise as far as the eye can see, a beacon to the Stars of our destruction.

I cut down one Soulless, two, then three. Seeing a small pocket form between me and the next approaching undead, I seize my opportunity.

Dropping my sword, I quickly summon my Gifts, blasting away the Soulless nearest to me with a torrential gust of air. Then I raise my hand, water streaming from my palms towards the huts, dousing more than half, but many still burn.

It'll have to do.

A Soulless reaches for me. When I crouch down to retrieve my sword, Griffin stabs it in the eye.

"How many more are there?" he asks, color returning to his cheeks as he swipes a blue glittering hand in the air, flipping several of them ass-over-end into the swarm.

"I don't know," I growl, wiping the sweat from my brow.

Frustrated, I don't have time to think of strategy when faced by the unceasing horde of Soulless. I swing, stab, duck, and slice, felling one creature after another, but they keep on coming.

Raising my dagger, I stab another in the ear canal, when a new cacophony of screams reaches me. Snapping my gaze to the East gate, I watch as dozens of Soulless flood into the city.

Before I can figure out a way to handle this new development, roars sound behind me. I whip around to the sight of a line of demons attacking the barrier.

"Dear gods," I breathe, watching in horror as the line of guards collapses beneath the onslaught.

Some of the Soulless stop to feed off those holding the line, but most crawl past, entering into the heart of Seboia.

Sensing a Soulless behind me, I spin and swing downward, slicing through its face with a roar. Frustration powers my limbs. Fury scorches through my veins. Fear thunders my heart. Guilt labors my breaths.

I. Warned. Her.

I warned my mother and the Kings Council this would happen. That the Breccans had instilled traitors on our lands and were actively working against us.

Yet they did *nothing*.

Refusing to see the truth, they allowed blindness and fear to govern their actions. Now my kingdom bleeds, for the cowardice of kings and queens.

Glancing between Kace and Griffin, I see the same grim acceptance on their faces as it is on mine, knowing that none of us will be leaving here alive.

Needing no words, I give them both one last brusque nod, and I fight. I fight for our brethren who died today. Fight for the kingdom I failed.

I'll fight until my very last breath and pray to the gods that I can buy some time for my loved ones to escape. For Aurora, Theon, Trip.

For Lena.

But as I'm hacking and stabbing, contemplating my death, the Soulless suddenly just stop. Stop snarling, stop growling, stop feeding.

They cock their heads to the side in the grotesque, unnatural way they do, and sniff.

"What's happening?" Kace asks, his eyes wide as he watches the creatures scent the air.

"I don't know," I reply, sharing an uneasy look with Griffin.

A whistle suddenly pierces through the sounds of snuffling and the Soulless instantly jerk their heads back, releasing a series of disconcerting clicking sounds.

Then, as one, they turn to face the brothel.

A deep-rooted fear, one I've been taught since birth pricks at me. It crawls along my skin in warning as I watch the Soulless respond to the whistle as a slave would to its master.

As they would to the Gods Cursed. Not really wanting to but knowing I must, I inhale a deep, fortifying breath and lift my gaze to the source of that sound.

My breath halts in my throat when I see Lena standing on the roof of the brothel.

"What is she doing?" Griffin asks, brows furrowed as he glances between the stilled Soulless and Lena.

"I don't know."

And I don't care. She shouldn't be here.

I took steps to ensure she wouldn't be.

Even when the inn exploded and I heard her voice, I knew she was set free, but Zander was supposed to watch over her. To protect her.

Where is he?

Passing my gaze over the roof, I find both Amara and Tristan crouched beside her with their bows strung.

And the male standing at her back, still shirtless but appearing as stoic as I've ever seen him, is Zander.

You're dead.

Lena walks forward, every step controlled, methodical, and confident, her plaited hair swaying with each calculated motion as she stops at the edge of the roof.

"You think you know death, because Desdemona's venom runs through your veins."

She unstraps an obsidian dagger from her waist, starlight jewels glinting beneath the moons.

"But not even she knows what true death is. For she is of the Void, and only the Stars can grant such Gifts."

She pricks her forefinger, blood beading beneath the point, and raises her arm over the edge, letting a single droplet fall to the ground.

At the scent of her blood, the Soulless stir into a frenzy like none I've ever seen. More frantic and desperate, their bones clacking together in bloodlust as they shove past us to rush towards the brothel.

“Come, little demons,” she coos, unsheathing the sword from her back. “Let me show you that true power lies not within the Void, but with the Stars.”

Then, all I can do is watch as she steps off the roof and vanishes within a swirl of shadows.

CHAPTER 30

DARIUS

I can't see her.
Can't hear her.
Can't feel her.

All there is beneath the howls of the Soulless are brief glimpses of their claws and fangs, before they, too, are swallowed up by shadows.

One of the undead crashes into my back as it rushes to join the horde, dismissing my blood for that of more tantalizing prey. Swinging my sword, I sever its head and roar. I roar my pain and grief. I roar my rage. I roar as I swing and slice, stab and pierce. I roar my wrath as I charge through the masses, killing those of the living and those of the dead blocking my path to her.

Griffin stabs a Soulless through the heart and shoves its corpse aside. Kace kicks out at one and then swings, cutting off its head. Both fight by my side. Neither of them says what we all know to be true: that Lena can't possibly have survived. But I can't admit that aloud. Can hardly even think it. Just imagining her cold corpse with that glowing crimson filling her eyes and those unnatural fangs descending...

***No!* I can't bear the thought.**

We finally reach the edge of the swarm, none of the creatures registering our presence. Quickly sheathing my dagger, I

summon my Gifts and raise a shimmering orange palm, parting the horde with a blast of air to reveal Lena with a dagger in one hand and her sword in the other, with a pile of corpses at her feet.

"Holy shit!" Kace says. "Look at the way she moves."

It's like a dance; every motion elegant and fluid, yet fast and efficient. Needing no more than a single strike, she cuts down one Soulless before turning to deliver death blows to another.

She's beauty and death bound in a single package, and absolute perfection.

Lena stabs a Soulless in the side of the head and turns, flinging her dagger past a sword-wielding Zander to pierce it through the heart.

Its body falls, revealing another undead behind it. Zander swings his broadsword over his head. Arching downward, he buries it into its head and cleaves its skull in two. His motions are more powerful than Lena's, but just as graceful and efficient.

Realizing their prize won't be so easily caught, some of the Soulless begin to take notice of our arrival. One such creature crouches before me, its mouth elongated and fangs dripping with blood.

It hisses, then springs forward. But its momentum stalls when it's thrown to the side from the arrow speared through its skull. A barrage of arrows suddenly swish through the air, piercing hearts and eyes, dropping Soulless after Soulless until there's a ring of corpses surrounding us.

"Unbelievable," Griffin whispers, staring up at Amara where she's crouched beside Tristan on the roof. Both of them string arrows and swiftly fire into the throng.

They're all extraordinary.

Their fighting style is entirely foreign, yet their skill is unparalleled. Far surpassing all my guards combined. Almost equal to my own. But no matter how skilled they are, they're still only four against the overwhelming numbers of the Soulless.

Now seven.

Readjusting the grip on my sword, I stab up into an undead's chin, spearing through the top of its head. Swinging overhead and then downward at an angle, I slash at another, slicing its torso in half.

I kill another and another and another. Their eyes dim and their shadows disintegrate, but they still don't let up. When one falls, four more pop up.

"Why don't you just die?" Kace grunts, stabbing at one's heart with a dagger but missing when it swipes at him with its claw.

Growling in frustration, he buries his dagger into its face all the way to the hilt.

Griffin cries out when a Soulless slashes at his arm from shoulder to wrist.

Dispatching the demon in front of me, I fling it aside and charge towards Griffin, severing the creature's arm above the elbow before cutting off its head.

Another barrage of arrows slams into the Soulless circling us, giving us a small moment's reprieve.

"We need to get out of here," Griffin grits out, clutching his arm. "We can't win." He glances up at Amara on the roof, his brow pinched in worry.

My gaze darts to Lena. She's covered head to toe in black blood and still dispatches any that come near her, but her movements are beginning to slow as exhaustion sets in.

"Grab Zander and get to the roof," I order Kace and Griffin. "We'll escape on the other side. I'll get Lena."

"What about the people in the brothel?" Kace asks. "There are still survivors."

"We can't help them." It pains me to say so, but it'll be a

miracle if we make it out ourselves.

I'm not risking Lena for people I don't even know. I would lay down my life for them if it was just mine at stake. Or even Griffin or Kace's. We are dutybound to do so. But none of them matter anymore. Only her.

Lena wipes her brow with the back of her hand, smearing black blood across her forehead as she looks at all the undead surrounding us. Then she glances up and meets my gaze, her smile filled with relief when she sees me. At the sight of her smile, the terror I felt when I saw her step off the roof returns tenfold and I move faster towards her. A feral desperation fuels my steps, knowing that the feeling won't abate until I have her in my arms.

Focused on me and me alone, she watches my every step with a similar need. Until her amethyst eyes suddenly snap up and she peers over my shoulder with a strangled cry. Then, with a speed I've never seen from an immortal, let alone a human, she whips her sword over her head and throws it, the blade flipping end over end to skewer the Soulless lunging at my back.

Fuck me, that was close.

Chuckling in relief, I turn back towards Lena. But that chuckle quickly morphs into a roar when I meet her shocked gaze just as a Soulless stabs its claws into her shoulders and bites down on her throat.

"Lena!" No, not her. Anyone but her.

Not my Lena. Not the woman who's so kind and gentle, but fiery and fierce. Who makes me laugh and play. Who couldn't give two shits that I'm a bastard. Who doesn't even blink an eye in the face of my wrath. Whose stoked a fire in me that I fear will never be doused.

I sprint towards her, pushing my legs faster than I ever have before, trying to out-speed the venom injecting into her veins, the blood pouring from her neck, the death looming at her back.

This is all my fault. I never should have left her side. I should've locked her away in the Palace Keep. Kicking and screaming, if need be.

Now, in the face of my foolishness, the only good, pure thing in my life will bleed out in front of me, becoming the very abomination I despise.

She tosses her head back with an agonized scream and jerks within the fiend's grip as he ravages her throat. Then a new terror, one I never would have expected, makes me skid to a halt mere steps away when I see her head snap forward and her eyes begin to glow with an eerie light.

Not of crimson, but of amethyst. Then she releases a rage-filled roar with a mouthful of fangs.

"What the fuck?" Kace barks, rooted to the ground right beside me, Griffin no less shocked on the other side.

Grabbing the Soulless by the hair, she rips it free from her throat and hisses in its face. Then she places her other hand at the base of its neck and tears its head from its shoulders with her bare hands.

When another one barrels toward her, she retrieves her dagger and stabs it in the chest. Then she spins, doing the same to the next one.

"Zander!" she calls out as she crouches down and rolls, coming up behind an undead and stabbing it in the back. "End it!"

Zander cuts down two Soulless, then glances back at her and jerks a nod, no hint of surprise at the sight of her fangs and glowing eyes.

Shock seizes me once again as I watch his palms and eyes begin to shimmer glittering gold, the gold crawling up his arms and chest, into his neck and the lower part of his jaw, illuminating his veins. And with a flick of his hand, gilded fire streams from his palms, shooting a hole through the heart of a Soulless rushing towards him.

Then spearing through the creature following at its back. Then skewering through another and another and another, toppling Soulless after Soulless on a wave until the only ones left standing are the living.

The night quiets once again, only disturbed by the panting breaths and broken sobs of the surviving few. But I can't hear any of that as I watch Lena crouch before a corpse. All I hear is the mindless roaring in my ears.

All I see are Lena's fangs and glowing amethyst eyes. Her strength and superior fighting prowess. All the signs I missed. Her strange markings and beauty. Her accent. How even the most common knowledge was unknown to her. Or how when she drew blood from my lip, she drank from me. *Fed* off me.

What a fool I've been.

Spinning lies and half-truths as a spider does a web, she convinced me she was an innocent human, manipulated me into believing she actually cared for me. But it was all an act.

I was so blinded by lust, I was willing to sacrifice my entire kingdom, to shame myself into becoming an oathbreaker, all for this being that's neither mortal nor immortal, but a... *thing.*

My natural born enemy. One I'm duty bound to destroy.

LENA

Crouching before the corpse, I pull my dagger free and slowly wipe it clean on the Soulless' soiled tunic, dread raising the hairs on the back of my nape. Hearing the thunk of multiple footsteps closing in on me, I sheathe my dagger and peek out the corner of my eye, watching the survivors form a circle around me, eyeing me as warily as they do the Soulless.

Amara and Tristan drop down from the roof to join Zander, their hardened expressions telling me all I need to know.

They saw me.

Rising slowly to my feet, I pause to blow out a shaky breath and turn to face Darius.

But the person I find myself standing before isn't Darius. This male looks like Darius, yes. Same eyes, same face, same hair. But with the lines bracketing his lips, features carved from stone, and death in his gaze, this isn't *my* Darius.

The Gods Wrath.

"You lied to me," he says with tightly leashed anger, hands fisted at his sides.

"I didn't," I reply quietly. But even I hear the lie in my voice, the guilt in my tone.

He slowly walks toward me, my body responding to each crunch of his boots. Not in desire as is its usual response, but with the need to flee from this person wearing Darius' face.

Visibly trembling with suppressed rage, he lowers his head toward mine. "You made me believe you lov –" Clenching his jaw, he turns his head to the side and squeezes his eyes shut. "You betrayed me."

Oh, gods.

"Listen to me, Darius," I plead, raising my hands to his cheeks. "On my life, on all the Stars above, I swear to you I did not betray y –"

"Shut up!" he roars in my face, knocking my hands away. "I'll not hear another word from that lying tongue of yours!" I flinch, shaking my head as he snarls, "You pretended to be human."

"I never said I was. Everyone just assumed."

"And you let them," he sneers. "When all along, you're a Gods Cursed."

I shake my head, wrapping my arms around myself. "I'm not a Gods Cursed."

"Then what are these?" He snatches up my arm and drags me to his chest. Uncaring of my wounds, he smears blood across my skin as he traces his thumb along my markings.

"I was born with them." Just as he was born with blue eyes and black hair, I was born with fangs and markings covering my entire body. If I could rid myself of them I would. I never asked to be who I am, what I am, but he should understand that better than anyone.

"As a Gods Cursed would be," he retorts, his face so close to mine I can see every spark of glacial fire in his eyes.

Temper beginning to rise at his hypocrisy, I tear my arm free and point at my cheek. "Do you see Desdemona's rune? No, you don't, because I'm not a Gods Cursed."

His gaze strays to my cheek, a knot forming between his brow as he inspects it. Seeing his hesitation, my body begins to loosen in relief. But then his gaze hardens once again.

"Maybe not, but *this* is a curse." He grabs me roughly by the chin, jerking it up. "These lips. Your eyes. That face." Pain radiates through my face as he digs his thumb into the hollow of my cheek, hissing, "*My* curse."

I grab his wrist and try to pull free, but he pinches tighter, refusing to release me. "What are you going to do now?" I challenge, my voice sounding bolder than I feel. "Kill me?"

"I should."

I rear back in shock, pain, Darius following me with his iron grip.

He means it. I see the truth in his eyes. So much hate and

scorn, his pupils blown wide in a maddened rage.

But he can't believe this of me. Not after everything we shared. Not after what we've come to mean to each other. There has to be more behind that hate.

Bracing myself, I feel for the bond, searching for a small hope, a sliver of something that'll let me know I can't possibly be tossed aside so easily. And a small sob escapes me when I find that the once vibrant link that ties us together is now devoid of all life and blackened to a parched husk.

A dagger suddenly appears on the ball of his throat.

"Let her go," Amara says from where she's slipped partially between us, her voice cold and unyielding. He growls but remains unmoving, glaring down at me. "Let. Her. Go." Amara digs the blade deeper and punctures his skin, blood beading beneath the point to slowly drip down the column of his throat.

Darius growls, the dagger vibrating from the sound as he bears down on the blade, drawing more blood to flow down his neck in a steady stream. He grips my jaw harder and I bite back a wince, feeling the bruises already begin to form, before he gives me one last snarl and releases me, tracking my every move as he walks backward.

"Silas, escort them to the city gates."

A large fae with red hair moves toward me and reaches for my arm. When I feel his skin graze mine, rage and pain swell within me and I round on him, fangs snapping out with a hiss. "Don't. Touch. Me," I seethe.

He gasps and jolts backwards, a move echoed by all the other survivors.

"There she is," Darius says. I whip my glowing gaze to him and see the same face that watched me with adoration only hours ago, now watching me with a face contorted in disgust.

Griffin moves to Darius' side, drawing his attention to him.

"You can't send them out there. It's too dangerous."

Darius jabs a finger in my direction. "I don't want that *thing* in my city any longer."

That *thing*. I'm a thing now. Not a lover, not a friend, not even a person. Just another cursed beast. Tears burn at the back of my eyes and I swallow back the cry that wants to escape.

"She saved us," Griffin says calmly, unflinching from Darius' wrath. "They all did."

Darius glances back at us, coldly passing his gaze over me and my companions. I know what he sees. My glowing eyes and fangs. Amara's single starlight jewel. Zander's illuminated veins. Tristan's strange markings. All of us are so different from them, so foreign. A dangerous unknown.

He curls his lip in contempt and says gruffly, "Be gone by dawn." Then he turns his back on me, calling out to his guards as he moves deeper into the human district.

Jaw aching from his punishing grip, I watch Darius with ragged breaths, reliving every moment of this horrid night. Each hateful word he spoke to me slashes at my heart, drenching my soul in blood and anguish. Unable to bear it any longer, I turn to leave, but find the red-haired fae blocking my path.

"Glowing eyes." He sucks in a breath. "I know you."

Tiger shifter.

"You don't," I reply as I brush past him, trying to hold back the tears as I pass the Gods Garden, clamping down on the sobs in my throat when I leave the market district. But as I near the inn, my vision becomes blurry and the tears begin to spill over.

"Lena, wait!" Amara calls out.

Pausing on the porch steps, I glance back at a solemn-faced Amara, with Zander and Tristan standing at her back.

"I'm so sorry."

"Don't be." I wipe away my tears. "I should've known better."

Shaking my head with a watery chuckle, I add, "The cursed are forever damned."

Anger flashes in her eyes. "You are *not* cursed; you're blessed. Any being with two eyes and a heart would know that."

"Darius has a heart." Biting my lip, my voice cracks. "It's just not meant for me."

"Lena…" Her face falls and she ascends the steps, but pauses mid-step and grits her teeth when I stop her with a raised palm. "I'll kill him for this."

"No," I reply harshly, recalling Zenith's prophetic words. "He is not to be harmed."

Amara's lips flatten, but she nods in acquiescence.

Once I'm certain Amara will heed my command, I shut my eyes and drop my head back on the beam at the top of the steps, slowly stitching myself together as I create another scar in addition to the sewn gashes already strewn across my patchwork heart.

With an audible sniff, I open my eyes and push off the beam. "Zander, Tristan, I want you two to dispatch any remaining Soulless in the city. Amara and I will pack up and salvage what we can."

Glancing up at the smoking, gaping hole where our rooms used to be, surveying the destruction I caused in my panic, my tears instantly dry as my grief twists into rage.

Darius had the audacity to accuse me of betraying him, when *he's* the one who caged me. He bound and chained me like the monster he believes me to be, knowing the torment it would cause, feeling the sheer agony of my pain through our bond. Yet he did it anyway. But that's alright. I now know what type of person he is and realize how wrong I was about him. It'll make everything that follows that much easier.

Because creatures like me aren't meant to be caged. Only unleashed.

CHAPTER 31

DARIUS

"Yours," Lena whispers, pressing her forehead against mine. "Only yours."

Clenching my hand around iron, I shove the memory aside, wrenching it from my mind and shredding it to a mutilated heap, the same as Lena has twisted me. I replace it with the image of her fangs and glowing eyes. Of her tearing a Soulless' head off with her bare hands. The sounds of her eerie hiss.

Feeling that ache in my chest begin to throb, I glance back at Kace and Griffin as I pull open the door to my mother's meeting room.

Adelphia paces back and forth before her throne. Garbed in a thin dressing gown and her long blonde hair draped loose across her shoulders, it's apparent that news of the attack drew her from her bed. Likewise for Theon, who sits before the stone table, eyes at half-mast as he rests his chin in his palm. Neither of them take notice of our arrival.

A petite blonde suddenly smacks into my chest.

"Thank the gods you're alright," Aurora says, squeezing me around the neck. "I was so worried." She drops down before I can even raise my arms, hugging Kace and Griffin just as tightly.

"We're fine," Griffin says, rubbing her back. "Where were

you during the attack?"

"Here." Arms falling to her sides, she steps back. "Tristan and I had just made it back to my chambers when we heard Lena's call." Her lips flatten. "He locked me in."

"Good man," Kace says, giving me a pointed look I ignore, unwilling to have a repeat of the argument we had on the way here.

Aurora lowers her head and wrings her hands. "Is he…"

"He's fine," I say and she squeezes her eyes shut, blowing out a shaky breath.

Another casualty.

It's not enough that Lena betrayed me, carving at my once beating heart until there's no life left to give, but did she have to do the same to my sister? Tristan may not be whatever manner of abomination Lena is, but he is different. He wouldn't be with Lena otherwise. None of them would be. And now it falls on me to tell Aurora.

Is there no end in their warpath?

"Aurora, something happened tonight."

"We already know." She smiles, her green eyes lighting up to bounce between the three of us. "It's a miracle, isn't it? They killed them all."

"It is," Griffin replies, shaking his head with an awed chuckle. "They saved our asses."

Giving Griffin a warning look, I grab Aurora by the shoulder, dragging her attention to me. "Aurora, Tristan isn't who you think he is."

Her expression hardens. "I know who he is."

Releasing her, I groan, scrubbing my face. "Aurora–"

"I *know* who he is," she enunciates slowly, eyeing me beneath thick lashes.

Growling in frustration, I run my hands through my hair, fingers tangling into the crisp hairs matted in dried blood.

Can't they see what I see? Don't they realize what they have done? These people lied to us. Betrayed us. They're not our friends; they're our enemies. Yet each one of my companions seems determined to see past that. To forgive when they've given us no reason to.

Griffin's right. They did save us. But I'd be willing to bet my life that they're the sole reason we were attacked in the first place, and that's something I cannot forgive.

"Next time, then," I say, both of us laughing between kisses. "Next time."

Dismissing them as much as the memory, I nudge past Aurora. Theon gives me a relieved smile and pats my back when I sit beside him.

"Are you injured?" my mother asks, passing a clinical gaze over me.

I shrug, glancing down at the Soulless blood smeared across my vest and arms, inhaling the scent of smoke and burnt flesh saturating my skin. "A few scrapes and bruises, but nothing more." Except for the hollow ache within me, but that's not what she's asking.

She nods, drawing her robe tighter around her. "How did the Soulless get in?"

"The East gate."

"They broke it down?" Aerin frowns, handing me a crystal tumbler filled to the brim with amber liquid. "The gate should have held."

"It was open." I pause to swig from my glass, swishing the whiskey across my tongue before adding, "From the inside."

Someone gasps.

"Traitors!" Aerin growls, slamming a fist on the table.

"I had already assembled a team prior to this to search for any possible Brecca sympathizers." Resting my forearms on the arms of the chair, I hang my now empty glass over the side. "After this, I'll pull them from their duties and have them focus solely on that."

Guilt flashes across Adelphia's face as she jerks a nod, but there's no vindication at the sight. In normal circumstances, I wouldn't hesitate at the chance to say I told you so, but I'm too tired to deal with the ensuing argument. We don't need to be fighting amongst ourselves on top of everything else. What's done is done.

"How many died?" Theon asks, drawing my attention to him.

"The numbers are still coming in, but I'd say a few hundred humans, at least. Fae and immortal?" I place my glass on the table, bobbing my head. "Around fifty or so."

"Stars save us," Aurora whispers, placing trembling fingertips to her lips.

The Stars won't save us. They've forsaken us.

"There are still a large number of humans unaccounted for," Griffin adds, seating himself between Kace and Aurora. "We believe some may have escaped through the gates after they were turned."

"Could they be in the city?" Adelphia asks, a new fear crossing her face as she clutches the hem of her gown.

"All Soulless that managed to get past the human district were destroyed," I reply tonelessly.

With a hole to the heart. The same way the Soulless in the human district were killed. I don't know if Zander hunted them down after the attack or if he killed them all in that single strike, but any Soulless we came across while searching the city were already dead.

Zander's power … the might behind it. I've never met a shifter with magic like that. Nor with gold, fluorescent blood. I should have figured there was something wrong with him when I saw his jewels for the first time. Shifters don't manifest jewels like that. No one does.

"What is she?" Adelphia asks, her expression hardening once more.

My lips flatten to a slashed line as I shake my head. "I don't know, but she's not human. None of them are who we believed them to be." My gaze wanders over Griffin's clenched jaw, Kace's accusing glare, and Aurora's pursed lips, defiance and stubbornness wafting from each of them.

Adelphia rubs her temples, her silk teal dressing gown flowing around her slippered feet as she ascends the dais to sit upon her throne. Placing her elbow on the arm of the crystal throne, she rests her chin on her fist.

Seeing her somber face, the wrinkle between her brows, and the forlorn expression on her face, I realize she doesn't have one of her many masks in place. Even with her children, she's never without one. It's a rare opportunity, one I refuse to allow to pass me by.

I push my chair back, each step slow yet purposeful as I move towards the foot of the dais. "What are we going to do about Brecca?"

"I don't know," she says quietly, staring off at nothing.

"You need to send me up into the mountains."

Her back stiffens and her eyes dart to mine. "No."

I groan and pinch my nose, completely baffled as to how she can still refuse to see reason. "Mother, we have no other opt-"

The door suddenly slams open, banging against the wall with a thunderous crack. I spin towards the sound, my heart galloping within my chest when I see none other than Dalenna Nectallius.

"Your Majesty, I need to speak with you," Lena says, striding purposefully towards the throne with Amara, Zander, and Tristan following at her back.

"How did you get in here?" Aerin shouts, unsheathing his sword and standing before the Queen. "Leave at once!"

Adelphia sucks in a sharp breath, her shocked gaze snapping to Theon at her side, then to me. "The wards are down."

The unbreachable wards. The wards no one, no human, no fae, no immortal, no Gods Blessed wardbreakers can break. Only the gods themselves have the power to do so.

Yet, Lena did.

Griffin and Kace move swiftly to their sides as I move to intercept their path, placing my body as a shield between the Queen and whatever ungodly creatures stand before me.

"Get. Out," I snarl at that cursed face.

As one, they all stop, but none of them make any move towards the door. Lena's gaze snaps to mine, her amethyst eyes cold and unfeeling, showing no sign or care to the male with whom she shared her body only hours before. No sign of guilt for destroying that very same male hours later. Just an unfeeling void, as she herself described the gods once before.

"Step aside, Darius," Adelphia says.

I remain unmoving.

"*Now*, Captain."

I clench my jaw at the order, recognizing the finality in her tone for what it is, and take one slow step back. Then two, but no more than that. Just enough to clear Adelphia's line of sight, but close enough to intercept these creatures if they wish to cause her harm.

"Where are my guards?" Adelphia asks.

Aurora cries out, slapping a hand to her mouth, and my gaze snaps to the doorway, seeing the guards' slumped forms.

"They're fine," Lena says, tossing a flippant hand over her shoulder. "They're taking a nap." Her gaze wanders to the Queen, speaking directly to Adelphia. "I need to speak with you."

"You've said as much," Adelphia replies, her tone calm and regal, her mask firmly set in place. "Since you've gone to so much trouble -"

"It was no trouble at all." Lena smirks. "We just walked through the door."

Adelphia's expression doesn't shift, but her chest expands with a steadying breath. "What do you wish to speak to me about?"

"The attack today is just the beginning," Lena claims. "You've noticed the increased activity from the Soulless? Even before today?" Adelphia nods. "The same has been happening throughout the continent. The King of Brecca-"

"So there *is* a King," Theon cuts in, a worried frown pulling at his lips.

"There is," Lena says factually, still holding Adelphia's gaze. "The King of Brecca has been watching you for years, biding his time while building his army and amassing weapons. Magical and otherwise." She gives me a pointed look and my breaths stall in my lungs when she adds, "They plan to attack."

"When?' Aurora asks, speaking directly to Tristan as she ambles toward him. Griffin stops her with an arm around her waist, her features contorting into misery when Tristan ignores her, staring straight ahead.

"A month," Lena answers her. "A couple weeks more, if you're lucky." Lena takes another step closer to Adelphia, but nothing more as Kace, Griffin, and I move in sync with her. "If Brecca attacks you as you are now, Cascadonia will fall."

Lips pursed, Adelphia drums her fingers along the arms of her throne. "You've been here over a month. Why haven't you told us sooner?"

"It would have jeopardized my mission."

Adelphia gives her a droll look. "Which is?"

Lena considers her for a moment. "We're searching for someone."

"Who?"

"That's not your concern."

Adelphia clenches the throne, her knuckles whitening as she leans forward. "You are in *my* kingdom. That makes it my concern."

Lena laughs, a cold, arrogant tone I've not heard from her before. "One would think so, but it doesn't." Adelphia's lips tighten in response and Lena's laughter cuts off. "Trust must be earned, Your Majesty, and you haven't earned the right to this knowledge." Lena's gaze snaps to mine, an accusing light flashing beneath. "None of you have."

"Who are you?" Adelphia asks, searching Lena's face with a furrowed brow.

"Me?" Lena shrugs. "I'm no one."

"Where are you from?"

"Nowhere."

Quickly losing patience, Adelphia says through clenched teeth, "*What* are you?"

Lena says nothing, wandering towards the table as I follow along, careful to keep myself between her and the Queen. "A being with access to a vast amount of knowledge." She plops down in a chair, casually holding my mother's gaze. "Someone who knows how to kill the Gods Cursed."

Someone gasps, probably Aurora, while I stand here stunned, my feet rooted to the ground in shock.

But Lena gives us no time to recover as she barrels on. "Your people believe the Cursed are invulnerable, but you're wrong. There is a weapon of sorts, stored deep within the Mandala Mountains that can be used to kill them. It negates the Goddess of Death's power."

Our people have searched for years to find a way to destroy the Gods Cursed. To cure the Soulless. But every trail led to the same conclusion. Only a god can defeat a goddess' power. But maybe we missed something. Maybe there really is a way to defeat them. Hope kindles within me but it quickly dwindles, morphing to rage when I remember who my source of information is.

"Nothing can defeat Desdemona's powers," Adelphia speaks my thoughts.

Lena continues as if she hadn't spoken. "I can show you the path. Teach the trusted few," she nods toward Kace and Griffin, "how to wield it. But it is imperative that the location of the weapon remains secret. Which is why in exchange for my assistance, I will require a member of the royal family to accompany me." Her gaze lands on me.

"You want my son?" Adelphia whispers, her head slowly swiveling in my direction.

Lena stiffens, visibly swallowing. "For the expedition, yes."

Something flashes within Adelphia's eyes, but I'm unable to decipher it before it vanishes.

"You ask too much."

"I haven't asked for enough," Lena quips. "I give you my word no harm will come to him."

Adelphia rises from her throne. Theon reaches for her, but she jerks out of his clutches as she descends the dais, slowly rounding the table to stand on the other side of Lena, derision and scorn lining her face as she stares down her nose at the abomination so flippantly holding her gaze.

"You say trust must be earned, yet you've proven yourself nothing but a liar and refuse to answer any questions." Her robe slips, but she still appears every bit the regal Queen she is as she flattens both palms on the table, hissing, "I will not entrust my son to the likes of *you*." Her face shutters, an unemotional mask slipping back into place as she straightens, clasping her hands over her abdomen. "You saved my people tonight, and for that reason alone, I will grant you safe passage from the city. Darius, along with his Commanders will escort you to the gates. But once you leave, never return. For if you do, your life will be forfeit." She glances over Lena's head, pale green eyes touching down on Amara, Zander, and then Tristan. "*All* your lives."

Aurora stifles a sob.

Rounding the table, Adelphia ascends the dais and lowers herself into her crystal throne, jerking a regal nod.

I don't hesitate.

Stalking towards Lena, I banish all thoughts of her smile, the sound of her pleasure-filled cries, that raspy laugh, the feel of her skin sliding against my own. Determined to rid her from me, mind, body, and soul. Hoping there's enough of me leftover once I do.

I stop beside her chair and she drops her head back and lifts her gaze to mine, a sorrowful smile tugging at her lips. I grit my teeth at the feel of her warm, soft skin as I curl my fingers around her upper arm, mentally preparing myself to drag her out of this city and my life for good.

But then her smile suddenly tightens to slashed lips, her amethyst eyes harden, and my blood runs cold when she commands sharply, "Amara."

Shrieks sound behind me and I snap my gaze around, sucking in a breath when I see Amara, the once human Amara, now with an illuminated starlight jewel, glowing diamond eyes, extended fangs, and her once brown hair streaked a brilliant, fluorescent white.

She whips up a glittering palm and a diamond ward snaps into existence, slicing down the center of the room and splitting it in half, trapping Aerin, Theon, and Adelphia on the other side.

"I apologize, Your Majesty." Lena reaches through the ward to grab a grape, holding Adelphia's gaze as she slowly bites into it. “But I believe you've misunderstood me. That wasn't a request.”

My breaths rush out of me as my heart rams against my chest. That power. That diamond power. It was Amara. It was hers all along! The one who created the ward in the courtyard that day. I almost thought I had imagined the feel of it. The way it crackles along my skin, raising the hairs along my arm, how the power doesn't hum but sizzles, popping in my ears. The way it crushes me beneath its supreme feet to drown me in its divinity. But it doesn't belong to the divine, does it? Not to a god known to us. Nor to a fae or an immortal. It belongs to a seemingly human Amara.

Adelphia lifts a trembling finger and touches the ward. The scent of burnt flesh along with a sizzling sound reaches my ears as she cries out and jerks her hand back. She peers down at her blackened finger and lifts her gaze. Not to Aerin, nor Aurora, not even to Theon, but to me.

“Darius.”

At the plea in her eyes, at the sound of my name spoken on a fearful whisper, I instantly snap out of my stupor.

I flick a glittering orange palm to shoot an orb of fire towards Amara, but it vanishes with a bored swipe of her hand. Kace and Griffin rush her from the sides. She flicks both hands and diamond chains spear from her palms, shooting towards them and binding their arms and legs, both tumbling to the floor with a loud smack.

Sprinting towards her, I whip up a hand and a stream of fire streaks towards her. It vanishes. I raise the other hand and another flamed stream flashes towards her. That one vanishes as well. I do it again and again and again, rapid firing one after another as I rush forward. The fire never touches her, but with every swipe of her hand I'm that much closer.

When I'm only a sword's width away, I raise both palms with a roar and blast into her, the orange flames coalescing into a massive funnel of fire.

Unable to vanish my assault with just a swipe, Amara braces her feet and holds up both hands to keep me at bay. The flames billow out and begin to lighten as I blast into her with one last surge of power. Releasing my Gift, I quickly unsheathe the sword from my back and swing it up and over my head, aiming for the crook of her neck as I slice downward.

But before my blade can even graze her skin, a small, leather clad foot suddenly rams into my chest, flinging me across the room to slam back against the ward.

Feeling like my chest has been caved in, I wheeze in a breath and push off the ground to stand, but I'm halted by the obsidian and starlight dagger pressed against my throat.

"As you can see, Amara's wards are more powerful than your Gods Blessed's," Lena says in that lilting, raspy voice from where she's crouched before me. "It cannot be dismantled by anyone or anything. Not your Wardbreakers, not your fire, not even in her death. If you had managed to kill her, they would have been trapped indefinitely."

Looking into those glimmering, amethyst orbs, I'm baffled as to how blind I was. How could I ever have thought she was anything remotely human? The way she tracks my every motion. That young, yet ancient depth that simmers within. Even the color was a sign all in itself. This abomination with her cursed face and bewitching eyes and enchanting scent could be nothing less than the predator she is. The predator she has always been.

"You will join me in the mountains," she orders, her features sharpened for all but those plush, heart-shaped lips. "I will show you the path to the weapon. Once we return, Amara will release them."

I bare my teeth at her. "How can I trust you to keep your word?"

She lifts the hand not holding the dagger and grazes her fingertips over my face. My brows, my cheekbones, along my jaw, my bottom lip. She then skates that hand down to flatten above my pec, digging the dagger deeper into the ball of my throat as she presses up against me and brushes those blood red lips against mine in a faux tender kiss, sharing her breath with mine as she whispers, "Because you have no other choice."

Feeling her breasts crushed against me, her scent invading my nostrils, the taste of her breath on my tongue, I feel the something that she broke inside me change, twist and deform, morphing into a volatile, convoluted mass of rage and darkness, reforming me into the monster so many claim me to be.

I grab her by the wrist and snap it back, the dagger falling from her grip with a startled yelp as I wrap my hands around her throat and squeeze. Her mouth rounds into an O, her eyes widen and begin to glow, and fangs snap out as she bats at my hands.

Shouts sound all around me. Hands tug at my arms and shoulders, ripping out my hair. But I notice none of that. All I hear are my own screams of hate.

Because I *do* hate her. I hate her for betraying me. I hate her for imprisoning my family. I hate her for forcing me to do this, and I hate the feel of her blood slickening my fingers from where I've torn open her wounds. I hate that I already miss her laugh and her touch and our once vibrant, but now blackened bond. I hate that she made me love her and I hate her even more that I still love her. I hate that I can only roar my rage, my pain, and my hate as I watch the ungodly, unnatural, yet breathtakingly beautiful glow in her eyes begin to dim.

But what I hate her for the most is my inability to truly hate her at all.

"Darius, stop!"

Adelphia's shrill cries finally break through my haze and I look up, seeing Tristan with a dagger pressed to a sobbing Aurora's throat and Griffin and Kace struggling against diamond binds. Snapping my gaze to the side, I find Zander with glowing eyes and gilded veins crawling up his neck and into his jaw, with a glittering gold palm pressed up against the ward. Beneath that shimmering hand flattened against the ward is a cyclone of gold flames, whirling around the screaming, hunched over forms of Theon, Aerin, and my mother.

I toss Lena aside, her head bouncing against the floor as a mortal-appearing Amara drags her onto her lap.

Watching Lena cough and sputter, grazing her fingers over the blood smeared, black and blue fingerprints marring her neck, I force my hands to remain still, ignoring the warring feelings of hate and guilt at the sight.

Lena moves to all fours, trying to stand but stumbles. Amara reaches for her, but she swats her hand away, those amethyst orbs boring into mine as she rises to her feet.

"Amara will…" Lena's voice cracks, her voice hoarsened to a mere whisper as she addresses Adelphia. "Amara will give you and Theon full access to your chambers. And as an act of good faith, we will release your guard. He can come and go through the ward as he pleases."

Aerin looks to Adelphia for approval before hesitantly sticking a hand through the diamond ward, then even slower, stepping outside its perimeter, giving Adelphia a brusque nod on the other side.

"I suggest you keep the number of people who are aware of your imprisonment to a minimum," Lena says to Adelphia. "You have many enemies within your kingdom. More than you know."

Lena pivots to face me, holding my gaze for a long moment.

Neither of us say anything as we stare at one another. Her expression shifts and contorts, torment suddenly flashing over her face, but it's gone so fast, I'm sure I imagined it.

"Go pack," she says, her features hardened and unfeeling once more. "We leave at dawn."

Then she turns her back on me and strides toward the door, Amara, Tristan, and Zander following at her back.

EPILOGUE

I have an itch. A tickle. Right on that narrow strip of skin that separates my nostrils. It's been there for some time already, strengthening in its annoyance by the second. But I make no move to scratch it. Not even a twitch of a finger. Only a fool would dare to shift their attention from beneath that arctic, impenetrable stare. And I'm no fool. But it appears that I'm surrounded by them.

A sniff.

"Quiet!" Garth barks from beside me, kicking out at the trembling human.

The human cries out, toppling over and catching herself with her bound hands, but does as she's ordered, sitting back on her heels and bowing her head.

Gods, I hate him. I hate the cold and this fucking place and the beings lining the wall. Seeming to be carved from the very same ice outside these slate palace walls, they don't even move. Don't fidget or shuffle. For all but the swirling, ruby flecked shadows marking their cheeks, they're frozen sculptures, staring at me with unnatural glowing eyes. Feeling the frigid burn of those stares burrowing all the way to my bones, a shiver wracks through my body and I instinctively huddle into my fur cloak.

Then I stop myself and straighten my shoulders, refusing to show any more weaknesses to these demons. They already look at me like they're salivating for my blood, moments away from pouncing on top of me and claiming my soul for themselves. No, if I want to make it out of this cavern they call a throne room alive, I won't move so much as a single muscle as I force my gaze to remain fixed on the bare chested man sitting upon the throne of bones, bones with curved points dipped in onyx, the same bones in the crown that circles the man's head.

"More humans," the King of Brecca says, passing his icy gaze over the two dozen bound humans kneeling at our feet. "I gave your lord explicit instructions to bring me immortals and fae in this batch."

"This is what our lord was able to procure," Garth says with a boastful lift of his chin, no sign of reverence in his tone.

The King's lips flatten. "My goddess will not be pleased if your lord decides to renege on any more of my terms-"

"We would have procured those who are gifted if your Soulless had managed to get past the human district," Garth cuts in, sneering up at the King.

Yep, surrounded by fools.

The King blinks, giving me a small reprieve from that bottomless pit of cruelty, before his lids lift once again, sucking me back into the void. Pushing off the throne, he descends the dais. A Gods Cursed holds up a fur cloak at the bottom of the steps and the King pivots to the side once reaching him, giving me a glimpse of the onyx shadows marking the entirety of his back before the Cursed slips the cloak over his shoulders.

Garth doesn't break the King's gaze during this act. Neither does he when the man slowly walks towards him. But when the Cursed lining the wall prowl towards us, their steps in sync with one another as they surround our group of thirty or so males and two dozen humans, that bravado slips and he drops his chin to his chest in a subservient position.

The King stops before Garth, his massive form dwarfing the average size male as he arches over him, inhaling deeply. A small whimper escapes Garth, his arms and legs trembling, and I curse my lord for choosing the insufferable ass to be our mouthpiece. I regret even more that I hadn't uttered a single word in opposition when the King straightens and snaps his gaze to mine.

"You are to tell your lord that I expect double the amount of immortals in the next batch."

I swallow. "Of course." I'm not sure how he's going to do that. Since the kingdoms have caught on to our efforts, they're much more watchful now. It was difficult just to get the humans in this batch. But there's no way I'm telling the Gods Cursed King that. "I'll relay your orders."

"You may go."

"H-h-he may go?" Garth asks with a stutter, peering up at the King with a wary, yet hopeful look.

"Yes." Eyes glowing, the King's arm lashes out, his hand fisting into Garth's hair and jerking his head to the side. "*He* may go."

Then his fangs snap out with a snarl and he strikes down on Garth's throat.

At the sound of Garth's screams, I turn my back on him and my brethren, walking as calmly as possible towards the throne room doors. Ignoring the sight of the Gods Cursed converging on my comrades as I step over the threshold, ignoring the feel of their metallic-scented blood splattered on my face as I pass through the hall, blocking out the memory of their gurgles and cries as I slip between the palace gates.

My only concern as I begin trekking through the mountains and return to my homeland, is to forget that I ever came to this gods forsaken wasteland.

To forget the warning in the demonic glow of those glacial blue eyes.

To be Continued…

THE BLEEDING REALMS

A NOTE FROM THE AUTHOR

Thank you so much for reading ***To Bleed A Kingdom,*** *The Bleeding Realms, Book 1*

If you have enjoyed entering this dark world, share it with other readers by leaving a review!

ABOUT THE AUTHOR

Ella Dawes has always held an unhealthy fascination with fae, vampires, magic and romance—and you'll find all of the above in her books. She loves to write alpha heroes and the fierce heroines who clash with them, in all their glorious complexities and fatal flaws.

When she's not writing her own fantasy worlds, Ella can usually be found between the pages of another or watching Game of Thrones reruns. She married her very own book boyfriend and they live in Michigan where they try—yet continuously fail—to wrangle their comically mischievous daughter.

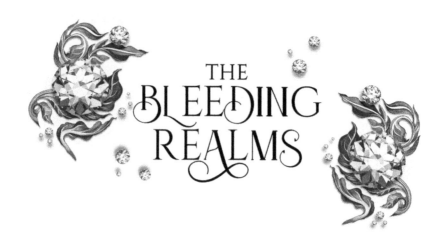

THE BLEEDING REALMS

ABOUT THE AUTHOR

Don't forget to follow her, to know a bit more about her and her upcoming books:

Website: www.elladawesauthor.com
Facebook: www.facebook.com/groups/elladawesreadergroup
Instagram: instagram.com/elladawesbooks
TikTok: https://www.tiktok.com/@elladawesbooks

Milton Keynes UK
Ingram Content Group UK Ltd.
UKHW040846220324
439740UK00021B/55

9 798989 269921